Joan Eadith lives ̲̲̲̲̲̲̲̲̲̲̲̲̲̲̲̲̲̲̲̲̲̲̲̲̲̲̲̲̲̲̲̲̲̲
Manchester, where she was educated ̲̲̲̲̲̲̲̲̲̲̲̲̲̲ a
nurse. She also worked in the University Dental
School and Royal Eye Hospital, and as a nursing vis-
itor. She has served her time as a wife and mother,
and now considers writing her career.

Also by Joan Eadith

DASIA
THE BLUE CORNFLOWER
CYGNET OF MELMERE
HOSPITAL GIRLS

Ivy Violet

Joan Eadith

WARNER BOOKS

A *Warner* Book

First published in Great Britain in 1993 by Warner
Reprinted 1997

A CIP catalogue record for this book
is available from the British Library.

ISBN 0 7515 0367 3

Typeset by M Rules
Printed and bound in Great Britain by
Clays Ltd, St Ives plc

Warner Books
A Division of
Little, Brown and Company (UK)
Brettenham House
Lancaster Place
London WC2E 7EN

Contents

v

CONTENTS

CONTENTS

Ivy Violet

CHAPTER 1

The Gramophone

The summer air was awash with sounds of the waltz, and Ivy Violet – in her heavy blue cotton frock and white calico smock – was so in love with the music that she hoped the whole of Hulme would hear it. She hoped it would spread through the breezy sky and reach even Clopton Street and curl its way round every street corner pub from the dancing bear ale houses of Chester Road to all the jug and bottle houses round the music hall at Hulme Hippodrome, whose owner enforced total abstinence from alcoholic liquor in his establishments.

A Viennese waltz . . .

The liltingly joyous tones bathed the whole row of small, red brick houses in Clark Terrace and followed her through the wide open door of number 4 and into bright sunshine.

She was thirteen and off school with a supposedly 'bad chest', for most people suffered from chest ailments where she lived, but in reality she was helping her mother Phillis who went out to work.

What a glorious day . . . Her body soaked up every rapturous second. Even the dull green medallion oilcloth beneath her bare feet felt warm and friendly as she danced straight out on to the flagstones, her chin lifting to the skies in rapture, her chestnut hair swirling round her shoulders, and her sparkling grey eyes paying homage to fine weather, because today it was St Swithin's Day, the 15th of July 1910. If it rained on St Swithin's Day it was supposed to rain for a further 40 days and 40 nights.

There was a sudden crash.

'Look where you're at. You young elephant!' Ma Chadwick edged away, but too late as Ivy Violet lunged against her plump muscular arms, and a whole wicker basket of washing fell to the ground near the sparse bit of grass, known as The Green, in front of the houses.

In some ways, Clark Terrace was one up on most of the other street houses in Hulme. It was a law unto itself – tucked away behind the back of Lawton's Commercial Hotel, and a decaying four storey brick monolith inhabited by Mellers the printers. But on the south side, there were enough lower, single storey huts and brick shacks to allow plenty of light into this small secret haven so near to the centre of the city.

It also had the added advantage of narrow gin-nels at each end of the tiny row of ten houses, so that most strangers were deterred from cutting through to tread the ancient, unevenly flagged path.

The unadopted bit of cobbled road skirted a few square yards of open land strung with washing lines and stout, weatherworn wooden posts, accompanied by two long faded clothes' props.

Ma Chadwick glowered at Ivy Violet as the young girl hastily smoothed the washing back into the basket. It had missed toppling out by a mere fraction.

'My God, child – it was only me new steel-boned corsets as saved me, and if all that load had been soiled again it would have been two days food gone. I depends on all that washing from Ellamina Street. Some of 'em's as rich as Lord Mayors down there.'

Ivy Violet stared.

Steel-boned corsets. She shuddered. Then she said insolently: 'How can you afford them posh steel-boned corsets then – seeing as how you're living from hand to mouth? Or has the Lord Mayor's wife passed them on, she's fat enough — '

'You scraggy little demon! All you Hiltons just about take the biscuit for cheek! An' why aren't you at school? If you was mine I'd belt you til — '

'Well I'm *not* yours, Mrs Chadwick, and how I can be an elephant one minute and all scraggy the next?'

Then, as Ma Chadwick ignored her and moved towards the washing line, Ivy Violet's exuberance waned, because Ma Chadwick had hit her where it hurt the most – her scragginess. She was only too well aware that most people described her bluntly as 'poorly developed', and that her worst enemy, buxom Maisy Fowler, next door but one, said she was a flat chested little worm, because she was still in liberty bodices with rubber buttons round the edges.

But the music on the gramophone had captured her senses so much that mere mortals soon faded away to a chuntering murmur in the city air.

Ivy Violet's neatly curved eyebrows rose a fraction with a quirk of inward humour: at least *she'd* never need to wear corsets that looked like a suit of armour. Old Mr Foster said she had a body like a sylph when she'd struggled to free herself, in his corner shop yesterday, after meekly asking him for a packet of washing soda and some dolly blue.

Johann Strauss . . . Vienna . . .

The Music of the Spheres, it said on the record . . .

Her heart began to beat with sudden growing passion. Oh to be swept away in the arms of an amorous dancer, a tall handsome courtier in a white wig and a blue velvet jacket at a grand ball in some golden palace like at Hobbs's cinematograph round the corner and upstairs above the church hall.

Waltzing, waltzing . . . ROMANCE.

But was she ever going to find that in Clark Street – except on a His Master's Voice gramophone?

And not even that was paid for, but almost stolen for her by Merrick who worked in Kershaw's music store.

Merrick had loaned it to her secretly whilst Henry

6

Kershaw tested out an amazing Pianola, that looked like a piano but played the music all on its own when you pressed the foot pedals. All you had to do was to finger the ivory keys in any sort of flourish you wanted – and it looked as if you were a real pianist.

It was for rich Mrs Tremelow from Wilbraham Road near Longford Park, and Merrick (said everybody round where the old fuss-pot lived) was going to hear her playing music from *H.M.S. Pinafore*.

'I don't worry about you having a flat chest, Ivy,' declared fourteen-year-old Merrick one day in secret as he pressed against her lovingly and gazed at her solemnly from a mass of spots and blackheads.' My brother Frank says it's the bottom 'alf not the top 'alf what matters.' Then he went a bright scarlet and hurried away.

'Where in heaven's name has *that* come from?' roared Ivy Violet's mother, Phillis, when she got back from town. 'I heard the row all along Stretford Road. And you off school with a cough. Get rid of it, sharp. It's not got here by honest means – that's for sure. There's not one person in this patch as can afford a solid oak cabinet gramophone, including us, and if I'm not wrong – it's that little pest, Merrick Jackson from Kershaw's who's wheeled it all the way here in that old pram.'

Ivy Violet said nothing. Mother was wrong this time. Merrick had brought it in a really nice cart made from orange boxes and lined inside with half a cotton blanket to prevent scratches and two special tyres from a broken bicycle.

She loved him dearly. He was so kind. She was trying to get him to eat a bit of raw yeast every day. It was supposed to cure carbuncles, and carbuncles were the very worst end of spots and boils – even though they both knew that in the end they'd go. But whenever would it be?

She herself seemed to be escaping them but Mother reminded her scornfully that this was because she was 'too much of the skinny scarecrow and her woman's parts hadn't got into her blood-stream yet.'

'And just as well too,' observed Phillis sharply. 'The uglier you stay whilst you're young the better, then you're less likely to be set upon by womanisers.'

Sometimes Ivy Violet wished Phillis was not so sharp but she knew her stepmother had a good heart and was always trying to keep her on the straight and narrow.

Her own mother had died soon after the birth of Ivy Violet's youngest brother Roger who was now eight, and Jos Hilton had married Phillis a year after Vi died – in 1903 when he was thirty-six, and Phillis was twenty-nine. But Phillis had never had any children herself.

She worked at the fustian mill as a checker: seeing there were no faults in the cotton corduroys and velveteens; and coping in Clark Street with Roger, Ivy Violet, seventeen-year-old Kenny, and Bryan Hilton aged twenty-two who was due to go and live with his fiancée Pauline in Old Trafford. Pauline was an only child and lived in a big house with attics where he could lodge until they got married. This prospect however was only viewed with cautious hope by the rest of the Hilton family as he had been engaged three times before in the previous year and always some dramatic catastrophe had brought it all to a close. The first time was Myrna Donkins who was under the age of consent, but kidded him along she was two years older. The second was Moira Hemmingway who fell in love with the best man who was already married and caused a real dust-up. Third was Felicity Smithson who had not believed that the horse – from the horse and trap all arrayed for the wedding in white satin ribbons and was taking Bryan Hilton to the church in Lavendar Street – had needed to have a new shoe on the way. And because he was half an hour late she had hysterics and refused to go on with any of it, much to Phillis's relief.

That night Jos Hilton was back from his three days a week job as a warehouseman in Cornbrook (which he fitted in with selling firewood) and everyone was squashed into the small kitchen round the large wooden table. There were three layers of tablecloth: the old grey felt one that hid the bumps in the coarse wooden table surface, the white starched cotton one which had to last a week, and finally a small cheap cotton one placed on diagonally. When they were all thanking God that their father had married a good cook and careful manager: For what we always receive, may God be praised . . . Whilst they were all sat there in front of the blackleaded and gleaming fire-range, sweating in the summery air and stuffing down sausage and mash, home made bread and rhubarb pie, their bountiful provider Phillis started to talk again about the gramophone.

'I know it *looks* very nice, Jos,' she said as she cleared some plates into the scullery, 'and I can see that it's a very good quality cabinet and it was very kind of 'im to bring it round . . . but you mark my words – there'll be trouble.'

Ivy Violet smiled at her father.

He was a kind, thoughtful man but he didn't spend much time at home if he could help it. Mostly he spruced himself up and went to Charlie Bradstock's pub, sometimes accompanied by Phillis if she was not weighed down with darning and ironing.

Bradstock's was their nearest local and was often called Cocky's because it had a bright green cockatoo in a cage which the regulars swore could say 'What a thirst' and 'Bloody boozer'. However the only real, but suspicious claim for this language prowess came from Harold Trench who let it be known he was a ventriloquist immediately after Cocky had outdone himself with a stream of bloodcurdling expletives.

'I'm open to any genuine offers,' beamed ever hopeful Harold. 'Weddings and childrens' parties is me speciality but they's a bit thin ont' ground at present.'

There was also a piano there providing regular singsongs. Not to mention actors who were partially resting, and those who fancied themselves as actors, and did not rest at all. Not until they had inflicted themselves on everyone else, reciting long lugubriously dramatic poems, and telling jokes in the smoke laden and beery den with the flickering oil lamps, gas mantles, and pictures of local boxers on the walls.

'I agree with Aunt Phil,' Bryan said, wiping some bread round and round on his empty plate so hard that its dark blue border with the faded trace of gilt suddenly glowed again with polished pride. 'We should get shut of it right now afore a bobby knocks at the door.'

'He's only borrowed it, our Bry.' Ivy Violet glared at him petulantly. 'He'll be taking it back tomorrow, when old Kershy's out again visiting mother Tremelow. Merrick reckons he's quite gone on her and is just like her little lap dog.'

'That's enough of *that*,' said Phillis. 'Girls of your age should be seen and not — '

'Heard . . . You're just like a gramophone yourself, Mam. But the music's not as good.'

'You *impudent* young hussy! How dare you speak to me like that. Tell her, Jos!'

'Shut your glib little trap and leave this table if you've nowt better than that to say,' said her father frowning.

'You're just a jumped-up little know-all,' Kenny said, who worked as a messenger boy in the city, gleefully piling in with his own donation. 'Phillis does right to complain.'

'You're the worst girl in Clark Terrace,' piped eight-year-old Roger. 'Everyone says you're bossy and stuck-up, and cheeky.' He looked round the table in triumph, then ducked as Kenny tried to slap his head. It was all right for older, working boys to say things, but not for little squirts of his age.

Ivy Violet suddenly went all pale inside. Why did she always get attacked? She was quite quiet really, if people didn't nag her. All she ever did was try to defend herself.

As soon as their evening supper was over, Phillis made the boys put the gramophone back in its orange box home in the washhouse in the back yard and then turned to Ivy Violet. 'Tomorrow morning, you'll just wheel that wretched old wooden carriage and its cargo right back to where it came from, and if old Kershaw's place is still shut you can leave it round their back. And if it gets damned well pinched it'll be that Merrick's fault because it's nothing to do with us and that's final.'

'B-but Ma . . . aaam — '

'Don't you Mam – me! If we're caught with that we could be locked up for receiving stolen goods.'

'But it's *not* stolen. He *lent* it me . . .' Tears began to well up in Ivy Violet's large grey eyes.

'Tell that to the judge and jury,' Phillis said.

That night as Ivy Violet lay in the rickety little three quarter bed in the small box room she shared with Roger, she thought miserably about her life. Oh yes, she knew it was better than some people's. At least she wasn't crippled, like nine-year-old Molly Simpkin from her friend Tilly Simpkin's family in number 2. Or half blind, like Klancy Chadwick's strange little husband in number 1. Or deaf and old like Mrs Platt who was eighty-six and lived with her bad tempered bachelor son, Monty aged sixty-four.

Why was it that in some other parts of the world, and even here in England, there could be wonderful princes, full of love, and dancing waltzes with beautiful young damsels?

And why was it shown in films and on the cinematographs, whilst all the time she was just stuck here? . . . And even poor Merrick who was her true love was covered with spots.

Where was the true land? Surely not in the streets of Hulme?

She lay back against the lumpy flock pillow, and sighed woefully and moved Roger's elbow away from her stomach, as she dreamed of changing her name to Imogen Violet Young, the initials of her own first name. Maybe with a handle like that the world would be her oyster?

Imogen . . . Violet . . . Young . . .

Young and free . . . Dancing and dancing. For ever . . . To Viennese waltzes . . .

Then she started to think what better name Merrick could have when all his spots had gone . . . Michael, Earl, Raymond . . .

But his first name was far too long to try it all with initials, and suddenly she fell fast asleep.

*

The next morning, in Merrick Jackson's house it was a fiasco for poor Merrick for – unknown to Ivy Violet – he had been cursed with some very unfortunate circumstances which were not his fault.

The silver framed, sepia photograph on the marble mantelpiece signalled a higher standard of comfort than those in Clark Terrace. It showed Merrick's brother Frank, aged five in a beautiful broad linen collar which was settled on his small shoulders by a wide band of delicately crocheted edging about two inches deep, above the crowning glory of his velvet suit.

Merrick himself was propped up on cushions, on a bamboo cane chair beside Frank, wearing a long frilly embroidered robe. Signifying top quality, the photographer's flowing signature was at the bottom.

Both their father and mother were lively energetic types, and all the family was overfed. Even though it never seemed to show in spite of the popular foods of the day being plentifully shoved down their thankful throats every day. Foods ranging from plum duff, suet dumplings, and black puddings, boiled beef, brawn and potted meat, pig's trotters and tripe, beast's heart, ox liver and chitterlings, to pickled herrings complete with roes, cod steaks, and tinned sardines, cabbage of all colours in all guises, lentil soups and Lancashire hot-pots. There were also home made rice and sago milk puddings on Sundays, muffins and funeral cake, rock buns, cheese scones, custards, pies and jellies. And all were well devoured by the never ending and ever hungry, boil-blessed and bony youths.

Al Jackson, Merrick's dad, helped to build barrel organs in a small, unhealthy dust-ridden workshop owned by a Mr Angeloni near the Bridgewater Canal. The best ones were intricate pieces of equipment, artistically decorated and capable of playing a succession of different, but familiar musical airs, and Al Jackson was relatively well paid, often earning as much as twenty-eight and sixpence a week depending on the hours worked. A full day was from seven in the morning until nine or ten o'clock at night – depending on how busy they were.

Many of the barrel organs became collectors' items in wealthy families, and organ grinders themselves were still common in the City roads and streets. Often the organ grinder was accompanied by a small monkey wearing a little red tasselled fez on his frail-looking, hairy skull, and dressed in a small, sleeveless bolero. A tin can would be strategically placed to beg for money and one of the monkey's limbs manacled to the music machine as it crouched with chattering teeth beside its master.

The Jacksons lived not far from Alexandra Road in a substantial house with attics and cellars which was regarded as posh by the inhabitants of Clark Terrace. Mrs Jackson took in lodgers. One was a school teacher called Miss Trentham who was forty-five, and the other was a distant cousin called Archie Monks, who was twenty-five, and a bit of a lad; his only saving grace was that he paid his rent regularly, as did Miss Trentham.

Mrs Jackson herself, whose first name was Doris, made waxed cloth and paper flowers on fine covered wire, which she sold to many of the big shops round Market Street for Christmas, and hat decorations. She also styled people's hair for when they had special occasions and was an agent for ladies' and gentlemen's hair pieces, which brought in a pittance but was all to keeping the Jacksons above the dark racing rivers of gloom and debt.

Merrick always went to bed quite early. First because he had to get up early for work, and was worn out by the end of the day and anxious never to be late in the mornings in case ratty Mr Kershaw sacked him, and secondly because he wanted to escape from all the rest of the house.

He did not like Miss Trentham a bit after she once got him to clean her shoes for her when she had been on a country walk with the headmaster of the school where she worked, and Merrick had no option but to clean them.

Immediately, he realised she was trying to make use of him, and could see a future laid out for himself polishing her shoes every morning for ever and ever, while at the same time always having to be polite, because he knew she was a good lodger and his mother would not want to lose her. So now he avoided her like the plague, until he found out from his brother Frank that, thankfully, she had been out to the ironmongers and bought herself a new set of good quality brushes and dusters, and some Cherry

Blossom boot polish, and had announced in cheerful and dramatic tones to their mother that it was part of an independent woman's way of life to always clean her own shoes and that all shoe-shine boys should be banned from city streets and given more fitting employment. At the same time she hinted that she never seemed to see much of Merrick these days and hoped she hadn't done or said anything to offend him.

'He's such a sweet helpful boy Mrs Jackson, and terribly sensitive. No job is ever too much trouble for him.'

The Jacksons' other lodger Archie was a different kettle of fish as far as Merrick was concerned, he was the complete dandy and man about town with a mania for cricket. Whenever he met Merrick he mentioned the Tyldesleys until Merrick felt he would explode if he heard the name again. The Tyldesleys were synonymous with cricket and Merrick had not the slightest interest in the game and secretly dreamed of sailing away to explore the Antarctic like Captain Scott.

However, on St Swithin's Day evening the house next door but two caught fire just when Merrick was going to bed. It had started when the Quinceys decided to light the fire in their best front room because they were celebrating their daughter Maria's engagement. They stuffed the chimney with newspaper to burn the soot out and get it going, but the chimney caught fire and was soon blazing away. Then to their horror part of the burning chimney fell off and toppled backwards sending burning ash, soot and pieces of brick hurtling down in clouds of sparks which set fire to the roof of the wash house. Before the horse-drawn fire brigade had arrived there was a blaze which lit up half the road and brought in more crowds than the 1902 film called *A Trip to the Moon*.

It was a godsend no one was burnt or injured. The outcome was that all the Quinceys went to the Jacksons to get over the shock and were put up for the night on camp beds and mattresses. Merrick though did not go to bed until two o'clock in the morning.

And he overslept . . .

'We've overslept! We've overslept.' Merrick tore round in a complete flap trying to stir everyone, including all the extra bodies, but it had not the slightest effect, for people knew that this was the best excuse for 'lying in' they were ever likely to get in the rest of their lives.

When he arrived at the music shop, his heart fell a mile. Mr Donby Kershaw was not in but his wife Berenice (commonly known as Big Bad Bunnie) was standing there like the Duke of Wellington, with her chest stuck out and her jowls wobbling in righteous anger.

'Where on earth have you been, you naughty, naughty boy! And what's happened to that expensive, oak cabinet, gramophone we were saving for Mr Antrobus? It was promised for delivery – first thing this morning and there isn't a sign of it.' She hesitated and bit her lip, because she knew, deep down, how hard-working and conscientious young Merrick Jackson was.

'Unless of course, that's where you've just been, Merrick – delivering it to Ellamina Street. But if that was the case, Mr Kershaw should have warned me before he rushed off to Mrs Tremelow's about one of the pedals stiffening up on her Pianola.'

Merrick looked at her in innocent amazement, with a thread of lurking fear. He realised now that if Bunnie was hunting for the gramophone, it might mean serious trouble. 'Oh no, Mrs Kershaw, I'm afraid I really am late. You see there was a fire next door but two, and — '

'Never mind fires Merrick,' said Bunnie with mounting suspicion. 'What I'm interested in is that unique and very dear oak cabinet gramophone with a deposit put on it by Harry Antrobus. I know for a fact it was in this shop this time yesterday morning. In fact I actually saw you rubbing it over with that yellow duster just before Mr Kershaw went to test out Mrs Tremelow's Pianola. So don't you start trying out your lies on me. You'd better find it immediately, AND BE QUICK ABOUT IT!'

She turned away and went to the back of the shop where all the cardboard boxes full of concertinas and mouth organs were. They carried a stock of all sorts of smaller musical instruments fronted by one grand piano in the shop window, plus many different catalogues to order from and shelves full of popular sheet music, and a few orchestral scores like

Tchaikovsky's *1812 Overture*. There were also pieces for the piano like *Blumenlied* (Song of the Blossoms) by Gustave Lange (Arthur's original edition) or *Musical Novelties for the piano*, by B H Smith of Amsterdam and published by Keith Prowse and Co Ltd, for Gt Britain and Colonies . . . .

Merrick stood there uncertainly. It was slowly beginning to dawn on him in the haze from last night's fire shock that he had done a very stupid thing in taking Mr Kershaw's property round to Ivy Violet's so blithely. It seemed like another age now since the lovely weather of yesterday, when he had watched the delight and disbelief in her face as she looked in the orange box carriage and uncovered the gramophone. He knew she was often off school by command of Phillis to help out with housework under the pretext of various ailments, and he knew she would love to hear waltz music .

Even the slightest sound of a melody made her want to dance. She had even tried to teach him, but it was hopeless. He did not seem to have a scrap of rhythm in the whole of his body, even though he liked listening to his mother playing the piano, and he had once been a church choir boy for about two months.

The more he thought of the way he had 'borrowed' that gramophone the more he saw what an absolute idiot he had been. Whatever had made him carry out such a stupid plan? He had put a note in the shop ledger saying the gramophone was being loaned to a (fictitiously named) person called Mrs

Blacket of Fern Street. Ninepence of his own money, in Mrs Blacket's own name, had been put in the Kershaws' rusting old tin tea caddy to prove it, if any questions should be asked.

Yesterday he had regarded this as extremely unlikely, for he had aimed to get it back swiftly and secretly some time today . . . probably first thing that morning before work, but his plan had all gone sour from oversleeping.

Looking back he could see that it was another case of being caught in Ivy Violet's spell, for whenever he was with her, ordinary reason flew out of the window at the mere sight of her laughing, mischievous eyes, so that the whole world was a more exciting place.

But not this morning. Whatever should he do?

Merrick's young earnest face was clouded with fear.

Maybe he could manufacture some pretext to Mrs Kershaw about having to go out on a special message, he thought. Then he could go round to the Hiltons in the Terrace and swiftly bring the gramophone back here. Bring it into the shop the back way, then plead innocence as to how it got into a different place. Getting it there was the main thing, before old Donby Kershaw himself arrived.

He took a deep breath, and gulping nervously, he hurried towards Mrs Kershaw in the back room.

Just as his own brave plunge was being enacted, the shop door bell jangled heralding a customer, a tall, sharp eyed stranger hovering purposefully in the background. Bunnie Kershaw's attention was immediately caught. He was from the moneyed class, attired in a coat with a velvet collar and wearing a monocle for his eye.

Merrick waited not a split second longer: 'I'm afraid I'll just have to dash back home, Mrs Kershaw. There really was a fire, and I've left my notebook behind with some orders in it.'

He was off like greased lightning leaving her completely mesmerised by the advancing customer, whose false teeth glittered promisingly.

Merrick had never run so fast in all his life to get to Ivy's and back. And then to his relief, when he was almost there he saw her coming towards him carefully wheeling the gramophone.

'Merrick! What a bit of luck seeing you.' Her face lit up with a huge cheeky smile. 'You've no idea what a rumpus there's been over it. Phillis ordered me to get it back to you quick – before we're all put in jail.'

He smiled back at her and as they slowed down and walked in the direction of the shop their steps got slower and slower as he told her all about the fire last night. Then he said: 'Anyways, you'd best get back. You know what your mam's like. An' I'd better put a spurt on, and get shot of this in the shop before Bunnie traps me again, and before Donby gets back from his lady love's.'

They waved goodbye affectionately, and Ivy waltzed off deliberately with a bit of a twirling dance to celebrate yesterday, towards City Road, leaving

Merrick to trundle back to the shop, with the borrowed property.

Merrick decided to take a short cut to the Kershaws, a somewhat devious route which had the advantage of not being so noticeable as the main road. This brought him out by an entry close to Kershaw's back yard amongst a fine web of small back streets. But hardly had he started out on his chosen route when a horse drawn cab came clopperting along at the side of him and pulled up.

In the cab was Mr Donby Kershaw resplendent in his bowler hat, with his walrus moustache quivering.' What the devil are you doing sloping round these parts, Merrick? Why aren't you int' shop? An' what's my damned gramophone doing in there?'

Before Merrick could utter a word Donby ordered the driver to put the gramophone in the cab. 'I'll see you back at my place, lad,' he bawled threateningly as the bony little nag was set off with its extra load. 'And you'd better be pretty sharp with a proper explanation.'

Merrick's knees began to tremble and twitch as he ran hastily towards the shop , shoving the wheels of his empty orange box to record speeds. He was in for it now, and no mistake. All the way along the back streets he wondered how on earth he could get out of it all. His hands were sweating with terror and there was a streak of soot on his white Eton celluloid collar. Even one of his bootlaces was now undone and trailing woefully between his dark trouser leg and thick, hand knitted sock whilst the faded navy blue, winceyette cap he had worn since school days was completely askew.

He even began to worry about his orange box carriage knowing that it had been made during slack periods in the Kershaws' back yard and hidden at the back of their W.C. all ready for transporting Ivy Violet's wonderful day of surprise. If he returned the carriage back there it would be another nail in his coffin and it would probably be confiscated, he thought. So he left it in the back alley at his pal Tubby Watson's who lived on the way before reaching the music shop. He passed on a message that he would call back for it to a woman sweeping a stiff brush and swilling the front paving stones with soapy water.

His reception at work lived up to his worst fears. The Kershaws were waiting for him like a pair of pacing, hungry lions and placed in a condemning place of honour on top of a tall display stand was the gramophone.

CHAPTER 2

Merrick's Decision

'You know what you are, don't you Merrick Jackson?

'You are a delinquent.

'And you know what they does to delinquents? They puts 'em away in reform places like Withington Workhouses in Nell Lane where they 'as to work 'ard and is kept under proper control.'

Bunnie Kershaw was towering over him as he sat weakly on the small varnished wooden chair pressing his fingers so hard against the inside of his palms that his finger nails were white and bloodless.

They had even pulled the dark blue front blind down in the shop window, and turned the card to CLOSED whilst they proceeded to torment him in peace. The place was as gloomy as a Father Christmas grotto with the gas mantle wearing out;

and the air was now as smoke filled as a dockland pub as Donby pushed down more thick shag into the bowl of his pipe and let his wife enjoy herself.

Merrick was terrified. Surely she was wrong? Places like workhouses were only for paupers and people living rough, and the homeless and old people? He suddenly remembered old Karadoc Andrews across the back entry who had once worked in the workhouse and how he said there were prison cells there, deep down in a network of underground passages like the dungeons of the olden days. Here those who tried to escape the harsh and loveless life of the institution, or got drunk, or became abusive were shoved into the hellholes to quieten them down and even chained to beds of stone slabs.

He thought of his kind mother and father and his heart bled. Supposing he was put in one of those underground cells and left there for ever, just because he'd borrowed a gramophone?

He remembered the story they had been told once at school about a girl who was sent to prison for stealing a tulip in a city park; maybe it had been a long time ago but were things any better now? He looked desperately towards Mr Kershaw, surely he would not be party to having him put away in a workhouse?

Mr Kershaw had turned his face the other way and was staring at a spider's web on the ceiling. Then he muttered, 'It's a bloody good job I caught you, Merrick. And it's a damned good job that gramophone weren't scratched or owt – or that Antrobus feller wouldn't 'ave paid us a penny piece for it. Anyways that's as may be, but I do know that from here and now you're sacked. An' I never want to see you again.'

A spark of hope lit Merrick's soul. At least he hadn't mentioned dreaded Nell Lane, and as for Merrick himself he was only too glad now to vanish from their sight.

'I'll go right now, Mr Kershaw. And I'm very, very sorry for causing so much trouble. I never meant to actually steal it. I was just borrowing it for a day. I thought it wouldn't be missed . . .' He suddenly realised he had said all the wrong things.

'Borrowing it – for the *day*?

'Wouldn't be *missed*? Have you gone out of your mind, boy?' Bunnie's voice had risen to a shriek, and even Donby flinched slightly. 'Surely you don't imagine that a theft like that can be condoned? And you – caught red-handed by my own husband – sneaking it round the back streets of Hulme in our paid working time – no doubt ready to hawk it to a shady den of vice. Oh no, Merrick Jackson. Oh, no, no! The punishment has got to fit the crime, and you'll be reported immediately to the police.'

Bunnie's eyes glazed over with a look of complete satisfaction, but Donby Kershaw was clearly ill at ease. 'Mebbe if 'ee swears never to misbe'ave again an' 'as twopence a week knocked of 'is pay for the next six weeks, and swears ont' Bible never to do such another foolish trick for ever more Bunnie love.'

27

Then he added: ' 'Ee's very good at figures, and we'd never get another like 'im when it comes to stock-taking. I mean taking stock. No, what a means is: doing the books as to what we *'ave* got and *'aven't* got.'

His wife glared at him then said icily: 'The police will decide. Just you keep guard of 'im Donby whilst I sees if Tommy Birtwistle is round on 'is beat . . .' And forthwith she disappeared into the back kitchen.

The minute she had gone Donby said: 'You'd better scamper away, lad. Your face is the colour of chalk. Vamoose, quick. I doesn't want to see even the likes of you imprisoned in a workhouse. Pull up the shop blind as you go and turn that notice to OPEN.'

Like someone in an awful nightmare, Merrick stumbled away from the music shop, not even knowing where he was supposed to be going.

Ivy Violet had not reckoned on meeting Merrick again that same morning, and when she saw him coming towards Clark Terrace she was quite shocked. He looked like a different person. He was suddenly revealed to her – as the sun rushed from cloud to cloud in a windy sky – as a thin, white faced, anxious and spotty boy; an untidily dressed stranger looking for some place to hide.

As he drew nearer and saw her come out of the house they became somehow united again, as she sensed danger in the air.

'Merrick? Whatever's happened? Wait a minute.' She bobbed back in the house, thanking her lucky stars that the rest of the family were out as she grabbed her purse with its few coppers inside, dumped her new straw hat over her dark curling tresses, dragged on her green flannelette, braided blazer and best button boots and hurried out again.

'Merrick, you're shivering! What on earth is it?'

'Mother Kershaw's going to get the police on to me. It's over me borrowing the gramophone. She says I'll be sent to the workhouse in Nell Lane. I could be locked up for ever.'

Ivy Violet stared at him in disbelieving astonishment. 'They could never do that Merrick. The worst I've ever heard of is getting the birch. But that's for really bad things, like stealing, but they do say that sometimes the scars stay with you for life because it cuts into your flesh like a knife.'

'They say I stole it.' He hung his head and huge tears came to his eyes.

Ivy Violet tried to comfort him. She put her arms round him and held him close. Then she suddenly saw half the Simpkin tribe from number 2 standing watching them.

'Come on, Merrick – let's get somewhere else. We'll walk to Witty Park.'

Whitworth Park was a couple of miles away in the Greenheys area next to Oxford Road, and as they walked, Merrick poured out the full details of the Kershaw episode. 'Whatever can I do now, Ivy? I just daren't go home. Just think of the disgrace it would bring to our family and mother and father to have a son who's branded as a criminal. All there is left – is to run away. Right now.'

Ivy Violet went cold with shock, and as they sat down on a wooden bench in the park near the drinking fountain, she said, 'You can't just run away this very minute, Merrick. Where would you go? And what about money? If you vanished, your mam and dad would kick up a rumpus and go round to Kershaw's shop to find out where you were, or even get in touch with the police themselves. It'll just add to it all.'

He looked at her sadly, and she realised how beautiful his dark eyes were with lashes long enough for any girl. He was quite handsome underneath.

He gave a huge troubled sigh: 'I've burned my boats Ivy. I *have* to go. Yes. I know I'm not really a thief – but whoever'll believe that? People'll just add to it and add to it until I'm reckoned to be the biggest rogue in the whole of Hulme. I just wouldn't be able to stand it.'

For a few doleful seconds there was silence, then Ivy Violet took hold of his hand and said: 'I'll come with you, then. It was partly my fault that it's all happened . You only brought it round to please me with those waltzes. So if there's going to be trouble we might as well make it big trouble.' Then she said: 'Exactly how much money have you got Merrick'?'

'Two half sovereigns and fourpence halfpenny.'

Ivy Violet sighed to herself, she had only got sixpence in all the world. The main thing would be for

Merrick to try and find a job right now and for her to
do something to gain some extra money for herself.

'Your best plan Merrick would be to go to Shude
Hill market and try and earn summat sweeping up
and running errands, or else go to Central Station
and do some bag carrying for the toffs what goes to
the Midland Hotel. An' meanwhile, I'll look for summat an' all, and we'll meet back here at tea time and
see how it's going – then find out where we can
spend the night.'

He nodded eagerly, and looked much more cheerful as she waved him off. Then Ivy Violet made her
own way quickly to Nelly's, a well known hawker's
stall in Shude Hill where human hair was bought
and sold. It was tucked away on its own behind a
single large sycamore tree with a trestle table loaded
with bottles of special hair lotion and cures for bald-
ness, and hair-nets, and special soaps, and wigs, and
pictures of men wearing false eyebrows — 'He was
nowt but a curate's egg face until he bought a pair of
Manifold Eyebrows . . . Special glue provided.
Guaranteed for all weathers and profuse sweating.'
At the back of all this was a tall canvas screen with a
flimsy roof covering. It was similar to the sort that
fortune tellers and palmists and herbalists used
when giving people private advice, but it was often
rudely suggested by many that it was nowt but a
private peeing hole for the stallholders.

'So what can I do for you, young missy?' said the
man on the stall rubbing his hands slightly. He was
small and wiry with a bit of stubble on his face and

wore a mucky white silk muffler.

Ivy Violet summoned up all her courage, and putting on her Sunday best accent said, 'I want to know how much you pay for hair, please.'

The man's face was expressionless but his eyes were as bright as a ferret's: 'Depends on the quality, don't it, Little Princess? Was it that you knew someone with —'

'It's me,' she said haughtily with her heart thudding. 'How much would I get if you was to cut all this off?' She ran her childlike fingers through deep, shining, chestnut coloured strands.

'Couldn't say for sure, darlin',' he said guardedly as he glanced about. 'Depends on the quality. Length, colour, grades of fineness. It all counts. Depending on what the hair's going to be used for.'

'Can't you even give a rough guess?'

'Sorry, my sweet, but it all depends on the scissors, see and how easy it is to cut. The hair that cuts the easiest gets the most money, but no one knows until it's been cut. Understand?'

Ivy Violet stood there, befuddled and undecided. It was obvious that she needed the money desperately if she was going to run away with Merrick, and this was clearly the way to get it. But she had a feeling that the man might not be honest. Yet what other course was there? The plan to meet Merrick again at Whitworth Park would soon be here. Although she knew Merrick might not have managed to find work for today he might manage to get something lined up for tomorrow. But it was harder for girls. It was highly unlikely that she would have a chance of working on a market or running messages when she was so young unless she was a relation of the stall-holder.

Suddenly she said: 'I'll have it done. Do I have to go behind that screen?'

He nodded silently, then said hesitantly: 'What'll your parents say, sweetheart?'

'I ain't got any. I live with my old grannie and we's nearly starvin'.'

'She keeps you very well dressed, sunshine. Don't blame me when it's cut off will yer now?'

She shook her head, her legs like jelly and her mouth dry with fear as she sat down on a rickety chair dug into the muddy grass floor, with a tatty old sheet round her neck. The man, who was called Choppy, produced a huge pair of barber's shears and a large grey looking and chipped enamel basin, and proceeded to hack away round her ears and the nape of her neck, stopping every so often to attend to customers on the other side of the screen.

There was no mirror to look into when he'd finished. All she was aware of was the sudden blast of cold dampish air round her neck, and all the spiky bits of hair around her ears and tickling down her back, and a huge mound of fine chestnut hair lying in a light hump in the bowl and thick dark curls lying scattered over the earth next to the chair.

'A right lot off there, Miss,' said Choppy in slightly subdued tones. 'I should get home as soon as possible if I was you, and don't on no account tell your old ma where you was shorn.'

'Why ever not?'

'Because hundreds of others'll want the same style see? An' I don't want to take on extra assistants.' He pulled hastily at the sheet round her neck: 'Be off with you then, there's a good girl.'

She looked at him, stunned. Be off with you? Was she hearing right?

'What about the money?'

'Tarrarr then, Missy. It was a pleasure to 'elp yer out. Be off now, afore your old gran begins to wonder where you are.'

Ivy Violet's temper began to rise: 'You old *bugger*! You're supposed to be paying me for all that hair. I didn't have it cut off for nothing. I was *selling* it.'

'Less of that bad language you lying little tart. You want your head examining if you think I'd pay owt for that stuff. It wouldn't even stuff a caterpillar!' He turned away, ready to go back to his stall on the other side of the screen, but Ivy Violet was not beaten yet. Her face was red with fear and outrage, and tears streamed down her face causing shreds of wet hair to stick to her cheeks.

'If you don't give me what you owe me, I'll tell it to the whole of Manchester you big twister.'

Hastily Choppy fished in the leather money bag at his waist, and drew out a threepenny bit. 'Here. Now get going.'

'THREEPENCE?' Her voice rang out all over Shude Hill. 'My beautiful hair only worth threepence?' She picked up her hat and swiftly she put the huge mound of hair into it, leaving Choppy in a daze as she hurried away. But on the way back to Whitworth Park, with the injustice of it all still smarting, she noticed a small barbers and wig makers in a basement in Mosely Street. She hesitated. She was tired now and hungry. It was getting late and Merrick would be waiting for her, but her pride pushed her down the small stone steps into the poorly lighted room. There was one elderly man there with a white apron on and rimless spectacles on his nose. He stared at her quietly.

She held out the hat full of her hair. 'I cut my hair off. I need to sell it.'

He took the hat from her as if it was the most usual thing in all the world. 'It's very good quality, madam. I don't actually deal in this sort of thing but I know a doll manufacturer who might be interested. How much were you wanting?'

She was completely taken aback: 'Well . . . Half a crown?' She gulped uncertainly.

The sides of his thin mouth smiled slightly. 'It is rather a lot.' He went over to a heavy wooden cupboard where there was a drawer with hollowed out wooden bowls in sections for money, and drew out a silver half-crown, and handed it to her.

'Thank you sir.' Ivy Violet almost bowed to him, then leaving the hair still resting in her hat, in his small salon, she rushed out.

When she arrived at Whitworth Park, she looked round anxiously. There wasn't a sign of Merrick.

Bondavalli's ice cream cart was nearby, where they

sold ice cream, from a huge wooden tub which was embedded in huge chunks of ice. They also sold small jam doughnuts at a halfpenny each. Ivy Violet bought a halfpenny ice cream cornet sprinkled with raspberry and a halfpenny doughnut. She devoured them anxiously as she sat down to wait for Merrick. Where on earth was he? She licked her fingers slowly, then got up and went to the drinking fountain to wash away the stickiness, and while she wiped her hands on her best lace hanky, she worried even more. There hadn't been a trace of him round Shude Hill, and even though the streets were so crowded . . . there was always that chance of seeing the needle in the haystack . . .

She decided to try the other place they'd talked about – Central Station, near the huge shining, granite, multi-storey luxury Midland Hotel.

No sooner had she walked through the entrance and up the brew of the wide cobbled courtyard packed with every sort of cab – from a few old style single horse drawn 'coffin' cabs, and 'growlers', to hansom cabs, hackney carriages and open topped landaulettes, interspersed with private motorcars and taxis and the steaming life of fresh horse manure – than she spotted Merrick standing near a horse trough next to an empty cab where the horse was munching away at a bag of oats fastened round its head. Beside him was a heavy leather travelling trunk.

At first he did not even seem to see her.

'It's *me* Ivy. Merrick . . . Remember?'

'Ivy! I didn't recognise you at first. What's happened to all your hair? You look completely different!' He looked at her and was speechless for a few moments, then he said: 'Sorry about getting stuck here, but two women have just gone to see someone off on the train and they've left me to guard this. I'm expecting at least fourpence for it. They've been ages.' He looked tired and hungry.

'Have you had anything to eat?'

'A cup of Oxo and a balm cake. How about you?'

'Ice cream and a doughnut.' She told him about Shude Hill and he called her stupid to have done such a thing.

'It's not the end of the world, Merrick,' she said huffily. 'I was trying to help both of us.'

'Well you don't need to any more, because as soon as these two posh women come back for this trunk, I'm setting off to Wigan on my own, to my Great Aunt Charlotte's. She's very religious, and if I tell her everything, she might help me. It'll be better than going home. I just couldn't stand that . . . And if you run away with me Ivy it'll make things even double worse.'

'Supposing your Aunt Charlotte's not there? Supposing she kicks you out?'

'If she does that, I shall just walk to London, or join the Foreign Legion or summat . . . Anyways you get back home quick. Manchester's no place when it gets dark for a young girl on her own.'

'And it's no place for you, either, Merrick . . . Not in some places.'

The two ladies arrived back to claim their trunk,

while Ivy Violet hovered uncertainly in the background. They both wore huge silk covered hats. One hat had a deep crown and was decorated with a purple velvet ribbon and small fresh violets. The other was like a huge upturned soup plate with a border of artificial rosebuds and Ivy could see, enviously, that their dresses were of dark ankle length heavy silk and that they wore silk stockings and soft delicate leather shoes. How on earth did they manage it?

When they'd gone, Merrick produced a sixpenny tip. He and Ivy Violet faced each other shyly. It was the parting of the ways. 'I'll go now then Ivy.'

Then suddenly they were in each other's arms as they kissed, and Ivy Violet sobbed bitterly against his jacket.

'There's no need to take on as much as that,' he said. 'We're sure to meet again.'

'But when . . . when?'

'It's no use.' He turned from her abruptly. 'I must go now. This minute. Or I'll never make it.' He was shivering slightly. Then he deliberately turned his back on her and walked quickly inside the great cavernous railway station, lost in seconds amongst the crowds.

Ivy Violet walked tearfully down the railway brew and on to Lower Mosely Street. She started off for home, never for one instant thinking of using her newly acquired wealth, the half-crown, and getting on a tram.

No. Somehow she just wanted to be sad and wallow in everything that had happened that day . . .

When she got out of bed this morning she never suspected what changes were in store for Merrick, and how she herself had almost changed the whole of her own life by nearly running away with him.

Time was beginning to fly and dusk was setting in as she approached the small streets off York Street, wondering what on earth she was going to say to her mother and father. She knew there would be all hell let loose when she got back. She was never out much on her own; it was usually with relations or friends, and her father had always warned her never to hang around pubs, but to give them a wide berth. 'Pubs is all right for the likes of me,' he'd say, 'but there's too many real boozers about these days, and too much drink has been the downfall of many a poor devil once he get in t'streets afterwards. So always watch it, lass, and steer clear. An' if any man tries to attract your attention – take no bloody notice, just keep going.'

Ivy Violet was doing just that when she heard loud footsteps at a small junction. She half turned, but it was too late as a weighty, beer soaked body pressed itself against her and a huge heavy hand grabbed at her shoulder: 'Give us a bit sweet'eart. 'Ave pity on a man what's lost 'is blooming wife.'

Immediately her sharp young senses came to her aid, as she kicked him sharply in the knees with her boots and scratched at his face in a squirming, ruthless fight. Then, as she realised she was winning the battle she let out a huge yell with what bit of breath she had left: 'Get rid of this bloody monster. Get rid of him!'

There was silence in the street. It was as if she was calling to a dead world, until out of the darkness she heard more footsteps running towards her, and in seconds the drunken man was wrenched away from her, and a voice said: 'Are you all right, child?'

She stood there gasping and out of breath. 'Yes. Yes I'm all right thank you. Thank you very much.'

Then the voice in the darkness said with a steely inflection: 'Nay . . . never thank me Ivy Violet. I'm only your damned father hunting high and low for you!'

'I warned you right from the start, you stupid girl!' said Phillis aggressively, when Ivy Violet was safely home. 'I always said things would come to no good with him carting other people's gramophones to places where they shouldn't oughter be . . . instead of getting on with what he was properly about in that there music shop.' Then she glared extra hard at Ivy Violet and said: 'No wonder that drunken lout had a go at you, tha' looks a proper little slut with all that hair hacked off. I'll just have to tell everyone we thought you was suffering from ring worm, but made a mistake.

'So you'd better wear my blue georgette scarf over your head for Sunday school tomorrow, and wear it for school an' all on Monday and evermore til all that hair's growed back to a decent length.'

Ivy Violet hung her head in shame.

'The next thing to do 'll be to let the Jacksons know what's 'appened,' said her father. 'So it's no good you sittin' there expecting to be mollycoddled with tripe and onions. We've got to go right now, and you've got to tell 'em what you told me – about the Kershaws threatening the poor lad with Nell Lane Workhouse.

'Come on then! Look sharp!'

The Jacksons were having their supper when Jos Hilton and Ivy Violet knocked at the door. And when Mrs Jackson opened it, she looked startled enough to have seen a ghost.

'Come in do Mr Hilton. Come in both of you. What a night and day it's been. I never want to live through it all again. First that fire – then we went to Kershaws to find out what had happened to poor Merrick . . . and Mr Kershaw told us he'd been dismissed on suspicion of stealing. It was a terrible, *terrible* shock to us all. Our Merrick would never steal anything in a month of Sundays. He has a heart of gold.

'As a matter of fact I was just this minute going to get in touch with the police to try and find him. I wanted to go to them sooner but our Al and the lads wouldn't hear of it. Said it was best to let us sort it out ourselves. His dad and our Frank, and Archie, our lodger, are all out hunting for him, right now.'

'Don't go to the police, Mrs Jackson,' pleaded Ivy Violet. 'Merrick's on his way to his Aunt Charlotte's at Wigan. He just couldn't face you all thinking he

41

IVY VIOLET

was a thief. And the Kershaws threatened him with
the workhouse. It was awful. And most of it was my
fault really. He lent me the gramophone, just for one
day. He didn't know someone wanted to buy it. He
even put a deposit on it from his own money whilst
he was borrowing it.'

'My poor, poor lad. Fancy threatening *anyone* like
that, never mind a boy his age. And all the work he's
done for them. They can never say he's even been a
scrounger. In fact he's been a godsend did they but
know it.' Mrs Jackson sighed with sadness and relief:
'I'll get our Frank to bicycle over to Wigan the second he gets in; through the night if needs be. All we
can hope and pray is that Merrick's safely there
under her roof.'

When Ivy Violet got to bed that night, she thanked
the heavens she was in her own bed, even with
young Roger's limbs jabbing her. She realised now
there was more to running away than she'd thought,
as she wept long and silently for Merrick remembering about what he'd said – that if his Aunt Charlotte
turfed him away he would head for London and
even try to join the Foreign Legion.

The following morning at church she prayed hard
for Merrick, and at Sunday school in the afternoon
she could hardly be bothered listening to Mr
Witherspoon as he laboured about sinners and the
fates of the fiery furnace for all wrongdoers. She
often found Sundays to be a pretty miserable day,
only fit for looking forward to Mondays.

Her mother Phillis was adamant that she lived a

very religious life on Sundays with attendance at
church twice or even three times. Phillis even went
so far as not to allow any work activities on the
Lord's Day of Rest including such items as sewing,
embroidery, playing the mouth organ, or laughing
and larking about too much. Though strangely – to
Ivy Violet's mind – she was still allowed to clean her
father's shoes, darn her brothers' socks, do the washing up, and make the bread.

The treatment of Merrick Jackson did not go unno-
ticed in the neighbourhood. People could all
distinguish between real villains and young folk
who were put upon, and for some time afterwards,
Bunnie and Donby noticed a definite decline in the
sale of sheet music, gramophone needles, penny
whistles, and concertinas, the smaller items being
the mainstay of their trade.

Next morning, when Ivy Violet was setting out sluggishly for the iron railings and grey stone yard of
school, she met her arch-enemy, buxom Maisy
Fowler from number 5, who had just started work in
a local bakehouse, where she had some relatives. No
wonder she was plump – for they never wanted for
broken fruit pies or even the odd loaf brought back
by an irate customer with a nut and bolt resting in it
from some loose machinery.

'It was a good quality fruit loaf, that was,' said
Maisy telling the tale one day, 'so Mrs Dixon let me
take it 'ome.'

43

'What's 'appened to Merrick then, Ivy Violet Hilton?' Her voice had a ring of hidden glee. 'I just don't know what you saw in such a bony, rag-bag of spots and pimples. All I can say is it serves you right for stealing things from that shop. Sometimes you really give yourselves airs, don't you? Just as if you was a proper lady. Everyone in the terrace heard that music, last Friday afternoon ... Talk about SWANK. Anyway, as my Mam always says: Pride comes before a fall.'

Ivy Violet tried to ignore her but her heart was thumping with anger. She knew there was nothing Maisy would like better than a really good scrap with Ivy Violet getting the worst of it. Then thankfully, there was a parting of the ways in the main street as Maisie said: 'And don't you go thinking I'm skiving off work like you do off school – because I'm on shift work see? And tonight when I gets back from me shift, I'm going to *proper* dancing lessons ...'

... Proper dancing lessons ... Ivy dwelt on it enviously until the old familiar large red brick building with its mass of tall windows and the words: Board of Education, written in black letters met her. If only *she* could go to proper dancing lessons like Maisy Fowler.

Not that they didn't do dancing at school. No one could say that Manchester Education was anything but forward looking and progressive. She even knew there would be dancing this very day because Miss Smith was rehearsing them for the end of summer

44

term Country Dancing Display in the grounds of Kendawe Hall near Old Trafford.

Their headmaster said that a revival of old national dances was greatly needed. 'Savage people,' he once said, '*always* danced.' Then he looked at the whole school from his platform and into their sea of pale, uncertain faces and proclaimed in loud, solemn and rather miserable tones – 'that the gayest dancers were often the saddest and most down-trodden on earth.' This put Ivy Violet off slightly as she certainly did not want to become sad and down-trodden – even though school country dancing did seem to lead to this effect . . . and Miss Smith could get extremely ratty if anyone went the wrong way in some of the dancing patterns they had to make.

That day in school, as they got ready to Strip The Willow and do a Handkerchief Morris Dance, and a Sailor's Hornpipe, she thought longingly of leaving school at fourteen and saving up to go to a proper Prince and Princess dancing class . . . like Maisy Fowler.

That flowered path to proper freedom.

CHAPTER 3

The Scandal

By the time Ivy Violet's fourteenth birthday arrived in the following May a terrible shock had occurred.

Her good, kind father, Jos Hilton, had died earlier in the year from what was described locally as galloping consumption, leaving the whole family totally heartbroken, and very poorly off.

Ivy Violet found now that there was little time for romantic day-dreaming, and her own freedom became more curtailed than ever as Phillis insisted that she stayed at home and kept house.

'You'd earn a mere pittance at your age. You'll be far more good to everyone if you stay here and keep things running smoothly for me and Bryan and Kenny what's working, and look after young Roger. Then if you gets really desperate for a bit of money of your own, you might manage to get a bit of sewing to do from the posher end or even help Tilly Simpkin out, for a few coppers from time to time with all those kids of hers.'

Ivy Violet heard the words with gloom and dejection. Tilly and Arthur Simpkin were what everybody called 'brainy'. Tilly had actually been to college and been a teacher for a while, until she met Arthur who was a gardener, and after that they had both been in a tied cottage working for the landed gentry until the cottage was lost to them because Arthur suddenly decided he was an atheist and refused to go to church. He swore that this was the reason for his dismissal and not the fact that he ruined the camellias by dosing them with lime and told his lordship that it was easier for a camel to go through the eye of a needle than a rich man to enter the house of the Lord. So ever since then Arthur had taken on any work he could get, such as road sweeping. Whilst Tilly Simpkin scrubbed the steps and washed the marble floors of Owen's College, and attended Workers Educational Association tutorial classes on Economics and Industrial History.

She was a very thin dark-eyed and active little woman with red spiky elbows and scrawked back hair in a huge bun, whilst her husband Arthur was short and round. He was sloppily clad in old tweed cast-offs, and was forever shaking his head from side to side and sagely quoting from the Bible, with new theories daily on the origin of Jesus Christ.

Often Ivy Violet felt a thread of envy for the whole

family, for they always seemed to land on the best side of things, and Joseph who was fifteen already had a steady job working in a printing works, whilst Mark who was fourteen and almost the same age as herself also had a job as a grocery assistant.

The only family who now bore any resemblance to themselves in Clark Terrace were the Watsons at number 6. The Watson family had been orphaned because of a gas explosion a year ago and were being looked after by fifteen-year-old Sylvia Watson who was now her friend – because they were both at home.

Sylvia's brother, Henry, was eighteen and worked at the Grand Hotel, Piccadilly, in the kitchens, whilst Sylvia looked after Thomas aged six and Mary aged four.

It was a sad family set-up for Sylvia and Henry, and young Sylvia bore the brunt of it. She was pale and very thin with fine, mousy coloured, straight hair and her young bright eyes seemed to dwell in wells of dark circles.

The backs of her hands were forever scarred with blister burns from the fat of cooking, and the paper thin surface of her white legs was delicately veined in blue, like that of many older women, or invalids. But in spite of all this she was a lively, kind-hearted girl with a great sense of humour and a depth of understanding far beyond her years.

One day in June when Ivy Violet was still grieving about the death of her father and she and Sylvia Watson were hanging out clothes together on the small green, Sylvia said, 'You know, Ivy, I think it's only fair you and me should get time off . . . like others does. We's the only young 'uns as works the 'ole time without a proper break, especially me with our Mary still at home, and only four. The truth is, Ivy – between you and me, I'd like to go out for a couple of hours on Wednesday afternoons.'

She hesitated a moment then gave Ivy Violet a swift sideways look and fluttered her eyelids nervously. 'I've met someone, see? But it's our secret and not even our Henry must know about it . . . So if you come and stand in for me, I'll do the same for you as well.'

Ivy Violet's heart leapt with delight 'Oh, Sylvia, what a good idea. Of course I'll do it. And maybe I'll be able to get out an' all to some sort of dancing class if I tries to make a copper or two out of the Simpkin tribe – doin' their ironing or summat.'

And so the next afternoon Ivy Violet went round to see Tilly Simpkin at number 2 , Clark Terrace.

'What can we do for you, Miss Hilton?' Tilly said, as she stood trimly at the door like a little red-cheeked skittle doll with eighteen-month-old Olive hanging on to her long black skirts. Marion, aged three, with a large hanky pinned to her check pinafore and her small red nose and lips all chapped and running with a summer cold, peered up at Ivy from behind her mother.

Ivy Violet looked at them. Quite truthfully they were her only hope for a bit of cash. She could see Poppy aged ten in the background sitting in a low wooden chair making a raffia mat. Her legs were like two thin misshapen lumps of flesh in long black stockings and were encased in leg irons

Never for her – the chance to dance. Her only advantage over others in similar states was that at least she came from a reasonably literate family and was encouraged to read books that her mother borrowed from the library, and to keep her hands occupied. In fact Poppy was so stuffed with general knowledge that she never lacked for words. Poppy attended special lessons twice a week in the mornings. Tilly wheeled her to them when she had finished her own stint of early morning charring.

They had eight children all together. The other two young ones in the family were Trevor who was seven and nine-year-old Maureen.

'I came to see if you'd like me to do washing for you Mrs Simpkin?'

'Washing? What on earth for? Aren't we clean enough for you?' said Tilly acidly surveying the young dark-haired girl in front of her. 'What's come over you Ivy? Surely a young lady of your age has got enough to do minding her own business?'

Ivy Violet was nonplussed . . . She didn't want to antagonise Tilly – who was known to be quite an awkward customer at times. It was almost as delicate as trying to avoid a tripwire.

'I've got this sort of . . . well this sort of idea of starting my own personal laundry service see, Mrs Simpkin. And I thought I'd call and see if you was interested. I want a top class of customer, if you understand? People who want their clothes properly looked after and all that sort of thing. And I knows how particular and well read you are Mrs Simpkin and how you think it's every woman's duty to try and get on in the world and be independent . . .' Ivy Violet paused for breath and trembled slightly under little Tilly Simpkin's shrewd gaze, half expecting to be sent off with a flea in her ear.

A glimmer of a smile softened Tilly's face. 'Well I must say – you're quite right on that score lass. There are people who believe in women being educated in our day and age, and fending for 'emselves, tho' one 'ud hardly ever think it in this terrace or most of the rest of Hulme come to that . . . But thank goodness for people like the Pankhursts and the Duchess of Marlborough that's what I say . . .' Then she said: 'You could push our Poppy out to her classes if you wanted. They're in t' mornings and I'm fair knackered when I gets back from charring. Your best bet, love, would be to start yourself off as a sort of general help at your age, then find out what suits you best as you go on. I could pay you fourpence a week if you took Poppy backwards and forwards for me. How would that suit?'

Ivy Violet could hardly believe her ears, and when her mother Phillis came home from work that evening there was even better news, for Phillis had been promoted to a higher grade checker in the fustian factory.

'. . . so maybe I'll be able to give you a shilling a week for working at home,' she said generously. 'But mind you save it up and put it in the penny bank every Friday.'

All that night in her cramped bed with young Roger, Ivy Violet dreamed of how she could now change her life, as she saw herself dressed in rustling, pale ivory taffeta and carrying a magnificent peacock feather fan as, all scented and tastefully powdered, she sat in some salon amidst the wealthiest women in the realm, indulging in conversation. They would discuss the Veleta, the St Bernard Waltz, the Military Two Step, the Polka and above all the Viennese Waltz . . . (including suitable partners for each dance . . .) All this was accompanied by sips of champagne. Finally she would be escorted to her fiacre wearing a royal blue velvet cloak lined in satin with a small ermine collar and holding a fringed, beaded purse with a fine carrying chain of pure gold. Her escort a young gentleman who spent as much on cigars in a month as the price of a house in Clark Terrace.

But the next day the rain was coming down in torrents as she and Sylvia washed and scrubbed and then festooned their small family living quarters with wet washing which had been put through the wooden mangle in a lean-to shed in the Hiltons' back yard. It left both their houses full of condensation in spite of the glowing fires in black leaded oven ranges. The atmosphere hung in a rising cloudy, muslin haze of steam which darkened the peeling, bulging and grubby parchment-coloured wallpaper, as both girls breathed in the scents of borax and soda and boiled wet cotton. To be followed like night follows day by the ironing.

Two weeks later, after Ivy Violet had been initiated into wheeling Tilly Simpkin's ten-year-old daughter Poppy to her special classes, and had been paid, she arranged to go the following Thursday afternoon to her first dancing class at Madam Miranda's Dance Studio.

Sylvia waved her off cheerfully, for she had already had two of her own secret Wednesday afternoon rendezvous, and was pledged to keep the secret about Ivy Violet's own time off. At home Phillis knew only that Ivy Violet was getting a few coppers for looking after Poppy and was, naturally, placing it in the penny bank along with her other weekly dues, for the time when she might need it – from ten to fifty years hence. 'For at least,' Phillis said proudly, 'even if the worst came to the worst, it will always pay for a funeral.'

At this Ivy Violet was filled with remorse and shame, for she knew that in Phillis's eyes her secret classes would appear to be tantamount to dancing on her father's grave, since they were hardly out of the mourning period.

At dinner time on Ivy Violet's first Thursday afternoon off she had arranged for Sylvia to do some of the Hiltons' starching and ironing and to prepare the food for the evening meal. If by some dire chance Phillis or one of the others got home early from work or school Sylvia would say Ivy was out at the shops.

*

The dancing lesson was for one hour, from 1.30 PM to 2.30 PM and was going to cost threepence. Madam Miranda's fees varied according to the time and name of the day; how many pupils were in any particular class, and what their general standard of dance was. Threepence was her minimum charge, an introductory starting fee.

Ivy Violet hurried towards the tall, early Victorian house with its soot darkened red bricks and blue-black slated roof.

The windows were grimy and there were heavy dark blue hessian curtains in the downstairs bay windows, which were decorated with the shapes of moons, suns and stars in orange and yellow felt appliquéd on. Hanging in each window was a white card which said in plain hand written block capitals: MADAM MIRANDA – QUALIFIED DANCING TEACHER FOR ALL DANCING SKILLS – BEGINNERS OF ALL AGES WELCOME.

Overawed by the temerity of her own courage in daring to come to this special establishment, Ivy Violet pressed the bell and heard it ring with a thin wobbly tinkle. She knew it was not the same place as her sworn enemy, Maisie Fowler, went for her evening dancing. Maisie was now fifteen and still as plump, petulant and wanton as ever. Ivy Violet could never forget how she had once collared Merrick Jackson in one of the back alleys when he was thirteen and tried to lure him to some bushes in the park playground, to 'gaze on her raspberries'. 'Raspberries' referred to her bare nipples and other things . . . But thankfully Merrick had thought better of it and said he had to get back to do his paper round.

The place Maisie still went to for her lessons was expensive and stylish. It was along Upper Chorlton Road, near Brooks' Bar, and you paid a shilling in advance and a shilling a lesson for dancing, callisthenics, and deportment. The instructor was Miss Isobel Denderfield, a Member of The Royal Imperial Institute of Footwork, Italy.

Ivy Violet paused again before ringing the bell of Madam Miranda's the second time for fear of seeming too demanding. Now that she was confronted with her dream of real dancing lessons about to be fulfilled, her morale had dwindled to that of a rabbit.

Then the paint-peeled front door suddenly opened and a tall handsome young man with a dark, pencil thin moustache and a scented aura of brilliantine from shining swept back hair greeted her.

He led her inside, and hardly had she passed an aspidistra plant on a bamboo stand when she heard a loud female voice booming: *One* – two, three. *One* – two, three. *One*, two, three, SWING . . . *One* – two, three. *One* – two, three. *One*, two, three, *SWING!* accompanied by weighty thumping on a highly stretched piano.

'I think you're a bit early for your class,' said the young man giving her a long cool stare. 'She won't 'ave finished this 'un for another ten minutes, but maybe I'll be takin' your lot for 'er 'cos she as to get out t' bank and the 'airdressers.' Then his voice went posh and he said: 'This way if you please, modo-moselle.'

He ushered her into a side room which had a black horsehair sofa in it piled with people's outdoor clothes. A large monochrome picture was on the wall of Anna Pavlova dancing *The Dying Swan*; whilst facing it on the other wall was an engraved print of an artist's impression of King George the Fifth's Coronation.

Another person was already waiting there in a beautiful pink satin dress.

'This is Mrs Gibbons,' said the young man introducing them. 'And this is Modo-moselle Hilton.'

When he'd gone, Mrs Gibbons explained to Ivy Violet that she had itching feet and wanted to regain her youth.

Ivy Violet smiled and looked with secret envy at the wonderful pink satin frock with its huge bustle-like bow at the back. Surely Mrs Gibbons was at least eighty-four? It just wasn't fair for her to be wearing a dress like that and taking dancing lessons when girls like herself had to scrimp and save and wear ordinary starched summer dresses.

'Now just you have a proper honest guess at how old I am, lovey,' Mrs Gibbons said five minutes after a stream of non-stop talking in which she revealed that the young man who had let Ivy Violet in was Madam Miranda's one and only eighteen-year-old son who sometimes helped out with the dancing lessons, and that Madam Miranda's husband was doing important work abroad . . . 'But between you and me, dearie – I don't think he even exists . . . Go on then. How old am I? Be honest, now.'

'Truly, I've just no idea,' pleaded Ivy Violet wondering whether she should play safe and say something like seventy-five.

There was a quick silence, then Mrs Gibbons said triumphantly: 'I'm exactly fifty-one. Just imagine that. Most gentlemen say I don't look a day over thirty-three . . .' She nudged Ivy slightly: 'I'm down on me luck, see darlin' – an' this frock's seen better days. You don't get much for a threepenny lesson love, but beggars can't be choosers, as you well know.'

Ivy nodded politely, taking in the powdered baggy surrounds of Mrs Gibbons's puffy eyes, and the missing tooth on one side of her rouged mouth and her rather saggy neck. Surely she, Ivy Violet Hilton, would never look as old as that? Surely – please God – she would be able to wear a pink satin frock with a bustle bow before she was too old for it? She resolved to swamp her face in witch hazel and rose water from her mother's small medicine cupboard the moment she got home.

A few minutes later two more people arrived, this time unintroduced. One was a very thin boy with a large Adam's apple and staring eyes who was wearing heavy boots, and the other was a man with a walrus moustache and a limp.

'They aren't actually dancers,' whispered Mrs Gibbons. 'The one with the walrus 'tache occasionally helps out with the piano, and gramophone. He's called Cedric Fogg. And the young thin lad is a general dogsbody called Robin who's good at playing the tambourine. They're both proper young gentleman; as polite as princes – which is more than can be said for her own, mollycoddled, darling Lankylot who showed you in here . . . His real name's Lancelot, but he doesn't deserve it.'

At that first lesson, which consisted of a mixed class of ten people, including herself and Mrs Gibbons, Ivy Violet was soon to find that Madam Miranda's training repertoire seemed to only consist of: One, two, three – SWING; One, two, three HOP, and One, two, three STOP!

'But not to worry if it seems very difficult at first,' said Madam Miranda who was about the same age as Mrs Gibbons and hated Mrs Gibbons for being so insensitive to her instructions, and for being so well dressed. 'We shall all do better next week when my son Mr Lancelot will help us all. He would have helped us this week but 'ee 'ad to go to the bank for me . . .' She beamed at everyone and waved a plump bespangled arm. She was wearing a peacock blue velvet dress with a lace insert at the bust. Her eyes were compelling and as black as coal. But even so nothing she could do or say could lure Mrs Gibbons into her power even though Ivy Violet herself left her academy like a small quivering jelly.

As Ivy Violet hurried home to relieve Sylvia she began to wonder whether her dream of being a dancer had been a huge and ghastly mistake.

When she got back everything had gone smoothly.

Some hot-pot was simmering away in the oven and Sylvia had ironed a mound of clothes.

'You've done just as good for me when I go out on Wednesdays,' she said to Ivy Violet. 'Going out on Wednesdays is like moving into a fairy-tale world.' Then her mouth set in a firm line and she said no more.

The following week, however, all was revealed when Sylvia got back all smiles, and produced two gold sovereigns. 'It's usually only one,' she explained, 'but he said I deserved more.' Then, after Ivy Violet had sworn eternal secrecy she began to explain.

'It's a rich old man I once met, and I 'as to do 'im favours . . . like . . . Special favours, you understand? But 'ee never enters into me, and it's nothing like them awful, perverted postcards, showing what some people does, like we was once shown by Dreena.' She shuddered in horror, and so did Ivy for they had gleaned bits of the most amazing knowledge from group conversations. Knowledge which was like a fantasy and had nothing to do with the reality of their own innocent young lives.

'All I 'as to do is undress and walk round 'is bedroom with no clothes on afore I goes 'ome. 'Ee says it's a natural physic that's better'rn all the pill boxes in the world for a rich old man, and 'ee always gives me a full sovereign. 'Ee says it's better than going to Mosely Street Art Gallery.

'I 'as the run of his 'ouse as Wednesdays is the 'ousekeeper's day off and I sits in the drawing room, with bowls of sweet peas on shining, polished tables next to me . . . and oh . . . the scent . . . sitting there looking out on a garden, as we drink tea and eat chocolate biscuits. Today I saw a red admiral butterfly . . .' She smiled peacefully at Ivy and the subject of her outings was never broached again.

But it was different with Ivy Violet as she went back for her second secret lesson with Madam Miranda, on Thursday.

When she got there she was late and the class had just begun. More people than ever were there and none of them less than twenty-five. Cedric Fogg was playing the piano. Robin was rattling the tambourine, and Lancelot Derby, Madam Miranda's eighteen-year-old son, was in full control and loving every minute of it. There was power, rather than music and dancing in his smooth handsome face, as seven pairs of people (many pairs being female couples because of male shortages) swung about the floor in the mad fever of a wooden legged quickstep. They rocked from side to side like ships in distress as the overworked piano gathered speed and the tambourine rattled away like a storm warning.

Ivy Violet stood there a trifle overawed, and watched. Everyone had intense looks on their faces and male and female teeth were glittering like those of wolves gathered in a pack The men's ears were very red and the women's bosoms were pressed hard against the men's chests, whilst legs were apparently uncontrolled.

Was this dancing?

Was this the true flowery path to the Viennese Waltz, and *Tales From the Vienna Woods*?

To Ivy Violet it looked liked the new rag-time from America she had heard about and the actual dancing she thought could only be described as The Scare-crow Walk.

Lancelot caught sight of her standing there in her lavender coloured, square necked cotton dress, with its three rows of tucks bordering the skirt and slotted with its small piece of purple ribbon on the bodice, and immediately he gulped with barely hidden triumph, for there was no one else in the room to equal her. All the rest were but faded parodies of youth.

His smile was perfect beneath the thin pencil moustache, and his eyes gleamed with lust. A feature Ivy Violet herself was completely unaware of standing so far away from him. But not for long. With a few panther-like steps from his black patent leather shoes he slid elegantly to her side and pressing her exceedingly close, guided her quickly into the musical jungle.

'Good afternoon Miss Hilton,' he murmured. 'This dance is called *The Miranda Walk*. I created it specially for our academy.' His voice was now irritatingly close to her ear and he blew into it slightly as he spoke.

Quickly she lifted her hand from his shoulder and wiped her ear. She found him bothersome. Yet when she looked in his face it was bland and reassuring, and she noticed that many of the ladies there were eyeing her with undisguised envy. Even Mrs Gibbons in her pink satin frock, who was being manoeuvred by an elderly woman with a neck like a giraffe, gave her a slight wave of encouragement.

By the time the end of the lesson arrived Ivy Violet was in a complete whirl, for Lancelot Derby had danced every dance with her, as well as giving instructions to all the rest of them. Although he was suspiciously jerky in his movements with a sort of bubbling inner strength completely unlinked to the rhythms of dance and had a grip like an iron vice, she began to succumb to his animal magnetism. Especially when the session actually finished to the strains of a Viennese waltz played on the gramophone. She half felt like a true princess – having to leave the ball well before the clock chimed three.

'We must, *must* meet again, my little princess, my little Ivy Violet,' crooned Lancelot with a streak of urgency. 'How about this Sunday? Meet me outside 'ere at two sharp and we'll walk to Platt Fields. I'll get a small 'amper prepared by our servant Rene.'

By now Ivy Violet had swept caution to the winds, for she realised she was being courted by a real young man who lived in a more exciting world than her own – even though he wasn't quite a prince.

'You seem very sparky, Ivy Violet Hilton,' joked Phillis when she arrived back from work to see the beautifully run home with the large wooden table neatly covered by a dazzling, white starched cotton cloth and set out ready for the evening meal. Quite unaware that it had all been done by Sylvia during Ivy Violet's outing to the dancing class she said, 'This domestic life doesn't half suit you. You're positively blooming!'

They all stared at her gratefully, and with a new respect as they demolished their gravy laden meat and potato pie and mopped the plates round greedily. It was a much quieter meal these days without their beloved father. There was not the same banter and air of confidence. They all seemed more involved in their own personal thoughts and lives.

Ivy Violet's eldest brother Bryan, who was now twenty-two and a warehouse clerk, had been due to go and lodge with his fiancée Pauline but the plan had been postponed when Jos Hilton died. Now, however, the move was imminent, for he and Pauline were due to be married in two months time.

Meanwhile, eighteen-year-old Kenny was still working as a messenger in the city where, in the course of his job, he had met Alfred MacFarlynne who worked as a clerk for a firm of architects just off Albert Square near Manchester Town Hall, and lived in Salford.

Both of them were the same age and keenly interested in photography. Alfred lived in a large house with access to a dark room of his own where he developed photographic plates. They had more space and freedom to pursue their hobby – and with Kenny's father gone – Kenny spent days and even nights at his friend's home, surrounded by Alfred's own family which consisted of five young sisters and an older brother. The effect was that Kenny quickly became divorced from the simple, penniless life of his childhood home at number 3 Clark Terrace. He became a more worldly person who visited Miss Horniman's Gaiety Theatre in Peter Street in Manchester and learned a lot about music and drama, and about actors like Lewis Casson and Sybil Thorndike and about the concerts given by the Hallé Orchestra and choir.

The two boys were as different in looks as chalk and cheese. Though they were both of good average height, Kenny Hilton was thin and wiry with dark curly hair, Alfred was more weighty and fairer with blue eyes.

'Whatever's up with our Ivy?' said her young brother, Roger, on Sunday morning. 'She says she'll not be at church this afternoon helping out with the Sunday school teaching. She says she's got a special appointment.'

Phillis pricked up her ears and frowned slightly: 'A *special* appointment? On a *Sunday*? How in heaven's name can that possibly come about? Surely there's nothing in her young life that is more important than The Lord on our day of rest!' Phillis quickened her step to the scullery where Ivy was gainfully employed starching collars in a small white enamel bowl full of thick grey-blue translucent Robin starch.

'Our Roger reckons you won't be at Sunday school this afternoon then?'

Ivy Violet gave an inward groan. Trust him to

spread the word . . . It must have happened when she said she'd be going for a walk with a friend and wouldn't be at Sunday school to give out the religious transfers. Sometimes they had scented picture cards to give out. But this time there were beautiful transfers of flowers of the Holy Land, which you could soak slightly in a saucer of water and try sticking them in the front of your Bible, even though there were reports that they often just dissolved into bits once too much water got at them. As everyone was only given a single transfer, there was no second chance to get it right. (Ivy's ever hopeful brother, Roger, had been hoping she would be able to give him and his mates a few extra transfers.)

'It's nothing, Mam,' said Ivy Violet hastily concentrating on the collars. 'Our Roger should keep his nose out of other people's business. I just *mentioned* a Sunday walk – that's all. There's no harm in *mentioning* things. The Lord doesn't frown on Sunday walks as long as it's not proper work. He likes us to greet the fresh air and sunshine – else why did he put the sun there?'

'Just so long as it's walking in the direction of church and back to help that nice Mr Witherspoon with the Sunday school,' said Phillis. 'You couldn't do better than meet a good young man like Quentin Witherspoon when you're a few years older. How he's managed to remain single so long is a complete mystery to me. It isn't as if he has an invalid mother or anything.'

Ivy Violet sniffed haughtily. Mothers seemed to

spend their time deciding who were the most suitable humans for others to marry, Ivy thought, even going so far as to suggest suitable girls for boys to marry. She closed her eyes in mild disgust. And as for deciding on suitable husbands – it was downright cheek when most of them moaned and groaned for ever once they themselves were married.

Sunday was a beautiful summery day, and to salve her conscience Ivy went early to Holy Communion. Then she went to the morning service as well, working like a slave between times to complete every manner of household task she could think of, and trying to look thoroughly pious and unconcerned. Then, after a midday dinner of fresh runner beans and potatoes, and roast lamb with mint sauce, which was a fortnightly treat, followed by semolina pudding, she washed the pots. Then she was delighted to hear her mother reveal that she was going out herself for a bicycle ride to Sale Moor with a friend from work who was a widower called Freddy Mason, and that they would not be back until well after teatime.

'So mind you get to that Sunday school sharp,' warned Phillis.

As soon as Phillis had gone Roger said: 'Promise you won't say owt, our Ivy, but I can't go this afternoon, 'cos I've promised Maureen and Poppy and Trevor Simpkin I'd help 'em sail their boats in t' park lake at the rec.

'An' anyways – I knows *you're* not goin'.'

He stared at her in triumph, then his face became

cool and insolent. It was an armed truce as she watched him dash away to the Simpkin tribe at number 2. They were a law unto themselves where religion was concerned, for fifteen-year-old Joseph their eldest son, and his brother Mark were staunch members of the church choir. But, in their mother Tilly's words, 'Freedom to worship or not to worship has always been one of the facts of life in this 'ouse Ivy. And them that doesn't approve that freedom is hypocrites. Most of 'em round 'ere doesn't care a tinker's cuss one way or t'other. They only trains kids not to be heathens on Sundays just to get a rest for 'emselves on Sunday afternoons . . . But 'oo can truly blame em?'

Swiftly, Ivy Violet slipped into her best lavender cotton frock again. Then she looked in the ancient, grey cardboard hat box in Phillis's bedroom where she knew there was a creamy straw hat that Phillis never wore because it was too tight. She took it out and perched it on her own long and bouncing curls which had grown again. Even though they were natural they had been tied up in head hurting rags all night to make them look more like the neat corkscrew curls of past Victorian days.

She hurried off to Madam Miranda's, to meet Lancelot.

As she neared the low brick wall with its black painted iron railings topped by a row of fleur-de-lys, she was shocked to find no one waiting there. But her confidence was rewarded as moments later Lancelot Derby turned up, regally attired in a buff-coloured striped blazer suit, a white shirt, bow tie and boater. He was also carrying a small wicker picnic basket.

Her heart flooded with happiness and relief.

Ivy Violet was aware of the joys of walking in open spaces and country lanes and municipal parks for a Sunday promenade, for it always revealed to her that not every young girl in Manchester was shackled to Sunday school. She strolled along in the warm sunshine with what must surely have been the most handsome man in the world, past elegantly dressed women with parasols, a Salvation Army band playing hymns in the distance, young children with kites and balloons and beautiful municipal flower beds arrayed in colourful splendour. Life could not have been more heavenly.

Lancelot Derby spent a great deal of time bowing and raising his hat to other young ladies and comely matrons who, he explained, had all been patrons of mother's dancing academy at some time in their lives.

Ivy Violet was overcome with shyness. Her normal cheekiness was lost as she walked along with Lancelot who she thought of as a Greek god. She had very little to say, which did not matter in the least as Lancelot was able to air his views on every subject under the sun. She thought this was a good sign, for she had heard it said that men who talked a lot were less likely to compromise women because their brains were on another plane. Not that she expected anything other than gentlemanly behaviour, but a girl always had to be on her guard.

Once they were in Platt Fields they strolled to a park seat beneath some willow trees. Lancelot opened the small wicker picnic basket and drew out a bundle of brawn and pickle sandwiches covered in a white damask dinner napkin. Then he produced two small pale blue china plates and two more napkins to spread on their laps. The sandwiches were followed by currant buns and ginger beer, most of it rapidly consumed by Lancelot whilst Ivy Violet endeavoured, to her own disadvantage, to eat at a delicate and ladylike speed.

'I thoroughly enjoyed that,' he said, licking his lips and hastily wiping his thin moustache. 'We must do this again some time. But now I think we should be walking home. Time waits for no man.'

Ivy Violet nodded. She was in a complete daze of compliance. If he had suggested paddling in a park lake she would no doubt have agreed. Even so, she was pleased that he suggested leaving early as she did not want to arouse Phillis's suspicions about Sunday school.

When they got back to the front entrance at Madam Miranda's Lancelot said: 'If you just come in for a few minutes whilst I leave this picnic basket and freshen up – I'll walk you home.'

It was the last thing Ivy wanted. The sight of him walking her home to Clark Terrace would be condemning her as a scarlet woman – especially on a Sunday – and at her tender age. In her heart of hearts she knew he was not quite the type of sober looking young man suitable for her part of Hulme in broad daylight.

'It's quite all right, Lancelot. I can see my own self home. I've truly enjoyed our afternoon outing.'

He looked at her askance. 'I couldn't let you walk home alone! Just imagine if anything happened?'

She was puzzled. 'But what on earth could happen?'

'Look, my little angel, you just do as I suggest, and come in for a few minutes whilst I dump this dratted food holder. There's no one else in. It'll all be completely private. Mother's gone to see her sister in Chorlton-cum-Hardy.'

For a moment, Ivy Violet felt a thread of unease. She sensed a streak of coarseness and bullying emerging, for the honeyed accent of the dancing class, with all its 'Modom-moselles', had long since vanished into a sharp unhampered local accent. But she was waylaid again as he suddenly gave her a charming toothy smile and murmured: 'Have faith in me my little bird. Just come in and wait for a few seconds and I'll show you some wonderful pictures of my mother, painted in her heyday. They are upstairs in her small private salon.' And before Ivy Violet could think or utter another word he was pulling her with a powerful grip up the wide staircase covered in Turkey carpeting.

He put her in a room while he went to dispose of the picnic basket and freshen himself up. He pointed out that if she wanted to do the same 'there is a

71

small boudoir bathroom facility just in the corridor opposite'.

Ivy Violet looked round the room with mounting nervousness. It was quite true that there were some lovely pictures on the walls of dancers, and there were a number of framed posters of music hall programmes featuring the name in very small letters of someone called Minna Derby. All she was interested in was getting back home.

She went and stood on the landing and called: 'Lan . . . celot.'

The house was still and silent with glimmers of sunlight coming through a small, stained glass window on the landing and from fanlights above the bedroom doors. It was as if she was the only person on earth. Then suddenly she heard the noise of a door open downstairs and he came hurrying towards her so quickly that she was almost bowled over. He stood close against her panting. 'What was it my darling?'

'N-n-nothing. I just wondered where you were that's all. I'll have to be getting back home.'

'Of course you will. What did you think of the paintings?' He led her downstairs as they spoke and her spirits lifted.

'They were beautiful . . .'

'But not as beautiful as you, Ivy Violet.' He stroked her hair gently, and pressed himself against her in the hall.

She did not quite know what to do. Then before she could say anything he had planted what she thought of as a horrible French kiss on her mouth;

the sort that she and Sylvia knew could often lead to pregnancy and even worse. She nearly fainted with fear, then pulling herself together she lunged out with one huge push. She made for the front door which fortunately opened easily.

She ran down the road like someone running for a tram, her heart thudding with disgust and shame. How could he possibly have used her so? Probably because it was an easy way to get at any maiden, for there were no cumbersome buttons and tapes to undo, or layers of clothes to wade through. She could see now that it was the most vulnerable piece of her body for any man to plunder, without warning. Any man, but certainly not any *gentleman*.

As she neared home her thoughts fell to rock bottom with fear as the words of the past mocked at her, words urged as a warning to all young girls: 'Never let them get their tongues in your mouth else you might end up wi' child.' At the time few young people knew where children came from: possible places ranged from the midwife's bag to being found under a gooseberry bush. The *human* event bore no relation to cats having kittens or dogs puppies for most children assumed that mothers and fathers had more magical ways of begetting their young than the so-called 'animal kingdom'.

'Wherever have you been?' said Phillis when she got back. 'Where's your prayer book and Bible? And what's happened to your gloves?'

Ivy hurried into the scullery to avoid her gaze, and started to cut some bread for tea. Then she called: 'Did you see Mr Mason then Mam? Did you get to Sale Moor on your bicycle ride?'

'I did that. We had right good bit of exercise. Get that tea poured out. And did you stay behind with that nice Quentin Witherspoon then?'

'No, he never mentioned anything to me,' called Ivy Violet, feeling that this was an entirely honest reply since she had not even seen him.

When she came back to the living room Phillis looked at her suspiciously. 'Still in your best frock? And not even a pinny to cover it – whatever's been going on?'

Ivy hurried past her to hide her fear and clattered upstairs calling as she went: 'I'm not a prisoner – just because it's Sunday, our Mam. I don't look at everything *you* wear and tell you whether you should be wearing an overall, or if you're wearing boots, or shoes, or clogs.'

At tea time there were only three of them, Phillis, young Roger and Ivy; Bryan was tactfully tucked away at his lady love's, Pauline's, and Kenny was out with his friend Alfred. But even so Ivy Violet was on tenterhooks as the meal progressed in case young Roger should give the game away.

Then just as she was sweeping the last crumbs from the table and was thankful to be disappearing into the scullery again, she heard Roger's piping voice: 'I can't help sucking me thumb, Mam. It's not 'cos I'm a baby at all, it's just that it 'urts and smarts. I scratched it see?'

'Go and get some iodine on it this minute then.'

'That'll make it smart more'n ever.' He stared at her sullenly. His straight sandy hair was unevenly fringed across his pale forehead.

'Do as I say, and less of your cheek. Bring me that iodine bottle an' t' cotton wool.

'How did you scratch it?'

'Int' pond at park – fixin' Trev's sailin' boat.' He gave a sudden gasp, and put his fingers across his gappy mouth where his two new front teeth were only half grown, realising too late that he had burnt his boats.

'You what? You mean to sit there and tell me that you've been in the park with that Simpkin tribe on a Sunday afternoon?' Her voice rose to a bellow: 'IVY – just you come here immediately, and bring that bottle of iodine off the shelf whilst you're passing.'

Ivy's knees weakened to blancmange. Trust that little blab mouth she thought. She walked slowly into the room. She had already changed into her white working smock and dark skirt. She wiped her hands slowly on a towel.

'What's all this then? Did you know he wasn't at Sunday school with Mr Witherspoon?'

Before Ivy Violet could say a word Roger revealed all. 'Course she didn't 'cos she never went herself, either. Me n' Maureen, n' Poppy, n' Trev saw 'er with a man with a black moustache when we was going t' rec. An' they was carrying a picnic basket.' He beamed at them both looking impressed by his own truthful description of what he had seen.

Phillis looked shocked and put a hand up to her

head. No wonder her own hair had suddenly gone so grey. Then she turned on Roger and shouted: 'Get away from this table!

'You're a very, very naughty and disobedient boy! Get upstairs to the bedroom and don't come out til I say.'

Then turning to Ivy Violet she said: 'And as for you *Miss*, there seems to be a lot of explaining to do.'

Any kind of deceit spotted by the inhabitants of Clark Terrace was talked about endlessly so that everyone knew of Ivy Violet's outing with a tall unknown stranger with a black moustache. Many opinions were floated on mischievous summer breezes:

'Oh yes. I've seen them quite often. He's twice her age, and they say he's a married man with four kids.'

'Oh aye. I know 'im all right; it's that son of Charlie Barnsgrove's, what tried to run away to sea last year when 'ee were thirteen. 'Ee's gettin into a right little tearaway – growing a 'tache at 'is age. It's a case of lock up yer daughters with 'im about.'

'Well yes. Actually . . . Yes I do know the young man in question, he's from a very high flown family. No I did not say fly blown – even if his moustache is a bit thin.'

The only person who kept quiet and helped Ivy to weather the storm was Sylvia. But even to her – the best keeper of secrets – Ivy was too shy to tell her exactly what had happened. She nursed the episode close to her own bosom with growing forebodings and said that Lancelot had not behaved very well towards her and that she had no intention of ever going back to Madam Miranda's again.

'But that doesn't mean you can't still have the time off to visit your rich old man, Sylvia,' she said. 'It's just that I don't think the place I went was any good, and anyway I'm not really interested in dancing classes any more.' She tried to smile cheerfully but underneath her heart was breaking.

One day about a month later when she thought all the fuss was at last forgotten she met her old enemy Maisy Fowler from number 5 – who usually tried to avoid her. But today was different. Today Maisy was as friendly and outgoing as a summer butterfly.

'Ivy Violet – Well I never! Who'd think we live so near yet hardly ever meet? I expect you've heard the news about Merrick?'

Ivy shook her head coldly. She and Merrick had never been in touch since their running away episode.

'He's coming back for good at the end of the week to help his Ma out.' Then Maisy added: 'My . . . you aren't half putting on weight, Ivy, for a young girl. I'd say you was three months gone if I didn't know better. But then you always did envy me my flesh didn't you?'

Ivy could hardly believe her ears. Her face went as red as fire as she sprang towards Maisy ready to hit her but Maisy was saved as Monty Pratt (who was a bad-tempered sixty-five) and his old mother Molly (aged eighty-seven) from number 4 Clark Terrace came shuffling along the street towards them.

Ivy knew she was getting plumper but most people just called her a bonny lass. She was always hoping that once she escaped from Clark Terrace for ever then she would get back to a wonderful slimness rather than a bony scragginess. A few people said that her extra weight was puppy fat. Then as the small thread of inner guilt and fear reared to the front of her mind again a terrible thought struck her: Supposing she *was* fertile and with child? As the childish gossip had warned.

She was filled with a cold dread.

'By the way Ivy Violet.' Maisy hesitated with glee. 'What happened to them dancing classes of yours? And you being Lankey's bit of fluff?'

Ivy stared at her in dumb misery.

'That's what comes of going to a tinpot place like that. I knew as soon as you went there you'd meet your doom. It's only for tarts, and everyone in the proper dancing world knows what Lanky Derby is.'

The next morning when Ivy Violet got up she felt sick with worry as the porridge she had eaten swayed about in her stomach. She felt like running to the W.C. every second.

'Whatever's wrong with you?' Phillis said, as she hurried off to work. 'Are you sure you'll be all right?'

Ivy Violet nodded forlornly. Supposing at this minute she was growing a small Lancelot within her?

She went sluggishly about her housework and

seemed to be doing nothing but eat ginger biscuits, and lumps of cheese. She had at least four ginger-breads, and normally she hated them, and the Cheshire cheese was crumbled to bits in its dish completely devastated.

By the time Phillis came back in the evening and the meal was over Ivy Violet was in a state of morbid hysteria. She imagined that she must have unwittingly allowed herself to become pregnant. Fourteen was very young but it wasn't impossible, she thought. All she could do was lie on her bed in a daze of fright.

'There's summat worrying you child,' Phillis said shrewdly as she stood at the bedside with a glass of water. Then stroking Ivy Violet's sweating forehead she said: 'Has it anything to do with when you went out for the walk with that young man?'

Ivy turned away and hid her face under the sheet.

'I happened to meet Mrs Jackson today,' said Phillis. 'She said Merrick was coming home.' Then Phillis added: 'We had a bit of a chat. I doesn't see her often, but I told her you'd met up with her cousin's son from Platt Fields way and was walking out with 'im.'

There was sudden silence.

Ivy Violet stayed hidden under the sheet and Phillis looked idly up at the bedroom ceiling. Then with a sudden streak of fury she ripped the sheet away from her cowering daughter and bellowed: 'You're a damned deceitful little madam! And it's not often I'm driven to swearing.

'Merrick's Mam hasn't got any cousins with sons! And that's not the half of it, you underhand little devil. It's being said in the terrace that you've been cheapening yourself with someone years older than yourself with a seedy reputation – from that harlot's dancing class.'

Ivy Violet climbed hastily from the bed and stood there wringing her hands. 'It was only the once, Mam. I *swear*. I never knew he was a womaniser; *honest*. I never went back there again. I went there because I wanted to learn to dance proper, and it was the only cheap place.'

'You learn more than *dancing* at holes like that,' said Phillis acidly, as Ivy began to moan and weep. As the weeping did not stop Phillis said: 'Well at least no harm's done and you've learnt a good lesson early on in life.'

'B . . . b . . . but s . . . s . . . supposing I'm with child Mam?' She burst into another torrent of weeping.

Phillis stared at her aghast. 'You WHAT?'

As Ivy Violet sat with red rimmed eyes explaining what had happened, a well concealed smile hovered at the corners of Phillis's mouth. 'Yes love. They're quite right to spread the message that French kisses can lead to babies, but it's not quite as easy as that. Thank the Good Lord!'

For the next half hour she sat there explaining the facts of life to Ivy Violet in full detail. It was not a task Phillis had ever ventured on before. Her own generation had been told little and only knew bits from gossip. For most people there was often not even an illustration of the reproductive organs of the body or any true information about this side of life. Boys were left to glean information from fathers and older brothers, and girls from any female unprudish enough to come forward with the revelations.

'Not that I knows the proper medical terms meself love, but at least you'll have a proper idea of what really happens. Even the best of men don't mind trying their luck if they think they can get away with it.' Then she added hastily: 'Except for real gentlemen like Mr Witherspoon.'

Ivy Violet's recovery was remarkable. In another hour she was completely back to her old self.

But in other parts of the terrace the stain on her character had become like a pool of indelible ink. When Merrick Jackson arrived home at the end of the week – tall and handsome with never a boil or carbuncle to be seen – he was warned by his mother to have nothing to do with her for she had grown into a cheat, a liar and a young girl of easy virtue.

CHAPTER 4

The Ball

Merrick Jackson had mixed feelings about being back home. In many ways he had come to appreciate living with his strict, well-organised Aunt Charlotte whose background was that of the coal mines and cotton mills of Wigan.

She had seven grown up children and scores of relatives, and when the true story had been revealed about Merrick and the gramophone she found him cheap lodgings nearby and a job in a small iron smelting and steel-making factory as an assistant ledger clerk. The wooden hut where he worked was black with soot and the small windows were almost opaque with grime. It lay in an unpaved, potholed yard bedded with ash grit. The smoke and fumes from the iron smelting turned his complexion to a dull yellow at times. But the comradeship of most of the other men working there widened his adolescent horizons, even though he began to think that he might live there for ever. He found himself a girlfriend called Imelda, at a local dance, who went with him for country walks and encouraged him to get some more education.

Wigan was in the forefront of mining engineering, mining plans and technical education for boys. Most girls though had to make do with working in the cotton mills or in the garment trade.

Just after his sixteenth birthday Merrick received a letter from his father saying that his mother was becoming lame with arthritis and suffering from bronchitis —

> ' . . . Archie Monks the lodger is quitting to get married son, so your ma and me think you'd better get back here to help out, especially as your brother Frank is wanting to sign on in the Mercantile Marine.'

A few weeks later, with the blessings and a few affectionate tears from his Aunt Charlotte, Merrick came back to Hulme. He was half an inch taller and a world wiser as his sad girlfriend Imelda waved him goodbye and they swore to meet as often as possible.

At first, it was as if he had been away a century. Then after a few hours of settling in and having something to eat, and getting all the local news, he said cautiously: 'How's Ivy Hilton going on from Clark Terrace?'

There was a frosty silence.

'I think all that's best forgotten son,' said his mother quietly, ' . . . after all the ructions she caused. She was at the bottom of all that gramophone palaver. She could have easily ruined your whole life with her selfishness. I can't think how she managed to get you so tied round her little finger. But it's best forgotten now.'

There was an uneasy silence as Merrick thought about the new girlfriend he had left behind in Wigan. Imelda was more like a sort of sister. But Ivy Violet? He shook his head slightly; she was an unknown quantity.

'The best thing tha' can do now Merrick is get along to evening classes like you was doin' in Wigan and keep on wi' them studies, so as to get some proper certificates,' his father said. 'Then tha' can help out at home and take on some casual work with the hope of getting some sort of apprenticeship in a regular trade. Even though you've nearly missed the boat lad.' His father shook his head knowingly: 'Sixteen's a bit late for apprenticeships in many trades.'

Merrick nodded silently. How different it all was now. Even some of the furniture downstairs had been altered. The books in his bedroom and his boyhood mementoes and toys had all been packed away in an old tin trunk. The curtains in the back kitchen window had been changed from green to dark orange. The whole picture of home had been ruined. But he knew deep down that nothing was ever just a picture and he felt a pang of terrible sadness.

'We must all count our blessings, son.' His mother smiled at him comfortingly: 'It's good to see you back so fit and well. At least we're all still alive and kicking – and not like poor Phillis Hilton losing her husband Jos. What a shock that was. I daresay that's what sent young Ivy Violet off the rails a bit. They say she went quite du-lally, with a no-gooder from one of those afternoon hops. Maisy Fowler's mother told me all about it. Maisy is getting to be a real good looker; a catch for any young man. And such a lovely personality. Her mother says she's hoping to become a music teacher and have her own private academy, but meanwhile she's working at the greengrocer's.'

Merrick nodded sympathetically, but really his mind was more interested in Ivy herself. Fancy her turning out so bad, so quickly – since he went away. It was almost unbelievable. But he knew his mother never told lies. And as for Maisy Fowler?

He quivered slightly and began to think about his heroes Captain Scott and Ernest Shackleton on their Antarctic expedition. And how Captain Scott discovered land for Edward VII using sledges to travel over the ice, pulled by teams of Eskimo sledge dogs across the vast regions of frozen snow. There was something more comforting about all that than thinking of Ivy Violet and Maisy Fowler.

*

As for Ivy Violet herself, she was wallowing in the depth of depression. Life was dragging on without a single bit of excitement or romance as she stood there ironing in the living room. She heated up the heavy black and shining flat irons for the mountains of family laundry including sheets from the Simpkin tribe who were paying her a few coppers but expected each sheet to be dolly blued and perfectly starched. She stared beyond the muggy interior gloom towards the heavy net curtains and the outdoor brightness.

Phillis threatened her daily: 'The sooner you get out to work to a place where you can't just do as you please during the day, the better.' Phillis seemed to have forgotten that it was she who had deprived Ivy Violet of a chance of getting out into the wider world by making her stay at home. But the tune was different now. 'The sooner you get away from that little tart Sylvia's influence my girl, the better it'll be,' she said. 'Oh yes, I well know she's to be pitied being left to bring up those two young weans herself and keep house for her brother, but there's many others been in the same boat and they never became an old man's darling. She's just a sly little puss and the sooner you get away from her influence the better. You mark my words Ivy Violet, Miss Sylvia Watson is on the slippery slope to complete ruination and soon you'll be slithering after her.'

'And how do I do *that*, Ma?' yelled Ivy Violet angrily one day, with her cheeks burning in fury as she stood there with the sweeping brush. 'Just explain if you will how a girl like me, tied all the time like a prisoner and slave to Clark Terrace, and with never a penny to her name can get out and find work? *It was you what made me a skivvy in the first place!'*

Phillis looked at her with a trace of dry compassion: 'I may not be anything special, and I may only be your poor old stepmother who bears all the brunt of you, but at least I knows the difference between proper talk and untidy talk. It wasn't me *"what* got you working as a skivvy". I presume you mean it was me who at that certain time thought it would be a suitable idea for you to stay at home and be the housekeeper.' Phillis was speaking like cool cut glass.

Ivy Violet glowered at her and muttered 'unpaid drudge' under her breath. When Phillis had flounced away she blessed Sylvia Watson for being there and sometimes giving the dark clouds just the hint of a silver lining with her descriptions of luxury and splendour only a few miles away. Sylvia was the only person, apart from heroines in weekly magazines, to shed the faintest ray of romantic hope.

Ivy Violet stopped ironing at last and put the irons in a corner of the kitchen range. Maybe she would just have time to sit on the doorstep in the sun, she thought, and sew a bit of her dance dress in time for the Spring Ball that Sylvia had told her about. It was a mid-summer affair which other people in the terrace had never heard of – not even Phillis. It was where all the arty people went and where Sylvia's sugar daddy Mr Horatio Porter was taking her. And he'd said Ivy Violet could go as well if she wanted to – even though he'd never even seen her. He said it was an honour to be partner to two beautiful young women. He had given Sylvia a dress length of deep blue velvet for Ivy Violet because he was a rich draper in the wholesale trade.

The thought of going to a ball and dancing proper Viennese waltzes and polkas, instead of just a cheap local, pay-at-the-door hop like some of the places in Manchester, filled Ivy Violet with ecstatic zeal as she undid the bundle of blue velvet carefully wrapped in brown paper which stretched itself out into the shape of a half stitched up, hand sewn frock.

It was taking a long time and was the first party dance dress she had ever made. It was done with French seams to give the seams as much strength as those done on a proper sewing machine. Firstly small running stitches were sewn on the right side of the material as if you were making a mistake. Then the frock was turned inside out and another row of the tiniest possible running stitches sewn along another seam beyond the line of stitches already sewn. It gave perfect results and was not just 'tacked together' like some dresses more cheaply machined. Her friend Sylvia had taught her. Sylvia had made a beautiful frock in deep crimson taffeta with huge puff sleeves and a very low, boat-shaped neck. But her own was planned with a plain vee neck and sleeveless with a very modern gently flared skirt, unlike the old-fashioned hobble things that some rich women still wore, all swaddled at the ankles so that you minced about instead of taking proper steps. Sometimes she crept downstairs in the night when everyone was asleep to stitch some of the seams and hems.

When it was finished she planned to have it fashioned across the shoulders with a remnant of white muslin and two revived artificial pale pink roses that Tilly Simpkins had once chucked out, which Ivy and Sylvia had carefully restored to a fresh brilliance.

Her eyes grew dreamy at the thought of her frock's final glory as she imagined the luxurious ball with all the wonderfully rich women of Manchester there, with their ostrich feathers and jewels, and their rows of pearls and beautiful ivory fans. And the men in evening dress.

Would she stand with Sylvia and Mr Porter at the top of some wide and thickly carpeted stairs with wrought iron balustrades and wooden banisters leading down to the huge ceremonial hall; a place alive with music and the scent of flowers, with elegant sprays of soft yellow mimosa in great pot vases?

Would they be announced by some loud voiced, bewigged and handsome flunkey in a gold braided jacket and a cravat of frilled white lace at his throat? 'Mr Horatio Porter, Miss Sylvia Watson , and Miss Ivy Violet Hilton . . .'

She sighed to herself in a moment of heavenly bliss, and accidentally stuck the needle in her finger causing a spot of blood to fall on the dress. She cursed silently, sucked her finger and wrapped up the frock hastily in its brown paper parcel.

When Phillis got back at tea time she had some surprise news. 'I think I've found you a job at last love. It's high time you had a normal working life at last, so as you can better yourself. Much as you don't appear to believe it, I really have been trying to find something all these months. But it's been very hard for me to seek out anything that might stand you in good stead for later. I certainly wouldn't like you to end up as a kept concubine in a gilded cage – such as young Sylvia is heading for. You're worth more than that Ivy Violet.' Phillis allowed a flicker of affection to escape across her face. 'Anyway I think summat's just about cropped up because I was talking to Winny Jackson whose cousin Conny works in the Diamonta sweatshops round the back of their gowns emporium not far from Samuels in King Street and she reckons they need an extra girl for tacking in linings and doing padding.' Then Phillis glowered and said: 'What's up? You spoilt ungrateful little monkey. I expected you to be really thrilled, yet you've got a sulky bottom lip fit to sit on!'

At once, Ivy Violet tried to look delighted, but they both knew it was a sham. She felt guilty. Perhaps she should have kept her trap shut about being a slave to the wash tub, the posser and flat iron because at the moment life wasn't too bad. Especially with the excitement of getting her frock ready for the Spring Ball in a few weeks' time. If this job Phillis had found for her started immediately it could well muck up all her arrangements. What chance would there be of any independence if she had to work all hours just to give Phillis her wages? Ivy Violet thought of how she and Sylvia were able to have long and intimate conversations and reveal their innermost thoughts to each other on the ways of the world, discussing the more interesting aspects of men and how they should be dealt with.

'They want you to start on Monday morning,' said Phillis, voicing Ivy's worst fears. 'You don't need to be there 'til eight thirty because you'll need to see Conny Jackson to be told what to do and to be introduced to everyone, including Mr Dempster the overseer. Miss Jackson is in charge of all the junior work staff in the sewing room. I think you normally have to start at seven fifteen each morning and do all the wet and dry dusting and sweeping, both morning and night. Then at the start of each day you change into a sewing overall and put out the patterns and materials, scissors, pins and all the rest on the work benches Anyway I'd better not get you muddled but Conny'll keep you right. They're very short of girls at present. One of them never came back from her honeymoon and three more are off with bad backs.'

The more Phillis said, the more Ivy Violet's heart fell. It was obvious that the place must be a hell hole if everyone was always being away. She had heard from other people that some of the supervisors behind posh gown shops were absolute birds of prey, pecking the very flesh off a young girl's bones in order to serve the rich pickings of the master.

Her mouth began to pout even more. How on earth could she get out of it after always moaning that there was nothing she wanted more than a job of her own, away from home? It dawned on her that finding a way towards what she thought of as a proper lady's life might have more thorns on the way than she had ever imagined. By the time she got there she could be some fading old hag of about forty and not even married to anyone decent.

'For God's sake get that look off your mug,' simmered Phillis. 'There must be thousands of girls would jump at it. Just imagine working in the best part of the city for a famous fashion house. Every damned apprentice – even lads has to do that to get on, and you're no girl that's going to get things easy in life – you're just not pretty enough. You've got to be someone with the looks of Maisy Fowler, and be able to play the piano before that can happen.

Maisy Fowler.

Ivy Violet seethed inside at the very sound of her name. It was reported that Merrick Jackson was never out of the greengrocer's shop where she worked these days and twice she had seen them herself, walking out together towards the Boskin Memorial Hall when there were dances on. She remembered that Maisy had been dolled up like a dog's dinner with a hat the size of a bin lid and Merrick had walked beside her. Merrick had looked as if he was in a strange dream with his nose in the air and wearing a cheap grey bowler hat and grey spats as if he were some ancient prime minister.

The following Monday Ivy Violet jumped out of bed with savage intensity to go to her new job. She caught the tram to Albert Square and made her way along the back of Kings Street to the huddled quarters of Diamonta Gowns.

A small heavily studded door on the ground floor was slightly ajar. Next to it was a polished brass plate the size of a sardine tin with the word DIA-MONTA engraved on it. The door led into a dark narrow passage lit by gas. Chocolate coloured walls led up some stone steps to another door with a glass window. A bell by the side of it proclaimed WORK-SHOP.

Nervously and with miserable fatalism Ivy Violet pressed the bell which was answered immediately by a thin pale girl. She had hair like mildewed straw and bleary running eyes, a red nose and a pinched looking mouth. She clutched a large piece of grubby white gauze to catch her sneezes. 'You bust be Biss 'ilton,' she snuffled. 'Bleased to beet cher. I'b Conny, Winnie Smith's cousin.'

When Ivy Violet staggered home that night after a day of indescribable misery and discomfort in a badly lit, badly ventilated room full of coughs and sneezes and the air full of fluff and particles, she wondered how she would ever manage to tackle the next day. Phillis asked her how she had got on and hardly believed her when she said everyone had colds and the whole place was awful.

'Colds? At this time of year? In this beautiful weather?'

'Beautiful weather, Mam?' Ivy Violet shuddered. 'Not in there it wasn't. The place was so horrible you didn't know whether it was December or June and everyone seemed to have asthma. They did. Truly.'

Phillis stared at her suspiciously and shook her own head slightly in wonder. Not wonder at the working conditions but wonder at Ivy Violet's vivid imagination and her ability to make the worst of a bad job rather than the best.

'They had these irons an' all, Mam, and I was set on to iron piddling bits of material, and it had to be very carefully done, an' if you damaged a bit or scorched it you was liable to have to pay for it out of your wages.' Ivy Violet looked at her appealingly: 'It was ever so good of you to get the job for me, Mam, but somehow . . . I don't think it's quite what I'm lookin' for.'

An awful puce colour welled up into Phillis's cheeks. She could hardly believe her ears . Whatever was the next generation coming to? 'You . . . don't think it's what you were looking for? You? Whatever has an impudent girl like you got to do with it? What you went there to do was to *work*, me girl. Work like all of us 'as to do, for our daily bread, and you were extremely lucky to land in a place like that where the cream of society goes to get kitted out. Very lucky indeed

'So just think on and get a good wash and get to

bed early ready for tomorrow.' Then she gave Ivy Violet a slightly affectionate pat and said: 'No need to take on so, lovey. It'll get better every day, just you see if it doesn't.'

Ivy Violet nodded and went early to bed. She wondered how Sylvia had got on. She thought of her stints of sewing her own ball gown – sitting there in the quiet sunshine on the doorstep. What a contrast!

For the rest of that week it was like being in some terrible prison and the only bit of light came from the pay packet awaiting her at the end of Friday's work – for at least they didn't have to work a week in hand. As they queued up at the table where Mr Dempster the overseer sat – with his huge walrus moustache and gigantic beefy hands – handing out the pay packets as Conny called out their names, a slight streak of optimism flared up in Ivy Violet's heart. At least she had survived the week even if she did know that she would probably have some money knocked off her wages for some very slightly scorched pieces of pale blue satin. They were ever such small pieces, she thought, and there was a huge bale of the same satin on one of the shelves in the huge store room.

She smiled quite perkily at Mr Dempster who ignored her, then went towards the clothes' pegs to her hat and coat and undid her pay packet. It felt quite fat as with excited young fingers she undid the top and felt inside. There was a statement inside listing her pay for the week: it was four shillings.

Underneath it said: 'Minus ninepence for faulty iron-ing and damaging of materials', followed by a short personal note scrawled by Mr Dempster which said: 'Thank you for your week's work. Some of our reg-ular girls will be back again next week.'

She read the words slowly again. Surely she hadn't been sacked? She went to find Conny and ask her.

'Yes dear, that's right. Just the week. That's all. Thanks for helping out. Nice to see yer. Tarrarr.'

Ivy Violet walked back home and felt heel blisters begin to rub against her badly fitting shoes. Tears began to well into her eyes. She wished with all her heart she had someone to turn to, like the heroines in books where strong young men (completely unlike the ones who lived around Clark Terrace) swept del-icate damsels into their athletic arms with firm and comforting gentleness.

She knew deep down it was just a fantasy. For a start, she was not all that delicate. She had been described many times as buxom, bonny, and a 'good hefty lass' by many a man old enough to be her grandfather.

It soothed her to imagine this other, more roman-tic scene, and she cheered up as she thought again of going to the Spring Ball with Sylvia and Mr Porter. After all, she might . . . just might . . . meet the man of her dreams there. Perhaps it would be like a fairy tale after all, and change her life for ever?

Then it all faded. She was within sight of her own front door and the small green with its washing line and old grey clothes' props outside the row of little brick houses where she lived.

She was going to have a lot of explaining to do.

The Spring Ball was at the Old Hall, off Piccadilly in the centre of Manchester. The Old Hall was a building as ornate inside as outside. On three storeys with carved stone pinnacles aloft in the sky and massive, arched, eight-pane windows; each pane being as big as the wall of a room in Clark Terrace. And the whole place ablaze with light as people moved up the stone steps to the marble entrance with tiled mosaic floors. Decorated iron balustrades on curved stairways led to the main hall itself.

'Going *there*?' said Phillis in quiet disbelief and looking quite pale, for she thought Ivy Violet must have taken leave of her senses. 'Going there, this Saturday? How can a young penniless girl like you possibly be going there? What will you wear, for a start? Who's taking you? And if it's some respectable person – why haven't they been to ask my permission?'

Then she relaxed slightly, and she said: 'Is it something Maisy Fowler's invited you to?'

The fact was that since Ivy Violet's unproductive week as a potential career girl in the rag trade, Phillis had made a great deal of effort to keep her from slipping back into bad ways at home with Sylvia. She had got her a job as a shop assistant at Bobby Byrtle's – a cobbler and shoe maker – near the greengrocer's shop where Maisy Fowler worked. Four small shop fronts were constructed from the front rooms of some larger, family sized, street houses. Old Bobby Byrtle lived with two elderly sisters carrying on his trade. The Byrtles were highly regarded and Bobby was looked on by most people with affection and considered a fine craftsman, if very untidy where the shop itself was concerned, and a little absent minded.

Bobby Byrtle's last assistant had gone to work in a posher establishment but he took to Ivy Violet straight away: 'You and I's going to get on lass. I know it. But I doesn't stand for hanky-panky or tantrums or followers hanging round shop doorways. The pay's three and six a week, lad or lass, and tha' mun't be afraid of a bit of muck and hard work. If tha' sticks w' me long enuff tha'll know as much about makin' boots, shoes and clogs as any in the land.'

Ivy had stared at him with deep interest. He was a small and pale little man of about fifty who smoked a pipe with hands all weathered and gnarled. He wore a thick leather apron, a flannel shirt, and coarse hodden trousers done up with string tied round each trouser leg at the calf, above thick, dusty boots.

To show his serious good will he gave Ivy Violet two shillings and told her to buy herself a pair of large overalls.

'Now you couldn't have done better than that,' said Phillis when Ivy got back from her first day of working there. For once Ivy had to admit Phillis was right. She realised that in a strange way she had struck lucky for she was virtually in charge of her own little domain in the dark and rather cosy little shop where working people brought their clogs to be repaired, and the rich took the trouble to find it to get their shoes made. Although she was always on the go and the work was noisy and mucky, and there was plenty of tidying up and sweeping to do, at least there was no back-biting and she had no one nagging her. On the contrary, his sister Aileen, all dressed in black and wearing a huge apron, brought them both a cup of tea and a home-made currant bun at ten o'clock each morning.

'Has the cat got your tongue?' said Phillis to Ivy Violet as she pressed her to give more details about the ball on Saturday. But Ivy remained as close as a clam – silently busying herself with cleaning out a cupboard in the back kitchen, until Phillis marched away in a temper with frustration.

Then on the Friday before the dance fate struck – Phillis came across a big brown paper parcel in a suitcase under Ivy Violet's bed. Phillis had been hunting for the suitcase everywhere. Normally Phillis knew exactly the whereabouts of things. She could spot immediately if a box of matches had moved three inches along a shelf or if a cup had been replaced the wrong way on a cup hook. Phillis looked at the package for some seconds, then seeing it was hastily wrapped and not fastened she decided to look inside. Placing it on the bed she unrolled the crumpled brown paper. Loose folds of blue silk velvet silently flowed over the shabby bedspread along with a trace of white muslin and some pink roses.

Her mouth fell open. Whatever was Ivy Violet doing with a frock like that hidden under her bed? The dress must have cost a fortune!

Holding it to the light she looked at it more closely and examined the seams. Hand stitched – every bit of it. Frocks like that would only be found in places like Samuels, or Kendals.

She began to feel quite sick. Had Ivy Violet stolen it whilst she was working at Diamonta? She thought she must have stolen it in the hope of going to the Spring Ball and picking up some rich sugar daddy just like Sylvia. Perhaps she had even stolen some money to get it or had some secret lover?

With quivering hands she wrapped up the frock again and put it back in the suitcase under the bed.

When she saw Ivy Violet later in the evening she said as casually as she could: 'Oh, by the way love – do you happen to have seen my suitcase? I may be going away for the weekend. Freddy Mason has suggested we have a part of Saturday evening and Sunday visiting his mother in Sale Moor. She's getting very old and lives alone.'

'But I thought you always went on your bicycles, Mam?'

'Well, yes – we do normally but that's usually just for a day out. This time we'd be staying the night there and going on the tram.

'Oh and that's another thing, love,' said Phillis

with wily calmness, 'that's really why I wanted you to tell me a bit more about this ball you mentioned tomorrow. Because it looks like you and the boys will be on your own for the night. I do think it's only fair you should give me the proper details about it instead of trying to make it look as if it's an everyday hop that Maisy and Merrick Jackson might be going to. Surely you won't be going with them? That Merrick's never been here since before he went away to Wigan?'

When Ivy Violet realised that Phillis would not even be there to see her setting off for the ball, and would not be back until it was over, she was over-whelmed with relief and she told a vague white lie.

'It was really a sort of dream, Mam. Even if I had gone I wouldn't have had my own partner to take me or even my own money to go.'

'Nor a dress neither,' said Phillis casually hoping to wheedle the whole story from her.

But it was not to be. For as soon as she mentioned the word dress Ivy turned her back and left the room calling: 'Oh by the way, Mam, I've spotted your suit-case upstairs. I'll just get it.'

Ivy Violet removed her parcel which she hid under the chest of drawers and brought the suitcase down.

Phillis took the empty case from her daughter. Should she accuse her here and now of stealing a beautiful and expensive party frock, from her place of work? Or should she wait to see what happened next? Rather than have some sort of family row she might not be able to control? She was not in the mood for letting anything disrupt her overnight weekend with Freddy Mason. She decided to ignore the whole thing until next week.

Changing the subject entirely she said: 'So I hope you'll manage whilst I'm away then, and I hope you'll do the sensible thing and go to church on Sunday and give my regards to Mr Witherspoon.'

Ivy Violet's face shone with pleasure: 'Oh, I'll do that all right, Ma. I'll definitely go to church.' They both gazed at each other for a few seconds of guarded silence, full of hidden thoughts. Then normality reigned once more.

On Saturday morning Ivy Violet was working in Bobby Byrtle's the cobbler's. The machine chugged away in the background, while new irons were hammered on clogs.

The smell of fresh leather, shoe dyes, and sweaty shoes mingled with the smell from traces of manure from shoes people had not bothered to wipe clean (Ivy Violet had to clean these). Ivy Violet prayed for the time to pass as quickly as possible until six o'clock so that she could then go with Sylvia to Mr Porter's mansion. Here they planned to have luxurious baths and array themselves in all their finery.

'We're in real luck,' Sylvia said one day. 'His housekeeper'll be away visiting her brother in Hoylake. She's got used to me being there, because she knows which side her bread's buttered – but I don't think she'd take too kindly to another one of us appearing.'

Ivy's mind could think of nothing else but chris-
tening her wonderful home-made frock as she
busied herself taking in shoe repairs and chalking S,
or S & H, or P for patch, on the soles of boots and
shoes and took them through to the racks at the back
of the shop where Bobby was working. She bought
the newly repaired shoes back to the counter with
their price tickets and names on. On the shelves
behind the counter were stored tins of boot polish,
dusters and brushes that he sold; there were also
some heavy leather belts for trousers, which were
often used as razor strops for cut-throat razors and
for punishing disobedient children. Next to the belts
were leather braces, and dog leads and leather boot
laces hanging from hooks. And on special display –
a leather chest and back guard suitable for coalmen
to wear, specially made to measure by Bobby, along-
side some beautifully made leather gaiters for young
ladies and children.

Ivy Violet stood in the midst of it all with her long
dark hair carefully plaited and coiled. She was wearing her new brown overall. The shop door bell rang.
Flooding the shop with light and noise from outside,
a familiar figure walked in. He was wearing a grey
flannel suit and sweating slightly.

At first, he didn't even recognise her as he handed
her a small paper ticket and said: 'Are Miss Fowler's
satin shoes ready yet? She brought 'em in to be dyed
pink.'

Suddenly their eyes met. 'Ivy Violet! How long
have you been working here?'

She looked at Merrick calmly. 'Not long. How're you going on then?

'I've seen you int' distance sometimes.'

There was an awkward silence. Ivy Violet looked at the shoe ticket. 'When did she bring them in?'

Merrick flushed. 'I think it was last week. But he swore they'd be ready by today because she wants them for a special dance.'

Ivy Violet's spirits dropped. Don't say they were going to the same one that she and Sylvia were going to. Maisy Fowler was the biggest trouble-maker alive. She stared at Merrick. Fancy coming all the way back from Wigan and getting in *her* clutches. 'Is it the Spring Ball you're going to – tonight?' she asked.

He looked at her, amazed. 'Spring Ball. We're not in that league! Anyway, what about you? How do you like working here then? I'll tell Maisy. I don't think she'll know.'

'Don't think she'll know, Merrick? What's come over you? She's the biggest gatherer of gossip in the neighbourhood.' Her voice faded.

She couldn't get over how handsome he looked, and how self-assured. His brown hair was thicker and wavier and made slightly blonder by the summery weather. His eyes were like boat shaped almonds, and almost green, the dark lashes were as long as any girl's beneath the thick eyebrows.

She felt quite shabby and ashamed standing there in a twill overall. Her legs now felt like jelly. No wonder she had heard it said what a bonny young pair he and the beautiful pouting Maisy were.

'I was real sorry to hear about your Dad, Ivy. It must have been an awful shock.'

'Me Mam's none too well. But at least she's still here.'

There was a mournful silence.

'Are you still keen on doing the proper dancing? Maisy said you was walking out wi' some young man from Madam Miranda's. Even courtin' like.'

They both stared each other full in the face. They both knew what the gossip had been.

Spots of angry colour rose in her cheeks, and suddenly for the first time in his life Merrick fell in love with her. He stared at her as if the angel of the Lord had made the Annunciation like in pictures in the art gallery. He began to go hot and cold with the panic and realisation of it, and stood there trembling slightly and wondering what to do. Was it a blessing or a curse? And how long would it last?

But her angry words brought him to his senses: 'I never was and never will be walking out with him, Merrick Jackson. And if anyone's been saying different they're nobbut a pack of lying demons. Maisy Fowler may or may not be your precious girlfriend – but it's nothing to do with me and I don't care a fig. I never have liked her and I never will. She's a stuck-up, spoilt little trouble-maker. All I'm sorry is that she's got you in her clutches enough to have you running round here to collect her shoes.'

Merrick stood there overwhelmed by a dumb helplessness. He stared at her. Her hair was shining suddenly with a glossy warm sheen, her cheeks risen to angry roses above large honest eyes. His heart was in turmoil. All he wanted to do was to stay beside her – like their childhood days; blot out Maisy and catch up the time lost when he had been in Wigan. He wanted to see her face alight with joyous enthusiasm again and her eyes sparkling with adventure; feel the smoothness of her firm and friendly arms and her body close to him, as her lips parted into one of those huge mischievous, carefree smiles of the past. Why had he rejected her? Why had he turned away in the flood of gossip which had met him when he returned?

He stayed there motionless in the shop as a new, older Ivy Violet went away and brought back the pink satin slippers. Putting them in a paper bag she said: 'And I hope her feet don't swell as much as her head seems to. Goodbye then Merrick. See you sometime.'

He smiled bleakly. 'S'pose so. Tarrarr then.'

When he had gone, Ivy Violet sat down on a wooden stool, and for a few moments was overwhelmed with a terrible grief, as a huge sad longing reminded her of those earlier days of childhood innocence and love, now cast aside by Merrick for Maisy Fowler. Why had he done it? Why had he rejected her? Oh Merrick . . . Merrick. She mouthed his name soundlessly, then brushing her hand hastily across her eyes, she pushed him away from her mind.

On most days, Ivy Violet went home for her 40

minute dinner breaks. There was 10 minutes walk, there and back, which left her another full 30 minutes. This time when she got there, Phillis had her suitcase packed and was all set to go off for her short weekend with Freddy Mason on the tram to Sale.

Forty-year-old Freddy was sitting there on a kitchen chair. He was in a lightly striped summer suit with a straw boater slung on the back of his head like a halo of confident good nature and drinking a glass of ginger beer.

Freddy Mason's main occupation was as a commercial traveller selling umbrellas, sunshades, parasols and window blinds. Until now he had never really considered getting married. But lately, as middle age began to loom, he surmised that a good woman would be a comfort in his future years to warm more than just his slippers, and 'no nonsense' Phillis Hilton just seemed to be what he was looking for.

She in her turn enjoyed his forthright cheerfulness and completely ignored his tendency of hoping to be waited on.

'Now mind all I've said,' admonished Phillis as she gave Ivy Violet a short sharp peck on the cheek. 'And if you've nothing much to do tonight you could just go through the work basket and darn some more of your stockings. You've been getting really behind with them, and you could put some Silvo on all the forks and spoons and polish the brasses. And don't forget to give my regards to Mr

Witherspoon at Sunday school. Goodbye then dear.'

'Goodbye Ivy,' said Freddy. He patted Ivy Violet's shoulder with a plump hand and giving her what looked like a sly wink said: 'I'll look after her.'

Ivy Violet nodded and smiled politely, itching for them to get on their way, so that she could check on all her own paraphernalia for the ball that evening, and prepare the evening meal ready for when Roger and Kenny got in. She was not really very keen on Freddy Mason. He was so different to her own father, and he was over familiar for a person she hardly knew.

'What's all the hurry?' said Kenny as he and Roger shovelled down their cheese and onion 'tatty pie' which Ivy Violet had managed to have ready before she rushed away.

'What about all the clearing up?'

'Where are you off to?'

'And mind you don't stay out late, our Ivy Violet,' said ten-year-old Roger cheekily, 'or I'll tell Mam.'

'You mind your own business, sneaky guts,' snapped Ivy Violet as she rushed from the house with a thumping, excited heart, 'or I'll tell Mam about you and Maureen Simpkin tampering with Mrs Nutall's canary when she left it in the yard in its cage. How it was you two who let it escape.'

'How did you know that?' yelled Roger in alarm.

'Never you mind. But just think on . . .'

Ivy and Sylvia had planned to meet at the corner of Ellamina Street rather than be seen setting off together from Clark Terrace.

'We'll go by cab to Mr Porter's,' Sylvia said.

'By cab?' Ivy Violet looked stunned. She had never travelled anywhere by cab in her whole life or ever had enough money to afford it. She stared wonderingly at Sylvia, marvelling at the calm simplicity of a young girl like herself who was dressed in a cheap calico frock and a coarsely woven straw hat, and had the plainest face in Christendom.

Sylvia smiled slightly. 'No need to look so shocked, Ivy.' She opened her purse. It was stuffed with ten shilling notes. 'Mr Porter sees I never go short. I just don't know what I'd do without him. He's a real gentleman.'

Whalley Range, where Mr Porter lived, was a spacious countrified area full of massive houses with stables, paddocks, and fields. He lived near Alexandra Road, not far from a park with a bandstand and ornamental pond, in a detached residence surrounded by laurel bushes. A rockery ran along all the garden paths which was made from great lumps of white quartz.

They did not go to the front door, for as Sylvia put it: 'It's not really fair to him, like. With us dressed like this. We're hardly better than hawkers selling pegs and such. It'll be different when we're all poshed up and we get in his car in the garage – 'cos then we'll just sail out in all our finery, like princesses.' Sylvia pressed the bell at the side of the back door, and it rang loud and strong.

A few moments later, through the stained glass panel in the green door, Ivy Violet discerned the small bowed shape of an elderly man coming to answer it.

He opened the door and smiled at them slowly. 'Come in Sylvia.' He looked at Ivy Violet. He had a fragile bony face and keen blue eyes 'I expect you are Miss Hilton, Sylvia's friend?'

She nodded. She was completely overawed. He was like an elderly gnome about to lead her into an unknown land.

'Show her upstairs Sylvia and take her to the dressing room. You've got plenty of time to get ready.' His hand rested gently on Sylvia's arm, and she nodded and smiled.

'This dressing room leads off from his own bedroom,' said Sylvia. 'Come and see the size of his mahogany bed. His wardrobe's big enough to live in.'

Ivy Violet stared in silence. It seemed so strange that a small frail gnome was surrounded by such gargantuan rooms.

As they busied themselves in his bathroom – which had a huge bath which filled with boiling hot water like a great Niagara – and dusted themselves with finely perfumed talcum powder and felt the luxury of huge, warmed Turkish bath towels, Ivy Violet could not resist asking how he managed to have scented things fit for women.

'They belong to his housekeeper,' said Sylvia as they slipped into their ball gowns. 'She always sees to it that he has scented talcum powder and bath salts in the bathroom. There's a picture of them both on his dressing table. She must be at least eighty now, so that picture must have been taken about ten years ago in the garden.'

Ivy Violet looked at the picture, and saw a huge woman of over six feet tall wearing a bustle and a sort of bowler hat with Mr Porter standing beside her. They both had very serious looks on their faces.

The Ball. Ivy Violet could hardly believe it as they entered the great hall in Manchester lit with sparkling facets of a thousand small crystal droplets from scores of chandeliers suspended beneath the heavily embossed ceilings. She felt quite intoxicated by the sudden vision of richness and colour. Heady perfumes intertwined with cigar smoke. Warm waves of human voices – in a pattern of laughter and joy – and music from the orchestra blended together in the background. Brass potted palm trees stood about on the dance floor with pink plush velvet chairs, and marble topped tables. Gilded dado rails decorated with wreaths and angels ran along the walls.

The only thing which had upset her slightly was an unknown man who appeared, just before they were announced into the hall.

'This is my partner for you, Miss Hilton,' smiled Mr Porter. 'He is my good friend Mr Alfonso Treadgold, and he is a very good dancer. Sylvia mentioned that you are very attracted to the art.'

Ivy Violet stared up at the huge man. He was wearing a purple satin cummerbund with his evening dress and looked even older than little Bobby Byrtle, the shoe maker. She smiled politely and as she put out her hand to him, he bowed slightly and kissed it gallantly. But as he raised his head to smile towards her she realised he had not a tooth in his head.

Ivy Violet's own smile froze for a second in confounded amazement. Don't say he had left his false teeth at home by mistake, she thought.

'Mr Horatio Porter and Miss Sylvia Watson,' announced the doorman. 'And Mr Alfonso Treadgold and Miss Ivy Violet Hilton.'

She stood there for a second in mounting irritation, as their names were announced to the whole of Manchester, even though no one was taking the least notice. She was now annoyed to think she had been deliberately paired off to an old man with no visible teeth.

Yet what choice was there? she thought. For she was here purely by the generosity of Mr Porter and was actually wearing the glad rags spawned from his own piece of blue velvet, and was wearing his housekeeper's talcum powder and had bathed in his sumptuous bath, not to mention arriving in his shining limousine, with only a shilling of her own in her small pochette.

They went to sit at a table for four and Mr Porter ordered champagne which arrived in a big silver bucket surrounded by ice.

'Alf is perfect at the Viennese Waltz,' said Mr Porter after they had all drunk each other's health.

'Might I suggest you try each other out?'

Reluctantly Ivy Violet allowed herself to be led by Mr Treadgold into the dance and was astounded to find that it was perfectly true – he was a perfect dancer. In fact he was so light on his pins and so masterful in the most gentle and unpressing type of way that she was whirled round the dance floor as if she truly was the belle of the ball, instead of being an untrained novice. And when she returned to the table she had to admit to herself that it was paradise to dance with him.

He was not 'Alf' to her. Oh no. From that minute on she thought of him as Fonzzy. During the course of the evening it was gradually revealed that Fonzzy worked in a counting house, which he said was very mucky work as he had to count out lots of money and it soiled your hands badly. He was also a rent collector for Mr Porter.

'I must apologise for the fact that my dentures are missing,' he said. 'I had some teeth out a few days ago and the new set haven't arrived yet.'

Ivy Violet gazed at him with a new respect. She was quite sure that she would never, never in her whole life have been able to face going to a posh ball without her teeth in. Especially if you were sat with anyone like Mr Treadgold, who kept telling jokes.

After the ball was over Mr Porter insisted that he would take Sylvia and Ivy Violet safely to their own doors, for it was well past midnight. And so in the full light of an almost full moon, his car slid to a halt in front of Clark Terrace, as the two girls thanked him for a wonderful evening, and they all went their separate ways.

'Can you see all't bedroom curtains on't move?' whispered Sylvia as they parted.

Ivy Violet nodded. She had also noticed something else. There was a light still on downstairs at number 3.

Were her brothers still up?

But when she got in it wasn't them at all.

It was Phillis.

CHAPTER 5

The Row

'Yes I *am* back here! No I *didn't* stay the night!' muttered Phillis grimly through pale, tight lips. 'Freddy's mother was taken bad with her angina. And having me staying there would have been too much for her heart.'

Ivy knew it wasn't true. She could read Phillis like a book, just as Phillis claimed to read her like one. Phillis had come back deliberately, to see what was going on. Ivy Violet began to tremble.

Phillis's eyes were smouldering dangerously as she looked at the blue velvet dress. Both girls had come back in all their finery and Sylvia had said she would bring back Ivy's ordinary clothes the following day.

'Get that thing off your back for a start,' hissed

117

Phillis. 'I saw it all through the curtains upstairs. Saw the car and that old man. It's just what I might have expected – you filthy little trollop!'

Ivy Violet froze with horror. How could anyone who claimed to love her call her that? 'Ma – you just don't understand. It wasn't like that – it —'

'I understand all right. I understand only too well.' Phillis gave a mighty lurch towards her and dragged at the dress, hanging on to the front of it so that it ripped. 'Get OUT of it!'

In tears, Ivy Violet stepped out of her beautiful frock, and stood there quivering in her petticoat, as with one angry swoop Phillis grabbed it up into her arms and deposited the whole lot into the fire grate where she kept it pressed in position with the long iron poker until it began to smoke and gradually catch fire.

'That'll teach you to bring your tarty ideas round here my girl.'

With a huge screaming sob Ivy Violet rushed to her bedroom and flung herself down, aware vaguely of footsteps from Phillis's own bedroom, and heavy footsteps going downstairs, and the sound of a man's voice. But she was too lost in her own grief at that moment to care.

Then after she had lain there in hopeless, emotional agony for about an hour, then undressed and put on her nightdress, she heard footsteps coming back to Phillis's bedroom and there was some whispering on the landing. She knew it was Freddy Mason and he was staying the night. Without waiting another second, and smarting at the hypocrisy of it all, Ivy Violet slipped on a coat. A few minutes later she was knocking at Sylvia's back door praying that Sylvia would not already be fast asleep. Her prayers were rewarded as a heavy eyed Sylvia unlocked the door and let her in.

'What on earth's happened, Ivy?' Sylvia's head was a mass of shabby looking curling rags. 'Would you like a drink of summat?'

'She's burnt my frock.' Ivy Violet collapsed in a chair as tears streamed down her face. 'How can I ever live there again?'

'*Burnt* it?' Sylvia stared in disbelief. 'What a terrible and wasteful thing to do. And all the time and care you put into it.' Sylvia tried to comfort her as the two of them clung together. 'She must have gone completely mad.'

'She did. She called me a trollop, and worse. But she's the one who's the trollop, Sylvia. She had that Freddy Mason hidden away in her bedroom.'

'What about your brothers?'

'I think Roger must have just kept out of the way and Kenny could have been out at his friend's.'

'What'll you do about work on Monday?'

'I'll just have to go from here, if that's all right with you? And wear the cotton frock and shoes and underwear from my shopping bag. And with it being Sunday tomorrow you won't need to worry much, because I shall get up early and go to church. An' if you let me make a jam sandwich I'll take it with me and eat it in the park. Then in the afternoon

I'll just go back there to Sunday school and see Mr Witherspoon. Just like Phillis would want me to do.' Ivy Violet's mouth set in a grim, sneering line.

'And then, what?

'I 'ope your Phillis doesn't come round here. She's got a real dander when she gets going.

'I'll just 'ave to not open the door to 'er. Unless she catches me out on't green.'

'I don't think she will come round, Sylvia. My bet is she'll be leaving me to stew in my own juice and expecting me to come grovelling back. Well, I can never do that! Not after what she did to my dress. She might as well've tried to shove *me* on the fire as do that to it. It's killed all my love for her for ever.'

The next morning, it was just as Ivy had surmised. She was informed by Sylvia that Sylvia had just seen Phillis and Freddy Mason leaving the Terrace together. Ivy Violet did just what she had planned to do. She felt, and looked a bit like Orphan Annie in her workaday clothes for usually she dressed up a bit on Sundays. She also felt very hungry indeed – existing on jam sandwiches, when Sunday was the day of the week they usually had the best meal.

After Sunday school, she hovered about near Mr Witherspoon half hoping he would offer to walk along with her with maybe the offer of an ice cream, or even a solitary fruit drop to curb her hunger pangs. But it was not to be.

He was in his best suit and wore a dark silk cravat and carried a brand new prayer book. All the time he talked to Miss Prentice, a new Sunday school teacher. She was a little older than Ivy Violet and lavishly attired in a lavender muslin dress and wore elbow length silk net gloves and neat little shoes with pompoms on them. She spoke with a very 'posh' voice and could play the harmonium, and had made one child stand in the corner in disgrace because he said that Joseph in the Bible had had a boat of many colours.

Ivy Violet was extra early getting up at Sylvia's, where she slept on a small, uncomfortable sofa. But when she arrived at her job, Bobby Byrtle was already at work.

'I canna rest as much these days, lass. I finds the early morning work soothing – and it isn't like having to go out anywhere to a job, like I did when I was a young lad working as a clicker in old Ely Blunt's little factory.' Then he looked at her shrewdly and said: 'Everything all right? Wouldst tha' like a sup of tea or bite to eat?'

Suddenly, Ivy Violet broke down and cried, as she told him how her mother had burnt her dress. 'And you've no idea how long it took me to plan it and make it and stitch it all, Mr Byrtle.'

'I have indeed lass,' he said earnestly, like some old warrior who was on her side. 'There's no need to tell me about how long it takes to plan and make and stitch things. She was a very wicked woman to have done it.' Then he said slowly: 'But what made her? She must 'a been right mad.'

'I was home late. I went to a dance in it. It was all a sort of secret.'

Bobby Byrtle realised now that it was better not to know the full story – or he might start to side with Phillis even though he was mentally deriding her. So all he said was that secrets never did anybody much good, and that if Ivy Violet was actually turfed out onto the street, his sisters might allow her to sleep in the attic for a few days until things settled down.

'Thank you very much, Mr Byrtle.' Ivy was genuinely touched, and somehow his offer raised her own pride as she realised that her only true alternative was to face the music and go home, as if nothing had happened, after work finished to where she belonged, even though she had sworn never to darken the door of number 3 again.

On the way back at teatime, she happened to see Maisy Fowler and tried to avoid her, but it was impossible.

'What was your posh ball like then?

'Merrick was telling me all about it. Fancy you working for old Bobby Byrtle. He's as daft as a brush. The last girl who worked there – Pansy – got muddled out of her mind with him. But I daresay he's harmless enough. Thank goodness I'm manageress at Micky O'Hara's Fruit and Veg. He treats me like a proper lady. He says he'd marry me if he wasn't married already and he'd buy me my own pony and trap, and arrange for me to give piano recitals.'

'I thought you were supposed to be walking out with Merrick,' said Ivy Violet coldly.

She knew all about Maisy, and how she was an only child until she was twelve, but now had a very spoilt little sister called Millicent, and how Maisy had always played the small fretwork piano in their front room. How she had been treated to expensive lessons yet had remained very bad indeed, rushing away on the ivory keys at the first line of many a Schubert melody, only to peter out and slam down the piano lid with a weak excuse.

'Did you go with Sylvia to it ?' said Maisy slyly.

'What if I did? It's nowt to do with you.'

'You was seen – that's why,' said Maisy, tossing her corkscrew curls with a gesture of glee. 'And mother said you'd had an awful row at your house and you was running away. And she said your mam's leaving Clark Terrace and going to live in Sale with her fancy man.'

'Well I'm *not* runnin' away am I? I'm going back home from work, just the same as you. And as for us all moving to Sale, it's just a load of lies, so you'd better watch your step.' Ivy Violet felt in a mood to hit her.

'I never is a liar!' gasped Maisy indignantly. 'My mother was told it by the rent collector. He reckons your mother has given him notice of moving out, and my mother might be getting your house for my Aunt Flo.'

Ivy Violet was completely stunned. Surely it wasn't really true? And why hadn't Phillis said?

'So you've finally decided to skulk back home then?'

observed Phillis dryly when Ivy Violet appeared. 'I'll have you know I had to get time off work to find out what was happening. I went round to see that little madam – Sylvia Watson – earlier, and she gave me a right mouthful of impudence. What she needs is putting over someone's knee and getting a right good thrashing. She's a jumped-up little good-for-nothing with pert ideas far and away above her age and her station.'

Ivy Violet stood there silently, then she said: 'I'm sorry, Mam, I didn't really want to cause you any trouble but — '

'Trouble? You've been nowt but trouble ever since I married your father – God rest his soul. Thank Heavens he never lived to see how you've turned out.'

Ivy Violet's temper rose to full flood: 'And thank heavens he never lived to see you carrying on with that horrible Freddy Mason, in our house!'

Phillis looked at her in shock. 'What ever do you mean, girl? How dare you say such a terrible thing!'

'It's you that's being terrible,' sobbed Ivy. 'He was in your bedroom, hiding, when I came back from the ball with Sylvia. I heard him. And I heard you and him on the landing, after you did that cruel thing to my beautiful dress.'

'He wasn't hiding. He just chose to stay up there out of the way because he didn't want to get involved in something which had nothing to do with him. And as for him staying the night. Yes, of course he did, but he slept in Kenny's bed – because Kenny was at Alfred MacFarlynne's, and our Roger slept on the ottoman.'

Ivy Violet stared at her sullenly. She felt a bit of a fool now – but even so she could not forgive Phillis for destroying her dress, or the way Phillis always wanted to think the worst of her.

Then Ivy Violet said: 'Well that's all right then isn't it? But what about you going to move to Sale to live with him and his mother? Maisy Fowler told me on the way home from work – and surely , if *she* said it, there's *no doubt* of the truth?' As she spoke Ivy Violet's eyes flashed with scorn, then her sense of cynical elation faded as she saw the look on her mother's face. Phillis had gone quite pale and remained silent.

Then Phillis said: 'I was going to tell you all this weekend. That was part of the real reason Freddy and I decided to come back here and let you know exactly what we have planned. But of course your behaviour ruined it all.' She raised her hand to silence any retorts. 'Anyway, that's all over now, and when Kenny comes back we'll discuss it more fully. There'll be no question of us all having to split up. Freddy and I will be getting married as soon as possible, and his mother will be sharing the house with us, as it's where they both live at present. It's quite a big place, and we'll all be able to live there.'

'MARRIED?' Ivy Violet couldn't believe her ears. 'To *him*? This house, here in Clark Terrace is our *proper* home. This is where my *proper* mam and dad used to live.' She knew as soon as the words were out it was the cruellest thing she could have said as she saw a look of downcast pain cross Phillis's face.

'Times change, and life goes on,' said Phillis as calmly as she could. 'I've done my best to be a decent mother to you all, and I know what I did to your frock was wrong. But it was a moment of fear for your own future. I know you'll never believe it but I was trying to protect you. Perhaps, one of these days, you'll see it my way and at least try to understand.'

Eventually, during the weeks that followed, the truth and reality of Phillis's plans began to sink in. The boys all accepted the new situation without a word. Bryan and Kenny shrugged their shoulders and said it would probably be an improvement, and they would still be able to carry on with their own occupations just as well from Sale. And Roger seemed really glad that he would be changing to a different school.

'And you Ivy will be far the best off,' said Phillis now they were on good terms again. 'You won't have to work for that old crackpot Bobby Byrtle in his poky little hovel any more. He only uses you as a drudge. You'll be able to get a really good position in service to some wealthy family in Sale or Brooklands and work your way up into something really respectable.'

Ivy Violet's heart sank. Bobby Byrtle wasn't a crackpot. He was a skilled craftsman and she would learn more about making handmade shoes from him than she could have known in all the world.

'I can't possibly leave there, Mam! Mr Byrtle's teaching me all about how to make shoes.'

'And about how to sweep up all the dust and rubbish and make him pint mugs full of strong tea, and run round buying him his tobacco, and working on the shoe repairs. And that's how it'll always be, Ivy Violet. For don't imagine that a young girl, working in a den like that, will ever make anything of it.'

Ivy suddenly summoned up all her strength to make a stand for herself. 'I'm just not coming with you to Sale, Mam, and that's all there is to it. Mr Byrtle's sisters say I can always stay in their attic if the need arises, and that's where I'll go, because I want to make beautiful shoes *for ever*, so there!' Then she stamped majestically out of the house, not really caring whether she ever saw another shoe again, but glad to have made a stand for her own independence.

But the following week an unusual thing happened.

Tilly Simpkin was wanting to get rid of an old iron shoe last. 'It's a damned nuisance. I mean just look at the stupid thing, it's only fit for a person with a foot as narrow as a herring. God knows what Arthur was thinking of when he dragged it home in the hand cart. But he's always the same, he just cannot resist accepting every bit of rubbish people palm off on him. I wouldn't mind, but we've already got a decent last for when he does a few family boot repairs, and many's the time I've used that meself for tacking up soles whilst he prates on about Buddha or what the moon's made of.'

Ivy Violet's face lit up at the sight of the shoe last. It wasn't of the slightest use to her but somehow it was like a sort of signpost in her life and a souvenir of her stand against having to move away from Clark Terrace and the idea that she should forsake her job with Bobby Byrtle.

'You can give it to me if you want to rid yourself Tilly.'

'But where on earth could you keep a great heavy object like that Ivy Violet?'

Ivy Violet looked downcast. Where indeed? 'It could stay in our wash house in a corner where we stacks the dirty clothes for washing,' she muttered, feeling slightly ashamed. 'Then I'd take it with me when we all move out.' Slowly she began to pour out her troubles to Tilly Simpkin. ' . . . and you see I quite like working with Mr Byrtle, and he's taught me ever so much about the shoe trade. I mean Tilly, why shouldn't a young girl like me be interested in making shoes?'

'Because it's not ladylike that's why,' said Tilly cynically as she pummelled away at a huge mound of bread dough. 'Oh no love, it's only a trade fit for men *that*. But of course it's quite all right for you to be chained to a big factory in a room like a school examination hall, for all the days of your life sat at a sewing machine, making shoe uppers and never daring to move. Oh, that's just fine, that is. It's what we was all put on earth for if the truth be known. 'Cos women doesn't warrant a proper trade, see? Either they's the skivvies or they's the proper ladies who wears the luxury shoes. There's no other way for 'em.'

Her face relaxed, and she smiled slightly. 'But of course you knows me by now Ivy Violet: I believes in equal rights for all, and God save the Pankhursts. The more education we can all get, the better.'

Ivy Violet looked at her – a small, wooden doll-like figure with highly coloured cheeks and dark, perceptive eyes – fit to tackle all the problems that came to the Simpkin family, and she was filled with wonder.

Fired now with the zeal for hard work and female dedication to a proper craft, Ivy Violet felt that she had found her path in life, as she watched all the rest of her own family pile their goods and personal chattels into a small horse drawn pantechnicon and move off to Sale. All the neighbours stood on their doorsteps waving them off. All except Tilly Simpkin who had far better things to do and think and talk about. One thing about her was that she was always completely unaware of how much influence her views had on others, especially young and impressionable girls. Not that it worried her for she thought, in her pragmatic way, that it was for people to make their own minds up in the end.

Bobby Byrtle's two elderly sisters were put in a flutter when they realised that Bobby's kindly meant and incautious invitations to his female assistant were being acted upon.

'We've never had anyone in that attic for years and years Aileen. It's full of old shoe patterns and bits of cow hide and half made shoes from the year dot. The floor is littered with those crumbling boxes of insoles and canvas backing . And tacks are everywhere.'

Dinah bit her lips together with a worried look. They were both in their seventies now and although they liked to help people the thought of having to clear out the attic was a wearying proposition.

'She'll just have to clear it out herself if she really needs a roof over her head,' said Aileen, putting her thin nervous fingers towards a wisp of silvery hair which had escaped from its tortoiseshell comb prison. 'Sometimes Bobby can be just *too* kind. I quite like the girl, but it's an entirely different kettle of fish when they live in the same house – especially at that tender age. They're a terrible responsibility.' Her eyebrows, still dark and well shaped, drew together in a steady frown.

Apart from treading on a tack, and having a slightly painful foot for a week, Ivy Violet had moved in gratefully to her new abode. To her it was like being the queen of all she surveyed, having a real room of her own with a pleasant dormer window looking down on to the labyrinth of nearby streets and back entries. What a change it was from living in the small backwater of Clark Terrace with its own communal washing green. Often she combed her hair and watched the never ending parade of neighbours and shoppers and tradesmen: ice cream men, lamp lighters, the local bobbies – strolling around in pairs; rag and bone men and old clothes' totters moving along briskly in their fragile carts and urging their thin overworked nags to keep up a good pace; heavy, carthorse drawn wagons of coal merchants and breweries, and the sound of their drivers calling in gruff, cheery voices to someone they knew across a street. And overhead, the pigeons, often caught and eaten by many families for a decent meal. Crows as well, and starlings perched on other attic roofs and birds on elderberry bushes in back yards; along with the ever present sparrows and a blackbird or thrush – in sparkling warm May sunshine.

Yes, it was quite a carefree life now for a young, hard working, seventeen-year-old girl with only herself to look after, cheerfully unaware of the good fortune of having landed in the nest of kindliness which Bobby Byrtle and his sisters Aileen and Dinah provided.

Today it was Wednesday and it was her afternoon off. She worked long hours – from seven in the morning until seven at night, but the shop was closed on Wednesday afternoons and she also had Sunday as the traditional day of rest. Through the window of her attic she saw Merrick walking along the street from the direction of the greengrocers where Maisy worked. She almost tapped on the window but thought better of it. She wondered whether he had seen the *Daily Mirror*. It was full of stuff about Captain Scott's tomb near the South Pole; and on the front page there was a picture of it amid Antarctic wastes. It reminded her a bit of the pyramid shape of a coconut macaroon, but instead of the red glacé cherry at the top there was a plain cross outlined against a beautiful sunset sky in a vast empty plain of frozen ice and snow. Close to this monument were Captain Scott's skis planted upright in a small pile of frozen snow. For a few moments the picture filled her with great sadness, and awe. She knew that Merrick would feel the same. She knew he always followed all the news about the expeditions.

On the next page was a large advertisement for Nugget Black Boot Polish, and underneath it another announcement about how the Children's Magazine told the story of the Antarctic heroes. It showed an excerpt from the only children's newspaper in the English language. It cost sevenpence a month which to Ivy Violet was very dear.

It portrayed a remnant from Captain Scott's own last written words in March 1912 – last year:

'Surely, surely, the country will remember . . .' it said. Then the actual last excerpt was printed for all to read:

'We are weak: writing is difficult; but for my own sake I do not regret this journey, which has shown that an Englishman can endure hardships, help one another, and meet death with as great a fortitude as ever in the past.

We took risks – we know we took them. Things have come out against us, and therefore

we have no cause for complaint, but bow to
the will of Providence, determined still to do
our best to the last.'

Ivy Violet shivered slightly and tried to sum up
the real risks she had ever taken. Up to now they
consisted of going to the ball in secret with Sylvia,
and coming to live in Mr Byrtle's attic. She read on:

'But if we have been willing to give our lives to
this enterprise, which is for the honour of our
country, I appeal to our countrymen to see that
those who depend on us are properly cared
for.
     Had we lived I should have had a tale to tell
of the hardihood, endurance, and courage of
my companions which would have stirred the
heart of every Englishman.
     These rough notes and our dead bodies
must tell the tale, but surely, surely a great rich
country like ours will see that those who are
dependent on us are properly provided for.
March 25, 1912   R.Scott'

The whole of the *Daily Mirror* was full of clear and
amazing photographs of Captain Scott's expedition,
taken by Mr Ponting who was camera artist to their
small band of five brave men on their epic 550 mile
walk across the relentless snow and ice, harnessed to
their own sleigh as they pulled their own provisions
along – wearing skis.

Ivy Violet stared long and hard at the rest of the pictures in the paper. She thought of her brother Kenny's friend, Alfred MacFarlynne, who lived in Salford and was a clerk to a firm of architects. He was mad on photography too. Just imagine if it had been him perishing in the snow. She could hardly bear to think of it now. Alfred was so interesting, and lively, and kind-hearted. Almost a girl's dream come true – if it came to marriage – with his pleasant personality and gentleness; as well as being well-heeled.

After wiping away a heartfelt tear Ivy Violet skipped through the rest of the paper noticing an interesting headline which said: BALLROOM BAN ON HUG-DANCES. It mentioned a plan to stop the graceless tango and revive minuets, and that the 'turkey trot' and the 'bunny hug' were being rigidly banned by matronly hostesses. She groaned slightly to herself, for although she had once longed only for Viennese waltzes, these days the tango and the bunny hug held much more excitement.

'Ivy Violet? Are you there? There's someone here to see you.' It was Miss Aileen's nervous, high-pitched voice calling up to her.

Ivy Violet put down the paper hastily and went downstairs. She was still wearing an overall over her yellow and white striped gingham dress, and her dark hair was long and unruly. She put her hand across her heart. Whoever could it be? Surely not Phillis or someone – wanting to cause yet more trouble? Since they had moved to Sale she had hardly seen them, except one of her brothers in the streets occasionally. Then her question was answered, as – to her amazement – she glimpsed Alfred Mac-Farlynne's earnest looking face peering up at her from the hallway as she peered over the banisters.

What on earth was he doing here? She felt an uncanny thread of fear . How strange to have been thinking of him only a few seconds ago. She never saw him very often – even when they had all lived in Clark Terrace. So why this?

She felt herself blushing slightly with shyness. Yet she was hardly ever shy. It was one thing having secret thoughts about him, but suddenly having to face him like this was different – as Miss Byrtle stood there between them with an enquiring look on her face.

'Alfred, how lovely to see you, and how strange, because only just now I . . .' Hastily they shook hands, and her words became quicker and quicker with sheer embarrassment, as she mentioned reading about Captain Scott in the paper and looking at all the photographs . . .

Her voice suddenly petered out.

He smiled at her cheerfully as if he was quite unaware of her shock at seeing him, then beamed at Miss Aileen and explained: 'I'm a friend of Ivy Violet's brother, Kenneth. Kenneth told me that Miss Hilton was free on Wednesday afternoons, so I called to see if she would honour me with her company for afternoon tea in town.'

Miss Aileen smiled at them both, and looked at

Ivy Violet who nodded. Then Miss Aileen ushered Alfred into the drawing room with its Brussels carpet, huge leather sofa, grandfather clock and a glass-domed case full of brightly coloured humming birds, whilst Ivy Violet went to get ready.

She was all of a flutter as she tried to decide whether to keep on her gingham frock or change into her blue silk poplin with the tiny buttons all down the front of the bodice. Then realising how long it would take to put it on and fasten it all she decided to keep to what she was already wearing and go in her straw boater. It was the first time she had ever been invited out to afternoon tea with a presentable young man in her whole life!

'I thought we could go to a little place that's open not far from Parkers and Sissons near St Ann's Church. And afterwards if you really don't mind I'll see if Chapman's the photographic dealers is open in Albert Square,' Alfred said.

They sat eating toasted tea-cakes in the small and smart café. The waitresses were dressed in neat black sateen dresses, white lace aprons and small head crowns of folded lace with long ribbons of black velvet decorating the back of their hair.

Alfred said, 'You must think it's a bit strange my being here on a Wednesday afternoon but all the drains are blocked up at work, and old Biddleworth's shut the place down for two days to have it fixed.'

Ivy nodded sympathetically. She knew the architect's office where Alfred was a clerk. It was on the third floor of a dark looking office block near the town hall, and the creaking, wooden lift often broke down.

'I expect – in a way – it's the best time to be off work in all this good weather,' she said.

Sunlight from the latticed window of the café glinted on their hair and showed up Ivy Violet's round, flushed cheeks and long eyelashes and highlighted Alfred's firm and gentle hands as he offered her the two tier silver-plated cake stand. A mass of chocolate eclairs, cream horns, meringues, and tiny sponge cakes decked out in coloured marzipan were laid on flower-patterned white paper doylies. 'What I really wanted to ask Ivy was . . .' he hesitated.

'Yes? Go on then.'

'Well . . . it's a sort of frightful cheek . . . but . . .'

'Yes?'

'It's to do with a photographic competition see . . . and it has to be a young lady as the model. Someone with long wavy hair like you . . . It's run by Le-Lani Hair Dressing. The ones who always have those pictures of beautiful young ladies advertising "Le- Lani: crystal clear, sheer and shining perfect hair." The first prize is a hundred pounds and there are ten runner-up prizes of twenty-five pounds each plus the lady's picture in a Le-Lani advertisement. Do you think? Would it be at all possible that you might consider?'

Ivy Violet burst out laughing, and Alfred looked slightly hurt. 'It's not that I'm not flattered, Alfred. It's just that I wouldn't stand a chance. I'm not a real good looker, like some girls.'

He stared at her in amazement. 'You are, you know. I've always thought it, but I never said anything.'

'What about your own sisters – surely one of them might oblige?'

'Melissa, Martha and Clara are far too young. Theresa's too bossy, and Virginia thinks such things are beneath her.'

'They're really beneath me, too,' Ivy said. Then she said at last: 'Per'aps I wouldn't mind doing it just as a joke.'

His eyes brightened: 'Would you really? You're ever such a sport. Kenny said you might. The thing is – with having these two days off work I thought it would be a good time to give it a try out. I know you've only got Wednesdays as half day and Sundays off because Kenny said, so I was half hoping you could come back home with me right now and I could try doing a few shots. I did mention it to mother and the others so it would be quite all right . . . if you'd agree?' He gazed at her pleadingly.

Ivy Violet nodded and smiled. She'd never been to his house even though Kenny spent so much time there, and she hadn't thought of doing anything else in particular today. 'Yes, I'd love to.'

'That's settled then!'

They both finished their tea and Alfred led Ivy Violet out of the café to the nearest tram stop for their ride to Broughton Lane, where there were some large family houses, which to Ivy Violet were like palaces. Alfred lived at one called Silver Birches. It had monumental stone gate posts with knobs on the tops, and a long curving driveway bounded by laurels.

She felt extremely nervous now. She was well away from her own territory, and although she knew Alfred slightly, she had never met any of his family – let alone coming to meet them in the guise of a photographic model. A vision of Phillis berating her came to her imagination. She knew that Phillis would say she had lowered her own dignity and self-esteem by agreeing to do this for Alfred, rather than meeting his family as a proper young lady in a decent manner, by being formally invited round for a meal.

It was quiet when they arrived, and Alfred took her around the back way. She was aware that if she had been invited out properly, they would have no doubt gone to the front door and rung the bell.

One of his sisters greeted them. Older than Ivy Violet, she had fair hair like her brother. She smiled politely but they were never properly introduced as Alfred asked where his mother was.

'She's gone to Mrs Mellowfields in the Polygon for an afternoon bridge party in aid of the Orphans Mission.'

'I'm just taking Ivy Violet up to my photography room to make a portrait. She's Kenny Hilton's sister.'

When they were both half way upstairs he said: 'That was Virginia,' as if he was a bit frightened of her.

'I want you to comb your hair out and make it like

139

a huge wavy shawl all round your shoulders,' Alfred said excitedly, once he had got all his camera equipment fixed up and had shown Ivy Violet where she was to sit. She had to remain perfectly still with her mouth set in a suggestion of a smile.

'I'm sure we'll win,' he muttered as his confidence grew and she sat there posed exactly as he had ordered.

That afternoon was the start of a growing friendship between Alfred and Ivy Violet. She became more and more involved in his passion for photography and found that most of her spare time was taken up with walking out with him as his regular young lady. Sometimes they were even accompanied by her brother Kenny and a rather superior girl he had met in Sale called Peony, who was an assistant school teacher in a small private kindergarten.

Both Ivy Violet and Alfred waited for weeks to hear the fate of the photograph of her that Alfred had sent to the Le-Lani competition. Then one day, out of the blue, Alfred grabbed her in his arms, squeezed her tight and swung her round. He revealed that they had won a consolation prize of twenty-five pounds and that Ivy Violet's photograph might be appearing sometime on a Le-Lani Hair Care advertisement.

'You've really helped me to make something of my photography Ivy. Really got me going. In fact only yesterday I had an enquiry from one of the large fashion shops asking if I could do quite a daring promotional photograph for their shoe department, featuring a young lady's ankles and displaying her feet in fashionable shoes. They want shoes that will catch the eye on the picture but they mustn't be the sort to be seen in any ordinary shoe department. They want something very bright and daring.'

They were both sitting in Alfred's garden drinking lemonade, and Ivy Violet realised how much the quality of her life had changed because of knowing him. It was almost as if he had unwittingly rescued Kenny and herself from a lower walk of life to one of brighter horizons bounded by comfort rather than hardship.

She smiled at him enthusiastically: 'I might have the very thing! Mr Byrtle gave me the most marvellous pair of slippers he once made which he said were just lying about and would probably never be used again. They're made of emerald green satin with dark green velvet bows at the heel – the heels are curved in the strangest way and dotted with diamanté.'

They both looked at each other in mutual triumph, and Alfred bent forward and kissed her. It wasn't the first time, but they were always kind, brotherly kisses.

Ivy Violet tossed her head slightly and laughed and pretended he had not kissed her. 'The only point about them is they're a bit small, but if it's just a display photograph of a pair of ankles you need, I could always gently half squeeze my foot into one of them for a few seconds – with the other shoe posed next to it as if I was just putting them both on?'

He looked at her with new wonder in his eyes. Alfred was a prosaic sort of person who was keen on photography but was a bit timid when it came to stepping away from formal ideas. He was what was known as 'the salt of the earth' – honest, true and very straightforward, as well as being extremely handsome. He was also sensible enough to see that Ivy Violet was a definite asset to him.

A few evenings later they took the shoes with them to try out.

The result was stunning. One of the pictures Alfred had tinted with colour. Ivy Violet's ankles looked perfect and the shoes themselves looked special and outrageously different from the usual run of the mill pictures.

'I insist that you share some of the proceeds as a partner – if anything comes of it,' he said generously.

Ivy Violet was over the moon. It was the first time she had ever been party to a real, independent business venture – apart from that day long, long ago when she had impulsively sold her hair to help Merrick out.

As she sat there so happily with her arm linked in Alfred's there didn't seem to be anything else in the world that could possibly make things more wonderful.

But the following morning when she got out of bed, she was amazed to find that it was quite a different story. Until now she had always got on well with Bobby's two elderly sisters Aileen and Dinah. Diligently they looked after her like their own daughter, soothing her and listening with interest to all the bits of gossip and news she passed on, and preparing her food with faithful promptness. But today as Ivy sat eating her porridge in the breakfast room she was interrupted by Dinah angrily waving the morning paper at her.

Ivy didn't take much notice at first. She knew how they fussed between themselves about every item of the news and what was happening abroad and what the prime minister or the king had said.

'Quite honestly I think it's nothing short of a disgrace that a young lady should flaunt herself in such a manner.'

Ivy Violet listened to the wittering as she helped herself to some more Lyle's golden syrup from the big green tin and allowed a golden trickle to fall from the spoon into a small pond of porridge.

Then out of the morning shadows she heard Dinah's voice say: 'I just don't know what possessed a sensible girl like you to stoop so low. Everybody knows that the models in those Le-Lani hair advertisements aren't respectable.'

Ivy put the syrup spoon back in the tin and stared. She was quite puzzled. Then before she could say a word Dinah had plonked the paper in front of her and was pointing with a thin trembling finger to the girl in the advertisement.

The girl had her dark wavy hair spread out like a

143

huge shawl and she was smiling brightly, whilst underneath it said in very small letters: 'All the pictures we show are taken from life and are true testaments to the perfection of Le-Lani Hair Care. Get your free trial offer NOW.'

Ivy Violet was truly amazed. It looked just like her, yet not like her. There was a certain brassiness about it. It was her frock all right, and the way her hair was spread out was exactly how Alfred had planned it for the competition. But here in the paper with that harsh newspapery smile, it looked – to say the least – a bit common. She began to wonder if Phillis would have seen it and her heart sank. Phillis would really think she'd gone to pot.

'I never ever imagined it would be in the paper,' said Ivy Violet with a weak gulp. 'It was a photograph competition that Alfred went in for.'

She began to hope fervently that none of Alfred's large family ever looked at papers or magazines with Le-Lani adverts in them.

Dinah said no more but as she left the room, Ivy Violet realised that things would never be quite the same again.

This was demonstrated a couple of months later when to Ivy Violet's alarm it was Aileen's turn to have a go at her. 'I've just been in Market Street,' Aileen said, 'and I could hardly believe my eyes. I saw this dreadful poster advertising shoes in one of the windows, and I'll swear those shoes in the picture belonged to us! They were some that Bobby made years ago.'

This time Ivy Violet was less inhibited by the news, for she knew the poster had been a great success and she was delighted it was getting such prominence.

'It's the advertisement feature I told you about, Miss Aileen. The one I helped Alfred with. It's been ever so successful – thanks to those wonderful shoes that Bobby made. It was ever so kind of him to have given them to me, but as he said they were only kicking around doing nothing, and now his fine craftsmanship is there for all the world to see.'

'YOUR shoes?' gasped Aileen. 'Those shoes were given to me by my own brother nearly 50 years ago. I spent years looking for them but he said they must have got lost.'

'That was really your own fault dear,' said Dinah reprovingly. 'You told him they were too small and too outlandish to wear, and when *I* offered to have them you refused, so he took them away from us in a huff.'

Without another word Ivy Violet went to the wardrobe in her bedroom and brought the beautiful green satin shoes to them. They were neatly and lovingly wrapped in their tissue paper, and her heart almost broke at having to part with them. But she knew now that both the sisters would never rest until the shoes were back in their grasp – even if they were left somewhere to gather dust again.

Aileen took them from her without so much as a thank you, and hastily hid them away elsewhere. Ivy left them both and silently wiped away the tears from her cheeks, knowing now that living here at Bobby Byrtle's was not going to be such a permanent situation after all.

In fact both the photographic exercises seemed to be causing nothing but problems, for Maisy Fowler had already had a few jabs at her in the street over Le-Lani Hair Care. 'I could have sworn it was you on that page Ivy Violet, but my how you've aged. You looked about forty in it and your hair was like coconut matting. Even Merrick said as much. I know for a fact I'd never lower myself to do anything like that – even if I was trying to get off with someone like Alfred MacFarlynne.'

Just before Christmas that same year, Ivy Violet received news from Phillis that Freddy Mason's aged mother had died, and Phillis and Freddy had decided to move into their own small house just off Marsland Road at Sale Moor, along with young Roger. Ivy's eldest brother Bryan was now well and truly married to his girlfriend Pauline; and Kenny, although still friendly with Alfred, had become more and more involved with Peony Bagshaw the kindergarten teacher and was now lodging near Sale Grammar School. They were in the Operatic Society together.

Meanwhile, Ivy Violet herself was still plodding away at Bobby Byrtle's. She had been somewhat redeemed in the eyes of Aileen and Dinah since she had looked after them while they were ill during an outbreak of influenza – having to empty their chamber pots and spittoons.

'What a blessing to have had you here to attend to even our most personal needs,' groaned Dinah tremulously as she slipped a spoonful of Benger's Food into her mouth and finished off the frugal meal with an iron 'Jelloid' which was recommended as a good 'pick-me-up' for all ailments.

In the Christmas post was a lovely lace-like Christmas card from Phillis with a Yule log and a robin in the centre. And inside, it said: 'Come and see us in our new house – Cornerstones, Ivy dear. Love from Freddy and Phillis.'

Ivy felt a warm surge of relief and happiness. She felt now that all that had gone on in the past was now forgiven and forgotten.

Maisy was getting very annoyed with Merrick Jackson, for in spite of her mother's good advice about keeping a grip on him at all times, Merrick was beginning to stray from her clutches. He seemed to be cooling off, even though he still went out with her religiously. But it was all becoming just as if they were some old married couple without any romance. All he ever seemed to talk about was his next meeting of the Novice Karabiner Club which was something to do with rock climbing. Its meetings were held in a small room in the Mechanic's Institute.

'You'll need to wean him off all that nonsense,' said Maisy's mother firmly. 'Your pa and I didn't bring you girls up to be cast aside and made into future grass widows by ropes and rock climbing. It's a phase he's going through. All that kind of thing is the pursuit of the rich anyway and Merrick Jackson still has his own mark to make in the world if he wants to marry a girl like you – with the talents of a budding concert pianist.'

But in spite of her mother's advice Maisy seemed to be fighting a losing battle as weekend after weekend Merrick made excuses about meetings and studied maps of wild and mysterious Derbyshire, Yorkshire and the Lake District.

'But Merrick,' she pouted, 'you never have time or the money for all that. We're supposed to be saving up to buy me a tapestry music stool and a sofa for when we're married. You've not got the time for such pointless, dangerous rubbish! What sensible wife wants a husband she has to worry about – every moment he's out of her sight? Even now you never have time to practise proper rock climbs. You've only walked up Kinder once with that terrible bachelor Sammy Broughton who tripped over a boulder and 's had a gammy knee ever more. And only one weekend in all your life did you ever go to that awful Borrowdale place in the middle of nowhere. Surely rocks don't mean more to you than ME?'

Merrick smiled apologetically. 'There's more to it than meets the female eye Maisy.'

'I'll say there is — '

'It's not only the rock climbing. At the club we have really good lantern slides about the Polar expeditions and journeys to the Himalayas, and climbing the Matterhorn in Switzerland.' He sighed slightly. How different it all was – that other life of natural adventure and physical challenge as men battled against the elements with their fellow strugglers.

'It's almost an insult to me, Merrick,' said Maisy with a warning anger in her eyes. 'No proper woman wants to be second to all that stuff. Promise me *faithfully* you won't try and get out of taking me to Blackpool Tower Ballroom on August Bank Holiday? Promise?'

He nodded, and smiled. Maisy certainly had a very assertive way with her and it could get exceedingly wearing. But most females seemed to be like that in the end – bossy yet vulnerable. Maisy stirred him with her voluptuousness. There was a compelling power in her curvaceous shape and a sense of warm security which made him feel he was doing the manly thing – courting a real, typical woman. The sort you could nod you head knowingly about with other men when the going got tough and she was nagging you to bits. But also the sort you knew would make a good housekeeper and keep things up to scratch in a home life full of creature comforts. Which was what most men seemed to go for . . . plus a family of course. For there was nothing a proper woman wanted more than her own little brood around her. His mother had always told him that. Yes, it was every woman's nature.

Quite abruptly he felt himself blushing with a strange guilt . . . Every woman – except people like . . . Hastily he blotted Ivy Violet from his mind, then with a sense of desperation cast both of them aside to dwell on the finer points of expeditions into vast unknown and unexplored territories. For that surely was where man's true freedom lay. . . .

Madge Fowler, Maisy's mother, was well aware what a plump, luscious creature Maisy was; she was also well acquainted with the 'soiled goods syndrome' which perpetuated the idea that no man worth his salt wanted goods already mauled by another male. And as for the truly rich men of mature years – excluding the classic unrepentant roués, who were grateful for small mercies – the rest of them still kept their weather eye open for a young innocent damsel who had no knowledge of her own inside.

Based on this state of affairs Madge could see that the way Maisy flaunted herself and thudded away on the piano with primitive abandon, she could well be taken advantage of by all and sundry. Unless she was carefully managed she was not going to be smoothed down enough in maturity to meet the Friends of the Hallé Orchestra or make her debut in the Free Trade Hall or the Opera House.

No, by the time all *that* came about, Maisy could be a faded forty with everything all a-droop.

Maisy's mother began to consider Merrick, thoughtfully. He was a sensible, serious, rather too young, man – callow in many of his ways and not yet on a satisfactory rung of the social ladder. There was nothing actually *wrong* with him, but her own dreams for Maisy had been much grander than her own simple family background in the small streets of Manchester. However, he had some very good points to his credit – including steadfastness, loyalty, and the way he had never bothered again with that terrible young tart Ivy Hilton – or even any other girl since he returned from Wigan. Mrs Fowler gritted her teeth slightly as she carefully summed up the situation. She took a deep, trembling breath. She had made a momentous decision. She went to the walnut veneered bureau in the overcrowded living room and took out a lined notepad and an envelope. Then sitting down at a small bamboo table covered by a heavily fringed, pink, artificial silk cloth, she began to write to her one and only sister Anona at 'North Pier View' in Blackpool.

Dear Noni,

Maisy and her young man will definitely be visiting you for August Bank Holiday . They are very suited to each other, and should make a good match. Maisy is mad about him . He is a good lad and I want it to stay that way. She was even mentioning the number of children she'd like when they are married, but I said if she wanted that many they would almost have to start right now . . . even though they're not engaged . . . (A joke of course, Noni – but we all have to accept the accidents of youthful passion, don't we?)

151

Hoping you and Bertram are in good
health,
Your affectionate sister,
Madge Fowler.

Anona Shuffleby read the strange letter over and
over again with a puzzled suspicious frown. Madge
could be very devious at times. She had been married over twenty years herself. Her husband Noel
was a semi-invalid with a bad chest who helped her
to run their three-storeyed red brick, boarding house.
They had no children of their own for which Anona
gave thanks. She had never liked them and never
would. She believed it was meant to be like that. She
also did not believe in accidental procreation outside the bonds of marriage. Reading between the
lines of her sister's letter almost seemed to suggest
that Madge might almost *welcome* such a terrible
thing happening, so she decided to put Merrick in
the attic and Maisy in the small box-room, right next
to where she and Noel slept.

No, she had not liked the tone of that letter one
tiny bit. No one was going to conceive in her domain
and that was final!

However, there was one small factor never taken
into consideration and it was Anona's inherent
meanness.

'She doesn't dish out much grub,' muttered
Merrick after they had eaten their supper when they
arrived the evening before the Bank Holiday. 'One
thin slice of brawn, a quarter of a tomato, and a slice

of bread and butter topped off by half a slice of funeral cake and a weak cup of tea isn't enough to keep body and soul together.'

'Sh . . . or she'll hear you,' said Maisy trying to put on a good face and longing to plunder a full box of chocolates. 'Beggars can't be choosers Merrick. It's very good of her to let us stay – seeing as we aren't paying her anything – though mother did say we should get her a nice vase before we left.'

That night up in his attic on a lumpy camp-bed, with the heat of the house rising to the small cramped room with its windows jammed shut from layers of brown lead paint, Merrick rolled about restlessly.

What a fiasco coming here with Maisy.

It was well past two o'clock in the morning and he had heard every church clock chime from miles around, not to mention the rumble of hot water pipes and chains pulling, deep in the bowels of the boarding house. Oh for the life of fresh air and exploration, he thought – yet here he was not even able to open the window for a bit of sea air and his stomach was lurching with hunger with as much noise as the incoming tide.

With a sudden spurt of anger he climbed out of bed and putting on his dressing gown and slippers he began to creep down the flights of stairs to the family kitchen in the basement. He had never known such a lack of good food in all his life. His time in Wigan had always been a memory of being well stoked up, and properly fed. It went without saying that he had been brought up to regard good food as his common right.

In the kitchen, a touch of moonlight brightened the room for a second before it was blotted out by a scurrying sky. There was a candle with some matches right in the centre of a scrubbed deal table. Merrick lit the candle and went over to a small wooden cupboard with a perforated zinc front similar to a meat safe. To his delight it contained three uncut loaves and a plate of unbuttered but stale looking curling white crusts. As he grabbed at the crusts in triumph he was startled to hear a slight movement behind him. Standing there in a long white satin nightie with an edging of soft white rabbit fluff, was Maisy.

'Merrick! What in mercy's name are you up to?' she hissed.

'What does it look like? It's starvation – that's what it is. I couldn't last the night out on what *she* gave us.'

'*She* is my auntie, Merrick. She's giving us a free holiday and don't you forget it.' Maisy came up close to him. Her breasts were wobbling dangerously.

'W – what are you doing here, anyway?' he stammered, mesmerised by the protruding outline of her nipples beneath the shimmering gloss. 'Why aren't you wearing your dressing-gown?'

'Because I didn't want to get it messed up in the kitchen. It's a very expensive one Merrick and it wouldn't do to get butter or jam on it – but I was so hungry.'

'Even though she is your auntie, and we're here free?'

She nodded silently, then whispered: 'She's got some biscuits in that fancy tin on the dresser. I saw her counting them last night. There were ten arrowroots.'

Maisy tiptoed with chubby, bare feet over to the tin in the moonlight. The candle flickered between them. Merrick was enthralled by her beauty. She was almost bursting from her nightie as she carefully took four biscuits and gave him two.

He took them from her in dazed wonder. It was like being blessed by some silken robed goddess.

Suddenly there was a noise. A door was being opened and some heavy treads sounded on the stairs close by.

They stared at each other in frozen terror. 'Under the table. Blow out the candle,' breathed Maisy, curling down – with Merrick following in breathless haste.

They were lucky, and by the time the plodding footsteps arrived at the kitchen door the moon had vanished again and the place was in complete darkness, as someone filled a jug with water and shuffled away again.

'You'd best go back to the attic by the small winding back stairs – through that door next to the dresser,' said Maisy. 'We don't want to be caught together like this in the main house.'

'Back stairs?' Merrick shivered slightly. 'Supposing I land up in the wrong place or summat? Wrong attic bedroom?'

155

'You aren't half a baby, Merrick Jackson. The main thing is to get out of here safely before we get another fright. I'll go first then, and you follow. I'll be better at thinking of something to say. Just you keep completely quiet.'

They crept to the door which was thankfully unlocked and he followed Maisy's glowing white silhouette. There was no need to have worried, it led directly to his own attic – to a door right next to a wardrobe, but behind a screen. If only he'd known in the first place – how simple his journey to the kitchen might have been.

No sooner was Maisy ready to get back to her box-room when there was a gentle tap at the door. 'Are you all right, Mr Jackson?'

He didn't reply but gestured to Maisy to hide under the thin cotton quilt on the camp bed. Then he let out one or two rather loud snores followed by prolonged silence, and soon the person outside seemed to move away.

Merrick went to the back stairs door behind the screen and carefully turned the key, then checking that the other door was also locked, he looked at his watch. It was nearly three o'clock.

'Surely you aren't going to lie there on the floor, Merrick,' whispered Maisy? 'We can both squash into this if we try. We'll just have to shape ourselves into a sort of double figure S. I'll get no sleep at all if I think you're lying there in that state.'

'It won't be for long, Maisy. You'll be able to get back to your own room once we're quite certain it's all clear.' His words faded as he felt her warm firm hand seeking his. She was dragging at his arm. 'You'll be quite *safe*, Merrick. I shan't eat you.'

Wearily but with subdued and growing excitement he did what he was told – mostly to stop her creating too much fuss which might easily have been heard by others. As he huddled in beside her into the figure S he realised that sleep would not take place just yet but on no account must they break the camp-bed.

They both rolled to the floor on top of the quilt and some time later there was another knock at the door. 'Are you all right Mr Merrick?' But this time the snores were genuine and when he did wake up properly again Maisy had vanished – as if it had all been just a dream.

Maisy was bubbling with some inner secret excitement when she arrived home. It was Merrick this and Merrick that every few seconds. So much so that her mother Madge began to wonder.

'Were the beds comfortable? Did you remember to buy her a vase?'.

Maisy gasped and put her hand to her mouth. 'The vase! We clean forgot. We were doing so many other things.'

Madge had mixed emotions. If Merrick had . . . Maisy and he must get wed as soon as possible. But if Merrick hadn't, she knew that someone else soon would.

Within a week she had wheedled the truth out of Maisy and by the end of the month, unknown to

Merrick, the bridesmaids' dresses were being planned.

The following day Madge received a terse little note from her sister in Blackpool:

'Dear Madge, . . . they seemed to enjoy themselves and I kept them well separated. I am having trouble with my waterworks at the moment so when I had to get up in the night, I knocked on the lad's door once or twice just to check everything was all right, and as for Maisy she slept like a log and almost missed her breakfast . . . from your loving sister . . . P.S. Don't expect me to put them up again for nothing as it comes very expensive and I half suspect they took extra biscuits from the kitchen.'

CHAPTER 6

Valentine Cards

On St Valentine's Day, 1914, Ivy was astonished and delighted to find two valentine cards to greet her in the post. She recognised the larger one from Alfred, because it was handmade, and had a small green slipper on it with interlocked scarlet hearts surrounded in a circle of fine Nottingham lace, and she recognised Alfred's writing on the envelope.

But the second love token was a puzzling surprise. It was a simple card with a red padded satin heart in the centre surrounded by a picture of snowdrops and aconites, with the words inside on a small beribboned scroll which said:

'Alas too late my heart I knew
That we belong – just me and you.
Be my Valentine
Forever mine . . .'

Ivy Violet stared hard at the envelope. The address was written in very careful copperplate writing. She felt a thread of unease.

She thought, deep down, that she knew who'd sent it – but it seemed quite unbelievable – especially coming from a married man. In fact –reading between the lines – it could seem as if it really *was* Merrick Jackson who'd sent it, and that even after so few months of married life with Maisy he was rueing his mistake.

Her heart began to beat a trifle nervously. Complications with Merrick were now the last thing she wanted. She had totally resigned herself to the fact that those childish early days full of mistakes were over, for now she was thankfully settled and courting a man she admired and loved – Alfred MacFarlynne, and nothing would shake it. Added to which she did not want to be the cause of trouble in Maisy's marriage to Merrick.

She sat there for a few moments brooding as she put the two valentines on her dressing table in her small attic bedroom. Perhaps it wasn't even from Merrick she thought. And if not, what did it matter who it was from except it was a charming and flattering surprise?

Her spirits brightened as she went downstairs into

the shop to start work. Her thoughts about Merrick vanished entirely when she looked on a shelf full of some shoe repairs. Tucked away in a dark corner was a stray alley cat in the middle of having kittens, amid howls of anguish as one after another, seven small, wet, blind, helpless morsels were licked into shape. A thin-looking grey and black brindled tabby cat began to purr contentedly.

It all made quite a talking point that day as plans were rapidly made to drown all the kittens as soon as possible. Aileen and Dinah started giving Ivy Violet instructions on which bucket to use.

Ivy Violet looked at them all in alarm: 'Oh no. I just couldn't!'

They looked at her puzzled.

'It's so cruel.'

'It'll be more cruel if they spend their lives being half starved causing a nuisance round all the back entries,' warned Aileen. 'We've already got two cats of our own and even those started off as strays. I know they're needed to keep down the mice and rats but it can't be allowed to get out of hand, and we certainly haven't the time or the money to feed them.'

'And even if we did,' said Dinah, trying to be extra kind and thoughtful, 'it would only happen all over again in a few more weeks somewhere. And it's no good relying on Bobby to do anything because he just ignores them altogether – plus all the messes they cause everywhere. We once had some shoes utterly spoiled by cat wee.'

161

Ivy Violet just gazed at them both and slowly shook her head. She knew they were quite right and it was the only sensible solution as far as they were concerned, but she could not bring herself to take away the life that had just forced itself into the world as she saw the mother cat lying there in the gloom, slowly grooming her brood.

Perhaps Ivy Violet's own family had been unusual for they had never ever had any pets except for a canary, once, and a goldfish. But even so there had been no shortage of cats, thin looking mongrel dogs, a monkey, caged rabbits, and pigeons, in the realms of Clark Terrace.

'We'll leave it till this afternoon, anyway,' said Ivy Violet as she went and looked carefully at the seven kittens. They were a motley crew, and two of them were obviously ginger toms. There was also a pure white one with a black spot on its back, a tabby one, like its mother, and two which were all black.

As soon as Aileen and Dinah had left the shop and Bobby was busy doing the repairs, Ivy Violet went upstairs and taking the unknown valentine card with its red heart on it she cut the cover off, and stuck the frontispiece to the top of a larger piece of card. Underneath that she wrote: 'Give a Valentine Kitten Token to the one you love. Beautiful kittens born today and ready for delivery as soon as their eyes are open. Get your free Valentine Token today from Miss Ivy Violet Hilton in the shop.'

Then quickly, whilst she was working behind the old wooden counter of the shoeshop, she made out

seven neat billet-doux from the receipt book, putting
a Valentine heart on each one and writing '*My Kitten*'
in curly decorative writing. Then she put the valentine card notice in the shop window.

She asked Bobby if – just for this special Friday
morning – they could have a gramophone record on,
something romantic like *Tales From the Vienna Woods*?

Bobby agreed. His eyes twinkled slightly. 'Tha's a
rum lass an' no mistake – but tha's a good worker.
Might as well shock the neighbour'ood – and let's
'ope it gets rid of all those little blighters in't corner
pretty quick, afore Aileen tries to get me to do summat.'

That afternoon Ivy Violet was staggered at the
effect caused by the valentine notice as the seven
I.O.U. Valentine Kitten notices were snapped up by
romantic and eager participants. Just at the stage
when there were only two still unspoken for, who
should walk into the shop but Merrick, his face
glowing from the cold, rheumy, February air – a
well-dressed young man in tweed knee breeches and
gaiters – and in his prime.

Ivy Violet saw him cast a surreptitious glance
towards the gloomy depths of the shop, then said: 'I
saw your valentine card notice Ivy. It looks really
good.'

Ivy Violet's face broke into a responsive smile.
'Yes. It's done ever so well. There are only two kittens left without future homes. Were you thinking of
getting one for Maisy?'

His neck coloured up slightly, as he pretended to

loosen his collar with a couple of fingers. 'No, not quite, but I think her young sister Milly'd like one. She'll be six in a few weeks.' Then he said casually: 'Was that card front – stuck at the top of the notice – part of a valentine *you* got?'

She nodded: 'I received one that I know was definitely from Alfred and also, I got that one in the window. I've no idea who sent it.' She looked at him hard and he looked away. Then she said: 'I expect valentine days are over now – for you and Maisy now you're married. Unless you ever send her one just for fun?'

He shook his head, and mumbled slightly: 'They're on the way out. It's what they did when our parents were young but it's getting right old fashioned these days.' Then with a flash of the old Merrick she once knew so well, he said impulsively: 'I wouldn't have even got *that* one if they hadn't had it stuck in't Co-op Fancy Goods from last year.' He suddenly went scarlet with embarrassment at the *faux pas* and moved as if to leave the shop as quickly as possible.

'Merrick. Don't go. Not without the cat token for Milly. Tell her it's a white one with a black blob on its back and she can come and see it any time. Do you think it will suit her?' She gabbled the words to try and pretend he had not revealed the truth, feeling a motherly desire to protect him.

He gulped and nodded as she stuck the small paper token in his trembling palm, and as she returned from the shop doorway to her work behind the counter she felt a strange mixture of both grief and comfort. Grief that Merrick was pining and unhappy in his marriage, and comfort that at last she had outlived all the slanders set against her and fed to Merrick in the past.

CHAPTER 7

Alfred's Party

' . . . Oh the moon shines bright on Charlie
    Chaplin
'is boots are cracklin'
For the want of blacking
And the 'ole in 'is trousers it wants mendin'
Before we send 'im
To the Dardanelles. . . .'

The outbreak of the 1914–18 War meant that in
Manchester and Salford almost every family was
personally affected by the call to arms.

Forthwith Lord Kitchener's famous recruitment
poster appeared throughout Britain with his finger
pointing directly at everyone telling them that their
country needed them. The cobbled streets of Hulme

echoed to the sounds of marching feet, with thousands of boys and men of all ages volunteering for army training, thus playing their part in the plan to get 70 divisions of infantry into the battlefields.

One of the training grounds was Heaton Park where men gathered – still in their civilian clothing and blue serge armlets, because there were not enough uniforms to go round.

By the time war was declared in August 1914, Ivy Violet's family had been affected. Everyone was immersed in war fever and patriotism. Kenny Hilton enlisted, and also Merrick Jackson – both of them joining the army; whilst others from Ivy Violet's Clark Terrace days were Mark Simpkin – who claimed to be a year older than he was for the army – and his brother Joseph who joined the navy. Most of these young men were promised that their jobs would still be waiting for them when they returned and that it would all be over by Christmas.

Sylvia Watson's brother, twenty-one-year-old Henry, also joined up, and many were the younger brothers and sisters who watched in puzzled fear as families were suddenly split asunder. Often, young boys gave false ages to enlist and were brought back home again by their parents; whilst smaller children asked the grown-ups what 'war' was, only to meet worried and strained faces as their query remained unanswered.

And, in the background, the music halls sang: 'Goodbye Dolly I must leave you', as Manchester Pals' battalions went off to fight the foe as part of

Kitchener's New Army to the tune of 'Dolly Grey' – many of them never to return.

Women manned the home front in the clothing and armament factories taking on many of the men's jobs and boosting the morale of the troops with vehicle driving, nursing, and running canteens. Even Phillis changed to war work, like many other women who were employed in what had been male territory, in armament factories, as Ivor Novello's song 'Keep the Home Fires Burning', was sung throughout the land.

But, in spite of declining hopes for an early settlement and the bombing by Zeppelins around Manchester, the start of food rationing and blackouts at night, the young unmarrieds like Ivy Violet remained cheerful and optimistic. They knew that all they could do for the best was to pray to God and try and live as normal a life as possible – for the sake of those who were already dying and wounded in the mud-bound trenches of the terrible battlefields.

Alfred MacFarlynne's call-up had been temporarily delayed due to damaged eyesight, caused when some photographic fluid splashed into them. This was hopefully a condition that might eventually be cured as Alfred eagerly claimed his desire to get across to France to join in the fray.

There were very few people who ever dared to say otherwise, and the only person that Ivy Violet knew of who did was a nephew of Tilly Simpkin's who registered as a conscientious objector on grounds of religion. He went to France as a stretcher bearer, but not before he had suffered the hate, violence and ostracism of many of his neighbours for bravely upholding his own pacifist beliefs.

On a breezy day in March, when purple crocuses were out, and delicate, butter coloured daffodils lay scattered everywhere, Alfred MacFarlynne took Ivy Violet to the garden of 'Silver Birches' in Salford and asked her to marry him. Ivy Violet was eighteen, and Alfred was due to be twenty-one in April.

'After we've been to see your mother, and Freddy, and hopefully received their blessing we'll announce it at my twenty-first party,' murmured Alfred ecstatically as he covered Ivy Violet's cheeks with small gentle kisses, and she stroked his hair.

The following week they went to visit Phillis and Freddy at Sale Moor to reveal the glad tidings. Everyone was delighted and the coming engagement was celebrated with a glass of port wine.

In some ways Ivy Violet knew she was lucky to have had no real fuss made about it. Mainly because Freddy was not her proper father. Also, Phillis, her stepmother, had always been a forthright working person, and when left as widow had no spare money, and was not attached to the old family customs of wealthier people, where a girl's fiancé approached the girl's father for her hand in marriage – often with a substantial dowry waiting in the wings.

There was still a strong element of these customs in Alfred's background, where the whole family, except Alfred's father who worked in the cotton trade, had chewed over the news of Alfred's startling announcement with their own strongly held opinions.

'Ivy Violet's a sweet girl, but rather young and unworldly,' said his mother tactfully. 'I had always rather hoped that he would have been less hasty and perhaps asked Penelope Malstruthers who is more his own age and type and has such a beautiful singing voice, and all that wonderfully calm self confidence. They were both such good little playmates when they were at Miss Kendal's at Riverside Kindergarten.'

'He couldn't have asked *her*, mother,' said Alfred's sister Virginia, scornfully. 'She's gone off all men entirely, and spends her time with Primmy Percival, wearing jodhpurs and discussing dairy farming, and carthorses.'

'I don't think Alfred should ever marry *anyone*,' said his sister Melissa who always carried a torch for slightly out of reach men who were either priests, monks, or young, anguished-looking curates.

'I don't, either,' Martha said, who had just enrolled at the new Loreburn Business College with a view to training for Civil Service secretarial work. She went on, 'At least not until he's over thirty and finds someone with plenty of money. Even our Ronald isn't engaged yet and he's much older than Alfred. And anyway we've got enough girls in our family already without another one pinned on at the side.'

'I've always liked Ivy Violet Hilton, and always shall, even if she becomes a deep-sea diver and never marries Alfred at all,' said Clara in her rather dramatic high-pitched voice as she took off her glasses and began slowly polishing the lenses. 'She's got lots of really bright ideas. She's just what Alfred needs.'

'I don't think she's really in love with him,' remarked Olivia with a certain cool spitefulness. 'She's more in love with his photography than him. I can tell when people are *really* in love. I was in love with Kenny Hilton before he broke my heart and went off with Peony. I wept buckets and buckets. I used to swoon every time he came near me, but I've never seen his sister Ivy Violet swoon. Nor is she ever likely to if you ask me.' Then Olivia hurried away because her latest young man, who was the Lord Mayor's nephew, was waiting for her in the hall with his new moustache and a silver-knobbed walking cane.

Alfred's twenty-first birthday party was a sumptuous affair and was held at the Smith-Blenkinsop Assembly Rooms in Higher Broughton. There was a large hall there built at the beginning of Queen Victoria's reign with an ornate marble-pillared entrance and eight imposing steps to climb to it from a sweeping driveway.

Ivy had never seen so many people at a private birthday party. They stood around in groups laughing and chattering and all dressed up. Alfred assured her that they were mostly family friends and relations. Although Phillis and Freddy had been invited, as well as Kenny and his lady-love Peony Bagshaw, both lots had turned down the invitation. Phillis and Freddy because they knew it was not quite their environment, but were pleased by the etiquette of being invited; and Kenny and Peony because they were going away to Llandudno on a coach trip.

The catering had been done by Tankervilles, a well known bakery and delicatessen. A huge decorated birthday cake rested on a solid silver cake stand. In the centre of which on the top tier was a castellated plateau and on this lay a big silver key with a ribbon on it, and the figures 21. A huge pig's head lay on the side table where all the plates and dishes were. Set in aspic with pale pink, pale lashed eyelids closed, intricate lacy patterns traced beneath the transparent and faintly yellow jelly across its cheeks and fore-head, whilst in its open mouth was a huge glacé orange complete with leaves. Everybody gazed at it in awe and said what a work of art it was, and what a fine specimen of a pig, and what lovely ears it had.

After a meal which included buttered asparagus, anchovy vol-au-vents, stuffed olives and pressed tongue, Alfred made his announcement about his engagement to Ivy Violet. Everyone drank their health with wine, and the cake was cut amongst much jovial applause.

Ivy Violet felt as if it was all a strange dream, as she smiled and nodded and sat there in a rather inex-pensive, blue, artificial silk dress from a Penny Bazaar. Momentarily she wished she still had the wonderful dress she made for the ball that she had gone to with Sylvia.

173

There was a music recital after their meal by an energetic lady in a brown velvet gown called Miss Bronsen. Ivy Violet tried hard to keep her eyes open and look appreciative as she sat next to Alfred's mother and father. Alfred himself had somehow become untangled from her and was sitting with two of his boyhood friends and another young man with long ringlets of red curls and wearing a flowered cummerbund round his waist. Some sheet music drooped casually from his long thin fingers. He was introduced as Mr Maximilian Dingle. He went up to Miss Bronsen, who had just bent her head slightly to everyone in pleased acknowledgement, and stood close to her by the grand piano as she took the music score from him.

In a quiet voice, Mr Dingle, who was generally known as Max, announced that he was going to sing 'Danny Boy'.

Ivy Violet gazed at him. She was completely mesmerised by his diffident and relaxed self-confidence. He was wearing a creamy, upright silk collar and a floppy, satin bow-tie round his neck. The arms of his shirt were very full and flowed from narrow cuffs where diamond cuff-links glinted, reminding Ivy Violet of gypsy dress. When he smiled she saw gold glinting from teeth and felt that even from his mouth there could be a small flashing diamond.

The moment he started singing it was as if the whole room was spellbound to total, perfect silence.

'Oh Danny Boy –

The pipes – the pipes are ca-l-ling
From glen to glen –
And down the mountainside . . .'

The passionate and sonorous tones sent a strange tremor down Ivy Violet's spine. She had never heard anything so perfect and compelling in all her life.

When the song was finished she joined in the standing ovation as people clapped and clapped.

'He used to be at school with me,' smiled Alfred a little later as the dancing began and he led Ivy Violet onto the shining wooden floor to waltz to music played by an ensemble consisting of Miss Bronsen, pianist; Alfred's older brother Ronald, timpani; and Max Dingle playing the fiddle.

'He's quite a lady's man if he allowed himself to be one, but he concentrates wholly on entertaining people with his music, and singing. His mother was a dancer and married into a wealthy family who made their fortune manufacturing bell wire which became a huge cable company. Sadly both his parents died young, and Max was brought up by his aunt and uncle, not far from here. Come over and meet him.'

Shyly, Ivy Violet allowed herself to be introduced, and felt herself trembling nervously as they shook hands. Smiling at her quite cheerfully, he seemed quite normal when he was not performing and was very pleased that she had liked the way he sang.

'It just shows what a good pal I am – to actually allow my betrothed to come into close contact with you, knowing the devastating effect you have on the fair sex,' joked Alfred, as they all laughed.

'Would I had met someone of the fair sex as wonderful as you have,' said Max, lightly returning the compliment.

That night when Alfred had seen Ivy Violet back to the Byrtles' shop, and had bid her a chaste goodnight, she could not get Max Dingle from her mind. She tried in vain to get to sleep with the refrain of 'Danny Boy' eventually invading her dreams, along with the hours chiming the way to early morning from a distant church clock.

Late April was wet and windy, but everywhere pale yellow primroses and rusty velvet wallflowers full of wonderful scent were in abundance. Golden winter jasmine, buttercups and daisies were to be seen in nooks and crannies, along with young fresh leaves of dandelion beneath bushes of pink flowering currant.

It lightened people's hearts that winter had finally flown as they walked past the small and iron-railed front gardens of those blessed with such luxuries in the streets of Hulme.

One day when boot and shoe repairs were doing a roaring trade and Ivy Violet was working hard, a stranger, an elegantly dressed young woman, came into the shop.

Ivy was now helping Bobby more and more with the actual repair work – for his eyes were becoming worse. The Byrtles had taken on Tilly Simpkin's fourteen-year-old crippled daughter Poppy in the shop as a sitting-down counter assistant and general clerk.

'Are you Miss Hilton?' said the girl to Poppy.

'No, but I'll ring the bell for her to come and see you.' Poppy pressed the small brass bell.

'I am in the right place aren't I? Is it true you sometimes make handmade shoes?'

Poppy hesitated and swept back her curly brown hair nervously. 'I'm not quite sure. I know Mr Byrtle did used to make all sorts of things, but he's getting old now and doesn't do as much – but Miss Hilton will certainly know.' Then to her relief Ivy Violet appeared.

Ivy greeted the unknown girl. The girl looked about the same age as herself and wore a two piece costume of finest crimson woollen whipcord with a large cameo brooch on its lapel. A small crimson feathered hat to match was perched on her pile of shining golden hair.

Ivy Violet gazed at her, and nodded respectfully. Her own attire consisted of a plain navy blue twill frock and a large worn calico apron. 'How can I be of assistance?' she said.

It seemed to Ivy Violet that a look of scarcely concealed shock flitted across the girl's face. 'I am right, aren't I? You are the Ivy Violet Hilton who's engaged to Alfred MacFarlynne?'

Ivy nodded, then said in slightly aggressive tones: 'I'm a working girl. I'm not one of them as can fill their time with socialising and soirées if that's what you were thinking.'

The girl suddenly laughed. 'Even I'm not in that league. I couldn't even get to Alfred's twenty-first with my fiancé Maxi Dingle because I was rehearsing for a play – and I wouldn't mind – but I only have to say "The toasted teacakes are here, madam", and iron a mountain of costumes back-stage in the whole of the two and a half hours of it.'

She looked hastily round the shop, then sitting on a bentwood chair next to the counter, she took off her buttoned ankle boot and said: 'I know it isn't actually a shoe – but it'll give you some idea of size and shape. Do you think Mr Byrtle would make me a pair of snakeskin shoes, if I got you the snakeskin? They're going to be all the rage, you mark my words. Maxi and I were talking to Alfred and he suggested I should pop round some time and see you about it.

Engaged . . . To Maximilian Dingle . . But of course why on earth shouldn't he have been engaged? Especially as she herself was engaged to Alfred. It was the most natural state of affairs in all the world. Yet somehow her heart sank and she felt ashamed of her romantic dreams and a traitor to Alfred, even though she knew it had all been a sudden moment of falling in love with an image of delight, so distant from her own general world. This girl, who now said she was called Garnet Swanson, seemed to highlight the fact that they were from entirely different settings, and that although Ivy Violet was now Alfred's wife to be, she had no really family backing or even comfortable family background in the sense that Alfred and his friends had. Mmmm . . . perhaps it was a strange way of looking at life but seeing this beautiful well-dressed creature before her she just couldn't help it.

As if sensing her thoughts, Garnet said cheerfully: 'Actors and actresses aren't rich people you know. It's just that I'm wearing my best today because I didn't know quite what to expect. But I am serious about the shoes.'

Ivy Violet hesitated. She knew in her heart of hearts that Bobby was getting past making and designing the exotic footwear of his younger days. But because of Bobby's teaching she could in theory, after all her own work, make some herself. Maybe? . . . In reality though? Could she? Would she really manage it?

'I'll just go and speak to Mr Byrtle, and see what he says – if you'd care to wait for a few minutes.'

'But of course. And do tell him that I can provide the snakeskin and that cost is no problem. Maxi is paying.'

Bobby was sitting in the back kitchen drinking a mug of tea. He looked pale and wan, but smiled as she walked in: 'Now then lass – what are they on at you for this time?'

Her eyes sparkled affectionately. 'Not one of those today, Mr Byrtle. It's a young lady who's a friend of my fiancé Alfred, and she's asking if she could have a pair of snakeskin shoes made.'

He shook his head a trifle gloomily and sighed: 'Snakeskin – what sort?'

'She didn't say – but she says she can provide it

179

and that money's no object. She's an actress and very fashionable. She's waiting at the counter.'

Bobby Byrtle drained the last dregs from his mug of tea, and stood up slowly. 'I'll come and 'ave a word. You see, Ivy – they expect the earth. They think that because they've got a bit of snakeskin it can just be magicked into summat different in the wink of an eyelid. Snakeskin's very hard stuff to work with and shoes made of it are often stiff and uncomfortable. But that's vanity for you.'

By the time they had arrived back at the counter, Ivy Violet could see no likelihood that Bobby would be prepared to spend his time on the shoes. Even so he stood there patiently and listened to what Garnet Swanson had to say.

'It's really to do with my young man, Mr Byrtle. He brought me the snakeskin as a special present from when he was abroad. He said it could all be softened up and made into a pair of shoes, and I don't want to disappoint him.'

'He's a lucky young man then – that's all I can say,' said Bobby dryly. 'I doesn't want to disappoint thee either lass and if it had been a bit of nice kid leather I might have thought the more of it.' He shook his head slowly and his mouth went down at the sides. 'No lass, me days of adventure are over where snakeskin's concerned. Mind you with it being so tough and unyielding it might just be the sort of job some enterprising young 'un 'ud have a go at. That is, if you can find any of 'em these days. Trouble is, they's all int' factories doing piece work.

They never sees a proper shoe through from start to finish. It's all the machine age now.'

Garnet Swanson's beautiful young face fell a mile. She was one of those people who thought everything was possible, because although she had not the means to do the impossible herself she was young, pretty and confident enough to assume that all the world would do her bidding.

'Is there *anyone* you could suggest who might do it, Mr Byrtle? I'd be so – *so* grateful.'

Bobby scratched his head slowly: 'Can't say as there's anybody I can think of these days as 'ud take on a job like this. There's not only the skin itself, there's the matching up of the patterns so's both shoes is the same. It's the sort of job fit to send someone barmy.' Then he looked straight at Ivy Violet with the slightest glimmer of a smile and said: 'There's only one person who might manage it without fading out, and that's my Miss Hilton – seeing as 'ow she's stuck me all this time. Though it's a chance you'd both 'ave to take and you wouldn't 'ave to moan if it didn't work out and the snakeskin was ruined. It's a question of what you and your young man want. A snakeskin memento in a glass case till kingdom come? Or this lass having a go at making her first pair of shoes in the hardest way possible, and maybe making a hash of it.'

The three of them stood there in silence for a few seconds, then Garnet Swanson said: 'I should be truly grateful if Miss Hilton would try and make them.'

Ivy Violet felt all the blood draining to her feet. Her head was in a complete spin. How on earth had she got herself in such an awful predicament? But on the outside she hoped with all her might she was looking calm. 'Yes, of course. I should be delighted, as long as everyone knows it's my very first attempt. All I can do is try my best.'

'Quite right lass,' nodded Bobby.

Garnet Swanson had explained that Maxi would call in with the snakeskin later in the week. After she had left the shop Bobby said to Ivy: 'Dinna fret thisel lassie – I'll help thee out if needs be.'

Some days later a whole bundle of snakeskin was left at the shop along with a pair of Garnet Swanson's own shoes for gauging the proper size. She would come in for some fittings while they were being made.

Ivy Violet had been out on an errand and when she got back, Bobby had sorted out the parcel and was carefully stretching out the snakeskin.

'The first thing Ivy lass, will be to do some design drawing suggestions based on the zigzag pattern of these skins, so tha'd better get tha thinking cap on.' Then he stared at it all again and said: 'But if you ask me I can't see you or anyone else making up this dratted pattern in any proper manner at t' moment. It just depends how pernickety she is. Some of these fashion proud women are so flibbertigibbet fussy that even one small dark, natural scale freckle on one shoe not matching the exact pattern on t'other, would be chewed over like a piece of stringy mutton.'

Little did Ivy Violet realise what she had let herself in for. Night after night she sat in her small attic bedroom trying to work out the final shoe design.

It became such an obsession that on one occasion she told Alfred she could not come out with him because she was so busy.

'Not today, of all days!' he protested, tugging at her arm urgently. 'Something's happened that may seriously change both our lives.'

It was Saturday evening and Ivy Violet, with much secret reluctance, left her work on the shoes and allowed him to take her back to his house to stay overnight and come back after tea on Sunday.

'I'm quite worried about you Ivy,' he said. 'All this shoe malarkey's getting out of hand. Sometimes I curse the day I ever mentioned to Maxi and Garnet that you worked for Bobby Byrtle. It's just not natural. Particularly for a girl shop assistant who isn't even trained in that sort of thing. I mean – how could you possibly have considered staying in on a Saturday night just to do that when you knew I was coming for you?' Alfred surveyed her with reproachful solemnity.

She sighed and laughed. 'It's a mystery to me too, Alfred. But that's how it was. I was just getting too immersed in it all and it took over. But I've pretty well got the shoe style worked out, now.' She gripped her large green, straw handbag with determination. 'In fact I've got the final sketch in here to show Garnet. Just in case by some mad chance we should meet them somewhere while we're at your house.'

When they were back at Alfred's she was surprised to find no one else in. 'How unusual. Do you mean to say they've all gone out to the same place?'

He nodded. 'A rather posh do, concerned with father being made president of Bellsover Cotton Institute this year. I was supposed to be going too, but the family gave me dispensation, because they knew we'd want some time on our own so that I could break the news to you.' Then quickly he said, 'And there's one thing I want to do more than anything else Ivy Violet. I want to take a special photograph of you tonight. One I can keep with me as a precious, loving token when I'm over there in France. As you know my eyes are completely A1 again and yesterday I received my calling up papers for the army. It's all quite sudden, and I have to report for duty next week.'

Ivy Violet stared at him. Somehow it seemed unbelievable, even though so many young men were joining up – including Merrick Jackson.

'Oh Alfred. What a terrible thing!'

Alfred's fair, good-looking face registered supreme consternation. 'You mustn't say such things, Ivy. It's unpatriotic. It's the duty of every physically fit man to answer the call and fight for King and Country.'

Tears flooded to her eyes as she stared at him, speechless. He put his arm round her as she began to sob. 'There, there; don't take on so. I'll be home on leave to see you, and you'll be able to send me plenty of letters giving me all the home news. They say that many women join knitting circles to make gloves and socks for the fighting forces, and they send regular parcels full of small luxuries like tobacco and cigarettes and sweets. It helps keep people cheerful. I'll be back – don't fret. This dreadful war'll be finished in a jiffy with all our lot over there. For heaven's sake wipe your eyes. I don't want you looking all pouchy and tearful on a photograph.'

When they were upstairs in what Alfred now called his studio, Ivy Violet allowed him to take a portrait of her head and shoulders, with bare shoulders and white muslin draped beneath and her dark hair loose and wavy. She held an artificial silk rose delicately placed just below her chin.

To her it was a sad occasion, but the gloomier Ivy Violet became, the more loving and cheerful Alfred became in his endeavour to cheer her up. He produced a bottle of sparkling white wine for them to drink each other's health and happiness.

As they sipped, and sipped . . . they grew drowsier and more relaxed on a huge, softly feathered settee. Alfred struggled to his feet and said: 'Look, we can't just drift away down here all evening in this state. We'd better go and lie down on my bed. Then if by chance anyone should call, they'll think everyone's out.'

Ivy Violet nodded. She was in a pleasant wine-laden daze, as they slowly made their way to

Alfred's room and lay peacefully under the eider-down. She could have gone to sleep if she had not been woken by being showered with kisses. The full force of his body pressed against hers and he groaned with passion. 'Oh my own sweet Violet. My dear one. How am I going to be able to leave you living all alone at the Byrtles'? If only we could already be married and together as man and wife for ever. Oh Ivy.' He went quiet, then tried to be cheerful again and said: 'On my very first leave we must be married by special licence – for both our sakes.'

For a moment Ivy Violet was impulsively caught up in his desperate passion as she clung to him and fondled him. But, as he tried to stray further with his hands she stiffened and came to her senses. 'No, Alfred. No. We mustn't.'

'We must. We must! Surely we can't be denied these last few moments of complete privacy togeth-er. Surely you wouldn't a deny a man going off to war this one last wonderful gift to carry him along the fearful road? A true mark of our own love and faithfulness? The ultimate goal of every man and wife.'

Ivy Violet could feel herself weakening as she struggled to escape from under the eiderdown. Oh how she would have loved to give him his heart's desire and prove that she really was his wife-to-be. But the strong moral training of her mother Phillis brought her back to earth. 'But we aren't man and wife yet, Alfred, and it would be wrong to pretend so. We're only engaged. No proper lady ever allows herself the pleasure of the bedchamber before the proper honeymoon. Alfred darling – I know it's worse for you than it is for me – but . . .' She put on her slippers hastily and combed her hair in case he should keep on trying to persuade her. Then, to her relief, they both heard the front door bell ring.

With surprising speed Alfred rolled out of bed and hurried softly to the bathroom in his stockinged feet to splash water on himself and freshen himself up. Ivy Violet smoothed out her clothes more fully and went to peer from behind the bedroom curtains at who was at the front door, but it was dark. Whoever it was pushed something through the letter-box and left.

'Probably the Parish News,' said Alfred as they both went downstairs.

Five minutes later both of them were sitting back in the drawing-room demurely playing Clock Patience with a very old rendering of 'The Lost Chord' by Sullivan being crackled out on a phonograph, by the distant voice of Mrs Ronalds, in readiness for the arrival of any of the family. Alfred had put it on specially for Ivy Violet since it was something of a collector's item.

The next morning, the weather was so good that Alfred asked his sister Virginia if Ivy Violet could borrow her bicycle so that they could cycle along the country lanes to Silver Moss Wood to have a last day out together before he reported for duty.

'Well, I'm not quite sure, Alfred. I spent a great deal of time polishing the handlebars with Zebra Metal Polish only two days ago, and I washed and polished all the wheel rims and hubs and polished the seat with beeswax and oiled the bell and the chain. I wanted to save it like that until I went out with Roderick to Worsley village.'

'We'd be very careful with it.'

'Oh all right then. But mind you are, and just see you don't get any punctures. You'd better take an extra tin of John Bull to put in the saddle-bag, and check on the tin of french chalk.'

'I might be a bit wobbly at first, Alfred,' Ivy said hitching her skirt above the chain guard. 'I've never been on a bike much – except to practise for a few yards on other people's – years ago.'

'We'll take lemonade and salmon paste sandwiches, and cinnamon buns,' said Alfred. 'And be back for afternoon tea. Then I'll take you back to Byrtles'.'

It was paradise pedalling along the winding lanes in the fresh spring air. There were occasional glimpses of the large city buildings stretching up from the hazy distant smoke below them. Skylarks sang overhead.

'When we're married in a month or two,' Alfred panted, 'we'll be able to do this regularly. Mother and father say we can live at home with the family until we get settled in our own place – for there's space enough for an extra one.'

Ivy Violet beamed and nodded towards him breathlessly. What a wonderful change it would be –

to be actually married and living at Alfred's. Whoever would have dreamed it?

Then she sobered down a little. But whoever would have dreamed there would be a war too – and that so many of her own friends and relations would be involved?

She trembled slightly as they sat beneath the budding branches of wild cherry trees. If only this day could go on for ever. And, as Alfred stretched towards her, she kissed him passionately with a feeling of terrible sadness.

On the way home Alfred said: 'P'raps it's as well nothing happened last night in my bedroom. I was a fool to try and encourage you. It wouldn't have been fair to you Ivy – even though we'll be getting married on my next leave.'

She nodded silently, thinking morbidly that this could be the last time she would ever have a day out with him again. At the thought of it her heart almost broke with grief. Oh how she wished now that she *had* succumbed to his advances up there in his bedroom. In case he was taken from her for ever.

Then she began to cheer up again because Alfred was so happy, and it was up to her to be happy with him.

Once Alfred was finally in the army Ivy Violet busied herself once more with work at the shop as she carried on making the snakeskin shoes for Garnet Swanson, and prayed daily for Alfred's safe return for his first leave.

And at last it all came true. She was married quietly by special licence in July.

'So now, you must come and live in Salford with the rest of us,' Alfred said.

But it was not to be . . .

CHAPTER 8

Other Paths

'Why on earth didn't you go and live at his home, then?' said Maisy Fowler with a slight sneer, as she waylaid Ivy Violet in the street.

'Because I wanted us to be independent married people, that's why. I know lots of people have got no choice. An' anyway, *you* never went to live at Merrick's, when he went, did you?' Ivy Violet glared at Maisy who stared back.

Maisy was now the size of a corporation tram. It was rumoured that she might be expecting twins, and in some quarters desperate for something more unusual to chew over, triplets.

'It was one night of romance just before Merrick went to France,' purred Maisy, 'and we'd eaten oysters. I've gone off all that sort of thing a bit now though.'

She could have said it all started with one night of romance on the floor of an attic in Blackpool. Since that moment of hunger and thirst Merrick had been bound hand and foot and everywhere else by stories of Maisy's forthcoming pregnancy, coupled with its non-arrival.

'I've missed two days Merrick, and I felt terribly sick after black puddings, fried bread, bacon, sausage, tomato and fried udder,' she would say. Or: 'I've been to the W.C. ten times since I drank those bottles of lemonade and that's a sure sign . . .'

Deep down Merrick accepted it as his fate – for wasn't it what happened in most cases?

Maisy stared at Ivy Violet challengingly. 'If it's a boy I'll call it Rupert Merrick, an' if it's a girl it'll be Arabella Maisy.' Then she said: 'What's all this about making shoes for a posh tart?'

Ivy Violet blushed scarlet. She knew Maisy was trying to put her down. 'Yes, it's true, but she doesn't happen to be a tart if you please Mrs Jackson. She's a very respectable friend of mine, and I've nearly finished the shoes. And they're better 'n any I've ever seen *you* wearin'. Once you can see your feet again.' Then Ivy turned on her heel and marched into Byrtles.

The shoes she had designed and slaved at had a cut-away pattern in the vamps which complemented the markings of the snakeskin giving a unique look.

'Tha's made a right good job of them lass,' said

Bobby generously. 'I doubt I could a done much better meself these days. The second pair'll be even better.'

Ivy groaned at this. 'Not *another* pair, Bobby. I don't think I could do another pair of handmade shoes for at least 20 years!'

He laughed and patted her lightly on the head. 'Maybees tha won't need to lass. Now tha's a married young lady, and looking for a home of your own.' Then he sighed and said: 'Well, all good things come to an end, and when you go it'll be time for me to hang up me clogs good and proper. We'll p'raps sell this place to Charlie Barnes's son and move out to some real country area like round where me brother and 'is wife lives in Altrincham.'

When the time came for Ivy Violet to finally present the snakeskin shoes to Garnet Swanson she was met with quite a shock.

'I know you'll think this is a terrible cheek after all the trouble I've put you to Ivy, but — '

'It was no trouble,' Ivy Violet said in amazement. 'It was a job I undertook to do, and it was marvellous experience for me. I'm proud they've turned out so well.'

Garnet Swanson's face became more and more troubled.

They were upstairs in Ivy Violet's attic bedroom, and at first Ivy Violet had the impression that Garnet was trying to appear extra bright and cheerful. But there was a feverish flush in her cheeks, and her eyes seemed too bright for comfort, beneath her beautiful blonde hair.

Ivy Violet frowned slightly. Garnet had put on quite a lot of weight, and her ankles were all puffed up. Her shoes at present were soft, cheap black leather with flat heels and very wide toes – the sort that old ladies wore.

'The truth is Ivy, I'm with child, and the doctor's told me I've got to rest more. No – no need to try and hide your shock. All I can say is that it's Maxi Dingle's and there's never been anyone else, but he's gone you see.'

'Gone?'

'Gone and joined up like all the rest. And he doesn't know about this.'

Then Garnet stared at the shoes sadly and said: 'I'll never be able to wear them in this state Ivy. And I just feel I never want to see them again seeing it was Maxi's idea to have them made . . . and how he went off and never said a word to me and hasn't even written . . . even though I know from other sources he's in contact with his relations.' She stopped, then went on, 'We had a row you see. He wanted me to live with him without being married. He seemed to think that because we'd done it once or twice I was just a loose woman. That's men for you.' Garnet pulled a delicate lace hanky from out of her draw-string bag and dabbed her eyes. 'I'll pay you for all your work Ivy – there's no doubt of that.'

Ivy Violet shook her head vigorously. 'I wouldn't hear of it Garnet. No, I quite understand and I don't mind in the least. I shall probably keep them all my life as a sort of memento, along with an old shoe last that a friend called Tilly Simpkin once gave me.' Then an idea suddenly struck her. 'So what are you doing now then?'

'Nothing really. I just get a few shillings from the Peregrines, this group of actors and actresses who tour round different northern towns. I'm a sort of general dogsbody for them as an assistant stage manager and a prompt, now that I'm *hors de combat*. My parents live in Stockport but I can't possibly let on to them what's happened. They thought I was already beyond hope when I took up acting. My father's a strait-laced business man. He thinks all actors are pansies and when he once saw Maxi wearing a floppy bow-tie he nearly collapsed. When we're not in lodgings somewhere I live above a bakery in Withington. At least it's warm but there's an awful lot of mice and cockroaches.'

Ivy Violet looked at her hesitantly. 'Would you be willing to share a flat with me somewhere else? Bobby Byrtle will probably be selling out and retiring soon and Alfred wants me to find a new place, though he isn't keen for me to live on my own. He really wanted me to go and live with his family, but I just couldn't face it. They're all very strong-willed and self-opinionated and I would have felt out of place in the end. So would you like to share somewhere with me?'

Garnet Swanson's face lit up. 'That would be marvellous. It seems almost too good to be true. And we wouldn't always be in each other's way, because I'd be away a lot of time touring during the day, and I could always be away when your Alfred was back on leave.'

Both girls smiled at each other, and Ivy Violet felt a huge surge of relief, for deep down she had been very worried about what she was going to do about future living quarters while Alfred was in the army. The only real, trusted friend she had had in the past – someone to confide in – had been Sylvia, who was now more than ever involved with the rich, gnome-like Mr Porter.

Mr Porter was almost like a grandfather to Sylvia if it were not for the occasional carnal sessions. Sylvia often said: 'Where would I be without him Ivy? Tied here keeping house and half starving to make ends meet and with our young Tommy and Mary to look after – and Henry gone to the war. You've no idea how he's cheered up my life and given me a bit of hope and comfort. Not to mention providing decent clothes for us all . . . so that I feel like a lady.'

Ivy thought back to the night of the ball . . . It seemed so long ago now. She wondered what had happened to Mr Alfonso, Fonzzy, Treadgold who worked in a counting house, and also collected rents for Mr Porter.

Was his huge body still tripping the light fantastic round all the notable dance gatherings of Manchester? Was he still escorting young maidens in their first ventures into Viennese waltzes? And most

of all what did he really look like with a good set of
artificial teeth? For she had never seen him from that
day to this.

At the end of September Ivy Violet's move from
Bobby Byrtle's shop was finalised with fond and
tearful farewells. All of them swore to keep in touch
with one another when Bobby and his sisters retired
to greener pastures.

Ivy Violet and Garnet Swanson had been found a
large, ground floor flat to share in Victoria Park
which was a salubrious area of huge houses. These
houses had their own private road entrances pro-
tected by monumental stone gate posts hung with
ornate iron gates to exclude the general public. A
friend of Alfred's father had divided up one of these
mansions into three flats.

The girls got on very well together. Garnet still
travelled round with the theatre group and became
fatter and fatter as the baby inside her began to grow.
There was no sign of its father, Maxi Dingle.

Then one day Garnet came home to the flat in
tears. 'I just can't manage any longer Ivy. I need to
rest far more than I do. Yet I just can't let down the
Peregrines. They'll be lost without my help. They're
in a turmoil of rehearsals for J.M. Barrie's *What Every
Woman Knows*, ready for showing in Bolton in two
weeks' time, as well as acting Sheridan's comedy,
The Rivals. But most of all, how am I going to manage
about sharing this flat with you?' Her lovely fair
rounded cheeks became pinched and drawn with

genuine anguish. She looked pleadingly at Ivy Violet and said: 'Is there any chance of your helping them out for a week or two until they find someone else to step in my shoes? I realise it sounds completely mad, but what can I do with no signs of proper income and the baby's birth getting closer and closer? But I do swear one thing Ivy dear – I promise on the Bible's honour to make myself scarce whenever Alfred is home on leave, even if it means walking the streets.'

Ivy Violet burst out laughing. 'Walking the streets? Don't put it like that Garnet. People are sure to mis-understand.' She put her arm round Garnet com-fortingly. 'If only you weren't so melodramatic. Things are never as bad as they seem.' But deep in her heart, she knew that things were often twice as bad as they seemed.

Then she said lightly: 'We'll just have to do a com-plete swap-over. I'll become Garnet Ivy Violet MacFarlynne, actress and dogsbody for the Pere-grines, and you can rest here at home in our flat as Ivy Violet Garnet Swanson, potential shoe designer for the wealthy and famous, and plan exotic patent leather shoes laced with military braid whilst you're resting your feet in carpet slippers until the baby arrives. Don't fret.'

The plan turned out to be a complete success during those Autumn months. The leaves turned to red and gold on ageing stone-flagged pavements; over pre-cariously laden street barrows wasps hung heavy in air rich with the somnolent smell of over-ripe plums.

The Peregrines were dedicated theatre players and welcomed Ivy Violet's help, which included hurrying to many a local off-licence to get Mr Fanackapan, the elderly trampler of the boards of Britain, his small tots of pick-me-up. It was always a case of dire emergency. 'Rum, brandy. Brandy. Brandy. Is it handy, Ivy. Is it handy?' he would say.

And then – like a bolt from the blue – just before Christmas 1915, when lamp flares flickered in darkening market places with a yellow and smoky glow, and dead ducks and geese hung on hooks ready to welcome the festive season, the dreaded, curt, official message arrived – that 2nd Lieutenant Alfred Mac-Farlynne was missing, presumed dead.

CHAPTER 9

St Crispin's Day

Because of the tragedy of Alfred's death on the battle-fields of Ypres in Belgium – she was officially notified as such six months later – Ivy Violet's life at the flat became a sort of nightmare. Events passed in a numb haze. Her good fortune, bestowed by Alfred's father's friend Mr Barber telling her that she and Garnet and Garnet's baby daughter could live in his flat rent free indefinitely, was accepted with silent gratitude, yet hardly even a word of thanks. The two girls and baby Crystal settled into a new way of living, with both of them immersed in theatre work, much of it linked with entertaining the local troops and war-workers in the factories. The result was that by the time the Great War came to an end Ivy Violet's whole way of life in Manchester had completely changed.

*

It had changed for Merrick Jackson too as he limped past Bobby Byrtle's old shop. He had lost his right leg during his stints in Gallipoli and France. Yet life seemed sweet. For here he was back home living in Coriander Street, a real family man with beautiful, plump, well-bred Maisy and their four-year-old twin dumplings Rupert and Arabella. Bobby's house and shop were empty now – the Byrtles had moved to Altrincham – and it was in a poor state of repair. Merrick gazed at it longingly. Maisy's widowed mother had just died and left them some money from the proceeds of her brother's drapery business in Leigh. He had amassed a good trade linked with various supplies for all the thousands of German prisoners of war who had been stationed there.

Merrick stared and stared at the old mucky shop. If only . . . Oh if only he could get out of his rut in Coriander Street and start afresh by working for himself. But he knew that Maisy had other ideas for the windfall . . . Plans of moving out to Edge Lane in Stretford, and buying a car, and sending the twins to a private school, whilst he still worked as a clerk in a poky little third floor shipping office. He had never ever managed to catch up on a formal apprenticeship in the engineering trade. But now with this money. Maisy's money . . . Oh to be his own master.

He kept looking and looking at the old shop, remembering it as it was in his early youth. He recalled conversations with old Bob, and how Bobby had proudly show him a picture of the coat of arms of the Edinburgh Cordwainers on its blue background with a clicker's knife resting beneath the crown of their patron saint St Crispin. 'That's the sign of a good craftsman Merrick lad . . . A noble and skilled trade . . .'

But what about himself? Own Master? Master of what? What was *he* best at – standing here, nearly twenty-four, with only one decent leg and a fulsome over-bossy wife and twins to look after? Was it too late to try again?

Maisy herself had no doubts at all what her role in life was to be. 'With this money,' she said time and time again, 'I shall be able to train properly at last to be a music teacher, and have help with the house-work, and take only the most talented pupils, for displays at Stretford Town Hall. So that we can move in our own proper cultural circle along with that Mrs Blombispham, and her 'All Through the Night There's a Little Brown Bird Singing', and Toby Arbuthnut whose hobby is playing a xylophone made of Manchester slates and owns fields and fields of rhubarb.'

In past centuries the 25th of October, St Crispin's Day, was kept by shoemakers everywhere as a holi-day with processions, and banners, banquets and music. But Ivy Violet, in her busy life with Garnet, was almost unaware of it, for she had never made another pair of shoes, even though she had redesigned and decorated a great deal of footwear. These were used in various types of plays by the Peregrines. She could transform a ladies' plain black-leather colonial slipper with its silver buckle, into a brocade covered eighteenth-century extravaganza of gold and silver threaded galloon. Or give an ordinary plain boot the appearance of being a two tone gaiter boot with a leather cloth top, or make an ordinary court shoe into a scarlet and satin laced dream.

So, it was by pure chance that on St Crispin's Day in October 1919, Ivy Violet came face to face with threads of her past, all in the same autumn afternoon. She was in Sale making one of her infrequent visits to see Phillis and Freddy at 'Cornerstones' and they were all taking a sedate walk in the nearby park, close to the bandstand.

'Well, I'll be hanged,' gasped Phillis, 'surely that's old Bobby Byrtle with his sister Dinah. My God they don't look a day older. That Altrincham air must be working wonders. Fancy them being here in Sale!'

Phillis marched across to them in triumph with Freddy and Ivy Violet hovering in the background. A man of about eighty in a double breasted overcoat and tweed cap emerged from the gentlemen's urinal and also made his way towards Bobby.

Ivy Violet saw them all shaking hands and heard Bobby introduce his friend from the gents as Cuthbert Garter who had once worked with him in the shoe trade. 'We allus makes a point of calling in on 'im here in Sale, on St Crispin's Day, doesn't we Bert?'

'Aye that's right lad – tha' does that. We allus goes for a little sup and bite of summat, and 'as a walk int' park.'

Then Bobby suddenly spied Ivy Violet. 'Well I

never. Ivy lass. What a surprise! And 'ow's life treating thee, girl?'

Ivy felt herself blushing. She was tongue tied with shyness. What could she say? So much seemed to have happened since her days in the shop. 'Oh, not so bad, Bobby.' She nodded nervously towards his sister Dinah who gave her a gentle, rather detached smile but took no part in the conversation. She was sitting on a wooden slatted park seat with wrought iron structural decoration. Her whole body was covered in an ankle-length, grey worsted costume and her thin white hair encased in a large velvet hat. A feather boa curled round her neck.

A four-year-old boy was scampering all over forbidden grass, beyond the green metal hoops warning people not to trespass, and was being loudly chastised by the over-posh voice of his mother. A small girl of the same age was trying to reach up and press the brass knob on the drinking fountain a few yards away.

Ivy Violet recognised them immediately.

The mother was resplendent, attired in bronze kid boots and slimline coat bordered in moleskin with a neat head-hugging hat to match. Underneath the outfit, the curvaceous figure was well corseted.

'Come here *immediately* Rupert.' Then as Rupert ignored her and began to run round an oak tree followed by his twin sister, Maisy turned to Merrick, dressed in tweed plus twos and Balmoral brogues that wholly disguised his artificial leg, and said in a loud voice: '*Do* something can't you?'

She looked cautiously towards Merrick as he stood there woodenly, and her heart bled for him. She knew about his leg. How strange to meet him like this. She began to wish she had dressed up instead of being in plain flannel hat and coat.

They smiled at each other. Long lost souls silently reunited whilst others absorbed themselves again in gossip.

Ivy Violet was strangely affected by the coincidence. Yet how often had she heard of people going as far afield as Dunham Massey or even on long journeys to Blackpool or Southport, only to bump into neighbours from the street round the corner they had not seen in years.

Merrick took his small daughter's hand as he and Maisy joined the group at the park seat, and in no time at all Mrs Merrick Jackson was holding court as she explained to the whole of Sale how she and Merrick would soon be moving to fresh pastures and a new life of luxury in Stretford. 'We owe it to the twins. They're both terribly intelligent. Rupert wants to be a bank manager when he grows up. He can count and add up on his bead frame, nearly as good as me. And Arabella says she wants to marry a real prince, not just a fairy tale one.'

Everyone laughed indulgently, but Ivy Violet could see the look of determination in Maisy's eyes. For one fleeting second Ivy Violet caught Merrick's troubled gaze. Then she looked away quickly. Why was it he had so much innocent power over her that she always wanted to try and shield him from his own fate? It was clearly the biggest mistake he had ever made to have married Maisy Fowler. But who was she to say when his mother had already clearly seen to it? She knew there were more reasons than one for a man marrying a woman. But why did she feel so strongly about a childhood friend from barefoot days? Ivy Violet realised that the best way to deal with it was to try and ignore it. Her own life was complicated enough, never mind Merrick's.

On the way back to her Victoria Park flat in Fallowfield she felt depressed.

Merrick had, in a few moments of quick conversation, described to her how he had looked at Bobby Byrtle's empty shop. 'It's just a pipe dream, Ivy. There's nowt I'm really good at except as a ledger clerk in that shipping office.'

'What about music, Merrick?' Ivy had muttered in quick undertones. 'Even Maisy's interested in *that*. And you got quite a lot of experience working for old Henry Kershaw. There's never ever been another music place round there since he went.'

Merrick shrugged his shoulders despondently, and a streak of annoyance rose within her. 'Life isn't composed of "if only", Merrick. I'm not your nursemaid or ever have been.'

He suddenly smiled and grimaced. 'I wish you were, Ivy.'

Her eyes flashed. 'Less of that talk Merrick Jackson. Believe me I'd soon knock you into shape if you were with me, so it's perhaps just as well we both went our separate ways.' Then she softened and said: 'But I wish you all the luck in the world. You'll always know that.'

'And the same to you, Ivy . . .' He hesitated. 'All the *love* in the world, Ivy Violet.'

She felt tears smarting in her eyes and hastily moved towards Phillis and Freddy just in time to hear Maisy summoning Merrick to get going.

When she got home there was a total surprise awaiting her.

Garnet was standing there in utter radiance next to a man.

He was holding young Crystal firmly in his arms. It was Maxi Dingle. He was more handsome and brass-faced than ever with a coating of elegant civility.

Ivy Violet felt her heart thudding and her knees turning to jelly. He seemed to fill the whole place with his presence. The gentle female unity and peace had vanished like sudden autumn leaves swept away in a gale. His quiet, dandified, self-confidence was exactly the same, as his child glowed and chuckled in his arms and tugged at his red curling hair which was now cut very short. His suit was the palest dove grey, and he wore a heavy silk taffeta cravat of emerald green slotted and knotted into a sparkling diamond ring. He smiled at her with his gold glinting and ingenuous smile.

Who could resist him? This singer of ballads; this drawing-room idol? This purveyor of the liltingly beautiful and mournfully sad 'Londonderry Air'.

'He's come back to us for good!' cried Garnet with

delighted joy. For not only had Maxi Dingle come back from his stint in the war completely unblemished, he had been mentioned in dispatches for bravery. And as Garnet stressed to Ivy the following day when they were alone: a man in the aftermath of battle can do many strange things, like even deserting his own true love, and child. 'But it's all over now and we plan to marry.'

As Christmas drew near Ivy Violet became more and more uneasy with the situation, as Garnet became happier and more confident. Maxi had re-established himself in a full round of drawing room and high-flown musical evenings. Garnet busied herself as his secretary and agent, in between her other work for the Peregrines, so that Ivy began to feel like an outsider under the roof that she had originally provided. This wasn't all, for all the time she knew that she too was being swept along by Max Dingle's magnetism, as he encouraged her to concentrate on her shoe designs.

'I've found two young lads in their own small workshop Ivy. Round Hanging Ditch: Terry and Cyril Blantyre. They're sons of a cobbler, and will be only too pleased to work under your instructions.'

He then asked her to fashion a pair of wedding shoes for Garnet for their February wedding. 'The shoes will be a good luck token in that fearful winter month, Ivy. The moment Garnet puts on your slippers the sun will shine and spring will put forth its first tender shoots.' He looked at her with a melting gaze of affection. 'It's going to work out like heaven at last – for all of us. I'm here for good now.'

And so it seemed to be as their lives became a flurry of movement with every second packed with organising details for Maxi's own work or Ivy Violet's shoe design work. Garnet became more and more involved with the Peregrines and Maxi employed an elderly part-time secretary called Miss Myrtle whom he shared with Ivy Violet.

Yet, in spite of everything working like clockwork and faces wreathed in friendly smiles, and the money available to carry out their general plans, Ivy Violet still felt a shadow of foreboding hanging over her, as if she were being swept along in a river that could overflow and drown them all at any minute.

Garnet's wedding in February 1920 was at the register office. It was a bright, freezing cold day, and Maxi Dingle had hired a Rolls Royce for them all to ride in with his cousin acting as chauffeur in dark blue livery. The rest of them were wrapped in heavy wool with huge furs over their legs, and blonde haired Garnet was dressed in shoes – made by Ivy Violet – of stitched suede stripes, in maroon and royal blue with crimson ribbon bow fastenings, and a blue silk velvet coat , dress and hat, with crimson accessories.

No one was there to support her except Ivy Violet and some of the players from the Peregrines, for her parents in Stockport were still ignoring her, in spite of their grandchild, Crystal. 'It's my father, really Ivy. He's the one who's doing it. I know my mother would adore Crystal, but mother's entirely under his thumb, because he's so bombastic and has such a terrible temper. Perhaps when they've learnt to accept that we're legally spliced they'll begin to come round to it all.'

Spring appeared that year in a welter of golden forsythia, and pink flowering almond blossom around the flat in Victoria Park whilst Ivy Violet became immersed in more and more orders for her handmade shoes. She registered their trade mark sign so that each pair was decorated with curling intertwined letters IVY in silver against smooth white kid leather on the inside edge of each shoe and a small ivy leaf next to its size number.

Then one day, when Elsa the nanny had gone to collect Crystal from her kindergarten, Maxi came into the large studio room where Ivy was standing at her design drawing board. Absorbed in her work, she did not notice him at first as he went over and stood beside her.

She jumped slightly. 'Maxi. I thought you were out.'

He smiled at her silently, then picking up one of her pencil crayons he began to doodle with it on a scrap of paper, and said: 'I stayed around on purpose, Ivy.'

'Whatever for? If it's for messages or anything I'll be here all day. You know that. When Garnet has to stay overnight with the Peregrines when they're playing further afield I stay here to be with Crystal and Elsa.'

'That's what I want to talk to you about.'

Ivy Violet's heart sank. She tried to look slightly surprised, but deep inside she knew what it was.

'What?'

'It's about Garnet and the Peregrines. She's staying overnight far too often.'

'But how can she do anything else, Maxi? She's an integral part of it all. It's her life, just as your musical performances are part of yours. You often stay nights away, too.'

'It's different for a man.'

'It isn't different at all,' Ivy Violet said quickly. She narrowed her eyes at him provokingly, then said slowly: 'The war made a difference Maxi ... for us as well as you. We had to fend for ourselves more. Garnet was having to do that for quite a long time and the Peregrines proved to be a godsend for her. So why should you suddenly start complaining now?'

She could see his colour rising slightly. He hated women arguing with him. 'Oh, I'm not complaining, it's just —'

'Just what?'

'If you want the bloody truth Ivy, I think she's been taken over by Robin Kandyford, their new leading man. He's a complete womaniser. I'll bet his bed's warmed by them from morning till night.'

So she was wrong. She felt herself blushing with sudden shock, not at his revelations but because she had assumed it was about him and her.

Robin Kandyford? Surely it wasn't true? She had met him once or twice and he was a very good actor with rather bulging blue eyes. Garnet often talked about him but only in a general way.

'You've gone very silent, Ivy?'

'I just don't know what to say, Maxi. I think you're talking absolute nonsense.' Her voice faded a little.

'I'm not you know.'

Then to her horror she had been correct in her assumption.

'The fact is though – I don't very much care. We never were much of a match. I knew it all along. That's why I never came back to her after — '

Ivy turned away and stuck her fingers in her ears. 'I do *not* want to hear! Your married life has nothing to do with me.'

'Nothing to do with you?' He looked at her incredulously. 'How on earth can you say that when we all live together in this flat, and when you and I see more of each other than I see of my own wife, and when we even share the same secretary, and when I've set you up designing shoes.'

'And I set YOU up in this flat!' Ivy Violet's eyes flashed with defensive fear and anger. She knew she must stand against him or she was lost. She knew the potency of his masculine charm and forcefulness. She knew the smell of him and every intonation of his voice and every bit of clothing he wore, and the shape of his sudden smiles and his quirky sense of humour.

'Don't try to escape me, Ivy.'

'Escape you? Whatever do you mean?' A cold thread of fear shot through her. In a moment her racing brain told her she had been playing a game of make-believe where Maxi Dingle was concerned. It had been pleasant to wallow in a small brook of romance, knowing that nothing would really come to pass, because he was Garnet's husband. But now he was challenging her. She stared at him in secret anguish, her mouth slightly open, not knowing what to say. Then, summoning up all her strength, she willed herself to turn away from him and leave the room.

Hastily she put on her outdoor clothes with trembling fingers and hurried out of the flat and down the garden path to the main driveway, hurrying almost blindly to the main road where the trams were. 'A penny one please.'

The red and cream tram clanked along, jerking every so often as the driver quickly turned the handle knob of the horizontal, brass steering-wheel one way then the other – in the course of picking up and depositing passengers – gathering speed then jolting back down again.

She sat upstairs. But where was she supposed to be going? She got up hastily and wound her way down the narrow cast-iron steps, with Maxi's last few words echoing within her: 'Don't try to escape me . . .' She realised that he had made entirely the opposite effect. It had shown her another side to his character. An element of moral blackmail. A sort of threat. No matter what he might do or say in the future she would always remember.

She was behaving like an automaton now, a robot,

as she left the tram and walked towards the outline of Manchester Cathedral. She only knew she must find somewhere quiet to sit down and think. At last she discovered a small wooden bench on a hummock of grass, sheltered by a silver birch tree and close to some grey marble horse troughs. It was a small oasis away from the grinding noise and stink of bustling main streets and open trading places.

As she sat there, gradually relaxing to a more normal and less excitable state, her first thoughts were of Alfred. If only he hadn't sacrificed his life; if only God had saved him. What was the purpose behind it all when good people were lost so tragically?

She brought out a small lace handkerchief to dry her eyes, thinking of what might have been. How they might even now have been settled down together in their own home with their own children.

Slowly she rose from the seat and turned towards the city, walking towards Kendal Milnes, close to where her own shoes were displayed at Leatherways, an exclusive shoe salon for handmade footwear. Still in a daze of shock about Maxi she did not know how she was going to go back and face Garnet again.

It was ironic that all of them were living in a flat which had been loaned to her by Mr Barber, a friend of Alfred's father, and that they were all still living there rent free. In spite of their ability to now pay a proper rent. 'Don't rock the boat,' Maxi had once said. 'Don't look a gift horse in the mouth, Ivy. Rich businessmen like Charlie Barber should never be questioned when they allow you to live in their property rent free. They'd tell you soon enough if they wanted you out of it.'

No sooner had these words flitted across her mind – as she gazed in the window of the salon – than she felt a light hand on her shoulder. To her amazement it was Mr Barber immaculate in his city clothes with bowler hat, grey spats and a rolled umbrella. He smiled down at her with a somewhat amused look and his grey moustache quivered slightly. 'Mrs MacFarlynne, what a pleasant surprise. How are things?'

'Very well thank you, Mr Barber. It seems an age since we saw you. Garnet's little daughter Crystal is almost grown up!'

They both laughed, then he said: 'Look, why don't we go for a little light refreshment? Have you time?'

She nodded thankfully. It was just what she needed. In minutes they were in a taxi cab to the Midland Hotel.

'We can catch up on the state of the world with peace and cream buns,' he said, as they sank down into comfortable leather chairs, beneath chandeliers and subdued wall lighting. Then gazing at her shrewdly he murmured: 'I can see by the very look of you that prosperity has already arrived.'

Ivy Violet went scarlet. All the deep-seated guilt of living in his flat rent free surfaced. What should she do? Should she apologise? Or thank him profusely for his kindness? Or do as Maxi had suggested and leave it for him to say something?

'I notice that Maxi Dingle is doing well for himself. It must be a great relief to you to know that Garnet is now married and settled with him and able to cope properly?'

She began to flutter nervously. 'Yes. It is indeed, Mr Barber. We would have sent you an invitation to the wedding – but it was a very quiet, swift affair.'

'So I heard. And please – do call me Charles, Ivy. You see – I happen to know your part-time secretary Miss Myrtle.'

'R-really?'

'She used to work for me once upon a time.'

'H-how amazing. She's ever so good – she – works for — '

'Both you and Dingle. I know all that. I met her in a bookshop and she was telling me.'

Ivy Violet put a table napkin swiftly to her lips to wipe away a trace of cream and hide her embarrassment.

'Allow me to share a cab with you and run you back home Ivy.'

'It's terribly kind of you Mr Barber, but it's quite unnecessary. I really enjoy travelling by tram. I do honestly. I wouldn't dream of taking you so far out of your way. It was nice enough just coming here.'

'Nonsense, my dear. What strange creatures young women are these days. So dashed independent. Surely you'll allow an old buffer the pleasure of seeing you safely back home? What about a nice horse and carriage? Let's be civilised.' He smiled at her showing a fine set of teeth. There was not really much of the old buffer about him, Ivy Violet thought. He was tall and well-preserved, in his early fifties with a golden brown moustache, and no sign of silvering hair. Unless of course it was all tastefully dyed, or he was wearing a toupee?

Ivy Violet hesitated. The last thing she wanted was to go back home and be greeted by Maxi again – complete with Mr Barber in tow. For he would obviously be sizing up the situation with regard to his tenants. But what alternative was there without seeming completely churlish and unladylike? Ivy Violet allowed herself to be ushered into a hansom cab, where she sat in tactful silence with Charles Barber, large and warm beside her.

She was just dwelling on the misfortune of meeting him, when another misfortune occurred. The horse suddenly bolted and they were both flung back in the cab. It was a momentary bolt as the young driver pulled on the reins with all his strength and the horse reared in the air. It was pulled down again and quietened by two men selling fruit from a barrow.

'What's a bloody little sprat like you doin' with a hefty nag like that if you can't bleeding well keep it on its bloody 'ooves,' said one of them wiping sweat from his brow.

'You're Alby Trenchers's kid aren't yer?' said the other. 'Well, I knows this much, laddie – you'll not be driving that thing no more while I'm around.' Then looking very hard at Charles Barber he said in a loud voice: 'That there gentleman and young lady could have been mangled to bits on the cobbles and 'ad their souls flittin' about in the 'eavens if it 'adn't bin for us. All t' gold in the world wouldn't 'ave saved 'em if we 'adn't bin 'ere at the right time.' Then moving nearer to Ivy Violet's landlord, he said earnestly: 'I advise you to get out right now sir, whilst you can, and we'll deal with all this for you sir. I'll have you a proper motor cab here straight away sir. Where was it you wanted?'

Ruefully they removed themselves from the cab as a crowd began to gather. Hastily Charles Barber doled out a sovereign each to the two men and thanked them. Then hurrying away down a small side-street he and Ivy Violet made their way back to the Midland Hotel where he made a serious complaint about the whole incident.

'What we need is a stiff drink,' he said, later.

Ivy Violet sat there fanning herself with a small, ancient ivory fan from her bag and sniffing occasionally at her smelling salts, even though there was nothing the matter with her in spite of the sudden shock.

'An orangeade with straws will be sufficient for me, Mr Barber, but I quite appreciate your need for something stronger.'

While Ivy Violet was sipping delicately at her orangeade she was alarmed to see that Charles Barber was knocking back 'Old Tom' gins as fast as he could swallow them, and his speech was becoming slurred.

Whatever was she to do? Her commonsense told her to politely get up and go, and leave him to sleep it off in comfort. But at that moment of decision, he flopped forward half hanging sideways over his chair.

Hastily she tried to sit him up as unobtrusively as possible into a more respectable position. How on earth could she leave him in such a condition – her friend and generous landlord?

He opened his eyes blearily just as a uniformed messenger boy tactfully came to Ivy Violet's assistance. 'I think you'll need to get him out of here, madam, in case he causes a disturbance for the other guests. Should I tell the manager, or just order you a cab to take him home?'

'You'll do no such thing, you little perisher,' said Charles Barber coming round. 'You'll just do what you're told and get this 'ere young lady and me into a private apartment immediately so as I can combat my illness and recuperate from me accident.' Then he closed his eyes and flopped back again.

In a panic the young page disappeared and soon a neatly moustached manager arrived, and after a few swiftly muttered words to Ivy, Charles Barber was helped by three members of staff to the lift. He and Ivy Violet were taken to a first-floor room.

It had a divan in it and its own small bathroom where he was immediately sick.

'I can't thank you enough, Ivy – for staying with me in my hour of need,' he said. 'Have a look at those gramophone records in that cabinet and put one on.'

Ivy Violet stared in amazement at the stylish

walnut cabinet with its squat cabriole legs. How on earth did he know there were gramophone records inside? Then a horrible thought struck her. This sort of thing must have happened before.

'Get out one of those with the Hawaiian guitars and put it on.'

Ivy looked in the cabinet which had an opening lid at the top to reveal the gramophone itself – but found no sign of Hawaiian guitars.

'All I can find is an album of favourite hymns, Mr Barber, and two Bach sonatas.'

'Curse them – The God Botherers!' He began to struggle up from the divan where he now lay – his eyes bright with a sudden watery lust. 'Come here and sit beside me Ivy. We have a lot to talk about. I was going to discuss the rent of the flat. Perhaps we could come to a special arrangement. Seein' as 'ow you've all bin living in it rent free for so long.'

Ivy moved herself a little further from his grasp. 'I think we're quite right to discuss it Mr Barber. As a matter of fact it's been troubling me for some time that you have never been in touch with us since your first generous gesture. Garnet and myself will never be able to thank you enough for your kindness to two young women in a distressful emergency – looking for a home . . . Especially with it being so soon after poor Alfred's death on the war front.' She stared him full in the eyes, and saw him blinking slightly as his eager hands fell meekly to his sides.

He knew he had been put in his place, especially with the mention of Alfred.

221

'Well, all I can say Ivy . . . is I'm glad I've been of assistance to you both, which was my first intention. But I know you'll agree that times have changed a bit haven't they lass? And you're a woman of the world now – not to mention that man of the world – Maxi Dingle who never did need my roof over *his* head. So I think the time's come – if you don't mind me saying it – for the whole lot of you to clear out!'

His face was suffused to purple by the rising plight of his own indignity, which in his half-sozzled state he imagined he might be able to disguise by striking up what he implied was a strictly paternal relationship.

He began to walk warily round the room with his chin raised to a noble profile. Then, in deep sonorous tones, he said: 'By the whole lot, I didn't exactly mean *you* to clear out, dear. It was just a flash of temper on my part which unbalanced my good judgement. It upsets me to think what you have had to go through and how the others have used you. For some time, my dear girl, I have been considering the idea of allowing you yourself to stay in my flat – as was originally arranged – for some small monthly token of goodwill. Whereby we might be able to meet every four weeks or so . . . at some attractive rendezvous.' His voice quickened so that she could not interrupt. 'You see – dear child – for that is what you are to people of my age – it is obvious that you need some type of proper fatherly protection. If you don't mind my saying so Ivy, I feel that Mr and Mrs Dingle have been playing too much on your own good nature as well as mine, for we can both remember that the flat was to be for you alone – because of poor Alfred's death. Am I not right?'

He fixed her now with an almost unwavering eye as she marvelled at how well he had pulled himself together in spite of drinking too much.

Her brain raced along as she sat there in polite silence. In one way he was unwittingly helping her out of her own predicament with Maxi Dingle – for how could she continue living so close to Maxi, who had read her deepest emotions and knew that she was attracted to him? Yet how could she turn them out? Especially Garnet and young Crystal. And most of all, why should she be the one forced to leave her own home because of it all, leaving them all to sort it out with Mr Barber. She felt like walking out and leaving everyone to stew. Escaping from her whole life and starting off somewhere completely fresh.

But – there again – maybe Mr Barber's own suggestion was right about Garnet and Maxi leaving to find some other abode. Perhaps it would be the best way to solve all their problems. It would put responsibilities in the right places; the main responsibility lying with Maxi Dingle as a married man with a young child.

And as for Mr Barber himself and his idea of being a second father – to herself? Mmmm – she well knew the pitfalls of all that. It was a situation which would need careful handling. She would have to keep him well within gentlemanly restrictions. A sudden memory came to her of Sylvia Watson from Clark Terrace, and her own fatherly saviour, Mr Porter. No – this was a different league entirely.

But Ivy Violet's confidence was misplaced as she heard Barber say: 'You couldn't do better than to have a man of property like me looking after your interests, Ivy. I could bring you both fame and fortune if you were to allow me to take shares in your shoe business. The world is a tough place for a young, vulnerable woman in a commercial world. You certainly can't put your trust in people like the Dingles. They're these artistic, unreliable types, and often complete spongers. Maxi has always been known as an incorrigible womaniser in the world of musical soirées. Mark my words dear, and try not to look so sad. Take heed from an older man. Come and sit beside me, and I'll tell you the story of my life, and how I acquired Barnfeather Hall, and the tragedy of my wife – now dead and gone – God rest her soul.'

Ivy Violet decided it was time to go.

But it was too late as she found herself being trailed round the large room by a heavily breathing panther. She was now in the far corner away from the door; with Charles Barber now back on form she realised that to hurry towards the door could be her undoing. He had a large stride and was quite athletic.

She suddenly sank to the carpeted floor and let out a yelp of pain. 'Oh Mr Barber, help me. My knee has slipped out of joint again. Oh if only you knew the agony.' She let out a sudden shriek and he began to look alarmed.

'Sh . . . Don't take on so girl. It can't be as bad as that, surely?'

She shrieked again stretching quickly towards the bell-pull. 'It catches me unawares, Mr Barber – it's almost as bad as cramp. I must get back home immediately. But you stay here and rest.' As she uttered the words there was a tap at the door. 'Come in,' she bellowed. And as she said it she pushed past the young porter who had answered the bell. She almost flew along the corridor, not to the lift but to the stairs, finding her way to a side entrance. Gasping with relief as she found the outside noise and smells of the city streets, she caught the first available tram and made her way back to her flat.

CHAPTER 10

Longings

Ivy Violet stood in the large empty room with sunshine streaming through huge windows. She was drained of energy. She could hardly bear to see the place completely stripped of all the details from her life with Garnet and Maxi and infant Crystal. Her drawing board gone – all her shoe designs; all her office work; all signs of Maxi and his music; of Garnet and her work with the Peregrines; all vestiges of Crystal and her clothes and toys.

She had been staggered by the suddenness of it. First, there was a secret briefing from Garnet: 'We had this terrible row Ivy and he accused me of playing fast and loose with Robin Kandyford from the Peregrines. It was completely ludicrous! Poor old Robin would have been devastated. The only thing he ever does in his spare time is go fishing. Basically, he's completely terrified of women. I just can't imagine what got into Maxi. It must have been a brain storm. How can he have ever doubted my love for him?'

The next thing was Miss Myrtle, their secretary, standing in front of her, saying she was leaving immediately and returning to work for her old employer Mr Barber: 'Mr Barber has more or less bludgeoned me into it, Mrs MacFarlynne, and I can't deny that the monetary compensation will come in very handy. Even though I've enjoyed being here so much.'

Her whole life had been turned upside down. Until all this started she had thought *she* was making all the decisions. She agonised over what to do about Maxi and Garnet, and planned in her mind – on the way home from seeing Mr Barber – never to be left alone with Maxi for fear of them both regretting it. Yet when she returned on the tram, trying to harden her soul to its utmost, and ready to face them with an ultimatum about moving out, it had all been a damp squib. There was no one in when she arrived.

Later that evening Garnet and Maxi presented her with a letter, saying they had found a place of their own to live, in Heaton Moor, well placed for transport and suitable for both their careers.

'We'd been considering it for some time,' said Garnet earnestly, her golden hair glowing softly round her forehead as she held Crystal close to her. 'Then Maxi really decided to get a move on. It was almost as if he'd had a nudge from on high.' She looked happily at Ivy Violet.

Ivy Violet stared at them all with amazed calm as Maxi looked towards her impassively, avoiding her eyes. 'Yes,' he said quietly. 'I think it will all be for the best.'

So now here she was, into another year, a widow of twenty-five, completely alone in this empty flat of joy, sadness, and alarming passions. All her furniture, all her small solitary future, encased in a battered pantechnicon slowly winding its way back to old Bobby Byrtle's empty shop – yards away from the Clark Terrace of her childhood. She didn't know whether to laugh or cry. For what option had there been except the threat of constant hassle from Charles Barber if she had stayed in Victoria Park?

Outside the old shop Sylvia said: 'They're desperate to get the whole place let out, Ivy, or it'll just rot away and be invaded by rats , mice and beetles. You can see for yourself the state of those broken windows. It's getting worse and worse every day, but they don't want to sell it. They'd almost let you rent it for nowt. It never did well after Bobby sold up, and this last lot – the Pennyforths with their iron-mongery fiasco – were beaten hollow by the new cut-price bazaar along Bessemer Street. They've gone now – to try working on a small country estate, near Congleton, as caretakers.'

Ivy Violet put an advertisement in the evening paper for a clerical worker cum typist. Among the deluge of replies were two with the name Simpkin and their Clark Terrace address. She invited both for an informal chat.

Maureen was a polite young lady and appeared far more confident and mature than Ivy Violet had ever been at that age. She had a complete grasp of shorthand and typing. Her brother, sixteen-year-old Trevor, was as tall as a telegraph pole, and eager to act as messenger boy. It made her think of Merrick at the same age. How different they were.

'So how's dear Tilly going on?' said Ivy Violet with affection. 'I still have the shoe last that she once gave me. It's become a sort of mascot for handmade, personally-designed Ivy Violet shoes. What different days those were.' She suddenly saw them staring at her askance.

'Didn't you know, then?' said Maureen.

Ivy's face fell. 'No?'

Trevor's voice trembled slightly as he took over: 'Mother passed away nearly a year ago, and father had an accident at work and has to be at home all day.'

'How dreadful. I had no idea. Whatever must you have thought?'

'It's all right. We're used to it now,' Maureen said. 'We all manage quite well and Poppy is out of her wheelchair, even though she's still crippled. She works for a lawyer in the city. When you left home, our Olive was still a tiny tot but now she's nearly eleven and helps in the house a lot.'

Ivy Violet looked at them admiringly. What a credit they all were to Tilly and Arthur. She only hoped she would do as well if she ever had any family of her own.

'You've got the jobs,' she said. 'We'll meet again next Monday morning and get organised.'

And that's how it was.

Ivy Violet set to with a willing heart to utterly transform both the cobbler's shop and the old house attached to it.

No longer was she the young gauche assistant living in a top attic; the attics were now storage space for shoe samples of her intricately designed fashion shoes. They were doing so well that although she still used the shoemakers Maxi Dingle had found for her – the Blantyre brothers of Hanging Ditch – she realised she was going to need yet another pair of skilled hands to work on the premises. This time she was selective, and the work was geared to special orders for top class shoes, and any repairs or alterations. The final accolade arrived when, out of the blue, a mysterious order came from the offices of a crowned head of Europe. One of their staff had purchased a pair of velvet and brocade slippers whilst staying at Gawthop Hall in Lancashire. Ivy Violet could truthfully add: By Royal Appointment . . . on both her notepaper and the sign at the front of the shop which now said: 'IVY SHOES – Designed for Royalty at a People's Price'.

'You'll never guess what I've seen,' Maisy said to Merrick as he chewed at a rather tough mutton chop

231

the following Sunday at 'Chez-nous', their new home in Stretford. 'I was round near Byrtle's old shop when I was visiting someone, and it's all been done up good and proper. And there was this man in a hessian apron polishing the window. There's a dark green curtain on a brass rail along the bottom half of it now – so that you can't see inside. But on the top half of the window there's a great big swanky gold ivy leaf, with IVY SHOES written underneath and Designed for Royalty at a People's Price. Surely it's not HER?'

Maisy glared at Merrick challengingly as she swamped his black chequered edge dinner plate with some extra Oxo gravy, telling the twins to chew the bits of gristle ten times then swallow them. 'An' no, you *can't* wash it down with ginger pop, Arabella Jackson. What do you think God gave you teeth for?'

'To smile with, Mammy, and to grow into a beautiful lady with a lovely smile, and marry someone rich.'

'I never said no such thing, you little pest. But I know this much – it'll be no good spittin' that there gristle out if you're at the Lord Mayor's show so you'd better get used to swallering it.'

'But suppose I was sick, Ma?' Arabella's face went pale as the gristle churned round and round in her mouth. She began to retch and hold her hand close to her mouth, whilst her brother Rupert casually deposited a large piece of mutton fat and gristle from his own plate on to the carpet, then managed to grind it hard down with his foot into the swirling, surface pattern of sprays and foliage. 'I've managed mine all right, Mother,' he said.

'There! You see? Your brother will grow up into a fine strong man with manners to match.'

Merrick sighed morosely, his mind still with Ivy Violet. How on earth had she done so well? She was becoming a really prosperous business woman. But it was all right for her – a single woman with no family commitments. It was entirely different for a tied family man like him with a wife and twins. He suddenly felt the urge to escape that very moment. Walk out of Chez-nous with its dangling, rhinestone lamp-shade in the front room, forsake his life of ledgers and clerking on the third floor of Lagoon's shipping office and throw himself at Ivy Violet's feet as her faithful slave – for she had always been more of a true friend to him than Maisy ever was.

He had never realised until now the indignity of living with a woman like Maisy who had come into money. Her mind bulged from morning till night with grandiose schemes on how to spend it, and often when they were out the children referred to him as 'poor Papa' and to Maisy as 'rich Mamaar'.

But, as life went on at its terrific speed with the twins getting bigger and bigger and eating like young horses and both his wife and offspring demanding more and more of what Maisy described as the simple luxuries of life, like holidays in Bournemouth instead of Blackpool, Merrick forgot all about Ivy Violet. Except to assume that she was by now a complete millionairess, for he had never visited the old shop again.

Then, quite by chance a couple of years later, he got a strange shock.

It was spring and the local countryside was fresh with fields of green and pale shoots of young willow trees. In the narrow ways round Byrtle's shop there were bits of flowering currant escaping from back yards and people putting their aspidistras out to air, and beating peg rugs on washing lines with flat wicker carpet-beaters. Or placing cages with bright yellow canaries inside on the tops of old wooden tables for a few minutes sun while cats and dogs were out of the way, lazing in some dark kitchen.

It was on such a day as this that Merrick decided to stroll along the memories of his youth, which included Ivy Violet's end at Clark Terrace and Bobby Byrtle's shop.

As he neared the shop something strange seemed to have happened. He could not quite pin it down, but it had all completely changed. Yet how? The first quick glance gave the impression of it being just as Maisy had once described it. He stared hard. The green curtain covering half of the window was still there and the place appeared well looked after. There was even a picture of a leaf at the top of the window.

He stood there, puzzled, and forced himself to read the name over the shop front. IRIS VIOLA SHOES, it said. He blinked and read it again. Then looking at the picture of the ivy leaf he took a short breath. It was not an ivy leaf any more; it was exactly the same size but looked more like sycamore. And as if to tell him so were the small words: Sycamore Shoes. Proprietors: Esmee and Humbert Pennyforth: Shoes from worlds of fashion *you* can afford.

Merrick was intrigued. What had happened? He decided to go in and ask for some shoelaces and a tin of black boot polish.

As he was getting his change he said to a young female assistant: 'Excuse me but has this shop changed hands?'

Mabel Pennyforth scratched nervously at her tightly-drawn-back, mousy-coloured hair with her thin little pink fingers and gave him a chalky yellow smile.

'Oh no sir. My parents have always owned it.'

'*Always*?'

'Well, nearly always. At least three years. But they wasn't here themselves at first. It was loaned out to someone else who did shoes.'

'Were they called Ivy Violet Shoes?'

'Summat like that.'

Merrick waited to see if she would say anything else, but she just stared back at him, then, as he was all set to move she said: 'It was another woman what rented it from us. But it was too posh for round 'ere, and anyway she moved – so my mother and father decided to take it on themselves seeing as 'ow they owned it int' first place. We used to 'ave it as an iron-mongery – see? Then Ma and Pa went to keep 'ouse for someone. But years ago it belonged to a proper, very old cobbler see? So my Ma and Pa they decided

on following in 'is footsteps and making it a real
good place with cheap shoes in it like you can see.
Cheap shoes from all the world over – what ordinary folks can afford.' She was in full flow now and
looking quite feverish as if she was going to go on
for ever.

Merrick nodded silently, then said: 'Thank you.
Thank you very much. I'm much obliged.' Then taking his laces and boot polish he slowly made his way
back to Lagoon's shipping office, and sat there
brooding on his high wooden chair. What on earth
had happened and where had she gone? And worst
of all – why should he be worrying about it when it
had nothing to do with him?

By the time Ivy Violet left Byrtle's shop she thought
that during her stint of three years she had made
just enough money to buy a small place of her own.
Somewhere more leafy and countryfied. She was
feeling strangely exhausted. It was 1922. The toll of
years of hard work and struggle had caught up with
her; the last year had been particularly stressful. She
became quite depressed. What was it all for? Here
she was – a childless war widow driving herself on
and on and to what end? Work had taken over so
completely that she never went out anywhere,
except to visit her mother Phillis and Freddy at
'Cornerstones' in Sale. It was almost as if she was
becoming a recluse tied to work and frightened of
stepping out into the real world.

'Why don't you have a complete rest and come

over to stay with me and Freddy for a bit 'til you've sorted yourself out properly?'

Ivy had looked at Phillis silently. Up to now she had always been so full of hope. Oh – if only Alfred hadn't been killed. It could all have been so different.

'You're brooding again,' said Phillis. 'What you need is to get settled into a place of your own and maybe find another husband and have a baby before it's too late.'

CHAPTER 11

Maisy's Ultimatum

Ivy Violet sat idly picking out items of interest which packed the *Manchester Evening News*. She was lodging at 'Cornerstones' with Phillis and Freddy. She had recovered from depression. Everything had turned out far better than she had dared to hope, thanks to the support of all her friends and relations, including Maxi and Garnet.

The Blantyre brothers who made the IVY shoes from her designs knew of a place available at a cheap rent in the middle of the city. It was on the second floor of a small textile printers, in a cobbled back street, close to the murky Bridgewater Canal.

'In some ways a city office sounds really grand. Perhaps, it'll be a fortune in disguise,' said Ivy bubbling away with her old enthusiasm. 'Even though

I'd always thought of places further afield like Didsbury or Altrincham.'

'So now all you need to do, is to find yourself the perfect residence to match up with the City . . .' joked Freddy.

She nodded and began to look at the paper with more concentration, but the Houses For Sale were the usual motley lot and her attention wandered back to smaller local news items. Suddenly, she gave a disbelieving gasp.

'Found your dream house then?' Phillis stopped short as she saw the colour leaving Ivy Violet's face. 'Good heavens. Whatever is it?'

Ivy Violet hardly heard her. Her own gaze was still fixed to the page.

But it *must* be a mistake. Surely? She was speechless in the silence of the small sitting-room. Her hands lay lifelessly on the pages as Phillis stepped forward and lifted the paper away to see what it was.

And then she realised. 'It's the same name as one of your friends.?' She read it through again herself: it was a report that someone had been knocked down by a car and had died earlier that day in hospital. The name was Garnet Dingle.

It took about three months for Ivy Violet to finally come to terms with the fact that she would never see Garnet again. Being busy with the changeover in her own business affairs helped to an extent. The office in Manchester was soon established.

'It's a good idea to be working under your own maiden name again Ivy,' Maureen said one day. 'I presume we use the courtesy title of Miss Hilton, though they do say that in the old days it was the other way round and spinsters like me were called Mrs as a courtesy.'

'You'll be a true Mrs soon enough,' smiled Ivy Violet, feeling as old as Methuselah.

'Yes, Miss Hilton.' Maureen's face was aglow with fun. Ivy Violet thought how young and beautiful Maureen was now she had reached twenty-one. The whole world was at her feet. But most girls never knew it.

The day they were settled in the new office was a mellow and sunny afternoon in autumn. The ivy leaf was once more set in gold on the door and the words: 'IVY shoes – designed for royalty at a people's price' printed in small letters at the bottom of every sheet of writing paper.

At a party celebrating the opening of the new premises a small group of faithful friends and relatives joined in, supported by bottles of champagne, sandwiches and cherry cake. It was all provided by the Simpkins.

Just after the first round of drinks Maxi made a shock announcement in private to Ivy Violet.

' . . . so young Crystal and myself will soon be sailing the Atlantic to New York – to a street west of Broadway to fix up some musical performances in vaudeville and to make some recordings . . . Life must go on, in spite of the shock.'

Ivy Violet could hardly believe her ears, but to others who were less involved it was not surprising. They automatically accepted that Maxi was in show business, and living on a completely different plane. He was now acquiring world-wide fame through singing on gramophone records well-loved traditional songs; many of them Irish, Scottish and Welsh, which evoked great nostalgia for their homelands from those who now lived far afield.

Maxi asked her to do him a favour: 'I wondered if it would be possible for you to treat our house at Heaton Moor as your own whilst Crystal and I are away? Just use it entirely as you wish until you get fixed up with your own place? Mrs Reece the housekeeper will still be there. And don't look at me like that Ivy. I'm not offering you charity. It's purely my own selfish motives and a streak of gratitude. I don't want the place in mothballs for months – so feel free to use it for friends and relations, just as Garnet and I did at your place in Victoria Park, years back.'

'I'm completely stunned. I just don't know what to say,' gasped Ivy.

'You don't need to say anything. Just nod your head in agreement.'

Ivy Violet smiled with heartfelt relief, at least it would solve the problem of forever being under Phillis and Freddy's feet.

She nodded her head vigorously.

Mary Reece, the forty-year-old housekeeper, viewed the idea of Ivy Violet living at the large, rambling house at Heaton Moor with some alarm. While Ivy Violet had been renting Bobby Byrtle's old premises there had been a momentous and secret occurrence in Mary's own life. Just when she had settled for life with the Dingles as their trusted retainer – a woman dedicated to domesticity and household management and who had experienced no other intercourse with a man other than conversation – a travelling brush salesman of mature years and wearing an expensive overcoat arrived at the door. The place was completely empty, except for herself and a visiting gardener, for three weeks.

He was a square set man called Tranter Bartholomew, with thin, capable hands and a balding scalp of thin brown hair. He confided in Mary that he had one glass eye but assured her it didn't make the slightest difference to his working abilities. After half an hour of talking it was as if they had known each other from the cradle.

She blamed the whole episode on some strange hot flush during 'the change'. It was perhaps Nature's way of capturing the unwary or the fulfilment of the ever hopeful. With persuasive elegance accompanied by six different types of wooden handled banister duster to try out, and six long, adaptable, cornice cleaners, he wooed her in the drawing room and gradually worked his way up three flights of stairs with Mansion polish, Ronuk, Wonder Window Cleaner, lavatory brushes, and a carpet-sweeper catalogue. Then they were in a double bed with the blinds drawn – an entirely new and almost lost experience for Mary Reece, and one that she never in a month of Sundays expected to get any return or rebate for.

She was so unworldly and sure of her own encroaching old age that she put down all strange symptoms to 'the change'; and all signs of extra weight to her sudden madness for suet puddings, both savoury and sweet, and abnormal amounts of fresh Jersey cream.

To do him justice, her paramour remained faithful to her as gradually they discovered she was pregnant, a fact kept from the Dingles because of her tallness and her long and heavy all-enveloping skirts and aprons.

When she was four months into her pregnancy she suggested to Tranter that they should marry. 'It's up to you to make an honest woman of me. The quieter the better; a register office. I don't want to upset the apple cart with the Dingles, until it's all over with.'

She frowned slightly as her cheerful assertiveness left her. His face had gone like yellowing parchment. 'Married?' He looked at her in a daze.

'But of course, Tranter. We don't want our child to start off as an unwanted appendage . . . a terrible mistake.' Her voice began to falter. 'Whatever's the matter dear?'

His colour had changed to a cold shivering grey. 'I think it might be a sudden chill, a sort of ague. I used to get them during the War.' He tried to cheer up. 'I agree about it being a very quiet do.'

Then, one day when they'd been married two weeks, he said: 'I've got to go to Buxton tomorrow and it may take some time.'

It was the last she ever saw of him.

A month later a small news item appeared in the paper saying that Thomas Boodle alias Ronny Porter alias Tranter Bartholomew, had been charged with bigamy and pleaded not guilty. Later still Mary Reece heard that the case had been dismissed due to insufficient and faulty evidence given by his common-law wife who claimed to have borne him five children.

As she cradled her unchristened child, Hetty, in her arms, gazing fondly at the pink cheeked infant with her mass of thick dark hair and big brown eyes, Mary gave thanks to God that at least Tranter had not been sent to prison, and she wept silently.

Now, as she greeted Ivy Violet with cool demeanour no one would have dreamed of her secret dilemma. Yet by the time Ivy Violet had been in the house with her for a couple of days she had heard the whole tale, as Mary sighed with the relief of telling someone at last – including how her sister Flo was a widow of nearly seventy suffering from arthritis and not in the best of health for coping with a lively two-year-old.

'You must bring Hetty here to live with you immediately,' ordered Ivy Violet, in excited triumph. 'Let Flo be your guest for a change and enjoy this house with all its space. You've worked in it long enough – so why not reap the benefits? With your permission I would take young Hetty out for walks sometimes myself. I often think I'll never have children of my own, no matter how much I long for them.'

And so another deep and lasting friendship was made.

Maisy Jackson was feeling very sour. She picked on everything Merrick did. Mainly because Arabella had come bottom in her music grade after being coached for hours and hours by her devoted mother. Merrick was Maisy's only outlet for torture, as the twins took not the slightest notice of her.

Merrick felt as if he would go mad if he ever heard another bungled note of 'The Bluebells of Scotland' thumped out on the piano in the front room , or 'Oh Can You Wash your Father's Shirt?' played on two fingers by his son, purely to aggravate. And as if that was not enough, Maisy was already going on at him to move again – from Stretford to the Altrincham area. 'I met Mrs Arbuthnut in Kendals and she gave me her hand-written recipe for rhubarb fool. They've just settled into a lavish three storey house with an acre of garden near Bowdon Church, and their children all ride ponies.'

Merrick groaned. He was busy reading the *Daily Herald* in his small garden shed where he had hoped to get some peace.

'And I wish you wouldn't read that Labour paper, Merrick. The children go on far too much about Bobby Bear and Ruby Rabbit these days and Maisy

Mouse . . . It's very annoying Merrick especially when I'm mixing with people who read the *Sketch* like I do. So what do you think then, dear?'

Dear? He looked at her sharply. 'About the *Daily Herald*?'

'No of course not.' She fluttered her eyelashes and moved closer. 'You did well to collar me, love. I had lots of offers. There aren't many who has wives who gets money left to 'em . . .'

'And not many who know how to spend it so quickly either Maisy. The difference between your friend Hazel Arbuthnut is that her husband owns fields and fields of rhubarb fit for digging up and building on at the quickest opportunity, whereas I . . . Well, we won't bother each other with that dratted shipping office again, and the one leg. But it is a different life style Maisy. Surely even you can see that.'

'Nothing venture nothing gained,' said Maisy sulkily dragging at a piece of lace in the deep V of her cleavage. 'You're such a stick-in-the-mud, Merrick. That war didn't improve you, and that's a fact.'

'At least I came back alive, which is more than Alfred MacFarlynne and lots of others.'

'We know that dear, but can't you see what a good place Altrincham would be for us? It's ever so go ahead, and if we got a big enough place we could even take in weekly boarders or paying guests if we was stuck.'

'We are not doing that.' Merrick's ears went bright red. 'We either live on my wages – or nothing.'

'There might be something a bit smaller there then. No need to get so touchy.' Maisy was getting more handsome every day; her huge brown eyes were as soulful and devouring as ever and although her girlhood cork-screw curls had vanished, her new fringe and shaped shingle set in Marcel waves above a regal bust made her somebody not to be trifled with. 'And they have really good schools, Merrick: Altrincham High School for the girls and Altrincham Grammar for the boys.'

He glowered at her. 'You could do just as well any-where else.'

'I know, but even Mrs Blombispham lives in Hale these days.'

Merrick grinned savagely. 'She's the type who wouldn't so much as pass the time of day with you if you took in paying guests.'

'Oh . . . I don't know . . . She's from very 'umble beginnings.'

'Well I do know – so shut up can't you?'

The next day in the office Merrick brooded secretly about Maisy's obsession with moving. He just could not see the point of it. They were extremely comfortable where they were, near Edge Lane in Stretford. He blamed the money she had been left. She had just never got over it. All the same he wished he could move – away from these offices to something less restrictive with more prospects. But what?

At lunch time he went for a walk to Shude Hill and began to mooch round the second-hand bookstalls, where he bought himself a copy of *Hard Times* by Charles Dickens for threepence. Then after drinking a black and tan and eating a hot meat and potato pie in a pub near the Shambles, he made his way back to the office, stopping to look rather morbidly into the small poky window of a surgical rubber goods shop. It had a welter of large orange-brown rubber enema sets with hard black connecting pieces, artificial limbs clothed in heavy elastic bandages and leather trusses, abdominal belts and rubber sheeting. Here and there was a small leather case purporting to be 'A Gentlemen's Going Away' set – known by all to have enough french letters in it to keep the whole of the British Army supplied – and resting close to Dr Marie Stopes's *Married Love* and *A Wife's Handbook*, by Dr Allbutt, price tenpence.

Then, just as Merrick was nearing Oxford Road, he bumped straight into Ivy Violet.

At first they didn't recognise each other for she had Hetty in a small baby trolley and he was looking down towards the pavement.

'Merrick! I thought it was you, but I wasn't quite certain.' Ivy Violet's face was wreathed in smiles. 'How are you going on? It's ages and ages — '

Merrick stared at the child . . . She'd never said she had one?

'I noticed you'd left Bobby's old place then? Getting on a bit now?' Merrick said no more. He glanced at Hetty who was warmly dressed in a pink cloth coat, bonnet and gaiters.

'Yes. I'm in town now. My work place is just off

249

Whitworth Street. There've been a lot of changes. This is Mary Reece's two-year-old daughter, Hetty. I'm having a couple of hours off looking after her. Her mother is the housekeeper at Heaton Moor. It's Maxi Dingle's place but he's away in America. I'm only staying there 'til I find a place of my own.'

Merrick nodded. He was slightly embarrassed. It seemed strange to hear Ivy Violet talking about such posh set-ups. 'The shoe trade must be doing well then?'

She smiled at him. 'Up and down like everything else, Merrick. It's with it being the luxury trade. I've always got to be up to the mark on latest fashions. It's quite a different life to what might be called the proper shoe trade in places like the Rossendale Valley with all their slippers and sandals, and thousands of people employed. Oh – and by the way – I'm back to my own name Ivy Violet Hilton: Miss Hilton again, so why don't you come up and see me some time?'

They both laughed, and even Hetty started to smile.

'I might well. Perhaps one dinner-time.'

'Wednesday is a good day. I'm always there Wednesdays.'

'Wednesday it'll be then.' As Merrick waved them goodbye he felt a new hopeful cheerfulness rise within him. And when he got back from work that evening he told Maisy: 'I got quite a shock seeing her after all this time, especially as she had a little girl with her belonging to the housekeeper.'

'A fine tale. It's probably hers,' said Maisy cattily. 'If ever there was a person for getting involved with wrong types of men it's her. My mother always warned me she had a streak of the tart in her.'

Merrick scowled. 'That's quite enough, Maisy. You know it's not true.'

'Where did you say she lived?'

'In a large house at Heaton Moor by all accounts but it belongs to that Maxi Dingle whose wife died. He's gone off to America with his young daughter Crystal for a few months. Ivy says she hasn't actually found a proper house of her own yet.'

'Oh, *Ivy* does, does she? Sponging on others that's all she's doing. Too full of herself by half. Not willing to settle down and be a proper home maker. Which reminds me, Merrick, I've been out to Hale today and seen the most perfect family house for us in Albert Road, which we can afford to put a deposit on whilst we sell this one. We'll all go and look at it at the weekend.'

Merrick said no more. He knew he was entirely in Maisy's clutches and as he chewed his way through Lancashire hot-pot followed by jam roly-poly he happily accepted it, knowing deep down that now Ivy Violet was only a stone's throw away from his office, he could always go round and talk to her. It was as if a faint light was shining at the end of the tunnel.

Two Wednesdays later, on the spur of the moment, he decided to take up Ivy Violet's midday invitation.

He hesitated at the dark uninviting entrance, then

moved towards the lift. It was the usual rickety old cage, but when he arrived at the small rooms on the second floor he was dazed by their unpretentious grandeur. He just had not realised. The contrast with his own working conditions at Lagoon's shipping office was almost unbelievable. He thought of the shabby, dusty and cramped outer office he spent most of his life in, that had very ancient high stools and oak furniture darkened with a patina of grime and greasy furniture wax. Ivy Violet's place was a modern palace of clean windows and straw coloured venetian blinds. The light oak office furniture was plain and well designed. The walls were pale primrose, the doors and skirting-boards white. The brass door knobs gleamed. There was an oblong mirror on the wall reflecting the light, and there were fresh flowers on a small table. The carpet on the floor was solid multi-coloured Axminster.

Merrick felt he had entered a dream world.

'Merrick. What a wonderful surprise! I hoped you'd call but never quite thought you would. Have you had anything to eat?'

He shook his head. 'I mustn't stay long. No longer than fifteen minutes because of getting back.'

'Just enough time for Maureen to nip to the delicatessen and get us balm cakes and salami, whilst I make a cup of tea. How's life in Stretford?'

Merrick tried to suppress a groan. 'Not going to last much longer if Maisy has owt to do with it. She's wanting to clear out to Hale to a bigger house. Her eye's bigger than her bank account.'

Hastily Ivy Violet changed the subject. 'I've just had a letter from Maxi and Crystal. They've completely fallen in love with America, and they're now off to Hollywood would you believe? If it goes on like this they won't want to come home!'

They both laughed, and were joined by Maureen who had returned with the food.

'How's the shoe trade then?' said Merrick with his mouth full.

'Marvellous at the moment. There's just no saying how things will go these days. But at the moment I'm counting my lucky stars.'

'Don't make it too long before you call again, Merrick,' said Ivy affectionately, as he got in the lift. 'Keep in touch.' He nodded and waved. The short visit had been like a breath of fresh air.

'So where exactly did you say her marvellous office was then?' Maisy said to Merrick a few days later. 'The reason I'm asking is because I saw a whole batch of her Ivy Leaf shoes in a very posh shop in Altrincham when I was out with Hazel Arbuthnut. It only goes to show how anyone in today's modern world can make good with a bit of luck, because if she can do it anyone can. Oh and by the way, I've put the deposit on that house in Albert Road, Merrick. So it's up to you to get this one sold straight away.'

Merrick paled slightly with an inner fear. All he wanted these days was to settle down and count his blessings. The war and the injuries from it had been quite enough to cope with. It was madness for Maisy always wanting to be on the move when they were very comfortable in the house where they were. And just supposing, after she got to Albert Road in Hale, it became a complete obsession with her, so that she'd want to move yet again? For if that went on they would soon be truly penniless and the whole of their family life totally disrupted. Maisy never thought of the financial consequences, he thought, and the money left to her was running out as quickly and surely as an egg-timer. Unless he could either stop her or sell this one in Edge Lane with breakneck speed, which might mean letting it go quite cheaply.

Two months later the Stretford house was sold at a giveaway price and Merrick and family were all getting ready to spend their first Christmas at 'Seedly' in Albert Road.

Ivy Violet was alone in the dining room of the Dingles' house at Heaton Moor. She was kneeling comfortably beside the flickering embers of a glowing fire, peacefully toasting muffins with a four-pronged brass toasting fork. Outside, beyond the brown, sateen-lined velvet curtains, a sudden November flurry of snowy winds howled round the chimney pots.

Hetty was in her baby chair, which was the sort that transformed from dining-table height to a normal seat for a toddler. It had a wide tray bordered with coloured, wooden beads on metal wires. Hetty was banging a spoon, and waiting for her tea. It was her mother's night off from her housekeeper's duties and she was out visiting her sister Flo.

Ivy Violet buttered the warm muffins in the fire-light as she thought about the most recent letter which had come this morning from Maxi. It had disturbed her. It was from Hollywood and talked a great deal about the film industry.

'It's another, sunnier world out here Ivy. Hollywood is the up and coming place for anyone who wants to get a foot on the ladder in the movie business. Mr Cecil B. de Mille makes sensational pictures. The costumes for the women are wonderful. If only you could see the numbers of really stylish *shoes* they wear. Rows and rows and rows of them . . . I'm going to look into it for you and see if I can get you some orders.'

Tears welled up in her eyes. Just supposing he and young Crystal never came back? Or they just came back and sold this house then returned again? She was getting quite entrenched these days, especially having an adorable toddler round the place. Strangely, she herself had no wish to travel to a place like Hollywood, even though she loved going to the pictures. But the idea of selling her shoes to them was a good one. Trust Maxi to think of it, she thought. He had been a terrific support to her from the moment she had met him – when Alfred was alive. What a man. What charisma. She frowned slightly, remembering the past. But – what terrible uncertainty for any woman who tied herself to a man like that.

She noticed there was no mention in the letter of when they would be actually coming back.

Quite suddenly she felt very lonely, and a bit isolated as another Christmas approached. She pondered over her future again.

When she had given Hetty her meal and had eventually tucked her up in her cot in the nursery bedroom, which had once been Crystal's, she came downstairs and washed up the tea things. Then she opened her office books and began to check all her arrangements for the following day. Tomorrow was Wednesday again, and immediately Merrick came into her mind. She cheered up. Perhaps he would pop round at dinner-time again at the office and see her?

Merrick hesitated, shivering slightly in the damp foggy air outside the entrance of the old printing works building where Ivy Violet's office was. He was undecided whether or not to call in yet again. It was becoming a sort of habit. At home when he had occasionally mentioned it he noticed that Maisy did not like it at all.

'Why tell me where you've been, Merrick? Are you trying to make me jealous or summat? I'm just not interested in her nor ever have been and you know what I think of her morals. If indeed she has any. It wouldn't surprise me if she has more than just you popping in at dinner-times.'

A slow flush of anger spread over Merrick's face as he silently left the room swearing never again to mention going to see Ivy Violet. What on earth had induced him to mention it in the first place he was not quite sure. He was not normally a person to analyse his own actions, but he suspected that Maisy's talk for hours and hours about the places she and Hazel Arbuthnut had visited, and the number of men who had made advances to them in the course of a normal morning coffee outing, may well have sparked his own mention of seeing Ivy Violet.

Merrick stood there still undecided about his midday visit, then he turned away firmly. All these meetings, however harmless, were becoming an unnecessary and ridiculous habit that did him no good whatsoever where Maisy was concerned. And if he went on with them there would be the added sense of constant deception based on never being able to mention the visits to Maisy in case she made a scene.

Having decided he felt much better and a huge surge of relief filled him as he headed towards his own office. It was not as if he'd sworn never to see Ivy Violet again, he thought. It was all purely casual. They were sure to meet somewhere at some unknown point in the future.

One thing he had not bargained for however was when the unknown point would be, as he suddenly heard her breathless voice beside him. 'Merrick. Thank goodness I caught you up! Had you been to my place? Isn't it freezing weather? I've been out this morning visiting department stores, about ordering shoe supplies, but I'm going back this minute if you think there's time for us to have a snack together? I got another letter from America the other day. Goodness knows when Maxi and Crystal will be back. But enough of them. How's Arabella going on with her new music teacher? and how did Rupert get on when Maisy found that wounded pigeon hidden in a soup tureen full of grass in his bedroom?'

In a few minutes he was back with her again, sipping hot broth, supplied by a small café round the corner. And in a further few minutes there was a steady hammering at the outer office door, as Maureen interrupted them hurriedly to say that Maisy was there in a huge fur coat and looking very dangerous.

'So this is where you both hang out to do it all is it? Very posh I'm sure. And if I hadn't just been in town myself and been near here looking for a cheap shirt factory next to the canal that Hazel Arbuthnut told me about, I might never have caught sight of my husband sloping off up 'ere in all this sleet and muck. You're an absolute disgrace Merrick Jackson.'

Ivy Violet's natural temper began to flare. It was as if they were two young girls again in Clark Terrace ready for a barney. 'Oh no he is *not*, Maisy Fowler. Everyone is entitled to do what they like in their own dinner-time, whether you're 'is wife or not. He doesn't follow you round Altrincham, do you, Merrick?'

Merrick opened and closed his fists desperately. 'Shut up the pair of you. I've got to get back to work. The fat really will be on't fire if I'm late. Old Turpentine's a right devil for punctuality especially when he's getting the books balanced – like now.'

But the two women were ignoring him completely as they let fly. 'I'll tell you this much, Maisy Fowler. If your Ma hadn't had your sister Millicent when you were twelve, which took some of the attention off Miss Queen of the May with her crimped corkscrew curls and her tinpot piano lessons, you'd have been even worse than you are now. You always were a spoilt brat.'

'You sly, jealous little besom! Just leave my Mam and our Milly out of it: nosey, little know-all Hilton with your fancy ways and deceit. At least my parents were respectable. Everyone knows that your stepmother — '

'Whatever you're going to say about Phillis,' said Ivy Violet in a cold steely voice, 'don't! Unless you want chucking down the steps.'

'The same applies to you, Hilton. You started it. You were the one who mentioned my mother and sister. And I'll tell you this much – if my husband ever visits this den of vice in his dinner hour again, you're welcome to 'im because I know hundreds of men round Altrincham who'd jump at changing places with 'im.' She was beginning to sweat a bit now. It was warm inside from the fire in the office grate and her fur coat was feeling like a furnace. 'Well I've had my say and that's that.' She looked round for Merrick and then called: 'And I hope it sunk in, Merrick.' But Merrick had rushed away ages ago, and even Maureen and Trevor had made themselves scarce.

Ivy Violet gave the outer office door an extra slam as Maisy left. The cheek of her. How on earth had Merrick ever got himself entangled with such a monster? If things went on like this, she thought, Merrick would be drained of all life. She was like a huge spider – especially in that gigantic fur coat – sucking every bit of goodness out of him, as he struggled helplessly in her web.

'I don't suppose Merrick will be visiting us again, Maureen,' she said later in the afternoon. 'I hadn't realised Maisy felt so strongly about it.'

Maureen tactfully kept her mouth shut. She knew that such a thing would never have happened in her own home. When they were small their mother Matilda Simpkin had thought about nothing but striving for female equality and spouting loud and long about female rights as she struggled to bring up the family decently. Maureen's father, Arthur, and her mother had been completely united. Her father would no more have thought of calling in on another woman in his dinner hour, unless it was a relative, than the man in the moon. Nor would he have had the chance because her mother would have known about it even before it happened and nipped it smartly in the bud. For when her father had once been a road sweeper, her mother Tilly knew every cobble of the streets he swept and every building and house on the routes and who occupied them.

'Least said, soonest mended, Ivy,' said Maureen sympathetically, as the normal office routine took over again.

Merrick was exactly two minutes late when he got back to Lagoon Shipping but Horace Turps the chief clerk was waiting for him. 'Two minutes forty seconds late, Jackson – and trouble ahead. Blandersbunt wants to see you in the inner sanctum straight away.'

No sooner said, than Miss Marsden, Blandersbunt's personal secretary, was standing there like a policeman on point duty. She was wearing a long navy blue serge skirt, a thick leather belt and a pin tucked white, poplin blouse surmounted by a mannish-looking striped tie in the shipping office colours.

Merrick was completely bemused. For a start Mr Hubert Blandersbunt was not normally in his office at this time. He was usually still in the Oyster Bar with some of his cronies, smoking cigars and drinking wine.

'Sit down Mr Jackson. It seems we have quite a lot to discuss.'

Blandersbunt's office was a huge mahogany room with dark panelling, heavy furniture and Victorian seats padded with evil-looking, black horsehair. Blandersbunt's short stubby fingers and fat palms lay across a pile of account books which Merrick recognised as coming from his own part of the establishment. And the one with the red taped spine and blue watermarked cover was the one he had actually been using this morning.

'I have not been out to lunch today, Mr Jackson,' said Blandersbunt ominously. 'All I have had to keep me going is a glass of ale and a piece of goose pie.'

'Is that so?' said Merrick nervously.

'It certainly is so, Mr Jackson – and believe me – there has to be a remarkably good reason for the owner of one of the best shipping offices in the land to give up his proper mealtime to interview one of his ordinary clerks.' (And to forgo superfluous food to stuff into his fat belly underneath his bulging waistcoat and gold watch and chain, thought Merrick in a sudden spurt of scarcely controlled rage.)

'Could you tell me what I'm here for then, Mr Blandersbunt?' Merrick felt his face glowing like a boiled, bright pink lobster.

'That's just what I want to know, Jackson. Why are you here when for years you've worked on the accounting books without a stain on your character?'

Merrick stared at him incredulously: 'I don't quite understand.'

'Just after you went out this lunch-time, it was brought to my notice by the chief clerk Mr Turps that the books were in serious disorder, and there was a discrepancy of 50 pounds, sevenpence three farthings, for this present month.'

Merrick opened his mouth to speak and then shut

it again. He was completely puzzled. How on earth could it be?

'Could I have a look at the entries Mr Blandersbunt? There must be a mistake.'

Blandersbunt thrust the book at him with an irritable flourish. The amount missing reminded him that he had an outstanding personal wine bill of similar proportions to pay for at Yates Wine Lodge. But how was a civilised man like him ever going to manage if he had robbers working for him?

Merrick ran his index finger carefully up and down the rows of figures in the gloom of the office. Then he stopped suddenly. There was a careful alteration at the beginning of November which he remembered well. He had been writing in the amount, and due to a disturbance caused by the office cat suddenly staggering across the room with what looked like a small rat in its mouth there had been quite a disruption and the column of figures had been splattered with ink by Ollie Potts, the junior clerk, who was standing close by waving his pen with a nib dripping. The result being that when all the fuss had died down and the page had been blotted and dried out, Merrick had to redo the figures by soaking out the ink and replacing the figures, then putting his signature in the margin to show that he was the one who had done it.

He stared at the line again. He realised that the figures had been carefully tampered with for a second time in precisely his own style of writing, with his own signature still lying in the margin.

Whoever would have done such a thing, and why? Was it in the crude hope of not being found out and stealing some money or was it simply a method of incriminating him personally and getting rid of him?

'So what have you to say, Mr Jackson?' Blandersbunt was staring at him stonily.

'I did make a mistake with the figures. It's true, and it's my signature. But there's been a second alteration.'

A huge sneer swept across Blandersbunt's heavy face and the side whiskers on his jowls almost went horizontal. 'A second alteration? What on earth do you mean, man?

'Do you mean *you* made a second alteration, or what, Jackson?' He gave a huge snort. 'Really, this is too much! It's just beyond belief. Surely you can at least be big enough to admit it and get it over with?'

Merrick ground his teeth together and stood there stiffly whilst his blood pressure rose. He felt like hitting Blandersbunt full in the face then and there, but he knew he was completely powerless.

Being suddenly confronted with the whole episode without even a second to consider what had actually happened, and who had actually perpetrated the crime put him at a distinct disadvantage. He thought that the alteration must have been made at lunch when he left the office. He sensed that during his own time in the office he would have spotted a second alteration, because his desk was near a window and there was more light than in Blanders-bunt's sombre office.

'I think my best plan will be to ask you to wait in Miss Marsden's office while I send for Mr Turps and inform him that you are henceforth dismissed.'

'Dismissed!' Merrick couldn't believe it. 'You're making a dreadful mistake, Mr Blandersbunt. I can assure you that every word I've said is completely true. Naturally I cannot say who has tampered with the figures or when it was done, but it certainly wasn't me . . . I . . .' Merrick began to break out in a cold sweat.

'That will be all, Mr Jackson. Kindly wait in Miss Marsden's office until Mr Turps arrives.'

As Merrick sat there in the office he tried to puzzle out who might have done it, and racked his brains to remember if there had been any other examples of deceit from the past.

Horace Turps was far too set in his ways to be able to alter the books. His own copperplate writing was stamped deep into his soul; and as for young Ollie Potts the junior clerk, he was such an untidy accident-prone lump that there was no chance that he could have done it so skilfully.

Merrick was at a loss to know what to do to prove his own innocence. But it was too late now as Mr Turps, accompanied by Mr Blandersbunt and witnessed by Miss Marsden, sacked him then and there. The only person who showed him any sympathy was Mrs Dove, the cleaner, who said it was all a scandal and of course he hadn't done it. 'I always knows an honest man when I sees one, love,' she said. But the rest of the office watched him go in paralysed, silent horror.

All the way home he was haunted by thoughts of what he would say to Maisy. He felt weak and ill. How on earth would they manage now he was jobless? Especially with Maisy's grandiose ideas. Apart from the disgrace of being sacked with no hope of even getting a reference. Indeed there could be charges of fraud pending if Blandersbunt wanted to pursue the matter. No doubt it would all be chewed over.

Merrick, pale and shivering, in his thick winter overcoat, limped painfully up the drive of 'Seedly' to his front door, in Hale. Already he could hear sounds of the twins romping about, and Maisy's voice in the hall.

Slowly and miserably he opened the door with his key.

CHAPTER 12

Angelic Ivy

That Christmas it was agony in the Jackson household.

'Little did I dream of the humiliation about to be piled on me and my family and all my friends and relations,' shrieked Maisy at the start of December. 'I promised Rupert faithfully that Papa would buy him a large Meccano set bigger than Donny Arbuthnut's, as well as a Red Indian tent and proper feathered head-dress. And Arabella's wept nearly all day because she won't be getting that fairy-cycle, and a doll that says Mama.'

'It's not the end of the world, Maisy. You aren't the only person with a husband out of work, and I'm trying my best.'

Maisy sniffed hard into her hanky as yet another

deluge of tears rolled down her chubby cheeks. 'But they don't all have 'usbands charged with fraud, Merrick. It's all *her* fault. It you hadn't got into them bad ways by traipsing round to that posh office of hers every dinner-time, it might never have 'appened. Of course *we* know you're innocent, but nobody else will and if you'd been paying proper attention to your books, and to any shady characters in that office instead of going round in a dream we wouldn't be in this state. It looks like the end of sending the twins to be properly educated now. They'll just have to go to elementary school. And I don't suppose Hazel will ever want her lot to mix with them again. She's very particular about things like that.' Maisy let out a terrible howl. 'And as for how we'll manage from day to day I have no idea, especially with winter being here. We'll have to use the cheapest slack on the kitchen fire and keep it smouldering with wet tea-leaves, and never go in the sitting room. We'll have to get back to candles again and an oil lamp, and stop eating butter. We'll have to live on scrag end and buy cracked eggs, and the children might even have to wear clogs to save on shoe repairs. Who would have dreamed it? Oh and by the way, you can sleep in the back bedroom from now on, Merrick. My nerves are too bad to allow anything else.'

In spite of his own misery at the whole situation, a glimmer of sardonic humour flushed through Merrick's soul. 'Won't that be a rather bad move, Maisy? There's the extra lighting to think of, and the washing of extra bed-linen, plus all the bed making and cleaning, and we shan't be able to have a daily help any more to do women's work.'

The only slight ray of improvement was that Merrick managed to get a day to day job helping out in Altrincham market. It was poorly paid, heavy, gruelling labour for a man with an artificial leg. However, he suffered it unflinchingly even though when he got home late at night he had to remove his artificial leg and put ointment and padding over the reddened stump of what had once been a healthy limb. If he kept on much longer with that sort of work it would be an ulcerating mass of flesh.

Christmas itself started out as one long row and wrangle because Merrick said he was too tired to go and have Christmas dinner with his in-laws. He knew they would not resist firing a few well-aimed arrows in his direction about his job. 'You and the twins go,' he said. 'There's nothing to stop you, and at least you won't have any cooking to do. I'll be quite happy on my own.'

'That's what's been the matter with you all your married life, Merrick Jackson – too happy on your own and ignoring your wife and family who've carried you along since the very moment I was left the money. No, I will not go on my own. What an insult to a wife to have to go away for Christmas on her own with young children to cope with. Not because she's some poor widow-woman but because her husband says he'll have a rest.'

So in the end they stayed at home. By virtue of a

wealthy lady from Bowden presenting Merrick with a small chicken because he was one of the poor who had been polite to her and seemed to be working hard, they managed quite a good meal. Gratified to discover that after their initial sulks at not getting the expensive toys they wanted, the twins had settled down to a compendium of board games, an orange each, some mixed nuts, bars of chocolate, woollen socks, and a brand new penny each.

Between Christmas and the new year of 1924 Maisy and Merrick were almost back to normal again. Merrick was allowed to come back to his double bed with Maisy – on the pretext of Maisy saving hot water for extra hot water bottles, but mainly because Hazel Arbuthnut had been very sympathetic about Merrick's predicament. 'I wouldn't let it stay at that, Maisy. If he was *my* husband I'd help him to battle through to the end to obtain full justice. How that poor, poor man must be suffering. *And* after losing his leg for king and country.'

Also the rhubarb season hadn't been quite as good as the Arbuthnuts had expected, so even their own wealthy offspring had not been given fairy-cycles and giant Meccano sets after all, but had to suffer educational jigsaw puzzles instead, and rather second-rate junior encyclopaedias full of articles on 'How to Clean Your Teeth' or 'How to Brush and Comb Your Hair Properly' or 'How to Polish All the Shoes' (Rule number one: Never try to put the polish on your own shoes with the shoes still on your feet and clean white socks on.) or 'How to Make Presents for Mama and Papa', and ending with a poem showing a witch and witches' cauldron which said:

'All children should be seen not heard,
Because not one was born a bird.
All children should be nice and quiet,
Unless they want to start a riot.'

Just before New Year's Eve Maisy said sweetly: 'Whatever do you think, Merrick? The Arbuthnuts have invited us to go with them to celebrate New Year's Eve in Albert Square, Manchester, starting with a dinner dance at the Grosvenor. Toby will take us in their car, and they've invited our two to go and stay the night with their three – with their nanny in charge. They said it will buck you up and act as a good omen for the coming year. Who said rich people hadn't got hearts of gold?'

Merrick nodded dryly: 'As long as they aren't a shipping firm run by Blandersbunts. All *their* gold stays behind bars. But at least we haven't heard any more from them over Christmas, and they haven't actually charged me with anything.'

'That's not the point, Merrick. Hazel and Toby think what happened to you is diabolical and that we should kick up a fuss about it, otherwise you'll carry the stigma of it for life.'

'It's all right for others to talk. You need money to even stand up for yourself against people like the Blandersbunts, Maisy.'

271

But the idea that Hazel Arbuthnut was actually worried about him, and that Maisy was showing signs of concern because of it, perked poor Merrick up enormously, as he began to think carefully about the whole dreadful episode and planned to do something about it in the New Year.

At first Ivy Violet had not been going to the New Year Celebrations in Manchester. It was a noisy rather crowded affair which she did not really relish, though she knew lots of families enjoyed going, particularly those with girls and boys in their young prime. It was Maureen who eventually persuaded her. 'I'd love to go Ivy but I've no one to be with. Trev's going but he'll be with his own pals.'

Ivy Violet nodded her head at last. 'All right then. But I doubt if I shall ever be persuaded to go again. I prefer to stay in and keep warm by the fire and just watch the clock and listen to the church bells and have neighbours like the Smiths calling to bring in the New Year, and drinking a glass of port wine with them.'

But once she was ready to go, and warmly attired in her long crimson winter coat with a beaver cape and fur hat to match, she began to look forward to all the excitement of welcoming in the fresh set of months, and having young Maureen to stay with her.

The whole of the area round Manchester town hall was crowded with noisy, fun loving, optimistic people. A few clowns decked in coloured paper hats and jumbles of paper streamers were busy trying to climb anything which was remotely climbable such as lampposts, drainpipes and large statues; while others played mouth organs, toy trumpets, whistles and cow bells as they waited for the town hall clock to strike twelve.

As everyone shuffled and swayed and moved in the vast crowd and people pushed to reach other people in the darkness, which was lit only by flares and oil lamps and gas light, Ivy Violet realised that she had lost Maureen completely and was entirely alone.

She did not worry too much; she had arranged to meet Maureen at the corner of Carriage Street outside the all-night cab office, off Cross Street, if by some chance they lost each other. 'If either of us hasn't arrived within half an hour, get a cab back to my place and I'll settle it up later.'

As soon as 'Auld Lang Syne' had been sung by the multitudinous, jostling crowd and as everyone fumbled about trying to grab hands, Ivy Violet set off to push her way through to the cab office.

Then, to her astonishment, just as she had managed to get to the outer edges of the gathering she noticed someone else pushing forward at the same time. They came face to face, the tips of ears and noses extra pink and fresh from the biting winter night, and strands of their hair covered in a fine damp grey haze of frosty steam . . . as they stared at each other.

'Ivy! What a place to meet! Happy New Year!'

Merrick smiled at her with shining, joyous eyes like someone just released from some form of detention. 'Maisy is somewhere about. We've come along with these friends of hers, but I seem to have lost them. Where are you off to then?'

'To meet Maureen at the all-night cab office. And Happy New Year to you, Merrick.' She kissed him lightly on the cheek. It was the first time a kiss had passed between them in the whole of their lives. 'I don't suppose we'll be seeing each other again this year at dinner-times any more after that row.'

He shook his head. 'I'm not even working at Lagoon's now. You probably won't know but I got the sack the very same afternoon that Maisy made the scene?'

Ivy Violet looked at him askance. 'The sack? You must be joking surely?'

He shook his head. 'Unfortunately – no.' He began to relate the whole tale, and his voice broke slightly betraying the hidden grief he had suffered over it all. 'But things are gradually getting back to normal. I have a temporary job as a market porter and Maisy's friends think I should make a fuss and get on to them at the shipping office as soon as New Year is over. The trouble is, it all takes money and time which aren't forthcoming at the moment, and Maisy herself just isn't the type to be of much help in that way. Although her friends the Arbuthnuts are anxious to be of use. They brought us here tonight.'

He looked at her gloomily as they sat on a wooden bench just outside the cab office. 'You've no idea what it's like, Ivy, to suddenly have turned into a sacked, penniless man with a wife and family to provide for and with a large fraud threat hanging over your head.'

A huge wave of motherly protection rose within Ivy Violet's bosom. What a terrible thing to have happened. Merrick was as honest as the day was long, she thought. She felt her heart beating angrily at the injustice of it all. But really she knew that it was nothing to do with her, even though they were so close and knew each other so well.

In a few more minutes, after she had offered Merrick her sympathy and told him to get in touch with her if she could possibly be of any help – but knowing, deep down that he would not – Maureen appeared, and they both took a cab back to Heaton Moor. She related in undertones and not using the name of the shipping firm, the awful fate of Mr J.

At Lagoon's office a smartly dressed and imposing Ivy Violet Hilton of IVY shoes handed her business card to the secretary Miss Marsden and asked to see Mr Hubert Blandersbunt. Miss Marsden was suitably impressed.

'I'm terribly sorry, Miss Hilton but Mr Blandersbunt is still away at present, but his brother, Mr Dennis is here. However he is out of the office but will be back in a few minutes if you'd care to wait in the reception office?'

With a slight inward groan Ivy Violet smiled graciously and followed Miss Marsden into a small glass and wood-partitioned offshoot containing a large, brown velvet-covered sofa, two wicker chairs, a small glass-topped wicker table with shipping leaflets on it and a glass ashtray decorated with a ship's steering wheel.

She was sitting there staring at the meagre trappings of such a rich concern when Mrs Dove, the cleaner, came in to wash all the windows. 'Oh excuse me madam, I didn't know as anyone was 'ere.'

'It's quite all right. Just you carry on. I'm waiting to see Mr Dennis Blandersbunt. Apparently Mr Hubert is away?'

'That's right, love. Mr Hubert's bin away since long afore Christmas, so Mr Dennis is in charge. Mind you there's no comparison. So if it's information you're wanting you won't get much out of him. Though I says it as shouldn't.'

'I expect you must have worked here for ages then – with knowing them both so well?'

'You can say that again, love. The name Dove has fluttered round these buildings since the year dot. When I started here at the beginning of my married life forty-five years ago, I used to remember old Ely Blandersbunt bringing them two in when they was just kids in tweed knickerbockers.' She gave Ivy Violet a short shrewd look. 'So what was you after then?'

'My name's Ivy Violet Hilton and I've come on behalf of my cousin Mr Merrick Jackson who was sacked just before Christmas, due to some terrible mistake. Mr Jackson isn't well enough to come himself.'

A light of interest spread over Mrs Dove's face as she sat down on one of the wicker chairs. 'I'm not surprised either. It was terrible the way Mr Jackson was dismissed. He was such a nice young man. Never 'urt a flea 'ee didn't, and in the end it was a storm in a teacup really because it was all about figures being altered in the account book. Then the next day when poor Mr Jackson had got the sack, the account book came back from Mr Blandersbunt's office with the whole page ripped out at that very spot, where all the trouble was, on the very day when Mr Hubert himself went away on urgent business. And isn't back yet, but away with what some say is nervous trouble, with him being at Juan les Pins to take the sea air, and 'is brother coming 'ome so sudden.'

Ivy Violet listened in startled silence.

'Then of course, the following week, Mr Turps left after 33 years of service after calling Mr Dennis a dishonest scrounger, which all the office heard. And himself was unfortunate enough to have a stroke but is now recovering and coming back again to do some lighter work, because folks do say that the Blandersbunts can't actually sack 'im because 'ee knows too much of everything that goes on including Miss Marsden.' She looked at Ivy meaningfully.

Ivy began to feel quite dizzy with the complications of it. 'So did they find out who actually did it then?'

'I'll tell you this in strict confidence madam – and it's nowt to do with me because I'm only the cleaner, so forget I ever spoke – but some does say that Hubert himself did it and the mistake was found out by Horace Turps. But others say it's a complete pack of lies and the Blandersbunts are as honest as your cousin Mr Jackson, and that it was done by *Miss Marsden*. So there love . . . we shall never really know and the evidence has all gone. But one thing is certain – it wasn't your Mr Jackson what did it – and that's a fact.'

A few moments later Mrs Dove was silently cleaning the windows, like a stranger. Soon she left the room with her bucket and wash-leather and wished Ivy Violet a kind goodbye, just as Miss Marsden walked in to say that Mr Dennis Blandersbunt was in his office and ready to see Miss Hilton.

Mr Dennis Blandersbunt was suave and well-dressed in a chalk pin-stripe suit. He had a curling moustache and slightly balding young head. Ivy Violet was greeted with effusive bonhomie: 'Sit down and make yourself at home. Now what can we do for you? I understand you have come on a personal matter and wanted to see my brother who of course has been absent for quite a while.'

As soon as Ivy Violet mentioned Merrick Jackson a guarded expression crossed his face and he tensed up slightly. 'Ah yes . . . So what exactly is it you have called about – Miss er – Miss?' He began to scribble restlessly with a fine, solid gold propelling pencil on his sheet of snow white blotting paper. 'Did Mr Jackson actually invite you to call on us?'

Ivy Violet nodded firmly. She did feel slightly

guilty pretending to be Merrick's cousin and the fact that he did not know of her visit. 'He wasn't well enough to come here himself,' she said.

'I understand he has a wife?' he said smoothly.

'He certainly has,' Ivy Violet said icily. 'But he didn't consider it quite fair to inflict further pain on his direct family by having to come here and go over it all again. So I said I would help because I have offices of my own in Manchester, as you will have seen by my card.'

'Oh yes. Of course. Please forgive me.' Dennis Blandersbunt looked about in a swift, reverent panic for the card.

They both waited for each other to make the next move. Finally he said: 'How is he getting on?'

'I don't quite understand you, Mr Blandersbunt. What exactly do you mean, apart from him having the flu?'

'Well . . . You know – about what happened.' He glanced at her sheepishly.

'How would *you* feel if you were an innocent hard-working person and it happened to you?'

'Quite. Quite.' He put on his most conciliatory expression. 'I'm afraid the whole affair was a bit of a hasty fiasco – made all the worse by my brother going abroad so suddenly. But anything we can do to alleviate your cousin's predicament will be carried out – even to inviting him to have his job back. Particularly as our chief clerk is off sick . . .' He began to fidget and scowl. 'Just tell Mr Jackson not to worry and that it's all under control and sorted out – and

that he'll be hearing from us in the next week or so.'
He stood up and held out his hand to Ivy Violet, but
was annoyed to see that she still sat there. 'When
exactly is the next week or so, Mr Blandersbunt? I
hope the letter will contain a full written apology
admitting your mistake and giving him a good character reference?'

'Yes, yes, of course. In fact I'll get Miss Marsden to
write it straightaway and get it all settled. How will
that suit?'

'Admirably.' Ivy Violet stood up at last and shook
hands with him, then she sailed out of the office in
full triumphant flood, feeling as if she had done the
best thing in her whole life.

A few days later Merrick received a special looking letter. It was waiting for him on his return from
working at the market.

He opened it somewhat cautiously for although
there was no marking of Lagoon's trade name printed on the envelope, the writing looked distinctly like
Miss Marsden's.

He read the contents with slow incredulity. What a
sudden and swift turnabout, after all these weeks of
silence and condemnation. He knew that Maisy and
her friends the Arbuthnuts were supposed to be
going to help him to sort it all out. But now it seemed
to be already done. The abject apologies stared at
him from the page with a plea to come back and join
the firm in his original position, and even a suggestion of some back pay.

Merrick stared at it sourly. He had suffered so

deeply that he was in no mood even to feel his heart lighten.

'Whatever's the matter, Merrick? Is it some more bad news?' Maisy was edgy. She had admitted to herself at last that they could not last out in their comfortable way of life as things were. That instead of concentrating on being a genteel and poorly paid purveyor of cheap music lessons to a few of her rich friends' children it might be better to get herself a steady job working in a shop again. Like she had done before she was married. Times were uncertain. It was rumoured that soon there would be a Labour cabinet in government if Baldwin resigned. Ramsay Macdonald would take over, which she knew would suit Merrick down to the ground, though they were all much of a muchness to her with their squabbles. Except that conservatives were at least more polite.

'It's from Lagoon's. A letter from Mr Dennis Blandersbunt, admitting it was all a bloody cock-up but not actually saying how it all came about and offering me my job back plus a glowing character reference. I can start next week.'

'But lovey. How simply marvellous!'

'It isn't marvellous at all Maisy. I'm not going back there after the way they've treated me. What did we fight that bloody awful War for – just to be made fools of and kicked about and treated like dirt in some tin-pot piddling shipping office?'

'I'll make you a nice cup of tea dear. You're a bit under the weather. It's only to be expected. Thank goodness they realised their mistake, before it was all too late.'

'It is too late, Maisy. The damage is done.'

Maisy gave a genuine howl of alarm. 'You can't really mean it Merrick, after all you've put us through. And after the Arbuthnuts 'ave bin so kind to us and said they would help you. You must've gone mad. Surely you don't want to spend your life slogging away with casual work ont' market with only one leg? You'll not last long at that, just mark my words. Only last week Mrs Portcullis 'oo lives down this very road heard of a man with one leg who lasted no time at all once he started on a labouring job.' Tears began to form in her large dark eyes. 'Surely you aren't going to let down your faithful wife and family? And to think of all that money out of my own inheritance I've spent on you, Merrick. You've got at least 20 lovely ties in that wardrobe and you never even wear them!'

'Working ont' market's at least a shade better than being cramped in that office tied to a desk all day doing figures for the rest of me life.'

'But not as well paid Merrick.'

'Oh I wouldn't say that. Some of 'em gets almost as much as I got in that dump.'

'Yes love, but they're younger and *fitter*. What you do takes skill – in that office, and I certainly don't want a husband 'oo's a failure just because 'ee wants to be one. An 'usband's proper job is as a provider, Merrick Jackson. So don't you forget it, and your proper job's back there with Lagoon's Shipping Office in town. Also it'll just show them what a proper man you are and how badly done to you were when you go back and face them again on Monday. So get your pen out straightaway and write and tell them so.'

With a huge groan of despair Merrick got his pen out, and the following Monday morning he was back in the office at his own desk, with a face as pale and bleak as a man who has been given the death sentence.

Dennis Blandersbunt came into the office and made a point of shaking hands with him and Miss Marsden brought him a cup of tea and a chocolate biscuit. Ollie Potts, the junior clerk, grinned all over his cheeky face and said he was glad to see him back and that 'old Turpentine' had probably gone for ever. And Mrs Dove, the cleaner, said he was a fool ever to have set foot in the place again after all he had suffered, and that even if Miss Marsden ever offered her even a sip of tea – never mind a biscuit – she would chuck it back in her smarmy face.

Yes. Merrick could see that his life was truly back to normal again at last, as Maisy informed him thankfully when he got home from work that the twins would not have to go to an elementary school after all. And she had got a new music pupil from a huge house with stables and electric lights.

Ivy Violet never mentioned her confrontation with Dennis Blandersbunt at Lagoon's Shipping Office from the very moment it was over. The fact was that she suffered from something of a guilty conscience.

She realised she was becoming what she had always sneered at in her youth – an interfering old busy-body – as bad as the people who had lived in Clark Terrace all those years ago. She knew that if Alfred had still been alive and some past childhood girl-friend had interfered in his working affairs, she would have been furious, no matter how noble the supposed reasons. She pretended that it had never happened thinking that at least it had done some good for Merrick.

But in Merrick's office, it was different. For a start, Mrs Dove had broadcast to all and sundry about the young woman 'who called to see "Mr Dennis" one day and 'oo was supposed to be very, very rich and made shoes for the 'ole of the Royals and was even going to supply them to the Blandersbunts.'

Then Dennis Blandersbunt himself sidled up to Merrick one day and asked him how his cousin was getting on who makes 'those posh IVY shoes'.

Merrick stared at him in amazement. 'Cousin? Do you mean Ivy Hilton?'

'Yes, that's right old man. Quite a flapper.'

Merrick frowned, completely puzzled, then nodded. 'It must be said that she is very capable, Mr Blandersbunt. She always has been. Were you wanting some shoes made?'

'No, no. Not at all. There happened to be a mention of them that's all. Someone we know.' Mr Dennis drifted away and the whole episode was at last forgotten, except by Merrick.

He spoke to Mrs Dove about it. 'So did Miss

Hilton come here then?' he asked.

'She did that, Mr Jackson. She came early in the year when you was still sacked. A very nice, refined young woman. We 'ad quite a conversation.'

Merrick nodded slowly and said no more. None of it was ever mentioned again. He cast Ivy Violet hastily from his mind and swore that he must never see her again.

The letter was long, and closely written. Its battered-looking envelope was covered in stamps from the U.S.A. Ivy Violet read it once more with total disbelief:

' . . . And so Ivy, I'm coming back to Manchester. Things haven't been all that great for Crystal with having no proper mother, and I don't want her to join the film studios where they groom the child actors. It would all have been so different if Garnet had still been here.

There's a good chance I might have been able to change my style to a singing cowboy in some of the talkies they're producing, but the whole thing's turned into a bit of a hotch-potch. Lots of money here and they say that the motion pictures will soon be an everyday affair . . .

Hope all is well with you. Hope to see you in a few months . . . regards to all.

Yours,

Maxi.'

When Ivy Violet showed Mary Reece the letter,

she too was perturbed. 'It means Hetty and I will have to move. I knew it might come to that in the end but didn't think it would all be so quick. He certainly won't want a small three-year-old girl he knows nothing about, chasing all round the place and treating it as her rightful home. I'll have to find him a replacement housekeeper.'

A wave of panic swept over Ivy Violet as she began to think of finding somewhere else to live. Her future looked uncertain even though she knew that in her world she was actually quite fortunate.

In the vast world Maxi was returning from it was a time of political upheaval (which many people blamed on last year's huge earthquake and fire in Japan, where over 72,000 people died). Manchester people begrudgingly gave thanks for living in a place where the only real tremors came from the underground rumblings of coal mines or some local blasting with dynamite. Many of them forecast that earthquakes of such terrible dimensions were to blame for things like Lenin dying and a man called Stalin taking over in the Soviet Union. But to Ivy Violet in 1924 it was merely a news item, and even the first Labour Government was of only slight importance compared to her problem of leaving Maxi Dingle's house as soon as possible along with Mary and Hetty. For now she was even considering inviting Mary to be *her* housekeeper, because she too loved little Hetty so much.

Ivy walked through town in a steady drizzle of rain pondering where she should look for a house or flat. Should it be somewhere like Didsbury or Chorlton? Or even Cheadle? There was a good private bus company between Cheadle, Baguely and Altrincham. And you could catch a 41 or 42 tramcar from Manchester to Palatine Road terminus in West Didsbury for twopence. For weeks the ideas of what to do and where to go governed her mind.

But she still had not got any further six weeks later when Maxi Dingle and Crystal arrived late one night at the beginning of May when all the cherry blossom was out, and she was alone in the house with Hetty asleep in the nursery.

She heard a key turn in the front door. It was a very light night and the man standing there in the open doorway was like a sudden giant dressed in a creamy white linen suit; such a contrast to the dark, working clothes of the grimy north.

'Ivy Violet! How wonderful to see you at last.' Maxi hugged her and put his arms round her with brotherly affection, whilst Crystal stood there smiling silently. 'I didn't intend to arrive until tomorrow morning, then I thought – what the hell – why moulder in hotel rooms just because of being so late getting here?'

He continued to beam with pleasure as they walked into the living room and sat down. 'How's tricks then? I just can't believe I'm here. You look absolutely blooming.'

She looked back at him quietly now, at his tightly cropped hair with hardly a trace of ginger curl to be seen. There was sudden silence; she broke it by nervously asking if they would like a night-time drink or a snack.

After a while Maxi said: 'I expect you were surprised by our sudden arrival. The truth is, I was offered a lead in a Gilbert and Sullivan and knew instantly that I couldn't refuse.'

She felt shy and didn't know how to continue the conversation. 'There's no real news. Everything is running very smoothly and the shoe trade is doing well. Mary has kept the house in tip-top condition, but it's her night off tonight. It's lovely to see you both again after so long.'

After they had eaten Ivy Violet made up their beds with white starched linen and placed hot water bottles in the centre of each one. Mary came in and told Maxi about Hetty, and Crystal went to her room and was soon fast asleep. Then they all had a glass of sherry and Mary broke her news about wanting to leave because of Hetty. 'I expect it's a bit of a surprise for you both sir, but I kept her birth a secret at the time. She used to live with my sister who's much older than I am but she found it too much to cope with. I have no husband so Miss Hilton invited us both to be here. I had planned to write to you about the situation before you got back, and I have found you a very good replacement – it's Jack Meadowcroft, the gardener's daughter Phoebe. She's a widow of twenty-eight and very competent and trustworthy.'

Maxi nodded and smiled drowsily in the warmth and comfort of his own home again. He was a little surprised by the idea of his housekeeper announcing that she was leaving, especially with a young daughter he had never dreamed of.

He turned to Ivy as his last port in a storm: 'Surely you'll be staying a bit longer, Ivy?'

'A little while. Just until I get settled in a place of my own if that's all right with you?'

He nodded towards them both with a slightly rueful smile of acceptance.

The following day Ivy Violet was up at six-thirty getting the breakfast room set out ready for Maxi and Crystal. She was in a sudden fever of anxiety to find other accommodation. If she stayed too long she thought she would be worrying about him and his comfort and getting too involved in his life. It had been different before when Garnet and Crystal were with him and they had all been a proper family threesome, for everyone kept a tactful distance from each other. And just supposing he met some other woman, or brought male friends round? Which he was quite free to do. No – she must get out as soon as possible.

She did not go to the office that morning. She rang Maureen instead. 'I'm going house-hunting Maureen. Maxi and Crystal came back last night.'

Things did not quite work out as she had planned. As soon as Maxi Dingle arrived downstairs, announcing that Crystal would probably sleep until midday, Ivy Violet's heart quickened at the sight of him. He strolled casually into the breakfast room which had a small oak table covered in a hand-

289

embroidered linen and set out with a willow pattern breakfast set. He soaked it all up with a sigh of contentment. 'Home,' he murmured towards the teapot beneath its tea cosy. He looked slowly over the hand-embroidered linen crash cover of lazy-daisy stitched flowers in Anchor silks, and pale yellow and pink hollyhocks made with french knots that Garnet had carefully sewn and at the small egg cosies next to the silver toast rack.

'First thing I'm going to do after breakfast,' he said cheerfully with his mouth full of toast and marmalade, 'is to buy a little sports car Ivy.' He gave her a swift, penetrating glance. 'D'you fancy coming with me?' His face was alive with energy and optimism.

She laughed and nodded, then said half seriously: 'And if you give it a test run I might spot a suitable place to move to.'

'Move to?' His expression changed. He looked puzzled and slightly shocked. 'Surely you aren't *truly* thinking of leaving here? Not in the cold light of day?'

'Even more so.' She nodded slowly. 'I was terribly happy with you and Garnet in the past but the time has come – now you're back to take over again – to settle down properly in my own little place.'

He ate the rest of his breakfast in quick, moody silence, as she stood in the other room gazing out of the window to the garden, half sorry now for what she had said. After all, he had only just got home and there was no need to make an issue of it when everything had been set for a carefree outing.

Suddenly she felt his hands resting gently round her waist and he was kissing the nape of her neck. 'Don't go Ivy. I've been so lonely. All the time in Hollywood I was thinking of you, here in Manchester.'

She pushed him away from her. 'No. No. We can't. We mustn't. It wouldn't be right. We would be bad for each other. You're lonely because of the shock of losing Garnet.'

She rushed from the room with tears of anger in her eyes. How dared he compromise her so, the moment he was back and they were alone together? How on earth was she going to survive it all? The last thing she wanted at the moment was to be hurtled into an affair with Maxi when she had her own life and work to sort out. She hurried upstairs to her room, flopped down on her bed and wept.

There was a tap at the door. 'Ivy. Please listen to me.'

Was he never going to leave her alone? 'Go away Maxi.' She jumped up and went to face him. 'Look, we can't start off like this. It's ridiculous. You have young Crystal to consider. We've both been married and we know the complications. We mustn't do it, Maxi. We mustn't.' She gazed at him hopelessly. 'If I stayed here with you, it just wouldn't work out however much we loved each other. It would all end in misery. I know it in my bones.' Then brightening up she said: 'Well at least we're getting it straight at the start. And knowing you, you'll be sure to meet more women in your life. To tell the truth all I'm really interested in at this moment is designing shoes – the very thing you encouraged me to do in the first place and I'm ever grateful for it.'

Maxi stared back at her impassively. He said: 'Does that mean you won't come with me to buy the car then?'

There was a few seconds silence as Ivy Violet hesitated, then she laughed and said: 'Of course I'll come. But I still meant what I said about looking for a place of my own.'

He smiled slightly in return. 'And am I never ever going to able to hug you again in a small moment of spontaneous affection?'

She pretended not to hear him as they set off, knowing that life at this moment was untrammelled paradise with no obligations, no worries, no attachments. It was just the present as they walked together down the tree-lined road deep in a scent of creamy blossomed rowans.

One day at a time. Perhaps that was the solution after all.

CHAPTER 13

A Rash Move

All the time that Ivy Violet was hunting for some-where to live that year, Merrick Jackson was secretly looking for a better job. For although the rest of staff had welcomed him back with open arms and the Blandersbunt brothers had been forced to eat hum-ble pie, the damage had been done as far as Merrick was concerned. He just could not settle even though he was given two shillings a week pay rise.

Help came to him from an unexpected corner, by way of Maisy.

'Oh yes, Merrick . . . and they're all going away for three whole weeks during the school 'olidays to France and Paris, and they'll be seeing that iron Eiffel Tower that's over one thousand feet tall. It's a mira-cle when you come to think of it, because Blackpool

Tower's only half the size. Hazel says they'll be going on one of them Cook's Tours, and they'll have a guide to show them round everything. But of course it's different for them – with all that rhubarb be'ind 'em.'

Merrick nodded his head a trifle sardonically. It certainly was different for them, and it was a miracle how Maisy still managed to claim the Arbuthnuts as their very best friends. The Jackson family were not in the same league where holidays abroad were concerned – even though Maisy always lived in hope.

This year they were going on a camping holiday in Derbyshire which the children had not objected to but which Maisy was viewing with complete alarm. 'If I so much as see a single bug or beetle in our tent Merrick I shall come home immediately and leave you to it. The sooner we manage something better, the happier I shall be, especially in a wet place like Derbyshire. Hazel was only telling me today that Thomas Cook, who started all those Cook's Tours, was born in Derbyshire in Victorian times – so can you wonder he moved to Loughborough and started arranging tours abroad to get out of this country to better weather?'

This conversation was followed a month or so later with an actual visit from Hazel Arbuthnut, after their holiday in France had taken place, showing plenty of photographic poses with the Eiffel Tower in the background.

'It was absolutely dee-vine,' said Hazel enthusiastically. 'I can't say it too often. So the moment you two get the chance, you simply *must* go on a Cook's Tour. Their organisation is truly wonderful, and Terry Mellorfield, our personal guide, said they're expanding their business in the Manchester area, and are looking for more staff. I'm beginning to wish sometimes that Toby had gone into something like that – instead of rhubarb – but it's a bit late to change when one reaches forty. We married fairly late, you see – mainly due to the War.'

A travel agency . . . Expanding their business . . . Merrick felt a rush of hope. Perhaps that was what he should do. Try and get into something like that, for at least there was a slight link with work in a shipping office – even if tours were mostly linked to motor coaches and trains.

The next day, during his lunch time, Merrick decided to call in at Thomas Cook's to pick up a brochure. He went up to the counter. 'Some friends of ours have just returned from abroad, and their guide Mr Terry Mellorfield mentioned that you needed extra staff in the Manchester area. Have you any official particulars? I know of someone who might be interested.'

The man rubbed his finger gingerly round the top of his tight, starched white collar, and grimaced: 'I do know they're looking for at least one extra – because I'm leaving at the end of this month to go to Canada for them on a twelve month contract. But you'll have to write in with an application. The closing date is tomorrow for applications.'

Merrick hurried back to the office and after eating

a hurried sandwich, carefully wrote out his application letter ready to catch the afternoon post so that it would arrive first thing in the morning. But his efforts to get it in the post were doomed as he was waylaid by their new clerk with a long and complicated tale about the chain not pulling properly in the lavatory. ' . . . Sometimes it can take as long as quarter of an hour to get a really good torrential gush. And I'm not afraid to say so.'

Merrick nodded sympathetically and said he would mention it, knowing that it was not the sort of message Miss Marsden would really want to convey to higher places. He put his letter in his pocket planning to put it in Thomas Cook's letter-box after work.

Yet again fate seemed to be against him. He had just got to the door of Thomas Cook's when a well-dressed elderly man in a lightweight grey-flannel suit with a sheaf of cardboard document wallets under one arm suddenly dropped them all because he had been stung by a wasp.

Merrick sprang to his assistance, carefully picking up the wallets as the man cursed and shook his hand and peered at his finger.

'Little blighter must 've bin crawling about between all that stuff. My God. What a jab! Think I'll pop back in and put some vinegar on it. Bring the files for me, there's a good chap.'

Merrick followed with all the files, then said: 'I was actually on my way here to drop this letter in. Where shall I leave it?'

The man took it and gave it a cursory glance. 'I'll see to it. Leave it with me. No need to worry. And thanks for the help.'

As Merrick walked out to catch the train home, he could almost have kicked himself. Trust that to have happened. The letter would no doubt be left lying on some office desk – never to be seen again. It was the sort of thing that often happened at Lagoon's.

A few days later, after he'd dismissed the whole episode, an oblong envelope plonked through the letter-box at home. Fortunately Maisy was nowhere to be seen at the time. He knew only too well that if she had known about it, so would all her friends and relations. And not before she had chewed over the whole act of his applying for the wretched job in the first place. 'What ever for Merrick? Surely you're happy enough where you are? Particularly with that nice rise. Oh I know Hazel was going on about those sorts of jobs in the holiday trade after they all got back from France – but it wasn't meant for you, dear, it was more for the children and their future prospects.'

He opened the envelope slowly, not really wanting to know the worst. Then to his delight he saw the words 'attend for an interview on Wednesday afternoon'. It was in two weeks time.

Hastily he folded the letter up and tucked it safely in the small desk bureau. It would just give him time to manufacture a dentist appointment so as to have the time off work.

When Wednesday arrived he was there for his interview with just a few unhurried minutes to spare.

'Anyone'd think you was off to a wedding or summat with that suit on, Merrick,' Maisy had said suspiciously. 'I hope you isn't starting those antics of visiting Ivy Violet again.'

He looked at her with mild scorn. 'Surely I have the right to change into my one and only second suit once in a while? You seem to have a new outfit on every day, and sometimes every hour.'

His spirits sagged a little though once he was in the small waiting room because there were six more men there. They were all turned out to band-box perfection with well-cut suits, shining shoes, and prestigious ties.

'Mr Merrick Jackson?' A middle-aged female secretary was standing there calling his name as six sets of eyes took note of him. He did not feel in the least nervous now, just a fatalistic streak of what will be, will be. He had nothing to lose. It would have been a different matter entirely if he had already been unemployed.

Inside the office there were two men and the oldest one sat straight behind a large desk with a massive glass paperweight on it. Next to the paperweight was a pile of blue envelope files. Merrick recognised both the files and the man as the man said: 'Wasp sting quite better now, old chap. But let's get down to business. I see you are at present with Lagoon's, a very well-established shipping firm with an excellent and longstanding reputation. Might we enquire why you want to leave?'

'I feel I need a job with more movement in it, sir,' said Merrick truthfully. 'I only have one leg – lost in the War, and it seems to me that because of it – it's better for me to be moving about more than just sitting on one office chair nine hours a day. I feel the need for more variety and the opportunity to explore new horizons in all senses.'

There was a deathly silence. 'Well I must say, Mr Jackson, this idea of a man with one leg wanting to move about more is a point of view we've never come across before in an interview, but we'll certainly bear it in mind in conjunction with your other capabilities.'

As Merrick walked along the busy city street back to his own office he felt neither pleased nor depressed as he began to think what he would say to them about his dental appointment. He hoped that a lot of extra work had not piled up while he had been away.

'You're soon back, Merrick,' said Dennis Blandersbunt when he arrived. 'You look amazingly fit for a man who's just visited Dr Fang.'

Merrick smiled slightly. 'It was just for a preliminary check up. Glad to get it all over with.'

The following week he received a letter – this time grabbed from the door-mat and brought to him by Maisy. It offered him a job in the offices of the travel agency as an assistant manager dealing with customers, with better pay than he was getting at present.

'I just can't bel-ieeeve it, Merrick. I really can't,' gasped Maisy. 'Who would have thought someone like you could do so well for 'imself, after all that upset you 'ad? It only goes to show what can be done with family encouragement and being looked after so well.'

Merrick smiled back at her calmly. He was redeemed at last in the eyes of the world where the Jacksons and the Arbuthnuts resided, so what could be better than that? He allowed himself a deep, secret, satisfied sigh.

'Looking for a nice little house eh? Looking for sum-mat fit for a young woman of substance, but only four bedrooms and with a nice big garden and plen-ty of room for an office ont' ground floor?'

Ivy Violet nodded cautiously towards Mr Trout in the estate agent's.

She was becoming more and more disheartened day after day, and as autumn inevitably approached, her dreams of being in a place of her own by Christmas were fading fast. She searched the length and breadth of Manchester for something she felt would suit her, until even her mother Phillis was berating her for being fussy and neurotic and spoilt into the bargain.

'Here you are,' Phillis said, 'moaning and com-plaining about not being able to find some impossible little palace of your dreams when most of the popu-lation is only too glad to get even a back-to-back to live in. I was hearing only yesterday of folks in town, with families to bring up, still struggling away in damp unhealthy cellars with earth floors, and beetles and woodlice everywhere not to mention rats.'

Ivy Violet sighed. 'You don't need to tell me it all again Phillis, and please don't mention how terrible things were when you were my age with all of us to cope with. My memory isn't that short. But times have changed. At least for some of us. And I don't want to live in sack cloth and ashes all *my* life.'

She was so busy house hunting in her spare time that she and Maxi hardly had time to say hello as they both got on with their own lives. Yet she knew she had to make a decision quickly for when the real winter came and they were indoors more . . .

Ivy Violet continued to gaze undecidedly at some photographs set in a special album, as Mr Trout, the estate agent's assistant, tried his best to enthuse. 'Altrincham's a very nice spot,' he persisted, 'yet it's the only place you never ever want to go. Only this very morning an extremely respectable gentleman from St John's Church area came in, wanting to sell his deceased mother's place in Blossom Street. That little gem I just told you about. Or if that doesn't suit I could maybe winkle you out summat round Bowdon or Hale Barns? They're on a direct route for the city; not too much travelling distance, and on the edge of beautiful countryside awash with thriving market gardens and nurseries; parks and entertainments; and good shopping everywhere. Well you should know that Miss Hilton – if you'd pardon the impertinence – because your own IVY shoes are sold there in high-class establishments. And my own wife bought some in that very spot near Bowdon Downs.'

Ivy tried to look pleased and interested about the shoes – for Mr Trout's sake – even though she was already well aware where every pair of her precious shoes went. She knew deep down that the main reason she always dismissed the Altrincham area was because Maisy and Merrick lived there, and that she was sure that if she lived even within a few miles of them, Maisy would say she was following Merrick.

'What about Stockport then? Bram'all Lane? Or more toward Cheadle Hulme? This same man whose mother's just died has an old maiden aunt who has just died too, who's left a real little jewel of a place right near station bridge – going towards Hulme Hall area.'

Ivy Violet looked at him with sharp suspicion: '*Another* one? The *same* man?'

Mr Trout looked down at his toes sheepishly. 'There is a bit more to it than meets the eye, Miss Hilton.' He gave a slightly embarrassed cough. 'I can't exactly divulge the exact truth about how he 'appened on the two of 'em, but take my word – sworn on the 'oly Bible – 'ee 'as got the two of 'em for sale at the same time. But let's put it like this – the lady 'oo moved out of the one in Cheadle 'Ulme wasn't dead by any means, and as to 'er being his *old* aunt – well we can only believe what we's told, but I do know she still plays hockey and is said to be the shape of a pocket Venus – if you'll pardon the description.'

Reluctantly Ivy Violet allowed herself to be slightly persuaded to go and look at the place in Cheadle Hulme. Mr Trout offered to take her in his car during his dinner break. It was a beautiful day and leaves on lime trees were turning to a vivid canary yellow amongst all the fluttering browns and oranges and deep warm scarlets of autumn.

The moment she saw the place, Ivy Violet fell for it. It was a low rambling house with greyish white stuccoed walls half covered in honeysuckle. The windows were latticed with the frames painted black. A large untidy garden was a golden riot of trailing nasturtiums, dahlias and purple Michaelmas daisies.

Inside it was panelled throughout in oak with plain white-washed ceilings. A few broken and dusty rush-seated chairs lay in a corner of the living room with the sun pouring in on them.

' 'Ee's asking a very moderate price. Says 'ee wants to get shut of it as soon as possible because 'is 'eart is broken.'

Ivy Violet hardly heard him. This was for her. It needed plenty of renovation, but to her it was perfect.

'Please offer Mr Bolger twenty pounds less than his asking price, and point out the cracked window in the kitchen plus the broken chimney pots. I'll look forward to hearing from you again from my main Manchester office address.'

They shook hands, then Ivy Violet returned home to her flat at Maxi Dingle's – her heart full of joy and satisfaction – as exactly a week after Christmas, she was actually moving into her own proper home at last.

'You don't *need* to go, you know,' said Maxi on the day she moved out. 'It's going to be hell without you here. Especially with Mary Reece and Hetty vanishing for good to her sister's.'

Ivy Violet knew he did not mean it. She had already met Mary's replacement – twenty-eight-year-old Phoebe, the gardener's daughter, who was a widow.

As she stood there in her new home in the midst of all the packing cases, alone in the oak-panelled living room, with a hard white frost lying on iron ground outside amongst black silhouettes of bare trees, she felt at peace with the whole world.

She had received offers of help for moving in and unpacking but she preferred to be in complete solitude. She went upstairs to the single bed which the removal men had put in a small box-room.

It was not until next day, when she woke early in the morning blackness in the small cold room, and heard the steady drip of water that she realised all was not quite so perfect as it had seemed the day before.

Hastily she dragged on her new red flannel dressing-gown and fleecy-lined suede slippers and went to trace the noise. As she entered the main bedroom, the sight she most dreaded met her eyes – a quick and steady drip of water from the flaking ceiling. It must have been pouring through all night. All the floor boards were awash with water and as she rushed downstairs to the dining-room she found that even more water was splashing into a huge pool on the floor.

Hurriedly she got dressed. She must phone a plumber. What idiocy. She had no phone and it was only six o'clock in the morning.

Shivering. she began lighting more of the gas lamps, thanking God that she had at least got those sorted out properly, with new gas mantles and plenty of wax tapers at hand. But oh for electricity, she thought, like she had in her office and had been used to at the flat.

She went downstairs in the icy gloom and made herself a cup of tea. A terrible thought crept into her mind. Had she made an awful mistake about this place? Was it to be a complete white elephant? Maybe in her haste to escape from Maxi, she had been carried along by a false sense of optimism?

As the early morning light began to filter through and she heard sounds of life in the nearby roads and the noises of railway trains and dogs barking and someone whistling, her confidence returned.

She lit two fires: one in the kitchen and one in the living room, then made herself another cup of tea, and some toast. Then she set off to find a good plumber.

It was not until the following spring that Ivy Violet could truthfully say she had settled down.

On a night in late April a distraught woman in a

torn, brown barathea coat and a scratched face confronted her. Without waiting to introduce herself she began to berate Ivy Violet for the condition she was in.

'You're to blame for all this,' she said tearfully. 'You, and him.'

Her pale amber eyes had a terrible stare in them as if she was not quite aware of what she was doing. She pushed past Ivy Violet with almost maniacal force into the hall and peered about with nervous aggressiveness. 'This is my rightful home. The place I lived for years before he got up to his tricks.'

'Come into the sitting room,' Ivy Violet said as calmly as she could. 'Or shall I take you to bathe your face first? Tell you what – come into the kitchen whilst I put the kettle on. I'm Ivy Violet Hilton. Surely we've never met before?' She put out her hand but the woman pushed it away angrily.

The woman's clothes were of extremely good quality, and her stockings, now laddered, were of heavy flesh-coloured silk with patterned clocks on the outer sides. She had no hat or handbag. Ivy Violet felt a gullible fool for having allowed herself to be treated with such rudeness, yet the woman seemed calmer now, and sat at the kitchen table with her head bowed. Slowly Ivy Violet poured out two cups of tea and offered milk and sugar.

As time ticked steadily away on the grandfather clock, the woman – who said her name was Claudetta Dresden – began to relax.

By the end of the first cup of tea, Ivy Violet had

been given the full picture of events. The more she heard them, the more her own heart sank.

Claudetta Dresden had recovered her equilibrium. 'So you see this house really *does* belong to me, because it was left to me years ago by my own long dead mother when I was Terence Bolger's common-law wife – the reason for that being that his own wife would never divorce him. I was young and foolish and in love with him in those days – for he was always a man with a bit of property in the area, and bits of buying and selling going on, so we lived very comfortably here. In fact we actually moved here when I was only eighteen years old, because it was better than his house at Chorlton on Medlock which we let out, along with many cheaper, and smaller properties.

'Then a couple of years ago he became infatuated with this little know-all harlot of eighteen – just the age of me when we lived here at first – who got him firmly wound round her little finger, and they both did their best to get me out.

'We never had any children so I had no one to turn to, and eventually I gave in and went to an old flat he owned in Chorlton, rent free, whilst she moved in here. It was a terrible blow, and I had a sort of nervous break-down, whilst he went from strength to strength.' She gulped miserably and tears came to her eyes. 'Then, to cap it all, he got rid of little Miss Delilah last autumn because he found her two-timing him, with a physical training teacher, and pushed her out, bag and baggage, and put *my* house up for sale.'

Ivy Violet's mind raced back to the transaction of buying the house. Why on earth hadn't it all come to light at the time? And, as if reading her thoughts Claudetta said: 'I was such an utter fool when I was young. Bits of paper and official documents meant nothing to me. I just handed them over to Terence for him to look after, and accepted this house from my dead mother just as if she had been alive and given me a casual box of chocolates for my birthday to enjoy. I was so young and naive and my mother was so good and kind over my not being properly married to Terence Bolger. She never once reproached me.'

Ivy Violet felt quite weak with alarm. What on earth was she to do? She herself had been extremely lax when she had bought the property. She had fallen in love with it so instantly and was so confident that her own income could put right any repairs in coming years that she had taken many things on face value and left the estate agents to deal with it all. Yet it was obvious that Claudetta was telling the truth.

Claudetta brushed her hand across the scratches on her face. 'These were done when, in a moment of spring madness, I called today to challenge my husband Terence Bolger and was confronted by his latest young paramour in his house in Chorlton. She swore he was out, even though I could see the smoke curling from his pipe in the living-room from the front door. She attacked me like a young tigress and said she was pregnant, and I was in such a state after it that I can hardly remember how I got here.'

They both sat in silence for a few moments. It

was getting late.

'How will you get back?'

'By tram. There's a good link-up service. I'm sorry to have unburdened it all on to you, Ivy. I realise it's not your fault. But how would you feel in my shoes at such an injustice?'

Ivy Violet nodded silently. They were two single women fighting their own battles yet inextricably linked. What a fiasco.

'We'll keep in touch,' Ivy Violet said. 'And I'll visit Mr Trout at the estate agent's again, who found me your place.' She hardly realised she had said the last two words but it was not lost on Claudetta as tears of relief ran down her cheeks. 'So you do believe me. Thank God.'

When she had gone Ivy Violet went up to bed with legs like lead. All her months of cheerful energy had drained away. All her future was in jeopardy again. How was she ever going to stand it all and what was she going to do? She knew that sensible, cool-headed people might have said: ignore it all, it was just the ramblings of a completely batty stranger and there was no evidence whatsoever of any truth, and that she Ivy Violet Hilton was the proper owner of this house. But somehow it was no longer like that for her. Her whole happy dream had been destroyed.

Yet she was so weary from it all that she slept like a log, only wanting to drown herself into oblivion until the morning when her work in Manchester would be waiting for her.

*

Ivy Violet was standing there facing Mr Trout. He was a bit taller than she was and about three times as large round the waist. His round red face was gradually turning to a faint mauve. 'I just can't make head nor tale of what you're trying to say, Miss Hilton, and you'll have to be quick because there's more urgent business to attend to.' He fixed her with a glassy pop-eyed stare. She could hardly believe it was nice Mr Trout who had been so kind and competent about selling Flagstones to her, only a few months ago.

Ivy Violet's face set to hard, grim determination. 'If you so much as move out of this office before I've finished what I've got to say Mr Trout, I shall follow you to the ends of the earth until I've had my proper and fair hearing. It's a very serious matter and I believe what Mrs Bolger said.'

His face changed to a supercilious sneer. '*Mrs Bolger*? She ain't even 'is proper lawful wife. 'Is proper missus lives miles and miles away. 'Ee's the one wot counts – not 'er. '*Ee's* the one wot's in the property market. You women's all the same. You just think you can chop and change about like magic. No, I'm sorry Miss Hilton but this time you've come a cropper if you want to muck us about like that. You bought the place fair and square at the time and that's 'ow it stays as far as we're concerned. We're only agents and that's all there is to it.

'We deal with 'undreds and 'undreds of sales and a lot of water flows under our bridge madam. Your little 'ouse flutter is just a speck in the rushing torrent of the trade, and if some gets drowned well it's nowt to do with us.' Then he said: 'The best thing you can do is get hold of Bolger yourself and sort it out with him.'

Swiftly, with small beads of sweat appearing on his brow, Mr Trout wrote out Mr Bolger's address and handed it to her: Meadowsweet Lodge, Barnfield Path, Chorlton-cum-Hardy. 'It's not 20 yards from the tram terminus, in its own grounds.' Then he hustled her out of the office before one of the two partners saw her.

Ivy Violet hesitated at the entrance then said: 'By the way, do you still remember telling me about that other place he had for sale in Altrincham? Did it ever get sold, or is it still on your books?'

He stared at her suspiciously then seeing that she seemed to be back to normal, he too relaxed. 'Aye, I remember well enough, and no it's still ont' books – so if there's owt you want to know about it, ask him about that an' all. Tarrar then.'

In her office that day, Ivy Violet was faintly distracted with what to do about visiting Mr Terence Bolger. She had no idea of what he would be like, and it would have been no use trying to ask Mr Trout, for even if he had told her, his would have been a different picture from her own. It was quite right when folks said 'speak as you find'.

Meadowsweet Lodge was what was termed 'A Gentleman's Residence'. It was a large rather grim red-bricked double-fronted house with a stone portico, and the usual wine cellars and a large billiards room. Ivy Violet was thankful that she had been sensible enough to take a cab there, instead of the tram, for the iron-gated entrance did not lend itself to the pedestrian.

She paid the cab man and rang the bell.

It was three o'clock in the afternoon and pouring with rain.

An elderly female servant in an ankle-length grey skirt and white starched apron opened the door. She stared passively at Ivy Violet, her plump face like a silent stone.

'Would it be possible to see Mr Bolger? It's a matter of some urgency My name is Miss Hilton.'

'The master's not at home to casual callers.'

Ivy Violet stood there hesitating and inwardly cursing. She sensed that Bolger would be a slippery type and hard to pin down except by being on the spot to see him – and at least it was evident that he was there.

'I know it sounds rather impertinent, but could you just inform him that I'd like to see him if it's at all possible? I shan't take up too much of his valuable time.'

The servant weighed her up slowly, starting at her feet in their expensive IVY shoes and travelling up inch by inch over her heavy, short silk skirt and matching pale blue jacket and cloche hat, and resting briefly on her plucked eyebrows and her powdered nose. Then, giving a mild sigh of unimpressed boredom, she said: 'I'll see if master's available.'

Ivy Violet hardly dared to breathe as she turned

her back on the front door and tried to be interested in the lawns and crimson flowering rhododendrons, until she heard heavy footsteps and the sound of a throaty cough from the hallway.

'What was it you were requiring Miss . . . er . . .?'

She spun round with relief to face him. 'Miss Hilton – Miss Ivy Violet Hilton.'

He was a heavily-built man in his fifties in light-coloured flannels and a dark blazer. His face shone with the soft summer tan of prosperity and his thick wiry eyebrows gave an air of decision making. She could see immediately that he was a perfect sugar daddy – complete with a large diamond ring on his finger.

He gave her a passing glare. 'You'd better come in then and say what you've got to say. That name rings a bell. Are you by any chance the lady I sold my house to in Cheadle Hulme?'

Before she could reply he had ushered her into the drawing-room and had swiftly closed the door. For a moment she was stuck for words. How was she going to approach the subject when he already had fixed ideas and referred to 'his' house?

'Settled in all right then?' he said brusquely.

'Very well indeed, thank you. At least until two nights ago.'

'Oh aye?' He stiffened and his voice took on a cynical turn. 'And what does that mean exactly?'

'It means that I had a visit from a woman in distress.'

He frowned and became uneasy, trying to pass it

off as a sort of joke. 'You never did? Well, would you believe it? So why come all the way 'ere to tell us that?'

'It was your — ' She hesitated unintentionally due to nervousness, 'wife Claudetta Dresden.'

He stared at her with narrowing steely blue eyes. 'My wife? I think there must be some mistake, Miss Hilton, my name is Bolger, not Dresden and my proper wife's name is Bolger. We seem to be at cross purposes and I suggest you leave immediately.'

Ivy Violet's brain was racing. She could see she was going to get nowhere, yet she knew she was now saddled with all the terrible ramifications of his crooked ways concerning her property, and although it had nothing directly to do with her she knew things were bound to get more and more complicated if Claudetta persisted in regarding Flagstones as rightfully hers and was constantly kicking up a fuss.

'I don't want to encroach on your privacy, Mr Bolger — '

'Oh thank you kind lady. Thank you very, bloody much.'

'What I really wanted to ask was if you'd do me a swap and let me move into your other property in Altrincham which is apparently still for sale and which I've already looked at?'

'Blossom Street? *Swap over*?' He looked quite purple. 'I'll have you know, young woman, that Pear Tree Round'us, near Blossom Street, is larger and in better nick than Flagstones ever was — '

'But not yet sold? According to Mr Trout.' Ivy

Violet began to talk very quickly: 'The fact is Mr Bolger that your wife called on me in a very distressed and dishevelled condition with a badly scratched face and torn clothes. She told me all her history and how my house was rightfully hers. And fool, or not, I believe her Mr Bolger. But the main thing is that after doing all the repairs to it and getting it just right for spending a happy life in, I now find myself saddled with all your domestic affairs, and I'm just not going to be able to stand it – because believe me things will just go from bad to worse and before any of us know it we could all be in the newspapers.'

She paused breathlessly and saw him sitting there pale and motionless. Then he nodded and said: 'You could be right there madam. But there's a lot more to it on all sides than meets the eye. Give me a few days and I'll be in touch with you through Mr Trout.' Then without another word he politely ushered her to the front door.

Two months later, and true to his word, Ivy Violet was living legally and reasonably in the other house – with many secret regrets – yet knowing how lucky she had been to land up in the place she had shied away from. Even though it meant living so close to Maisy and Merrick.

CHAPTER 14

The Arbuthnuts

Ivy Violet was determined to steer well clear of
Merrick and Maisy when she moved to Altrincham.
She was so efficient she actually managed to avoid
them for the whole of 1925, only seeing their shapes
in the distance when going into Boots or a brief
glimpse of them with rolled up towels under their
arms taking the twins to the swimming baths across
the road from the railway station. She dodged away
in another direction.

Then, one day in the winter of 1926, Ivy Violet was
thrown into close contact with Hazel Arbuthnut in a
closing down sale of a china and glass shop. Every
housewife who ever owned a fur coat was there

pressed one against another to form a seething mass of coney, beaver, moleskin, squirrel, and astrakhan backed up heavily by imitation leopard skin. Ivy Violet and Hazel Arbuthnut both grabbed the same blue and white jar with a Chinese plum blossom design. To their horror it fell to the floor between them.

Quickly Ivy Violet made her way to a shop assistant and told him of the broken pot . . . 'In case anyone steps on it and gets cut . . .' then slipped casually from the crowded shop and along George Street, followed swiftly by Hazel Arbuthnut.

'Excuse me, I feel I must compliment you on your presence of mind,' said Hazel with regal charm. 'It was my fault really, the way it dropped on the floor. I'm sure it wasn't particularly valuable. There were any number of them. They were obviously copies but extremely attractive.'

Ivy Violet looked at her a trifle coldly; she couldn't stand over-fussy women. 'It's done with now, even if it belonged to the Emperor of China in the year dot.' She smiled rather stiffly and went on her way. By coincidence she bumped into Hazel yet again, outside Altrincham Hippodrome in Stamford Street, where Ivy Violet was looking at the notices for the next show.

'Fancy us meeting again so soon,' laughed Hazel who had emerged from a small car. 'Can I give you a lift home? My name's Hazel Arbuthnut, by the way.'

Ivy Violet hesitated. Then she said: 'It depends

which way you're going, but if you're going anywhere near St John's Church?'

'Of course. I know it well. My friend Maisy
Jackson and I visit regularly. It has those wonderful
stained glass windows in memory of Canon
Wainwright.'

Ivy blinked slightly. Arbuthnut! Of course. Why
on earth had she been so dim? Merrick had occasionally mentioned them. The rich, rhubarb people.

'Have you always lived here?' Hazel said as they
chugged along.

'For just over a year, but I know the area very well,
and I've enjoyed settling here.'

'I didn't quite catch your name?'

'Young,' said Ivy Violet hastily. 'Mrs Imogen V.
Young. I'm a war widow.' The words rolled off her
tongue with childlike ease as she secretly recalled
that the name had been born in salad days when
she was a dreaming schoolgirl: Imogen Violet Young
from the letters IVY . . . And now she was using
them to protect herself – to retain this sweet untrammelled patch of life with no more repercussions
from Flagstones, or anywhere else. She was now
tucked up in what she regarded as her true earthly
abode, looking forward to a summer of laburnum
blossom, climbing roses, and honeysuckle, with
Mary as her permanent housekeeper, and Mary's
daughter Hetty.

'Where *exactly* do you live then?' smiled Hazel
with brazen, snobbish inquisitiveness, as they drew
near the church.

'Off Blossom Street, with a footpath to it,' Ivy Violet said as she got out of the car.

Hazel frowned slightly, not being able to place it.

'Thank you ever so much. It was dreadfully kind of you,' said Ivy Violet giving her a wave to speed the car away.

But Hazel was in no hurry. She was warmly clad in thick lisle stockings and lace shoes, a Harris tweed costume, and green felt hat, ready for an inviting, sunny winter's day. Her family were all safely out of the way, her three children hopefully with their noses to the educational grindstone, and Toby well immersed in orders for rhubarb from a major canning factory. She smiled again: 'Look – why don't you come round for coffee one morning? How about tomorrow, at ten thirty. I shall be free then?'

Ivy Violet shook her head sadly and called: 'Impossible. I work most days in town. Perhaps some other time. It was kind of you to ask.' She turned and hurried along the pavement, not wanting to get involved any further.

But fate seemed determined to catch her out as, a month or so later, when she was with Maureen at the Opera House in Manchester to see Jack Hulbert and Cicely Courtneidge in a comedy, who should she meet in the foyer but both the Arbuthnuts.

'Toby, this is the person I was telling you about. Mrs Young who lives along Blossom Street,' said Hazel, smiling at Ivy.

Involuntarily, and with not much genuine attention, Toby put up his left hand and groomed the tweaky end of his waxed moustache with slow studied care as he shook hands with his right. 'Pleased to meet you. Lovely show – what?'

'We're with some friends – the Jacksons,' explained Hazel smiling forcefully, 'but they're just away yonder in the crowd at the moment, aren't they Toby?'

'Mmm . . . Quite right my dear. Exactly right.'

Ivy Violet smiled and nodded. He seemed quite a pleasant man, and rather reserved. Not a bit like one would have imagined a rhubarb king. He was slim and medium sized with a well-cut dark, caped coat and a dark blue cravat.

'If you'll excuse me. I must go to find a friend.' Ivy Violet moved quickly away from all of them and was soon lost in the chattering groups of theatregoers, as she looked for Maureen.

Then suddenly her way was completely barred.

'Ivy Violet! What a terrific surprise! How are things? I heard you'd moved to Altrincham. This is Clementina by the way. She's the new star of that Chekhov play.'

'Maxi!'

Whilst she was talking to him Merrick and Maisy drifted past. She knew Maisy had seen her and was pretending not to have but it did not matter because she was on neutral ground.

Maxi told her about Crystal who was now eleven. His eyes fixed Ivy Violet's own in a deep, affectionate glance, while his lady friend stood by politely with smiling acceptance.

On the way back to Altrincham that evening with Maureen who was staying with her, Ivy Violet sat mostly in silence as Maureen chattered away about their night out. Her own mind was still immersed in the throes of seeing Maxi again and catching up on all his news. He was obviously thriving.

Then about a week later she received a telephone call. It was his voice. 'It's quite important Ivy. When could I come and see you – either at your home – or at the office? I should prefer it to be in Altrincham if possible?' His voice was serious and intense.

Whatever could it be? She became uneasy. It was good to have met him again, but not to get too involved. Now she was so settled all she really wanted was to be left to her comfortable life and to concentrate on her shoes in the hope that they would always be successful.

With a slightly sinking heart she agreed that it might be best if he came to Altrincham, if the errand was private and personal. 'Come here for midday lunch, Maxi, whilst Hetty is out with Mary. It's my home help Mrs Podmore's day off next Tuesday too, so we'll be entirely private.'

She heard his voice change with satisfaction: 'Fine. I'll be there for eleven-thirty.'

True to his word, he arrived exactly on time, brisk and smiling.

Just as they were half way through their midday omelettes he said casually: 'Don't you think it's time you took on another partner in the firm?'

The silver-plated fork slid from her fingers.

'*Another* one? Whatever for? Surely you're joking?'

He smiled at her calmly and reassuringly. 'It's no joke. I'd like to at least buy some shares.'

'*You* would?'

'Yes, me. Surely it isn't such a strange idea?'

'It's a bit sudden.' Ivy Violet was secretly astounded. 'I've been getting on perfectly well with just Maureen and Trev. It's all very simple and uncomplicated.'

'But you'll need to go on expanding. You can't just become static, because if things should take a turn for the worst – which is quite likely in these strike-ridden, jobless times – you might succumb to a rich businessman buying you out as if you were just a bundle of fish and chips in newspaper.'

Her face paled slightly. 'I'll wait until that day arrives.'

'But by then I might not be around to make the same offer.' His eyes met hers with quizzical irony. 'Better the devil you know – than the one you don't.'

They finished the meal with pears and cream in brooding silence. As he wiped his mouth on a dinner napkin and stood up Maxi said: 'Anyway, think about it. I'm lucky enough to have a bit of surplus cash at present and I want to invest it in something interesting. We'd make a formidable pair . . .'

When he had gone Ivy Violet lay on the chaise longue and looked up at the small glass chandelier hanging from the ceiling. Why, for heaven's sake, had he pushed himself back into her life? Wasn't it enough for him to live in comfort with his musical performances and his young actresses?

But the more she dwelt on the subject – the more she could see a grain of sense in the idea of having him as a partner, and at the same time getting a few more rich investors. His words echoed back to her: 'I'll take care of all that side. All you have to do is to keep on designing shoes.'

Maxi Dingle's visit faded like racing April clouds. Ivy Violet heard no word from him nor did she try to get in touch. She ploughed on with her shoes, and added yet another design to her book of original 'firsts', coupled with private shoe displays and launchings at various salons, boutiques, and fashion houses round the city.

One day after an IVY footwear display at a very successful mannequin show in Kendal's, she was approached when she was tidying up by a man in a grey cape coat, and she knew instantly it was Toby Arbuthnut.

'Excuse me if I'm incorrect, but didn't we once meet at the theatre? You are Mrs Young if I'm not mistaken? My wife often speaks of you and wonders how you're settling down. She rarely sees you at social gatherings.'

Ivy smiled apologetically. 'It's because I work. My time is limited where coffee mornings and women's clubs are concerned.'

His eyes were alight with curiosity as he gazed at the catwalk now covered in a white sheet. 'Do you work for this outfit then?'

She nodded cautiously. 'I work for IVY Shoes, if that's what you mean.'

'What doing? Typist? Clerking? I'll bet they don't pay you much.' He began to get slightly overfamiliar. 'You'd probably do better coming to work for a person like me. I need a smart woman around.'

Ivy Violet tried to look suitably impressed. 'It's very good of you to think of me, but I get by quite well thank you. However, if the occasion ever did arise when I was looking for a change, I'd get in touch.'

He lingered about uncertainly, and began to prod her with questions. 'What's your boss like then? Was it that fellow you were talking to at the Opera House that night – the one with the seductive blonde?'

His eyes flickered playfully, as Ivy Violet felt her temper rising. The cheek of him, and to think she had thought he was quite a gentleman. It only went to show that those cape coats he wore covered a multitude of sins when it came to judging females, she thought. Clearly, he thought she was in a lower station than his own – from where he was perched, at the top of his large spacious rhubarb leaf . . .

'As a matter of fact my boss happens to be a woman.'

'God help you, my dear. They always reckon they're the worst. Anyway it's been very nice meeting you again.' He did not bother to shake hands. 'I'll pass on your regards to Hazel. Quite a coincidence our getting together in here. You'd better be getting back to wherever you have to go in case the supervisor catches you. I only happened to be passing through to get our maid some black silk stockings, but don't forget what I said.' He put his hand to the small breast pocket in his waistcoat and withdrew a gleaming white card. It said: 'Toby Faversham Arbuthnut, Managing Director, Rhubarb House, Hanging Ditch. Purveyors of pure canned foods and bottled condiments.' Then getting out his gold-nibbed fountain pen he wrote on the back with a flourish, 'Call and see me any time T.F.A.'.

Ivy Violet hurriedly bid him adieu, slipped the card into her handbag, and went back behind the scenes for the final clear up.

Maximilian Dingle had just had the worst shock of his life. He had visited his private doctor and been given a dire warning.

He had gone to St John's Street in Manchester and been told by Doctor Flavious that unless he rested his voice completely for 12 months no one could be responsible for the consequences. 'All this laryngitis is a symptom of your vocal cords rebelling against the massive strain of years,' he said, 'so you'd better be prepared to change your life style.'

Maxi was utterly despondent as he drove back to his large house. He was hit by a feeling of loneliness. He was not a man to confide in his new housekeeper or one of his secretarial underlings. Since the time that Ivy Violet had left him the flat at the top of the house was rarely used except by acquaintances in show business.

He decided to ring Ivy Violet immediately and fixed up an appointment to see her. This time in her town office.

'She's in this afternoon,' said Maureen.

'Tell her it's urgent.' He rang off abruptly.

It was the beginning of July and Merrick Jackson and family had all gone to Port Erin on the Isle of Man for a week – even though it meant that the twelve-year-old twins, Arabella and Rupert, had to miss school.

Maisy was delighted not only with the holiday but also that Merrick was doing so well these days at a time when so many others were out of work. They were indeed in another bracket, as she described to her friend Hazel Arbuthnut the exact spot where their boarding house was. 'It's two minutes from the beach – facing the sea – at the lighthouse end.'

Meanwhile, Ivy Violet was entertaining Maxi with cool lemonade at a white, wrought iron table, close to the ancient walled pear trees. She had succumbed to his suggestions of partnership and the business relationship was now three weeks old.

'I must say,' admitted Ivy Violet as she smiled at him: 'It's much better having you to turn to, but on the other hand I do hope your voice gets better so you can go back to what you really like doing.'

He nodded as a slight shadow crossed his face. 'I'm sure it will. And in any case I wouldn't dream of moving out of IVY Designs now, even when my voice does get better, so it's all proved to be a mixed blessing of fresh horizons. He paused then said casually: 'I expect our main aim is to have as many investors as we can, and I think I've found one, but I don't want you to worry about it.'

She frowned. What now? Just when things seemed to be going so well. Surely not a stranger to upset the apple cart?

'Do you remember that night months ago when we met at the Opera House?'

She nodded with foreboding.

'Well, I bumped into a businessman who must have seen us there, and for some reason we got talking. He lives not far from here and his name's Arbuthnut. I believe he once met you when you were doing a fashion show at Kendals and mistakenly assumed you were an ordinary assistant.'

Ivy Violet's heart began to quicken with alarm. Not *him* for heaven's sake!

'Surely you d-d-don't mean Toby Arbuthnut from the rhubarb firm? He's a friend of friends of mine. But he has absolutely nothing to do with me. In fact I try to steer clear of them all.'

Maxi's face broadened into a bright smile. 'That's the bloke! Seems to have money to spare and isn't quite sure what to do with it.'

Ivy Violet was aghast. 'He knows exactly what to do with it – put it back into his rhubarb. It's absolutely ludicrous wanting to divert it into IVY shoes! Before I know where I am he'll have taken the whole thing over! It's different with you, because you were one of the people who got me started, and you understand the fashion trade. But him? With his purveying of canned foods and bottled condiments? *No thank you.*' Her face clouded over in puzzled amazement: 'What on earth's come over you Maxi? It was you who warned me in the first place about "mere businessmen tycoons" buying me out. It was one of your reasons for wanting to be part of it all. So that designer shoes weren't treated like fish and chips in newspaper.'

He looked slightly ashamed. 'There's no real reason why he shouldn't take an interest in IVY shoes, even if he is a rhubarb king. Some of those types yearn to be linked with more artistic fields. And the more serious investors the better.'

'Not for me thank you, Maxi and that's final.'

His lips set in a hard thin line. 'Please yourself,' he muttered coldly. 'But don't come crying to me in times of trouble in the future.'

She had never heard such fury in his quiet voice.

They both sat there in sullen silence. Then Ivy Violet relented. 'Perhaps I was a little rash, and as you say, the more investors the better. Especially with your being involved to balance things up.'

His face brightened again. 'Thank goodness you can see what I mean, Ivy. It's a purely financial partnership, and there'll be lots of legal safeguards for all of us. We could at least have a meeting with him about it? Let's drink to it.'

Ivy Violet relaxed slightly as they drank. Perhaps she was getting too pernickety, too small-minded and restrictive about her thriving business. 'Yes, you're right Maxi. I'm getting too narrow in my approach.'

Later, when Maxi had gone, she began to hunt for something. It was the small white card Toby Arbuthnut had so flippantly presented to her when she was working in Kendals on her shoe exhibition: 'Call and see me any time T.F.A.'

At the end of the following month Ivy Violet was in her Manchester office when Maureen announced that Mr Toby Arbuthnut was on the phone. 'He says he won't keep you long, but it's very important.'

She listened to him with a certain dry contentment. He no longer regarded her as Imogen Violet Young, the name she had fobbed him off with at the Opera House. He addressed her as Miss Hilton.

'I just wanted to apologise for the way I treated you when I met you once in Kendal's. I hadn't realised you actually *owned* IVY shoes and that the name of Mrs Young was just an everyday disguise away from the pressures of your busy life.'

What smarm. Ivy Violet's eyebrows rose a fraction. So that was why she had chosen the romantic name of Imogen V. Young all those years ago. How good of him to tell her.

His voice pressed on with polite persuasion: 'Actually, I don't know whether you're aware of it, but some months ago I was speaking to a mutual friend called Maxi Dingle, and that was how the puzzle of your name and your actual links with the shoes came to light. I felt quite a fool when I told Hazel your proper name and exactly who you were.'

She groaned to herself. She knew it was inevitable in the end to face being a proper resident of Altrincham and not be trying to dodge Merrick and Maisy, and the Arbuthnuts, like some dancing shadow.

'Names don't really matter all that much, Mr Arbuthnut, otherwise I would never have played about with them. After all, it's the way we treat people that counts.'

It sounded a trifle pious but even then he did not seem to understand. 'Yes, yes . . . er quite . . . You must come round for dinner with us some time. It's very difficult for men to know sometimes what sort of women they're talking to.'

She burst out laughing. 'I know exactly what your insults meant.'

'You did? Thank Heavens!'

'So what was the real point of this very important, *quick* phone call?'

'Actually it was to ask if you needed investors in your firm. Your friend Maxi Dingle said he was becoming a director, and he was telling me about it.'

There was silence. Then Toby Arbuthnut said with a meek tentativeness: 'I was wondering if I could join you as a sleeping partner — ' Realising in a panic the *double entendre* of his words he began to fluster.

Ivy pretended she had not noticed. But the idea

of him as a sleeping partner in the firm did not disturb her as much now, chiefly because of Maxi's own approach when they had talked about it. For as he had said, there was no reason why a man in rhubarb could not be interested in more artistic investments.

'Perhaps one day we could meet and discuss it together, Mr Arbuthnut. In Altrincham, at either my home or yours, along with Hazel.'

His enthusiasm waned slightly. 'Good idea. Although Hazel doesn't usually have anything to do with my business affairs. She wouldn't even thank me if I invited her.'

'Anyway, I'll leave it to you to fix up the next move, Mr Arbuthnut. Goodbye.' She rang off swiftly.

The next time Hazel met Maisy Jackson was over coffee at the Arbuthnuts' mansion – a splendid monster of Victorian enterprise complete with small turrets near Bowdon Downs. It had six bedrooms, two attics, large cellars, a billiards room, vegetable gardens, green velvet lawns and a pony paddock. The name of it was Damozell, and there were signs saying Beware of The Dog and No Hawkers or Circulars on rather better quality enamelled signs than where Merrick and Maisy lived.

'We'll go into the drawing-room,' said Hazel when Maisy arrived. 'There's a lot for us to talk about, and cook has baked some really good biscuits for once.'

Maisy sat there in luxurious expectancy. She adored going to Hazel's. She gazed with fondness at the grand piano and wished they had one – especially with her own musical interest. It did not seem quite fair for the Arbuthnuts to have such a jewel lying there hardly ever used when she would have played on it all day long. Or used it for home concerts with some of her star pupils.

Hazel brought in the coffee herself on a square wooden tray with brass handles which had a beautiful little tray cloth all handmade, with an intricate pattern in finest angular cross-stitch, in blue and pink and golden yellow.

'Toby might be joining up with that luxury shoe outfit IVY creations,' said Hazel triumphantly. 'It will be another silver arrow for his quiver, and quite a change from rhubarb.'

Maisy stared at her in uncomprehending and shocked surprise. What on earth was going on? Was she hearing things? She had taken two pink pills the night before and wondered if she had overdosed. She nodded and gave a polite smile just in case she had not understood.

'Apparently Miss Hilton has given us the option of visiting her at her own place near Blossom Street, or she will come here to discuss it. I do know her slightly already. It's that woman I once mentioned that I thought might have been a good friend for you and me – but I mistakenly thought she was called Mrs Young. She always said she was too busy to join in local things, as she worked mainly in Manchester. I had no idea she was IVY Shoes.' Hazel was beaming all over her face as Maisy's own plump countenance became more and more uneasy.

Whatever was Ivy Violet Hilton doing here of all places? She was obviously up to no good. Maisy looked grimmer and grimmer.

She was chasing Merrick! That's what it was. It was as clear as daylight.

'Are you quite all right Maisy? I don't want to be rude, but you look *awful*. I do hope it isn't these biscuits. I have to watch cook like a hawk sometimes.'

Maisy shook her head and tried valiantly to smile. 'So where was it you said she lived?'

'Just off Blossom Street.

'We must have her round for morning coffee some time, when she's free. She's ever so nice. Though I wouldn't think she's very easy to manoeuvre. She always seems to know her own mind.'

'I'm sure she does,' said Maisy through gritted teeth. 'I've a feeling I knew her quite well when we were girls, and I don't want to sound like a gossip, but she hadn't got a very good reputation regarding the opposite sex, but of course she was only about sixteen and I blame her family background. It was years ago and times have changed. But if it's the same person that I knew, she is very strong willed.'

There was a thoughtful silence as they drank their coffee, and Hazel Arbuthnut tried to look very understanding. She was slightly more liberal and less formal and dogmatic than Maisy.

Later that day when Maisy was in her own domain in Albert Road, she made a point of greeting

Merrick in a special way when he got back from work.

'Come into the front room,' she said. 'The twins are out and I've just brewed you a pot of tea. There's something I want to tell you before you have your proper meal.'

CHAPTER 15

All Claws

Hazel Arbuthnut did not tell Maisy Jackson everything that went on in her life, especially to do with Toby's business affairs. Partly because she did not know much about business. As long as Toby could find the income to pay for a mansion to live in, with essential servants such as gardeners, cooks and cleaners, first-class education for the children, and continental holidays (linked with business trips to sell rhubarb on the Rhine) which she occasionally went on, she considered life to be very satisfactory and never asked him too many questions.

This was the direct opposite of Maisy Jackson's life – where Merrick had his humble affairs dissected with cold precision from the second he left his house to the moment he got back.

Merrick had now found a friend of the same age as himself at the Bowling Club. Called John Throstle, he was what was termed 'a bit of a card'. He also had a very strict wife, so that at every available moment Merrick and John Throstle worked for the bowling club, both winter and summer, arranging outings and events to make money, and keeping the books in order.

Unknown to Maisy, the Arbuthnuts had already had an informal business meeting at their house with Ivy Violet, a solicitor and an accountant. This resulted in Ivy Violet deciding to accept Toby Arbuthnut into the financial side of IVY Shoes.

'Do you think we should invite Merrick and Maisy round for a meal at the same time as Ivy Violet Hilton?' said Hazel to Toby one spring day. 'It seems so strange that we now know all of them in quite an intimate way – yet they seem to keep well apart. Miss Hilton certainly never mentions the Jacksons and Maisy was quite rude about Miss Hilton's early background, yet I for one find Miss Hilton to be the most charming and worldly person, and she never seems a bit afraid of our two Alsatians, which I think is a good sign of character.'

Normally, Toby Arbuthnut would have left it all to his wife and shown only lukewarm enthusiasm for any of it. But at the sound of Ivy Violet's name his eyes brightened.

At first Hazel did not notice his interest. But when the boisterous enthusiasm continued to the extent of Toby suggesting that he should look after Ivy Violet at the dinner, and that she should look after Vernon Kettlehulme, their next door neighbour, who lived in a place similar to their own (and was a well-preserved fifty with a wife who had chosen to stay abroad), she felt slightly disturbed. It was so out of character for Toby to show interest in anyone else but herself and his rhubarb.

And so it was decided to arrange a dinner party for eight comprising of Toby and Hazel, Merrick and Maisy, Celia Blombispham of the caramel toffees, and her latest male partner, Henry Crabtree, a glass millionaire, Ivy Violet and what Hazel termed 'Vernon the rogue male'. Usually Hazel was straightforward and well-meaning, but now she was unsettled, and could not quite bring herself to be completely open about certain guests. Ivy Violet had no idea that the Jacksons would be there, and the Jacksons had no idea Ivy Violet would be there. Hazel thought that it was the perfect way to get everyone integrated into Altrincham society and into her own little conclave.

Ivy Violet looked in her wardrobe, and wondered what to wear. She felt something very simple was the order of the day and eventually chose an emerald green Molyneux dress with a tailored look. It had a V neck, a dropped waist and a short straight skirt. She wore a piece of costume jewellery with it – a silver salamander set in paste diamonds and pearls across her shoulder. These days her lustrous chestnut brown hair was shingled into soft Marcel waves, and at nearly thirty-one she was in her sophisticated prime – when a woman has just about learnt the art of making the best of herself – with good results.

In the Jackson household Merrick refused outright to go to the dinner party at all as it clashed with his Bowling Club activities. The years of reasonable prosperity had produced a husband who was asserting himself more. He had found his haven of like-minded souls who had no time for fancy affairs which bore no relation to their own 'family nights' full of potted meat sandwiches, jellies, and fruit cake, presided over by a gigantic tea urn.

'You can't just not go, Merrick!' roared Maisy with exasperation. 'It would be a complete insult to Hazel and Toby, and I certainly couldn't go on my own. It's just not done. And to think of all the years we've been here and known them and how I've always seen to it that we mix with the very best people; people of music and the arts – and you suddenly start to sink back into places like the Bowling Club, where they talk about nothing but the quality of their woods, the texture of the bowling green, and the length of the hose-pipe.'

Merrick sat there groaning inwardly, his spirits drooping even lower as he heard the next words: 'And I'll certainly need a new outfit for it. There was the very thing in Madam Zorina's in Hale. It was in her window only today – completely alone against a white satin background, a beautiful green and blue georgette frock with frills twisting round it like a heavenly helter-skelter from neck to hem, and all set off with a lovely sea-blue ribbon — '

'But we can't possibly afford anything like that Maisy! It's only a *meal* you're going to, at their house. We aren't going to a banquet to meet the King and Queen.'

'Oh, so you are going with me then?'

'I expect I've no option. But you certainly can't get anything from that Zorina woman's place. Even the Bowling Club know it's just a front for a kept woman, and it hardly matters whether she sells her frocks or not at those inflated prices.'

'I might try Pauldens then,' said Maisy purring with triumph. 'I'll ring Hazel and tell her we'll go.'

It so happened that Ivy Violet was late for her dinner appointment with the Arbuthnuts. She felt quite bad about it, but it was entirely unavoidable. Just as she was ready to go, poised in front of her own bedroom mirror in triumph, Hetty who was now five, trapped her finger in the toy box in the nursery.

'It's *bleeding*, Ivy!' she yelled, as she ran into the room over to Ivy Violet. Blood began to trickle in bright smears all over the front of Ivy Violet's emerald green dress, so that she had to take it off immediately and soak it in cold water.

'I'm supposed to be at the Arbuthnuts' already, Mary,' she groaned as she struggled into another frock.

'You poor, poor soul,' groaned Mary in anguish. 'I should have checked up on Hetty. I was down in the kitchen and never even heard her at first.'

Ivy gave a twisted smile. 'Nothing like being late

for dinner parties. They always think people who do it are just attention seekers. Anyway, thank goodness this is only going to be a very small, informal gathering. It shouldn't take me more than a few minutes to get there in the car, so there's no need to ring them.'

'Get going then,' said Mary. 'And stop worrying about Hetty. She's just playing you up a bit. She'll stop crying the moment you close the front gate, I swear.'

'Oh, *there* you are.' Hazel smiled at her with relief as she arrived. 'I hadn't said anything to the others about anyone being missing, because I knew you'd have rung if it was anything really serious. Anyway, just in time to start the meal so no real harm done. There'll be eight of us altogether.'

Eight of them? Ivy Violet's heart sank. She hated arriving anywhere in a rush and fluster and not knowing what she was in for. She began to wish she had put on her lemon moiré silk instead of this rather mundane striped frock which Hetty called 'Ivy Violet's deck-chair dress'.

Hazel led her into the drawing room and introduced her to the others. 'Dinner is about to be served. This is Miss Ivy Violet Hilton. She was inadvertently held up.' Hazel introduced her to everyone then Toby arrived and took charge. 'I'll look after you from now on,' he said boldly. 'Hazel will do the honours with Vernon.'

The whole introduction was so quick, followed by everyone being moved to the dining room and put into their correct seats by Hazel, Toby and a maid, that Ivy Violet was only vaguely aware that Merrick and Maisy were there. It was rather a case of her accepting them as a familiar integral part of her life and being slightly surprised to see them, but not having the time to register anything else as they were all sat down and bombarded by the hors-d'oeuvres.

Then, after a few delicate forkfuls of anchovy and mayonnaise, she realised that Merrick and Maisy were directly opposite her beyond the silver cande-labrum. Their mouths were too full to say anything. The rest of the meal was taken over with the antics of Mrs Blombispham's partner, Henry Crabtree, who had a very loud voice and jovially balanced at least 40 matches on top of an empty wine bottle and set fire to them. Everyone held their polite breaths and clapped with relief when the small charred mess was all over.

It wasn't until they had all been led to the library for coffee and liqueurs that everyone was speaking and mingling properly. It was then that Ivy Violet found herself alone with Merrick.

She was surprised in a way. She had at least expected some sort of verbal foray with Maisy, but Maisy was occupied elsewhere, waving her plump fingers delicately about in expressive pianissimo ges-tures close to Vernon Kettlehulme's neat grey moustache. They were discussing grand pianos: he invited her to pop round and see his grand piano sometime and told her the sad tale of his invalid wife who had to spend her time in warmer climes for medical reasons.

'Fancy you being here,' murmured Merrick to Ivy Violet. 'I never even knew you were living so close.'

'You're looking well,' she said slowly.

'You too.'

There was a shy silence.

Then Merrick said: 'I should have been at the bowls with my pal John Throstle. It's Maisy who likes all this sort of thing.'

'Well, it won't do you any harm once in a while. It's no good trying to get sympathy from me, Merrick. I'm not keen on it either, but it just so happens that Toby Arbuthnut is now part of IVY shoes.'

'You're joking?'

'I am not! It's a bit of a long tale – but that's how it is. I only hope it works out all right.' She paused, then said, 'How are the twins?'

'Driving us mad as usual. Arabella is thirteen and wants to be a ballet dancer but is covered in puppy fat, takes size six shoes, and is good at chemistry. Rupert wants to be a jockey, is covered in pimples, can hardly jump a pony over the smallest fence and is good at music. Arabella's teacher sees Arabella's future in Boots the Chemists, probably in their library department. And Rupert's teacher sees his future as a piano tuner. Anyway at least they're both fit and healthy and that's what matters most.

'How's your housekeeper's little girl?'

'Hetty? Oh, fine. She's four now and goes to kindergarten near Sandy Lane in the mornings.

Quite a little boss, by all accounts.'

'Influenced by you being around – no doubt?'

They both laughed, then looked solemn again as Maisy came towards them followed by Vernon, but even so Ivy Violet had felt a slight pang of self pity, when Merrick had so cheerfully mentioned his own children. She wished for one small child of her own. Then she brushed the thought away as sheer sentimentality. Life was being very kind to her at the moment, and Mary's child in her home was just enough, with none of the real hindrances and responsibilities.

Maisy ignored Ivy Violet completely. She spoke to her husband: 'Merrick, Vernon has invited us round for me to play his grand piano some time. It's a Bechstein.'

Merrick nodded politely. 'Very nice.'

'I was telling him how you were manager of a music shop when you were only very young and knew a lot about them.'

'Is that so? Yes. I did once work in a music shop – although it wasn't — '

'Vernon says he's always in on Wednesday evenings, and he'll be there this Wednesday,' said Maisy smoothly.

'I usually go to the bowling on Wed — '

'You usually go to the bowling on *Thursdays*, dear.' Maisy fixed him with a penetrating scowl, and Merrick gave a deep quivering sigh.

'Would you like to come too, Miss Hilton?' Vernon Kettlehulme was turning all his charm on. The invitation fell from the air like a small exploding egg, as all three of them recoiled with sudden surprise.

'No thank you,' said Ivy Violet hastily. 'Wednesday is the one day I can never manage.'

'In that case,' said the unquenchable Vernon smiling with hard-baked glee at his two handsome young women, and knowing that Merrick did not really want to visit him, 'why don't you ladies come round together on Thursday when Mr Jackson is otherwise occupied?'

There was a moment's stony quiet, then Maisy said: 'I'm not quite sure. I might have to look in my diary.'

'What about you then, Miss Hilton?'

Ivy Violet hesitated. She didn't like to see him snubbed completely, and Maisy and Merrick's plans had nothing to do with her. It might be better to accept and get the visit over with to put things in an amicable situation for the future. Also he was Hazel and Toby's next door neighbour and had obviously been invited to even up the numbers at the dinner party along with herself. The fact that he was old enough to be her father made it all completely respectable.

'Right-o then. Yes I'd be pleased to accept your invitation. On Thursday?'

He nodded. 'About seven-thirty for a meal. Along with Mrs Jackson – if her diary allows her.'

That evening when the Jacksons arrived home Maisy went at Merrick, hammer and tongs.

'You ruined the whole thing, Merrick Jackson. You

completely let me down. You're positively obsessed by that tin-pot Bowling Club. I never felt so humiliated in all my life as when he asked *her* to visit him as well – and all because you made all that fuss about Wednesdays.'

'But you were the one who mentioned *Thursdays*, Maisy. We aren't mind readers. If you ask me he was just out to have a pair of women fussing round him. He's a right menace. Mysterious wife abroad? Tell me another! Believe me Maisy – I've met his type many a time.'

Maisy's lips went tight with anger. 'How on earth can you be so uncharitable as to say that about such a gentleman, Merrick? He was the very essence of decorum, and he needn't even have mentioned he had a wife at all if he'd wanted to be truly deceitful. There are others of my sex who really are menaces, and who were there tonight. Oh yes, don't try to bluster. I saw both you and Toby Arbuthnut sinking to her feet like a couple of jellyfish, and you and her having that tête-à-tête like long lost souls. Whenever will you grow up and be your age, Merrick?'

Merrick limped quickly away in a storm of inner fury as he heard her ranting on and on – her voice lapsing to a louder, less prim style of younger days. 'She knows damned well nowt about decent grand pianos. That Ivy Violet Hilton is just a jumped up shoe repairer's assistant from the dregs of a back street shop with airs and graces above her station. At least I was brought up with a proper bit of culture. She's the type that twists weak people like you,

Merrick Jackson, round her little finger. And the less we see of her and her loose ways, once I've got this invitation to see Vernon's grand piano over, the better.'

But Merrick was no longer listening. He had gone to get his Bowling Club notebook, and as he opened it he was happy again.

Generally speaking he could stand quite a lot of Maisy's tantrums and tirades without it actually worrying him unduly. He knew men and women took a gamble once they got married, and overall, to be safely back in his own comfortable home with all his bowling fixtures to dwell on, and a charabanc outing to Clitheroe ready to be fixed up for the club, with his friend John, was quite an acceptable married state.

Merrick knew he was lucky having Maisy as a wife, compared with John Throstle's domestic setup. John's wife Veronica would not even let him go out without a hat on his head, and insisted that he ate the cheapest sardine in oil sandwiches, and had a tangerine for his midday meal at the Council Offices every day of his life. John longed for the occasional shrimp paste sandwich, and a proper orange, and confessed to Merrick that he had his weekly pocket money doled back to him from his wages as if he was a small child. Constant weddings, with all the extras, for his innumerable and weighty-looking daughters drained his resources.

In the end, as the weeks rolled by, it was the best summer Merrick had ever known in his married life.

The Bowling Club was running like clockwork. The greens were in pristine condition, and his friend John Throstle had come to an arrangement with his wife about pleasing himself when he wore a hat and having sandwiches with more variety.

For Merrick, even the twins were perking up a bit and becoming less of a weight round his neck, and as for Maisy? Well, he could not quite get over her placid demeanour over money. He had hardly heard a nagging word out of her for weeks, and she was looking wonderfully healthy, as if she had been spending plenty of time in the open air. The truth was, that in spite of Maisy's ardent protestations to herself after her first outing to Vernon Kettlehulme's – when Ivy had never arrived but had actually sent her housekeeper instead with her apologies – she had been out with Vernon six times. She always assured herself that she would never accept any gifts from him, but was always slightly disappointed when there weren't any. She rode in splendour round all the best local places in Lancashire and Cheshire on secret outings, until on their fourth outing he took to pushing bank notes secretly into her handbag, and pretending he had not done so.

Then the rot set in. First Vernon's healthy looking wife came home briskly from abroad and the outings stopped as quickly as they had begun. Secondly, there was the accusation from Merrick . . .

She was having a cup of tea on Sunday morning with him when the twins were out, when he suddenly said: 'By the way, what exactly *is* going on

Maisy? People say you're gadding about with that old crock Kettlehulme in his car. I couldn't quite believe it. You never mentioned it to me.'

Maisy went scarlet. 'He's a lonely old man, Merrick. I don't want to hear any more about it. No woman is a *complete* slave.'

'And neither is a man Maisy. You've kept surprisingly quiet about it all.'

'I wasn't keeping quiet. There was just nothing of interest to tell you about it; especially with it being to do with shop gazing. You know how you hate me going shopping. Seeing as I never even bought anything it was a non-event as far as you were concerned.' Then she said: 'And for goodness sake shave properly. You've got two small cuts on your chin and some stubble just round your cheek bone. You really are getting careless about your appearance, Merrick.' Maisy's skill at carefully aimed tit-for-tat found its mark as Merrick stroked his chin uneasily.

Two days later Hazel happened to bump into Ivy Violet in Turnberry's Tea Shop as they nibbled at banana ice cream sundaes in cornet-shaped glass holders, using very long handled spoons.

'Maisy seems to have quite taken poor old Vernon Kettlehulme under her wing,' said Hazel casually. 'Toby and I once saw them in Southport in the distance, and she's often seen driving round with him. It's quite touching really. Yet strangely, she never ever mentions it and neither do I because it's none of my business.'

Ivy Violet ate her ice cream in silence. She wondered if Merrick knew. A slight glimmer of a secret smile rose to her lips as she thought about how, a few years ago, Maisy had been nasty to Merrick over his visits to her office in Manchester.

Hazel looked at her with curiosity – then they both stared at their sundaes, and began to laugh.

CHAPTER 16

The Dramatic Society

'I'm a bit worried about you, Ivy,' said Mary half jokingly one day, as they sat in the kitchen drinking tea. 'You lead such a quiet life. It's beginning to be a case of *you* always being my sitter-in for young Hetty whilst I'm out courting. To my mind, it all seems to stem from that very first dinner date you had with the Arbuthnuts and met your friends the Jacksons.'

'Mary! What's got into you?' Then as Ivy Violet saw the hurt look and rise of colour in Mary's face she said thoughtfully: 'Perhaps you're right. Maybe I'll land up in a nunnery. I've clung too much to those past, happy childhood times. That's what comes of always living in the same place you're brought up in. Maybe I should have been whisked off on a magic carpet much earlier on.'

She rarely spoke to Mary of earlier times. Normally they lived in the present with all its busy domesticity and Ivy Violet's business affairs, coupled with the love they both shared for Hetty.

Then impulsively Ivy Violet said: 'You see, I've known Maisy and Merrick since the year dot. It's almost as if we're fated to follow each other about, even though I've mostly tried to avoid them. I even tried to avoid living too close to them here in Altrincham, but it didn't quite work out.'

'But why do you feel so strongly about them?'

Ivy hesitated. She was not used to being quizzed about her motives. 'I expect – to be honest – it's because of Merrick. There was such a bond between us when we were young.'

'You really mean, you loved each other,' said Mary quietly. 'I know what it's like.'

'Yes. And then I grieved when he turned to Maisy, but that's life isn't it?' Ivy Violet got up with sudden haste from her chair and sighed. Then she smiled and said: 'I'll try not to be such a nun in future, I promise. I'll look for something I can join.'

'Have you ever thought of becoming a member of our Bluebell Dramatic Society?' Hazel Arbuthnut said to Ivy Violet, as they sat in Turnberry's Tea Shop, eating toasted teacakes oozing with butter. 'It would be so nice to see you taking part in more of our local affairs.'

It was the New Year and Hazel was playing the maid in a comedy called *One Over the Eight* by a local writer.

Ivy Violet smiled and shook her head. 'I couldn't act to save my life, although my friend Garnet Dingle, the one who died, worked with a professional company for some time . . .'

She was nearly going to reveal more, but closed up. Although Hazel was a good friend of Ivy Violet's (now that she had realised that Ivy Violet was not going to try and steal her husband), especially as Toby was involved in her shoe business, there was a certain guarded distance between them from Ivy Violet's side.

It was quite a different relationship to the one she had had with Garnet, or Sylvia years ago when they could reveal anything and everything to one another. Being friends with Hazel was more a case of being with an intelligent, warm hearted, wealthy but very conventional creature, who was always looking for other people's small problems to chew over and pretend to solve in a way that she considered satisfactory.

Ivy Violet had been to a number of the Dramatic Society's current productions but they were a far cry from the professional group Garnet had worked with, who tackled the works of Ibsen and Shaw and Chekhov.

'You don't need to actually be able to act,' persisted Hazel. 'We're terribly short of prompters, and people to help out behind the scenes. We'll grab you, or anyone else with open arms, and with you a busy working woman you'd be able to arrange it all to coincide with the times you were available?'

'I'll think about it,' said Ivy.

As she travelled home she did think about it, and by the time she was back in her own comfortable round house with a log fire glowing in the grate and her grey and white cat, Podger, purring on the hearth rug she began to think not only of that but her whole life.

She was now practically thirty-two, and Mary's daughter, Hetty, was quickly growing into a school-girl. It made her feel old to see Hetty in school uniform attending the local convent.

Thirty-two. She gave a quick shiver. Where did all the time go? When she went upstairs she looked at her face in the bathroom mirror. It hardly seemed to have changed, except that her neck seemed a bit scraggy, and she looked harsher when she wore make-up.

For a few seconds she thought about the state of things in general. The fact that in this year – 1928 – women would be able to vote on equal terms with men at the age of twenty-one, and how the whole country was deep in unemployment and poverty – particularly in the North of England. For she was one of the lucky and prosperous ones now – but for how long?

A couple of weeks later, she decided, after all, to join the Bluebell Dramatic Society as a general dogs-body. For some reason she felt a bit lonely these days even though she had such a band of loyal friends and workers like Maureen and Trev, and Mary. Yes, she missed proper male company, yet in all her dealings with men, the only one she had been really intimate with was Alfred.

It annoyed her sometimes when people hinted that she was some carefree, childless woman giving and receiving favours all over the place. She once pointed out to Sylvia, her old childhood friend, when on a very rare occasion they happened to meet: 'Just because you mingle with a lot of men in your life doesn't *mean* anything.'

Secretly she still missed the past and the painfully short sojourn with her dear husband Alfred so much that she longed desperately now to meet a decent man she could settle down with.

As soon as she joined the drama society she saw the answer to her prayer. He was tall, thin, and rather pale with floppy black hair and a worried look on his face. He was the visiting producer for *One Over the Eight* and also for their present production *Storm in a Teacup*. Normally, he worked on programmes for the radio.

'Cedric Plane,' murmured Hazel as she introduced them.

In a few minutes Ivy Violet realised that Hazel also liked Cedric Plane, and by the time she went home that evening she was aware that Hazel was secretly and madly in love with Cedric Plane and talked about him and nothing else. She knew that Ivy Violet had realised her secret.

'Of course I know he must be a few years younger than me . . . perhaps your age. But age doesn't matter does it?' She said earnestly: 'It's the person inside that counts with all of us. Now honestly Ivy – for a start – would you have thought that one of the first people you'd meet there tonight would be Vernon Kettlehulme? He only joined us a fortnight ago as an acting member to give his invalid wife a rest. But what I'm trying to say is it's not the outside that counts, it's the inside. I mean – take Vernon. There he is, as old as the hills, yet he's willing to join our little society and have a go – and we in our turn are glad to welcome him and support him in his adventure on to the boards. That's the beauty of having a visiting producer like Cedric Plane who is so wonderful to act for. I've never known a man with so much talent and perception. So much kindness and love. Yes, love Ivy. I think he loves everyone of us.'

Ivy Violet nodded solemnly. There was no doubt about it that Cedric Plane was a very interesting man and a definite charmer; but he didn't seem to be a saint. In fact one of his attractions was his faintly befuddled straitlaced vagueness that might well hold a multitude of sins. Ivy Violet's latent imagination began to work: suppose that pale face and floppy black hair revealed some awful monster who hated every one of them? That was his attraction: that streak of mystery in his personality as he stared with dark grey eyes, clad in green velvet corduroy trousers, striped shirt and bow-tie.

Dutifully Ivy Violet began to attend the meetings

of the Bluebell Dramatic Society regularly. Hazel, mad with desire, was always at Cedric's side with soothing suggestions about scenery and timing, and making sure that Vernon Kettlehulme came in from the correct side of the stage instead of following the best legs and fattest bottom that happened to be passing. Ivy Violet was a maker of tea, assistant dresser and general dogsbody.

She and Cedric were different parts of the Bluebell Dramatic Society. He was its centre stamen, whereas she was somewhere at the beginning of the stalk. Then, one evening, three nights after the opening of *Storm in a Teacup*, there was a disaster. Primrose Jansen slipped on a wet patch near the tea urn and had to be replaced with only 20 seconds to spare by another Ladyship (Ivy Violet) to say 'Fosdyke!' and 'Thank you Fosdyke' in the scene with Vernon, as the understudy had vanished.

It was a scene where the gardener, Mr Fosdyke, came in and told her Ladyship that the slugs had attacked the lettuces – just when the vicar was expected for tea. Mr Fosdyke was being played by Vernon Kettlehulme, and the prompter was a retired elocution teacher called Penelope Arkinsall. A crucial scene as far as the drama went, it was Vernon's one and only entrance and exit, his star turn as he made his first bid for the footlights. He was word perfect and knew his part well. In fact he had perfected it with such precision that he had timed every pause on his stop-watch to gain the most dramatic effect possible, as he clomped on stage in heavy boots and gardening clothes and a piece of straw stuck in a battered old hat.

'Your Ladyship . . .' He paused dramatically, and as he did so Penelope Arkinsall's sharp, piping voice came in just before his next line as she hissed in a voice loud and clear enough for a prima donna at the Royal Opera House: 'The *slugs* have *attacked* the *lettuce*'.

Vernon stood there startled and demoralised and stared at Ivy Violet who was trembling like a leaf and wondering whether she should have already uttered 'Fosdyke!' as he repeated the words in panic, getting them slightly muddled: 'The bugs have attacked them —'

'FOSDYKE!' said Ivy Violet in her loudest voice. She was in a cold sweat as complete silence fell and the sharp voice of the prompter struck yet again: 'Vicar. Vicar.'

Vernon Kettlehulme gulped: 'And the vicar has gone for a —'

'Thank you Fosdyke,' said Ivy Violet in a miserable panic.

Everyone started to howl with laughter.

'And the vicar has gone for his tea . . .' Vernon stopped and peered round. Then standing up to his full height he glared at the audience and said: 'It's no good you lot all killing yourselves. I was word perfect before I came up here. It is Miss Hilton and that prompter that are to blame. There's nothing more off-putting than a bloody prompter being there before you when —'

Quickly he was ushered off the stage by Cedric Plane as the curtains closed and the whole place erupted into prolonged applause.

Behind the scenes it was pandemonium as a short interval was announced. It was decided to skip the rest of that scene and have a small musical recital instead in the last act to lull everyone into a dazed and uncritical state.

Meanwhile Mrs Arkinsall claimed she would never be able to lift up her head with pride again and resigned then and there as prompter. Cedric Plane accepted her resignation with respectful thanks, as he glared slightly in Ivy Violet's direction and said it was unfortunate that she had been roped in for the emergency in her somewhat green state.

Ivy Violet knew then and there that her days of treading the boards were over for ever. She realised too that Cedric Plane was not quite as nice as she had imagined as he commanded her to sweep up a broken saucer in the kitchen. As for Vernon, it might well have been imagined that he would have left the players for ever, but no. His face to face confrontation with his public, and their resounding applause, had fired an even stronger sense of duty in his loins as he began to ask Cedric then and there if there would be a good part in the next play for him.

'How unfortunate for you, Ivy,' Hazel said as they went home that night. 'But at least, on Saturday when it finally ends, he'll be taking us all for a celebration drink at the George and Dragon.'

'What a pity I shan't be able to go,' said Ivy with

inner relief. 'I have to stay in with Hetty.' Hazel tried to look sad, but Ivy Violet knew she was delighted to be able to concentrate on Cedric Plane on her own.

Maisy Jackson was reading the evening newspaper. There was a short report of the play by the Bluebell Dramatic Society. She could hardly believe her eyes – Ivy Violet standing there next to Vernon Kettlehulme – the cheek of her, and him a man with an invalid wife living at home!

Merrick shuddered slightly. He knew that Maisy had some very good points and her heart was in the right place where her own family was concerned, yet he never knew which was worst – her posh performances, or her attacks on Ivy Violet. Fortunately tonight he was able to change the subject quickly because he was able to announce that he had been offered a top manager's job with Sunsell Holidays in Blackpool.

In some ways he was sorry to have to pull up his roots again, especially with being so involved with the Bowling Club, but Blackpool had more than one bowling club and they were all excellent. Even Maisy showed no objection and her tones seemed delighted as she rattled on about going to live in a big house at Lytham St Annes.

As for Ivy Violet, she had no idea that Merrick and family were even moving at all, until one day Hazel, after going on at length about her passion for Cedric Plane and his latest production *Trapped in a Lift*, mentioned that they had gone.

'Gone?' Ivy Violet was startled. Perhaps, she thought, Merrick had lost his job again and they were about to slide down the slippery ladder of fate to join the bottom rungs.

'They went the day before yesterday with a huge pantechnicon. By all accounts the twins were heart-broken. Young children rarely like to change their surroundings, and they hate losing all their friends suddenly. I believe the Bowling Club had a special farewell do for Merrick arranged by his friend John Throstle, and they gave him a set of woods as a leaving present. But they all plan to meet again at matches.'

Ivy Violet felt thoroughly forlorn. 'Is he going to be doing the same type of work?'

Hazel looked at her with puzzled eyes. What a strange question to ask, she thought. Ivy Violet's concern and emotional shock seemed almost as if she was his sister or something . . . 'Oh goodness – yes. He's even in a better position there. A much better status. He's going to be the manager of three different branches in Blackpool, and Preston, with an office of his own with an Axminster carpet and an oak desk – according to Maisy – though how she knows is a mystery.'

When she was at home again, Ivy Violet began to brood. Tears came into her eyes as she realised that her friendship with Merrick might now be ended for ever. For there was never going to be any communication with her as far as Maisy was concerned, and whenever she had seen Merrick in Altrincham it had always been by chance. But now there was no chance because she hardly ever went to Blackpool or Preston except to visit shoe shops.

The whole episode was almost like a personal bereavement as she thought back to their early years. They knew each other so well. They only had to say a few words and each of them knew by one sentence the state of a situation. She gave a sobbing sigh. Ah well that's how it was in life, she thought. One's loved ones come and go, and people survived, often with far more hardship in their lives than she had ever suffered.

There was also another cloud on the horizon. Hazel also mentioned that Toby was in a very edgy state financially.

'In the strictest confidence Ivy, and I know it'll be something of a shock for you but it's better to be forewarned . . . we ourselves might, only *might* mind you, have to withdraw some of our IVY shares to bolster up the rhubarb.'

Ivy Violet's state of gloom lasted about a fortnight and was hardly helped by Hazel confessing to her that Cedric Plane had suggested that he and Hazel should have a night out whilst Toby was away in London.

'Cedric's getting really embroiled in *Trapped in a Lift*,' said Hazel, 'and he wants to go somewhere completely private like the Waldorf to study their lifts to get a bit of real colour into it, before he goes on to *Three for Tennis* with me in the lead.'

*

The following year, one day in February just before St Valentine's Day, Ivy Violet received damaging news from the Arbuthnuts.

Her involvement with the Dramatic Society had gradually waned as she became more and concerned with keeping IVY Shoes afloat. It was a time of slump and business enterprises were going bankrupt every day. A determined ruthlessness took over. She was thirty-three and had even discarded the niceties of female make-up. 'I am as God made me,' she said to herself. 'For better or for worse.'

She had changed her wardrobe completely, preferring to wear only tailored grey suits or classic black frocks cut in severe styles with only a single diamond as jewellery.

The bad news was that the Arbuthnuts were taking all their shares out of IVY shoes. Toby had become a declared bankrupt due to the collapse of rhubarb. Hazel secretly admitted that the child she was expecting in three months belonged to Cedric Plane and was the reason she and Toby were moving to Windermere in the Lake District, where they planned to live rather frugally, in a six-bedroomed house.

Times were very bleak. Ivy Violet saw her own shoe sales slipping and slipping. She even feared she would have to close her Manchester office and work entirely from home – even getting rid of Maureen and Trev because of the cost of their wages. Mary too might have to remove Hetty from the convent to an ordinary elementary school, because Ivy Violet would have to pay her less for being the housekeeper.

The news of this was a terrible shock to the Simpkins. Maureen was now twenty-six and considered herself to be a spinster for ever with her own neat little flat in West Didsbury. Trevor was engaged to a doctor's daughter, slightly older than himself, who came from Urmston and had once been crossed in love in her early youth by the rich son of a local baker who left her waiting at the church on her wedding day. This time, however, after courting Trevor for five years, she planned to get married at the register office.

'However will I be able to afford somewhere decent for me and Lotty to live?' said Trevor bluntly. 'This is the worst day of my whole life.'

'And where will I ever find such an interesting job again,' wept Maureen. 'All I'd get anywhere else is an ordinary typing job – but not even that with all this unemployment.'

That particular night Ivy Violet thought long and hard about what to do, then the next day she put forward her plan. 'I'm not pushing you, and it's only based on my own needs so think carefully about it. I've decided to sell the Manchester office and work from home. Meanwhile if you Trev, and your lady love, want to live with me rent free in Altrincham for a while, in exchange for a bit of all round help, and if Maureen is willing to travel into Altrincham three days a week to come here to work, I think we could manage until times are better. Even though it'll be a bit of a squash.'

They both agreed immediately. Maureen remarked that she might, after all, be able to get some other work to do as a nursing assistant to a dentist in Didsbury, during the other spare days.

To Ivy Violet's relief it all worked very well. In the next few months she struck even more good luck with a complete change of plan in her shoe designs. On Maureen's suggestion she concentrated on patterns for children's patent leather shoes, particularly ankle straps which were starting to be so popular with ten-year-old girls. Quite by chance they had found a small manufacturer who made cheap shoes for the general market with canvas linings inside the patent leather, rather than the double leather lining of higher quality, more expensive shoes. Ivy Violet found that even in these times of terrible hardship, her IVY ankle straps for girls, her patent leather boots for boy toddlers and all manner of other cheaply-designed but attractive styles sold all over the north of England in small shops and on market stalls. This gave her time to still keep up the threads of the luxury fashion shoes that she loved so much.

CHAPTER 17

Aunty Ivy

Maxi Dingle was in a fuming temper about his daughter Crystal. He had sent her to the best high school for girls he could find, but she had been thrown out due to some antics in the classroom involving imitation of the headmistress, and causing trouble next door in the boys' school.

'The only thing for you,' he said bitterly, 'is to learn what the proper adult world is like, and do some proper work.' Henceforth he got in touch with Ivy Violet to see if she could help him out, for Crystal had always regarded Ivy Violet as an aunt.

He arrived at Altrincham on a day late in August when everywhere was deluged by sudden bursts of rain and gales with interims of hot sun.

'You've just picked the right day to find me here,'

laughed Ivy Violet as he took off his heavy straw-coloured riding mac.

'Right? In this weather?' His face fell. 'I'm on my own. Everyone's away and I'm due in Scotland tomorrow, but I'm having problems with Crystal. I don't want to worry you too much because I know you're very busy but I'm very worried about her. It's no joke looking after a motherless daughter.'

They sat down together in the drawing room. It was as if time had stood still. They caught up on other news then Maxi spoke of his own problems about his voice.

'It's pretty well better now – thanks to a complete rest, and I'm booked up with musical engagements again.' He looked at her quizzically. 'Yet somehow I'm not sure I want to go back to it all. Anyway that's beside the point. To put it bluntly Ivy will you take on Crystal for a while and train her in the shoe design business?'

'Well – I . . . It's such a bolt out of the blue!'

Her brain raced as she tried to work out the best way to fit Crystal in, and where she would sleep. 'I'm sure Mary wouldn't mind if she slept in Hetty's room in the other single bed – for the time being. Just to see how things go.'

Fourteen-year-old Crystal was now what people described as 'well developed'. A bonny, rosy-cheeked girl with a sharp business sense and an out-going personality as far as her own age group was concerned, she was extremely pleased to get away from Hermisford High School and all its narrowness. In spite of her father's anger about her being expelled. But, in keeping with many children who had been over-cosseted for one reason or another, she had no sense of responsibility to the adult world.

Ivy Violet knew only too well what it was like at Crystal's age to always be with people who misjudged you – even though her own schooldays had been entirely different.

'I'll send her along to see you then, Ivy,' said Maxi at the end of their meeting. 'I can't thank you enough.' Their eyes met for a fleeting second in memories of times past.

'How would you like to come and work for IVY shoes?' Ivy Violet said to Crystal later. 'After all, it was your father and mother, amongst others, who started me off.

'You'd make a wonderful model for the popular market in shoes for young lassies. We could have photographs of your feet attired in elegant patent leather ankle straps to send all over the world.'

Crystal jumped at the chance. 'Aunty Ivy – how marvellous!'

Ivy Violet smiled. 'But don't think it'll be easy. I'm a very strict employer. You would have to work very hard and be paid accordingly.'

'Oh – yes – yes!' said Crystal flushed with effusive enthusiasm. 'I'll work from morning till night and do whatever you say.'

'It might well be no, no, before a few weeks are out,' said Ivy Violet warningly. 'We can but try.'

By the end of April Crystal had made herself indispensable to IVY shoes as she posed for advertisements, helped Ivy Violet on her visits to shoe shops and proved herself to be extremely attractive and vivacious to everyone concerned with the trade.

She has the makings of a real business woman, thought Ivy Violet cheerfully, but at the same time she was slightly worried because Crystal seemed cut off from people her own age as Crystal immersed herself in work. As if there were no tomorrow.

During 1930 the IVY shoes industry went from strength to strength. The trade in cheaper shoes for younger girls boomed and a steady market grew for Ivy Violet's luxury creations, which were still produced with the same craftsmanship by people like the Blantyre brothers of Hanging Ditch in Manchester.

'YOU – old?' said Phillis when Ivy Violet went to visit her mother one day and catch up on the news. 'You don't know what you're talking about woman. You were obviously born with a secret silver spoon in your mouth, when you think of what most people have to suffer.' Then she stopped and said shamefacedly: 'That was silly of me love, after you losing Alfred in the War and the hard work and trouble you've had, and the way you battled on to make a success of the shoes. What I really mean is that you're still very young, and in your prime. Folks always think they're into the realms of real old age when they start to get into their thirties, and another

lot are seeming to catch them up, but it's just a passing phase. I reckon you can only get to that when
you're about seventy, and even then you're as young
as you feel – so cheer up lass.' Then Phillis said a little truculently: 'If you're frightened of being an old
maid, or nearly that, why don't you join a proper
ballroom dancing group or summat. Something really respectable. The sort of people that go on outings.
You used to like all those polkas and things when
you were young and Merrick Jackson was a little
lad.'

'*Ballroom dancing*?' Ivy Violet stared at her aghast.

'Well it was only a suggestion. They do say it's
extremely soothing, and it's far better than the
Charleston and all that complicated modern rubbish
and even better exercise.'

'But I get loads and loads and *loads* of exercise,
Mam. I'm on the go the whole time. Why don't you
and Freddy try it?'

'I haven't the time either, love, otherwise I would.'

All the way home Phillis's jab about the old fashioned dancing niggled her as it suddenly brought
Merrick to mind. Perhaps he and Maisy had taken to
it. They were certainly in the right place – so near to
the Tower Ballroom in Blackpool. Maybe he'd given
up his bowls and gone on the rampage – doing vale-
tas or military two steps and saluting Maisy every
few steps. That should just suit her. Ivy Violet was
quite depressed. She knew it was because she always
felt Merrick had made a mistake – marrying that
awful girl.

When she got home she said to Crystal: 'How do you fancy an outing to Blackpool visiting the tower – just the two of us?' Crystal was also fed up; she had just split up with a boyfriend who was supposed to be the one for 'ever and ever'.

'Oh – Ivy – what a great idea.'

They set off early on the train and as they neared Preston the weather suddenly cleared with bright blue-grey skies and cold bracing winds which brought colour to their cheeks. There was a tea dance that afternoon. It was old-time dancing. There were all manner of age groups there from young mothers with children and a sprinkling of lads and lasses in their teens, to older more mature-looking men and women sailing round in their well-pressed, and carefully-ironed clothes.

At first, Ivy Violet and Crystal danced together so that Ivy Violet could teach Crystal the steps. They made a lot of mistakes coupled with much laughing. Then gradually they were captured by mostly fatherly men who seemed to know all the steps inside out Even so, Crystal was partnered twice by a boy her own age who admitted he was really supposed to be at school and gave her his name and address to get in touch. His name was Rupert Jackson.

Crystal put the scrap of paper with his name and address into the pocket of her frock, but not before she had torn a small piece from the bottom of the paper and returned it to him, folded up, with her own name on it. He quickly hid it in his pocket without even a glance and drifted away.

It was a harmless, simple day out which neither Ivy Violet nor Crystal ever forgot, yet even so Ivy Violet kept looking round at everyone in Blackpool wondering what she would do if she suddenly saw Merrick. But she need not have worried because there was never a sign of him. However just as Merrick was nearing Blackpool Tower that day after a visit to one of the tourist offices, he caught sight of his son. He frowned to himself. What on earth was Rupert doing round there when he should have been in school studying for end of term exams? Merrick never asked him. He feared that he would only be told lies, and even if he did it would only cause a row with Maisy.

When he got home, Maisy was sitting there talking to her sister Millicent. Millicent, twelve years younger than Maisy, was a quieter, more timid creature. She was clutching a tear-soaked hanky and had red-rimmed eyes. They had never got on particularly well. Now twenty-three and not yet married, Millicent was still suffering the disruption of being on her own after being the one to stay at home and look after their parents, who had both died. Consequently she had never been out in the world much, as far as jobs for women were concerned, and all she was skilled at was housekeeping. So to encourage her, Maisy had decided that she could come and be their lodger and help *them* in the house instead, which she had been doing for the last few months. Then, getting a bit fed up with being Maisy's doormat, she had suddenly found herself a job in a fashion shop in Blackpool.

The tears were the direct result of Maisy complaining about people who bit the hand that fed them and threatening to chuck Milly out completely if she took the job.

'We aren't just here to provide you with luxury surroundings, Millicent. My goodness, if you were in a posh hotel with furniture and comforts like ours, you'd have to pay the earth! I'm proud to say that I didn't offer you charity when you came here. It was on the understanding that you acted as our house-keeper and now you're wanting the cake and the halfpenny too. It just isn't good enough.'

'Come off it Maisy,' said Merrick angrily. 'We've got loads of room and we can easily afford paid help – particularly if Milly pays us lodgings' money when she gets her job. Your behaviour is diabolical!'

He went and stood beside Milly's chair and put his hand on her shoulder consolingly. He had always liked her.

Gradually Maisy subsided, and Millicent was allowed to stay as long as she transferred her belongings to the smallest bedroom, and promised to pay them six shillings a week.

Millicent was delighted. Freedom at last! 'I owe it all to you, Merrick. If you hadn't come in just at the right time to support me – I'd — '

'Forget it Milly,' smiled Merrick giving her arm a gentle squeeze. 'Make the most of it and good luck to you. It's been a real tonic having you about the house. Maisy can be very trying at times. Good luck with the job.'

When Crystal and Ivy Violet got back to Altrincham that day, in the November darkness with fog drawing in round all the houses, Mary and Hetty were waiting to welcome them. A good log fire glowed and crackled in the wide stone fireplace. Crystal escaped to her bedroom as quickly as she could and pulled out the name of the boy she had danced with in Blackpool on her memorable day out:

> Rupert Jackson,
> Sea Mead,
> Promenade Road,
> Lytham St Annes.

She stared at it for quite a while. She felt as if there was already a link somewhere but had no idea what it was.

Impulsively she decided to write back to him then and there, for why had he gone to the trouble of scribbling out his address if he hadn't wanted her to?

Dear Rupert,
    What a good day it was today at the tea-dance. It was great to meet you. I sure did appreciate it. My Aunt Ivy who came with me liked it as well. We are home at her place now. As I told you when we were dancing, I work for her helping to run her shoe company, but

some day I aim to run one of my own. Dancing with you was a thrill.

> Please write back,
>> I am,
>>> Your friend Crystal Dingle

Rupert struck lucky when the letter arrived, for it was Milly who picked it up and handed it to him when it dropped through the letter-box. If it had been Maisy he would have been cross-questioned for ever more, so instead of him being quizzed it was Milly herself who suffered.

'Did I see you pick up a letter from that floor and hand it over to Rupert?'

'Yes, Maisy.'

'Was it his name on the envelope?'

Milly coloured up indignantly. 'Of course it was!'

'You're quite certain it wasn't Merrick's initials – or mine?'

'I'm not a *fool*. It had his full name on it as bold as brass. A really confident hand.'

'*Bold* writing? Whoever would want to be sending him a letter in *bold* writing? He *never* gets personal letters.'

'Well he has today.' Milly beamed in triumph.

'I hope it isn't some little trollop trying to lead him away from his studies,' groaned Maisy irritably. 'That would be the last straw. It's been very difficult to get both him and Arabella to settle down properly since we left Hale.'

She raised her voice and called piercingly to

Rupert who was upstairs, but he ignored her as he read and re-read Crystal's letter. She had put no address on, just the date. Then, with a sudden lucky thought he fished in his jacket pockets until he discovered the tiny scrap of folded up paper with her address on it.

> Crystal Dingle,
> c/o Miss Ivy Violet Hilton,
> Pear Tree Round'us,
> Near Blossom Street,
> Altrincham.

His inside gave a strange lurch. He knew that area very well. There were small private orchards in many of the large gardens and he had often been there pinching fruit with other boys from school. The happy memories flooded back in pangs of sorrow. It was as if a ship had suddenly answered his distress signal. His heart flooded with hope.

He wrote straight back to Crystal in the most flowing language he could think of, the sort women were supposed to like from men – if the books his twin sister Arabella soaked up were to be believed.

Dearest Crystal,
My darling. How wonderfull it was to danse with you at the ballrom and fele yor hot breth on my cheeck and get your letter. I know you will not bileeve this but I know wear you live as I used to live in Hale, and I went to

school in Altrincham. Hopping to sea you
soon, may darling.
            Your loveing boy fiend,
                  Rupert.

He had written it in a hurry with no time to check
it, and only just had time to put it in the envelope
and seal it up, before Arabella came snooping round,
asking if he had seen the small hand mirror from her
dressing table.

'Who are you writing to?' said Arabella hovering
closer and closer as she tried to catch sight of the
address.

Her luck was in. Rupert was so nervous he had
hastily caught the letter with his hand and flicked it
to the floor.

Arabella pounced on it remorselessly and began to
read out the name and address in a loud, slow voice
just as Maisy was within earshot. 'Crystal Dingle,
care of Miss Ivy Violet Hilton.' She stopped. 'Isn't
that the person mother used to know when we were
all very young? The one she hates? I remember when
we were playing round a water fountain in a park in
Sale, and she was there. She lives in Altrincham. Ma
and Pa had a row about her.'

'Shut up and mind your own business,' growled
Rupert. 'I don't go round spying on everything you
do.'

'What's all this about spying on things?' said
Maisy. She had suddenly appeared and began
admonishing them as if they were still three-year-

olds. She walked across to the letter and picked it up.

The moment she saw the address she stood still. She read it and re-read it. She just could not believe it. What on earth was going on? She grabbed at the letter and said determinedly: '*I'll* have that – if you don't mind.'

But Rupert was there at the same time clutching her chubby wrist in his forceful young hand. 'Oh no you *won't*, Mother. It's my private property.' He looked at her with his thin boyish face full of fierce hate, and she quailed and looked helplessly round for Arabella who had already fled.

'What a terrible way to treat your poor old mother,' she whimpered.

'What a terrible way to treat me, Ma – when it's a private letter to my friend,' said Rupert, now feeling slightly apologetic.

'Your friend? Who is this so-called friend Rupert? And when did it all happen?'

He stared at her ruthlessly. He realised that he had grown up and from now on he had the complete upper hand. She no longer held hidden terror for him, so he could afford to be kind, could afford to tell her the truth if and when he chose.

'If you must know, I happened to bump into her and Miss Hilton in the Tower Ballroom a day or so ago.'

'But that was when you were at school?'

'Well, I wasn't at school then – was I?'

Maisy looked at him in a complete daze. 'I didn't even know you could dance.'

'I can't, but it's easy to pick up the rudiments. Lots of us go there from time to time.'

'But what about your studies?'

'What about them? I'll never do any good. My spelling's all to pot. It's just like yours. But I've ceased bothering about it. I shall probably try and join the army.'

Maisy went quite pale with despair. Rupert had no intention of trying to join the army, but it was the best way he knew of getting at his mother. No, what he aimed to do was to make lots and lots of money by studying world finance meticulously. That was his true aim in life from now on. There was plenty of time for it.

When Maisy had staggered away groaning miserably to herself, Rupert picked up his letter again, and taking his pen, wrote S.W.A.L.K. on the back of the envelope, then he kissed the letter, and took it to the letter-box as Maisy stood and watched him from the front drawing room window with a heavy heart.

She turned away mournfully. What was the world coming to? she thought. Had they done the right thing after all – coming to live here at Lytham? She drifted over to the piano and as her fingers touched the keys her old forcefulness returned and she thumped away at a small patch of a Beethoven sonata.

CHAPTER 18

1931. Ivy Violet's Big Mistake

Ivy Violet had a good thirty-fifth birthday party. It was a quiet personal affair with a beautifully iced cake made by one of Maureen's friends. There were no expensive presents, but Hetty had proudly presented her with a raffia shopping bag lined in sky blue taffeta, which she had been making secretly at school in needlework. Crystal had given her a slim bunch of creamy, sweetly scented, tea roses.

Deep down Ivy Violet felt proud on that day of the way her life had worked out. She was also proud of Crystal's progress and of how well she had trained her. One of these days Crystal could well be the owner of her own luxury empire, thanks to Ivy

Violet's careful nurturing. Yet her one regret was the same niggling old desire to have everything properly balanced with a really reliable and loving man in her life. She felt she had come to an age when she wanted to settle down and be herself with an intelligent male of her own age. Surely she deserved it? Life was extra hard for a woman on her own in the commercial world, for – as she thought – all the men she dealt with in her business were mollycoddled by numerous females of all ages, from mothers, secretaries, wives and girlfriends, to secret and not so secret mistresses.

There was champagne for her birthday party and as she sipped through its cool effervescence, her gaze drifted across to Crystal again who was talking ten to the dozen to her latest casual boyfriend Lester Warmesly, a seventeen-year-old who lived just round the corner, and was the son of a local barrister. He was home from college. What a contrast it all was to when she had been sixteen and her boyfriend had been Merrick.

She smiled at them and felt a rush of pleasure at the way she had mothered young Crystal. Crystal smiled back at her fleetingly.

When the party was all finished and Crystal was helping her to put away some of the champagne glasses, Crystal said casually: 'I'm afraid I shan't be at work on Monday, Ivy. I have a private engagement.'

Ivy was stunned. Never before had she had 'a private engagement' on a busy working day. 'Whatever is it, Crystal? It'll have to be something pretty worth-while. I was absolutely depending on you organising our ballet and tap shoes display on the children's shoes stand at the Dancing Years Exhibition in Manchester. Surely you know that?' Ivy Violet stared at her with ill-concealed shock. 'That shoe display was arranged months ago! Don't tell me young Lester's trying to get you off the hook.'

Crystal's mouth set in a hard sulky line as she turned and walked away.

Ivy Violet shook her head in despair. She usually coped with Crystal quite well – overall. However, she decided to ignore it. Least said, soonest mended was her motto.

The following Monday Ivy Violet was up extra early to get into Manchester to arrange their display. She was in a cheerful mood – especially with her finances being on the upsurge once more. She decid-ed to wake Crystal up with a glass of freshly squeezed orange juice, but was startled to see her door wide open and the bed already neatly made. Crystal had obviously heeded her words, after all, about being up extra early on this important day.

But where was she?

She called her name loudly: 'Crystal?' and was relieved to hear a reply from downstairs.

'Here, Ivy. Sorry I can't come with you – but I did warn you. Tarrar then. See you later.' The front door slammed shut.

Whatever was Crystal playing at? Ivy Violet thought. What a little minx. How dare she be so totally disobedient and disloyal? Normally when they arrived to display their goods at exhibitions, Crystal worked like lightning. They worked together with a perfect machine-like precision.

Ivy Violet was furious as she stamped into the Free Trade Hall where the exhibition was. Their goods had already been delivered, but she was completely alone as she began to assemble it all. She noted with grim bitterness that all the other people had others to help them. In her anger she dropped shoe boxes, mixed up shoe sizes and accidentally knocked down display stands in her haste to get it ready for public viewing.

Having no one to help meant she would have to stay at the stand and be unable to have a good look round the rest of the exhibition. To her relief as she looked across the aisles of other displays, she saw someone she knew. It was Bessie Bellini who was showing the brocades, velvets and heavy linen used in shoes.

Bessie waved and came over to her. 'Ivy Violet. All on your own? Don't worry, I've got my three daughters and a son helping me so if you ever want to take a bit of time to look around at the other stands or have a break we'll always cover for you.'

If it had not been for Bessie Ivy Violet would never have been able to walk round the hall. She gazed with interest at all the other displays and thanked her lucky stars that she still reigned supreme in the luxury shoes field.

Having absorbed all the new innovations on show

– from fancy bootlaces to luxury button hooks made of pure gold and mother of pearl, and shoes with all variety of patented easy fastenings and tins and tins of various shoe creams, cleaning powders and leather enhancers – she made her way back past all the stands concerned with dancing and ballet. People were there dressed as dancers to display the shoes. On one of the stands there was a girl in a tap dancing outfit made of scarlet satin and decorated in gold braid. The flared skirt was very short and on her head she wore a mock soldier's hat with a huge feather in it. Ivy Violet looked at her and smiled. Then her face froze. Crystal!

'Crystal? What in heaven's name?'

At first Crystal just stared ahead as if she was from a wax-works, then she looked down rather shame-facedly and muttered: 'Whatever I'm doing it's nothing to do with you, Ivy.' Then relenting a little at the hurt expression on Ivy Violet's face she added: 'If you must know, me and Lester Warmesly are help-ing out a friend whose father supplies metal taps for tap dancing shoes from his iron foundry near Ancoats.' Then Crystal turned away, just as if Ivy Violet was a complete stranger.

That day Ivy Violet could not wait to get home to tackle Crystal. But to her alarm as the grandfather clock struck eleven o'clock that night there was no sign of her, until a few minute later the phone rang.

It was Maxi. 'I'm not sure what it's all about Ivy, but she's here with me.'

Ivy Violet flopped down on a chair. What a fiasco

– having Crystal walking out as if she had not a care in the world when she had been so important a part of the exhibition arrangements. It was not as if Crystal was working for nothing, she was handsomely paid for all her work.

A week later nothing was any better, as Maxi rang again. 'I'm very worried Ivy, she isn't settling at all well. It's proving very difficult. I'm so busy myself, but never once has she offered to help. Instead she disappears all day long never saying a word.' His voice took on a pleading note. 'I know it sounds the most frightful cheek, but would you be willing to have her back with you, if I could persuade her?'

Ivy Violet's mouth set thinly. Her face these days was changing, and not for the better. There were small downward lines on each side of her mouth which only vanished when she smiled, and there were permanent frown furrows appearing on her forehead. 'I don't know what to say, Maxi. After all – she . . . it was me she ran away from. I *must* have people round me in the business world who are totally reliable.'

'Oh I know – I *do* know, Ivy, and I feel absolutely terrible about it, but surely if you could just give her one more chance? It's a hell of a problem her having no proper mother. If you could just try one last forgiving invitation to come back to you again? You've no idea how much it would mean to me. And I value our friendship so much.'

Ivy hesitated lengthily, then finally agreed. 'Very well then, but it really will have to be the last time, and then I shall look round for someone else to employ.'

She hung up the telephone receiver wearily as she thought it all over yet again, and was quite amazed when Crystal arrived back a few days later. But this Crystal was quiet and silent and sullen, and not a bit like the cheerful girl she had once known, as Crystal disappeared each day to some unknown destination.

Ivy Violet noticed that there was a definite time pattern, for Crystal was always available when she was being forced to work with Ivy Violet who could keep a tag on her; but the moment she was left to check on other parts of the business and make her own visits, she moved out of everyone's orbit. Ivy Violet decided to follow her to find out what on earth was going on.

It was after they had both been checking shoe stocks and further orders around Market Street in Manchester and were about to go for a cup of coffee.

'I think I'll skip the coffee and make my way back to Altrincham to get on with the accounts,' said Crystal restlessly. 'Then I'll be all set to go out with you later this afternoon when you get back yourself.'

Ivy Violet nodded. 'Good idea. See you later on this afternoon then.' She waved goodbye affectionately, but the moment Crystal was out of the coffee shop Ivy Violet was following her.

Relentlessly she kept Crystal in sight through the centre of the town, along all the shopping streets and out towards Stretford Road. Crystal walked along back street after back street. Nearing Ivy Violet's childhood territory not far from Clark Terrace, Ivy Violet saw Crystal glance towards a place known by older generations as Shabby Alley, which was noted for its huge rat population spawned from nearby derelict warehouses.

Crystal slowed down and walked along a row of small houses. She knocked at the door of one of the worst ones. It was in the centre of the row.

A youth about Crystal's age opened the door and greeted her affectionately as she went inside.

Ivy Violet shuddered. It was such a change from what Crystal was used to – to be entering what was a seedy broken-down slum.

She moved closer. There were grubby lace curtains downstairs with damp stains on them, and the brown paint on the door was bubbled to the state of boiling toffee.

She paused. Should she knock? Or just make note of the place, and at some later date tackle Crystal with the news that she had found her secret rendezvous? But before she could make up her mind the door creaked open and the boy faced her. He was in his teens and had well cut hair and an extremely good pair of what she secretly termed 'school' trousers on.

They gazed at each other for a second. She'd seen him somewhere else, she could swear it, but where?

By now Crystal was standing in the gloom behind him. 'You'd better come in,' she said coldly.

Ivy Violet walked in carefully and was surprised to find the place fitted out like a small office with a bentwood chair, and a typewriter on a table in the corner, along with a waste paper basket. There was also a set of shelves with books and files on them, and two old arm chairs with stuffing coming out of them in the centre of the tiny room. A striped cat washed its paws languidly near the empty hearth.

'I'll make us all a cup of tea,' said Crystal hastily as she moved to a scullery that had a greasy brown slopstone and single gas ring close to some enamelled tin mugs.

'No thank you, Crystal,' said Ivy Violet as politely as possible, 'but I would like to know what you and this friend of yours are up to?'

'UP TO?' Crystal glared at her aggressively. 'What's that supposed to mean? You aren't my keeper, you know? You're making a very big mistake indeed if you think that, *Aunty* Ivy. I don't have to answer to *you* for all my movements, let alone a spy who follows me about. Rupert and I are more than capable of looking after ourselves.'

'Rupert?' Ivy Violet looked at the boy again. 'Rupert and – and Arabella. Surely not?'

'That's right, Rupert Jackson,' said Rupert staring her out. 'Merrick and Maisy Jackson's son, except I don't live at home with them any more. We had a row and this is my home now. My home and *our* office.' He took hold of Crystal's hand as they both stood in front of her with cool defiance. 'You might as well know the truth seeing that you've come all this way to pry. We're in business on our own account, see?'

In business on their own account? What pie in the sky was that? Ivy Violet frowned to herself. It sounded like a half-baked pipe dream. How could a couple of kids like them possibly expect to make a living out of some small tin-pot business of their own?

'But Crystal works for *me*,' she said angrily. 'It isn't a joke shop I work in, it's serious trading. Crystal is supposed to be my faithful trainee – crucial to the whole organisation. That's why I came here to find out what was happening.' She looked at Crystal accusingly. 'To see what all these mysterious comings and goings in *my* working time were about. You must admit you do work for me, Crystal.'

'Not any more I don't,' said Crystal triumphantly. 'From this moment on, thanks to you and your interference, Rupert and me, and Lester Warmesly, are in partnership on our own account. And if you see Dad you can tell him.'

'But in heaven's name – what are you partners *in*?'

They both smiled a trifle smugly. 'You'll find out soon enough.'

Ivy Violet left the house in a sort of daze mixed with terrific anger. Two people their age and nowhere near twenty-one – swanking about running their own business. What gobbledygook.

To cool off she decided to walk back via Clark Terrace, and see how it looked, and as she caught sight of it tucked away at the back of Lawson's Hotel and Mellers the printers she became calmer.

The patch of washing green was still there and the houses were as good as they had ever been with a few added things like new doors and different windows. Number 2, where some of the Simpkins still lived, now had a small, rounded bay window quite out of keeping with the rest of the terrace, yet somehow attractive. She stared hard at number 3 where she had once lived. It had a pot dog in the window and criss-cross lead lighting on the glass.

It all seemed so different from the dramatic days when Phillis had destroyed her dance dress . . .

It was so quiet and peaceful with not an open door to be seen.

She strolled along to take a quick look at number 6 where Sylvia Watson had once lived. The whole of their orphaned family had moved to Levenshulme and had all done very well for themselves. Ivy smiled to herself. She was glad about that for they deserved it. Sylvia had always looked so pale and underfed. These days she was a real fashion plate.

She made her way through the narrow ginnel at the end of the tiny row of thriving houses in the heart of Hulme, which was a hive of memories for so many, then she made her way back to Altrincham.

As soon as she got in she rang Maxi and told him about Crystal. ' . . . I'm afraid I can't take any responsibility for her actions from now on Maxi. And as I said before, I can't possibly keep her employed in her proper job with all this going on behind the scenes. I shall just have to look round for another assistant; someone a bit older and totally reliable. It's terribly sad but there you are. What other option is there?'

There was a muffled groan at the other end of the phone. 'Thanks, Ivy. At least you tried. I expect it's half my fault because of keeping her so extravagantly topped up with a private allowance.'

'Private allowance?'

He gave a shamefaced sigh. 'I tried to make it up to her a bit because of Garnet's death. I realise it was stupid. She gets more in a year than many a hard-working man earns. She's really a very, very spoilt brat. I can see it now. The money you paid her was just extra icing, and now I fear that those two boys involved in this mad scheme will manage to fritter all the cash away. I shall try and find out exactly what it is they're up to.'

By the time the phone call was over Ivy Violet felt totally drained. It was essential to get someone else to help her as soon as possible. She thought of Trevor's wife but that was out of the question at present as she was expecting a baby and had been told to rest. Maybe if she put an advert in the local *Altrincham Guardian* it would help, though the thought of having to train up yet another young person from scratch after all the wasted time with Crystal, weighed heavily on her shoulders.

During the next fortnight, and after three advertisements in the paper under a box number she was still no nearer finding anyone. She was at her wits end. Had she worked all these years just to draw a blank?

Then, one fine day, in a mass of russet autumn leaves and turquoise skies, a car drew up and an exceedingly smart woman in brilliant lime green, with a silvery grey lamb coat and pill-box hat with a veil, rang her door bell.

Ivy Violet opened the door and gazed at the elegant figure with platinum blonde hair, pencil thin eyebrows shaded with green mascara and cheekbones softly rouged. It was Sylvia!

With joyous heart Ivy Violet led her into the sunny conservatory. They drank coffee and ate chocolates as they caught up on their lives. Ivy Violet described her present predicament.

'What a cheek Crystal's got – trying to compete with you,' gasped Sylvia.

Ivy Violet nodded fiercely. 'And if she uses my designs I'd sue her for every penny if it wasn't for the fact that, apart from being under age, Maxi is part of IVY Shoes!'

Sylvia looked at her calmly. 'Don't take on so, Ivy. Everyone's free to design shoes. They're very young and it might fade out completely in a few weeks when they find out all the real work and responsibility entailed. Meanwhile, if you're still without a helper I'd really welcome the job. I was working for Derrivale's Fashions, and then I had to go into hospital for a hysterectomy, because of fibroids. It was an awful shock because I'm so young for it, but there you are. Anyway, since then I've been doing very little except help out in a local book shop.'

Ivy Violet welcomed Sylvia into the firm and asked her if she could start work in about ten days.

'No trouble at all, Ivy. I know I'll enjoy every minute of it.'

The rest of 1931 ran like clockwork as Ivy Violet realised she had found the ideal working companion at last.

CHAPTER 19

The Sea-side

One day, as March winds lifted the clouds away in a hustling blue and white sky, Maxi knocked at Ivy Violet's door in Altrincham.

'Ivy. How good to have found you in,' said Maxi. 'I decided to call – just on the off-chance. It's just to say I've sorted Crystal and her pals out – and all that encroachment on IVY Shoes.'

She led him to the drawing room. 'I've just made a cup of tea.' She offered him some brandy snaps.

'It's really to do with a change of life-style, Ivy. My singing career is on the way out. I reckon I've had a good innings and shall concentrate on being an impresario from now on to help others on the ladder. There's lots of talent in Manchester and I've got plenty of contacts.'

As she stretched forward to offer him another cup of tea his hand brushed against hers and it was like an electric tremor. They both looked at each other. To hide her shyness she said: 'So how did you sort out the Crystal dilemma?'

He nodded. 'I saw all of them. Of course Crystal is doing amazingly well with her own small branch of the shoe trade.' A troubled look passed across his face. 'I tried to sort out all this nonsense about her saying you had accused her of stealing some of your shoe designs. It's quite laughable.'

Ivy Violet smiled enigmatically. How little he really knew.

Then Maxi said: 'Do you remember the time we nearly . . . ?'

Ivy Violet nodded hastily. 'It was a long time ago Maxi. It just wouldn't have worked out.' A sudden thread of fear ran through her. She knew she was no match for him. She felt herself dissolving like during those early days as soon as she was with him, yet she knew that to succumb would be a disaster. That had been proved time and time again by his own list of abandoned female conquests.

'Let's go to bed,' he said with sudden gentleness. 'Lets forget all our earthly troubles.' He gazed at her pleadingly, but she shook her head. He little realised the effort of will it had taken to refuse. Nevertheless he began to send her hot house flowers once a week.

'Why do you do it Father?' said Crystal one day. 'Why do you send her all those flowers when you know how badly she treated me – as if I was her personal slave.'

'She didn't mean you to be her slave. She was just training you in the trade and she did it damned well – or else you would never have been able to start off so early on your own account.' Then he added darkly: 'But you need to get out of the shoe rut, Crystal. You'll never be able to design the way she does. You're better at the theatrical stuff – dress designing for set shows and productions. I can get you any manner of work on that side.'

And so it came about that Crystal Creations went from strength to strength as designers for theatrical productions. But one day when Maxi was mooching about in his own home, quite by chance, he came across a sheaf of stiff cartridge paper. They were masses of small original shoe designs carefully and thoroughly measured, worked out as practical drawings, and all signed 'Ivy Violet Hilton'. He nodded his head with resigned disgust. So there *had* been something in the idea of Crystal pinching her designs. Thank God he'd steered Crystal, young Jackson and Warmesly away from that side of the market.

Taking the sheaf of drawings he placed them carefully in a folder and enclosed a card.

Darling Ivy,
    I've just found these. I realise now that the little wretch was not being honest with me when she said you had been wrongfully accusing her. But what can one do when she's

my own flesh and blood? Perhaps she's a chip
off the old block – and at least there's no
damage done now I've guided her little band
of distributors to pastures new, on the
theatrical side.

Yours for ever,
Maxi.

He got in the car and took the packet round to Ivy
Violet's office in Altrincham immediately.

Ivy was not there but her assistant Sylvia was.

Maxi had never seen Sylvia before though Ivy
Violet had often mentioned her. In a flash he saw the
slim figure and the waved platinum blonde hair and
the rather serious, kindly face with greeny blue eyes
beneath the thin pencilled eyebrows and immediately he was hooked.

He handed Sylvia the parcel, explained what it
was then said: 'Would you care to come out to dinner with me tonight?'

She nodded as if it was the easiest decision in the
world and three dinner outings later Maxi had pro-
posed to her and she had accepted him.

Ivy Violet noted it all with a mixture of wry sadness and happy amusement. Maybe this time with a
girl like Sylvia it would all work out, she thought. It
was almost as if a dynasty was being founded –
between them all in the business world – in a loose-
ly linked way as she and Maureen and Trev, and
Sylvia all continued to work together.

*

A couple of years later, as summer approached, Maureen arranged an office outing to Blackpool for the weekend. The May weather forecast for the weekend was perfect with not a drop of rain in the blue skies and the sun beating down as they all arrived at the Shoredene Hotel, near Cleveleys. There were fresh and invigorating views of sand and white breakers on the rolling blue grey sea. It was a small place of thirty bedrooms.

Even Maxi went with his wife Sylvia, Trev with his wife, Maureen with her new husband, and various other members of office staff with wives and sweethearts. Ivy Violet was with Mary and Hetty. She had decided to introduce Hetty to the ballroom in the Blackpool Tower just as she had once done with Crystal.

The afternoon dance floor was crowded as Ivy Violet took Hetty round it, but somehow for her the magic was lost. Although Hetty enjoyed every minute of it amid the music and laughter, and they had afternoon tea afterwards, all it seemed to do for Ivy Violet was to bring back memories of her own young life, so different from Hetty's, and make her long again for a child of her own.

When they arrived back at the hotel and supper was over and Hetty was safely in bed, it was Maxi who suddenly suggested they should all have a night out dancing, and everyone was in agreement.

'Double rations for me then,' laughed Ivy Violet as she explained where she and Hetty had been. 'Maybe I'm making up for lost time.'

'I'll allow you to dance as much as you like with my wayward husband,' joked Sylvia. She was generous and confident these days for her marriage to Maxi was working very well.

That night the atmosphere of the place was totally different from the way it had been in the afternoon. The ornate gilding and all the red plush and glittering chandeliers cast a glow of sheer magic as Maxi waltzed round with her and said she had turned down the chance to be his first and last love. But it was too late now he laughingly reminded her. He'd found another just as good. 'I can't say better because you didn't let me get far enough.'

'And just as well, too,' remarked Ivy Violet dreamily. The orchestra played its heart out. Coloured spotlights glanced about and caught at the folds of her flowing blue silk gown and made glass necklaces flash with a rainbow of sparkling colours in the restful darkness.

When the music finished and they had made their way back to the tables, Ivy Violet was suddenly aware that Merrick was there! He was sitting about three tables away talking happily to a younger woman. His hair was getting thinner now, but it was definitely him.

'What's caught your eye this time?' said Maxi as they drank champagne.

'Not what, but who,' said Ivy reprovingly. 'It's Merrick Jackson. He and his wife came to live here ages back.

'He's the father of Rupert who was with Crystal

when she first started her 'Creations'. I seem to know the girl he's with but just can't place her.'

'Invite him over,' said Maxi.

At that moment Ivy Violet and Merrick both caught each other's eye. Merrick limped over to her and asked her to dance. 'What a surprise – and after all these years? You'll have to put up with the jerky dancing. These days people seem to think it's part of the steps, and Millicent's used to it of course. So how's life treating you?'

'Very well thank you, at present. What about you?'

His face fell slightly. '. . . Not too bad. Mustn't grumble I suppose, but it's been a bit of a haul back to reality. She may have had her faults but she was a good wife, and I miss her like hell – even though I have got Milly to look after me.'

'Milly? What's happened? I don't understand.'

'Yes, poor old Milly. Maisy did treat her as a bit of a drudge when they were younger. She's the one who always drags me here. She's done it ever since Maisy died – to try and cheer me up. She leaves her old man at home on Saturday nights. Insists.'

When the music stopped Merrick and Ivy Violet went over to an empty table set well away in the darkness.

'Tell me what happened then, I had no idea.'

He told her with a slightly trembling voice how Maisy had been involved in a car accident when out shopping almost two years ago and had never returned home.

'It was an awful shock. At first I couldn't believe it.

403

I expect that's what finally sent Rupert away to find another life in the Merchant Navy, and Arabella to train as a nurse.

'I don't know what I'd have done if it had not been for Milly. She and her husband and two young children keep me going. I'm still the same old stodgy cup of tea Ivy, and even worse now I'm on my own. But at least I've got the local bowling club to keep my spirits up and they've just asked me to join their jazz band.'

They went back to Milly and then joined Maxi and the others, and by the time Merrick had drunk two glasses of champagne he had cheered up enormously.

A little while later, when everyone else was dancing and there was only himself and Ivy Violet sitting there, Merrick stood up solemnly and bowed. 'Can I tempt you to this dance, Miss Imogen Violet Young?'

As they swirled round slowly to the lilting, heart lifting strains of a Viennese waltz, Ivy Violet said: 'Did I tell *you* my other name then? It's the first time I've ever heard Imogen Violet Young spoken out aloud except by me. I thought it was still a deep childhood secret of my own, made up years ago.'

'You told me a lot of your secrets in those days, Ivy.'

'Did I ever tell you the name I'd planned for you?'

He shook his head. He wished he was a perfect dancer and had his proper leg.

'Michael Earl Raymond – but your first name, Merrick, was too long to try all the initials and I fell asleep.'

They walked back again to the plush covered gilded chairs, holding hands like young lovers in a bliss of perfect contentment, and the next time when Ivy Violet went on a weekend to Blackpool on her own, Merrick was there holding out his arms joyously towards her.

DASIA

Joan Eadith

Manchester, 1926. Sixteen years old, strong willed and
with a cloud of red-gold hair, Dasia Greenbow lives with
her parents and older sisters in their large, dilapidated
house. Working begrudgingly but resignedly in her
family's pawn shop, she one day accidentally opens a
letter addressed to her father – and discovers to her
horror that her family is not all it seems. In a desperate
bid for independence she runs away to her Aunt Dolly's
boarding house, and finds work as a maid.

But when a handsome young medical student, Hal
Wrioth, asks for Dasia's hand in marriage, her fortunes
seem to take a turn for the better – especially when she
then gets a job on the gloves counter of Baulden's
department store.

But in the depths of the Depression, no one's job or future
is secure, and although she can always turn to her
irrepressible Aunt Dolly, Dasia must contend with
hardship, pregnancy and the ever-present threat of the
bailiffs. Still there are youth and determination on her
side, and Dasia is determined some day to claim the
mysterious legacy that is promised to her . . .

Other best selling Warner titles available by mail:

☐	Dasia	Joan Eadith	£5.99
☐	Hospital Girls	Joan Eadith	£5.99
☐	The Blue Cornflower	Joan Eadith	£5.99
☐	Cygnet of Melmere	Joan Eadith	£5.99
☐	Skinny Lizzie	Elizabeth Waite	£4.99
☐	Cockney Waif	Elizabeth Waite	£5.99
☐	Cockney Family	Elizabeth Waite	£5.99

The prices shown above are correct at time of going to press, however the publishers reserve the right to increase prices on covers from those previously advertised, without further notice.

WARNER BOOKS
WARNER BOOKS
Cash Sales Department, P.O. Box 11, Falmouth, Cornwall, TR10 9EN
Tel: +44 (0) 1326 372400, Fax: +44 (0) 1326 374888
Email: books@barni.avel.co.uk.

POST AND PACKING:
Payments can be made as follows: cheque, postal order (payable to Warner Books) or by credit cards. Do not send cash or currency.

All U.K. Orders	**FREE OF CHARGE**
E.E.C. & Overseas	25% of order value

Name (Block Letters) _____

Address _____

_____

Post/zip code: _____

☐ Please keep me in touch with future Warner publications

☐ I enclose my remittance £ _____

☐ I wish to pay by Visa/Access/Mastercard/Eurocard

Card Expiry Date

_____